The

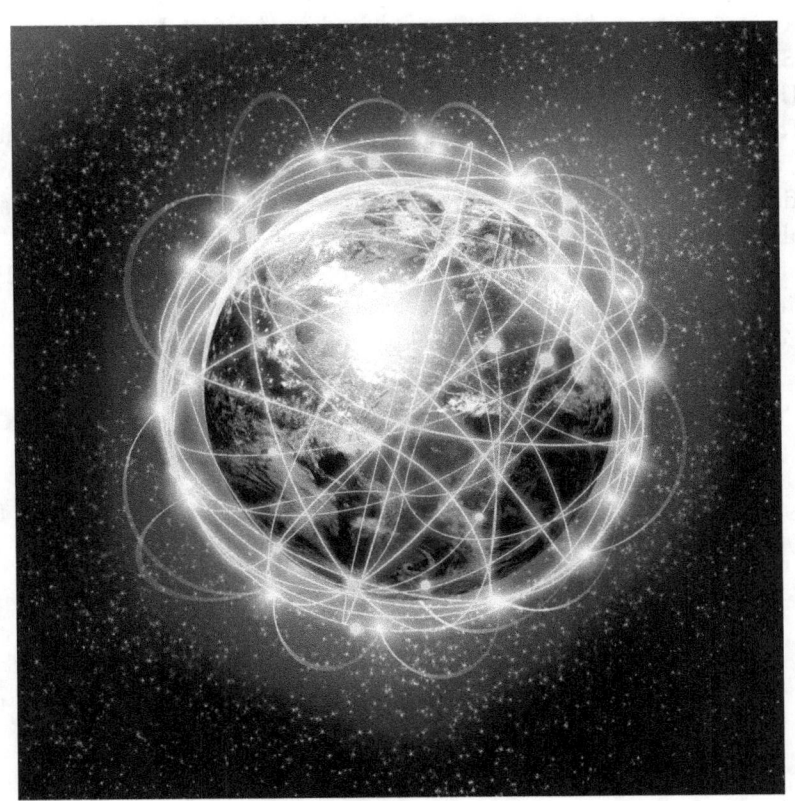

Intervention

by

Kenneth J. M. MacLean

The Intervention

Book 4 in the Potentials of Consciousness Series.

Copyright ©2023 by Kenneth J. M. MacLean

ISBN: 978-0-9996724-8-8

Contact the author at www.kjmaclean.com. Email: kmaclean@kjmaclean.com

Contents

Acknowledgments

A shout-out to Marshal Vian Summers for his *Allies of Humanity* essays. Summers presents a coherent and plausible outline of what the galaxy might look like outside this little rock. His 12-point summary of the Allies of Humanity briefings can be found at

https://www.alliesofhumanity.org/the-briefings/12-point-summary-of-the-allies-of-humanity-briefings/

Thanks also to Lee Carroll for his uplifting spiritual lectures.

Thank you to David Brin for his brilliant Uplift series of SF books.

Thanks also to the musicians who always help me in my writing, especially the monumentally talented Brad Mehldau and his trio with Larry Grenadier and Jorgy Rossy/Jeff Ballard, and the generational talent Kurt Rosenwinkel. Kurt and his Chopin Project – an astonishing jazz recording of Chopin's music – provided many hours of inspiration. Other musicians who helped to keep me inspired while writing this book:

The Bill Evans trio,
Roy Hargrove,
The Miles Davis quintet,
Sean Jones,
Taylor Eigsti and Eric Harland,
Peter Bernstein,
Gonzalo Rubalcaba,
Brian Blade and Jon Cowherd,
and the Mike Moreno quartet.

Introduction

There's a big wide galaxy out there and it has discovered spaceship earth. The galactics are already here. If you knew what I knew...well, you're about to find out. Some of this is beautiful, some of it is really ugly. Most of it is just unbelievable.

This isn't a comic book story about a guy who gets superpowers from a lab accident. It's not about somebody who goes on a Hero's Journey – you know, the stuff Hollywood movie makers and book writers shovel out every year. Good triumphs over evil, the nerd encounters the adversary and bravely fights through to victory. That's just small stuff for a very small planet. What's real is so much more complicated and unreal, and scary, and incredible.

The Intervention is beyond anything I could have believed. The worldwide lockdowns and forced vaccinations were just a trial run for the real thing.

Get set and strap in, it's coming to a screen near you.

(Note: mental plane communications are in single quotes ' '. Spoken communications are in double quotes " ").

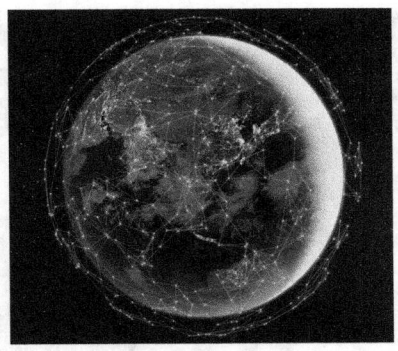

— 1 —

The very near future...

[Midland, Illinois]

My name is Philogene Rothman. I'm a satellite tech at Uploads, the company that manages the Space Grid. Elon Musk had the right idea back in the day with SpaceX and Starlink. Now the planet is surrounded by tens of thousands of small, Low Earth Orbit (LEO) communication satellites that bounce signals sent from the earth all over the planet. Even somebody living in a yurt in Outer Mongolia can talk and stream to anyone on the planet in 3D. But this system is enormously complex, because the satellites are moving in their orbits faster than the the rotation of the earth. So they are constantly moving in and out of stationary areas on the ground that send and pick up the signals. Basically, a satellite in low earth orbit is a moving target for computers and mobiles and networks on the ground.

Artist's conception of Space Grid.[1]

The biggest problem with the Grid is that satellites move slightly out of position in their orbits because they are only 200 kilometers above the earth's surface. A slight atmospheric drag disturbs the orbits of the little sats in random ways.[2] This can cause the signals to become distorted or lost entirely, and disrupts communications. When that happens people really get upset, especially the heavy hitters who pay the big bucks that keep the system financially solvent.

The Space Grid system was thoroughly tested before it went online. Uploads discovered pretty quickly that no matter how much sophisticated AI was applied to the problem, the Grid can never be fully automated. So techs like me are responsible for taking care of all Grid glitches. Almost no one can do it because the work is critical and time-sensitive, and there's a lot of stress. Satellite techs are rare and valuable, and are paid accordingly. Only a small percentage qualify out of the ten million who apply every year, and most of them flame out during the training.

The Space Grid is awesome, and so is my job. I work in a gigantic room with 30 consoles, all with human operators. The consoles have displays that are 3 feet wide and 2 feet high and show data on the orbital status of each sat, with optical keyboards for silently entering code. Huge display monitors circle the room, showing every Grid sector under management by the U.S. Uploads stations. Each screen is filled with hundreds of small satellites, each moving in groups, in a predefined pattern. In the middle of the room, hanging from thin, almost invisible wires, is one of the new lightweight flexipanels. This is a monstrous 150 foot wide, 24 foot high, brilliantly lit circular panel that shows all of the sats (satellites) in the Space Grid. It is almost invisible and looks like an illuminated area of space. The framework for the panel is a series of thin translucent wires, and the panel itself is formed from millions of tiny, translucent LEs (light emitters). It is astonishingly beautiful, and my eyes go to it often when I'm not making orbital calculations or correcting glitches the AIs can't handle.

I get paid a lot of money to do this, but for me it's easy. I see patterns in the way the satellites move. I read code like people read the labels on soup cans.

I was named Philogene after my maternal grandfather, who is French. I loved Uncle Philogene, but I prefer to be called Philo. I grew up in Palatine, Illinois, a suburb of Chicago, just before the Pandemic of 2020. My dad is a plumber and my mother teaches English Lit at the local community college, and is an avid reader of Shakespeare's plays. That's all you need to know about me, other than my swearing. I learned that from my plumber father, to the despair of my mother.

One day at work I was sitting at my console, monitoring my area, when I heard Jamaal (the head honcho) call me. "Hey Philo, get over here!" I knew that voice: the voice of panic. I walked over to another console in the C-block row, unit C-3. A young woman with an irritated look on her face got up from her chair, mumbling something about how she could handle it. I gave her a condescending, superior look that really annoyed her. I grinned at her and glanced at the screen, a 3D real-time view of the orbits of the sats in that area of space. I saw immediately that a dedicated group of 13 satellites was slowly moving out of position, perturbing the nearby satellites. This almost never happens, because the speed and position of the little comm satellites are programmed to follow unique paths. After two seconds of study I saw the pattern: a one in a million chance where the deltas of every one of the 13 satellites entrained each other in the same direction. The only way to solve this was by writing code snippets that would nullify the group perturbation (each of the sats has a small power supply that allows for minor course corrections). My fingers flew over the optical keyboard. Within a couple of seconds I could see that the satellites were beginning to work their way back into place. I strode confidently back to my console before it was obvious to Jamaal, and saw him frown.

"Arrogant asshole," I heard the woman say. I recognized the type: self-centered and competitive, just like me. It takes one to know one, I thought, as I settled back down into my chair and expanded the view on my display to the entire sector. Several hundred satellites floated in the blackness of space, with the earth approximately 200 kilometers below.

A few minutes later a man strolled over to my console, accompanied by a young woman in her early 20s. I had never seen either of them before, and I knew everyone at the facility. I didn't look up. "Who are you?"

He didn't answer, but I could feel him looking at me. I turned in my chair and looked into his eyes. I got a shock. Behind those eyes was an otherworldly presence.

"I'm Patrick," he said softly. I felt the spoken words resonate inside my head. I suspected that Patrick wasn't his real name, but it didn't seem important. "I saw what you did back there."

"Oh you did?"

Patrick ignored my snarky response. "I think I can, er, find something more exciting for you to do."

I took a look back to the console where the female tech was sitting. She had a knowing smile on her face, as if she knew I was going to get blasted for stunting her. Techs frown on other techs who show them up.

I looked at Patrick's companion, a remarkably beautiful young woman.

Jamaal walked over, angry. "Why don't you Space Force people recruit someplace else? Philogene is my best tech."

Patrick didn't even turn around. His eyebrows raised slightly, questioning me. I didn't hesitate. "Lay on, Macduff."

I saw Patrick's eyes sharpen. He clearly recognized the Shakespearean quote in its correct form, and I think he was a little irritated. "Come with me," he said in a command voice.

"Don't try that shit with me," I said. "I'm not a lemming you can order around."

Patrick's eyebrows raised slightly in hauteur. I looked directly into his eyes and got the impression that the man was a grizzled veteran of battles in foreign places I had never heard of. The young woman beside him clinched it. Unusual and exotic, with a perfectly symmetrical face, large eyes with violet pupils, and an ancestry I couldn't determine.

Patrick turned and walked away. I knew he was expecting me to follow him and I didn't want to give in, but I knew I was going to anyway. When the girl followed him I looked back at my boss. "Sorry Jamaal," I said.

I could hear Jamaal sigh as the three of us walked out.

— 2 —

I followed the exotic-looking girl as we walked out of the building into a warm late-October day. I saw an unusual cigar-shaped craft about the length of an 18-wheeler sitting at the far edge of the Uploads parking lot. A lifter! These are the new, cutting-edge electrogravitic space planes I had read about in the tech mags but had never seen. Back in the day they were called UFOs or UAPs. Only the military had the new lifters. But I was more fascinated with the girl walking in front of me. She had short blond hair and ears that came to a point, like an elf's. She had an air to her, a feel, that I had never encountered before. I'm 26 but I've been all over the world for my job and I've met a lot of people. She was unusual and I was intrigued. She never turned around or noticed me as we walked up a small retractable ramp into the vehicle. There were three other people in the craft, two women and another guy.

Patrick and the exotic girl went forward into the navigation area. I found a seat next to the guy, who looked as bewildered as I was.

The craft took off before I could question my seat mate. It was a really cool feeling. There was no impression of gravity at all, no pressure on my seat as we raised off the ground so quickly that we were a couple of miles above the earth's surface in a few seconds. Then the transparencies along the side of the craft opaqued, and I couldn't see outside. Wherever we were going, it wasn't to the grocery store.

About an hour later the girl came out of the forward compartment and told us, "We'll be on the ground in less than a minute."

We landed inside an underground hangar inside a huge cave. Patrick and the girl began walking toward a grey rounded door that led to a large elevator. The elevator took the six of us down very swiftly. Again there was the same feeling of movement, but without the inertia associated with gravity. Was this a secret Space Force military base? I had no idea where we were.

When the elevator door opened I stared into a huge but beautiful underground city. Rounded white towers of a natural-looking substance rose hundreds of feet into a bluish-green canopy illuminated by an appealing, uniform light source. The light had a nourishing quality, but it wasn't sunlight. The air smelled as fragrant as a flower garden. In the air I thought I heard a soft, tingling music. I didn't see any speakers and I couldn't tell where the sound was coming from. The sounds were soothing. I felt the tension release from my body.

Patrick and the girl were already walking toward a small egg-shaped craft, but the four of us stood, gawking in disbelief. I wish I had an image to show you of the city, because words are too pitiful to describe the magnificence of the place. It was as big as Shanghai, but the colors were all muted pastels, pleasing to the eye. There was no metal, wood, or glass here. All of the structures looked like huge, organic stalactites that you'd find in a cave, except they rose from the cave floor. The floor itself was covered with an algae-like substance that felt pleasant to walk on, and it emitted a multi-colored luminescence.

This was no military base!

Patrick motioned impatiently to us. "You can take the tour later. Get in."

I was stunned. This place felt totally different from anywhere I'd been in the world. It was exotic in a way that felt alien, but I felt a really good vibe.

"Where are we?" I asked Patrick. "I didn't know there were cities underground."

Patrick rolled his eyes and got into the vehicle, which was floating about a foot above the ground with no visible means of support.

The girl walked into the craft and sat down in the front, next to Patrick. I was irritated at Patrick for being a prick. I wanted to talk to her, but she seemed to have eyes only for the older man. There were six seats in the vehicle. The four of us sat down behind Patrick and the girl. I looked around at my three seat-mates, quickly sizing them up. The man was about 30, tall and lanky, and looked like an athlete. I noticed when he was walking how graceful his steps were. This guy had his body under control. Unlike myself and the two other women, he had almost immediately adjusted to this strange situation and was sitting calmly, surveying the craft with interest.

The two women were sitting next to each other, and I turned my seat to look at them. The first was petite and had short black hair. She looked like a scientist or an academic. The other girl was very tall and blonde, with a full figure, a Joan-of-Arc type. She immediately rubbed me the wrong way and by the look on her face she felt the same way about me.

Before I had a chance to introduce myself the craft suddenly took off. We didn't feel anything – this must be another inertialess craft. The sides and the top of the vehicle were transparent, and we all got a good view of the underground city.

The stalactite structures were beautiful.

Each of them was several hundred feet tall and looked organic, as if they had been grown in a huge garden. They looked like living quarters, and had little spiral walkways going around the structures. I didn't see anyone walking around on them, or inside. Each of the structures was in a group, and spaced peculiarly.

The ship kept rising; we were several hundred feet in the air now. The light covered the ceiling evenly and was indistinguishable from a real sky, but there was no source to the light as far as I could tell. We moved slowly over the tops of the structures for several miles, until they ended abruptly. The craft exited the gigantic underground city and we were now on the surface. I looked up into a purple sky with a sun that was a blazing pinpoint of light. The surface was hard but barren. It didn't have the colorful algae on it. In the far distance I saw buildings on the horizon, but I couldn't make out details until the craft sped up rapidly. The atmosphere here was perfectly clear. There were no clouds or dust to obscure the view. I wondered how far the buildings were.

Within a few minutes we were flying over a huge, ruined city. Miles and miles of broken buildings, as if a nuclear weapon had struck the city in some ancient war. I got the impression the city had been here for eons.

My companions were staring out of the transparencies, as transfixed as I was. I wanted to question Patrick but he was deep in whispered conversation with the girl. The craft continued now even faster, the surface whizzing by. I noticed a few grizzled trees, and a few waterholes where zebra-like creatures were gathered. By the position of the sun it was the middle of the day. The harsh white light from the brilliant sun starkly illuminated the surface and the crumbled buildings.

"This isn't earth," I blurted out.

"Whatever gave you that idea?" Patrick said sarcastically.

"But...we were only in the ship for an hour!"

Artist's conception of the organic towers in the underground city.[3]

Patrick ignored me and I was feeling really angry now. "What is this, some kind of simulation? I want some answers, and I want them now!"

I could see that my companions felt the same way.

Patrick turned to me. "If you're too afraid to continue we'll turn the ship around and you can go back to your boring job at Uploads." He spoke gruffly.

"I'm not afraid!"

"Then shut your piehole and enjoy the view." Patrick gave his attention to the girl beside him. They looked like they were communicating with each other, but their lips weren't moving.

Enjoy the view! Well, this place was beautiful in its own way. The ship itself was blowing my mind; how could anything go from one planet to another in an hour? I sat back in my seat, shrugging at my three companions as if to say, "We're here, let's see what happens."

At that moment the ship gained speed. The ground was a blur now as the ship sped on. Suddenly I saw a sliver of light on the horizon that got bigger and bigger and bigger as we sped across the surface. The ship began to slow down. I saw that this planet had one gigantic moon that was reflecting a soft, multicolored light onto the surface. Here, the light from the moon was much brighter than the light from earth's moon.

I had to acknowledge to myself that this wasn't a simulation, but I didn't have time to ask questions because the craft had slowed down and was now hovering over an opening in the rocky surface. As I watched, an egg-shaped craft (but much larger) came out of the opening. Our craft dived in. We were in another underground area, but this was much smaller than the city we'd left, although the architecture and the look and feel of this place was the same.

We dropped to the surface in front of a huge stone entrance that had illuminated symbols on each side. Light was streaming out of the opening but it didn't hurt my eyes.

The side of the craft opened, and Patrick and the girl walked out. I looked at my three companions. What else was there to do but follow along?

I was getting really angry now. I could tell Joan-of-Arc was feeling the same way. I approached Patrick and turned him around roughly with my hand on his shoulder. "We're not going another foot until you explain what this place is and what we're doing here."

Joan-of-Arc, who was almost a head taller than me, was right behind me. I could feel her glaring also at Patrick.

The older man sighed. "I hate these recruiting missions, but they have to be done."

The girl nodded knowingly. "All will be explained," she said to the four of us. "If you can be patient for just a few more minutes, you will be thoroughly briefed."

I looked up at the Amazon behind me. She nodded. The other two began to move forward, and passed us as Patrick and the girl continued down a magnificently lit entranceway that looked like it was meant for royalty.

Joan-of-Arc and I stared as we walked beside each other. The light was a golden color and allowed close inspection of the various statues, holograms, artwork, and light displays that filled the space. Just before we exited the entranceway I turned around and looked at the entire display. Each piece of art was complete in itself, but designed to be part of a larger composition. The petite woman was standing beside me now, her mouth open as she took it all in. Ideas and concepts were coming into my head when Patrick yelled at me again. "Philogene! Kelleye! Let's go!" The Amazon grinned at us. The other guy was already walking out of the entranceway. Kelleye and I followed. We turned the corner and emerged into one of a number of darkened caverns that were grouped together. Farther on, the small caverns led to a lighted area that looked like another of the huge underground cities.

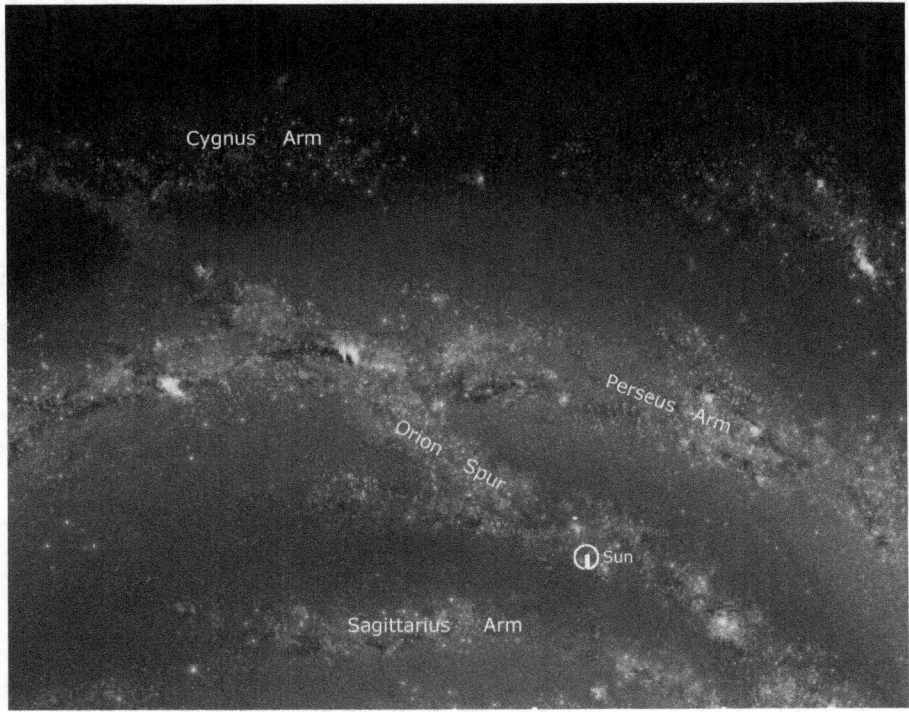

The Orion Spur and the sun[4]

As the four of us and Patrick and the girl walked into the cavern, a gigantic holographic projection filled the space. We started watching a short presentation about the history of earth and its relationship to the galaxy. We learned that the earth is part of the Greater Community, a local group of stars in the Orion Spur. The Spur has over a billion solar systems.

The Milky Way galaxy[5]

The earth sits in a geostrategically important position in the Spur, on the border between two gigantic corporate trading collectives. These trading collectives are very interested in the earth, and not necessarily in a good way.

After we were done the four of us just stood there, staring at each other. The situation "out there" is just as fucked up as on earth, except that galactic technology is about a million years ahead of ours.

— 3 —

Patrick had the look of a bored parent who had just watched a kiddie program for the hundredth time. "You guys get it now I hope," he said.

My cockiness about my little life was gone. My job at Uploads, which had seemed like an elite position, was as important as a rock thrown into the middle of the Pacific Ocean.

Patrick gestured to the girl, who introduced herself as Gwenneth (or something that sounded like that. I'm going to call her Gwenneth).

"You are on a planet in what you call the α Aquilae, or Altair, star system," she began, "within the Fenachrone Trading Collective. Our sun is brighter than yours, but our planet is further away than earth is from its sun. Like earth, Celeste is hidden in a solar system with a single star. You know the rest."

"So you're not from earth," I said, feeling like a dolt. "And this isn't earth."

The Amazon, who was standing next to me, hit me on the shoulder. "Thank you, Mr. Obvious."

I was ready to snark back when Patrick said, "Enough, children. It's time to introduce yourselves. If all goes well you will be working together as a team."

"I'm not working with her," I said.

"Philogene, meet Joann."

"Joann of Arc!" I said. "I knew it."

"The woman to your left is Kelleye," Patrick said. "She's a mathematician and a network analyst."

Patrick pointed to Joann. "Joann is a pilot, and a good one. Tested very high on the personal affinity scale. She's good in crisis situations and relating

16

to strangers. Your group is going to need an experienced pilot. That is, if you decide to join us."

"Good at relating to strangers? You could have fooled me."

Joann stuck her tongue out at me.

"The gentleman beside Kelleye is Joshua," Patrick said. "Joshua is skilled in hand-to-hand combat. You may need those skills, at least occasionally. When he's not fighting, you'll find that his diplomatic and arbitration skills are second to none."

I looked at Joshua. He didn't seem special to me. He hadn't said a word so far to anyone, and seemed to want to keep himself to himself.

"Appearances are deceiving," Patrick replied, seeming to read my thoughts.

"What about me? Why am I here?"

"You? You have the capability to be a superior remote viewer, hopefully a Seer. You'll find out exactly what that means in your training."

I looked around at my three companions, who were as baffled as I was. I saw Gwenneth smiling, looking at us fondly like we were a new batch of kittens about to be released from their cages into a new world.

"We're taking you home now," Patrick said. "This was just an orientation session, to show you that the earth is completely unprepared to face the integration of your planet into the Greater Community, which is already in progress. We will contact you when we are ready to begin your training."

On the way back the four of us were trying to make sense of what we had seen. My head was spinning with information I couldn't process. I couldn't deny that the world we had been on wasn't earth. According to Patrick's presentation, our little planet is on a busy trade route within the Greater Community, and lots of trading nations use our solar system, and the earth, like a truck stop. It was unreal to me.

Patrick was an enigma. Jamaal said that Patrick was Space Force, but I didn't believe that. He looked human, but was he? He had the look and personality of a human, but he seemed to belong on Celeste. Something didn't add up there. But Patrick was the least of my worries.

After a while Joshua spoke up. "Maybe we'll know more after we do our training."

Joann and I snorted; Kelleye said nothing.

I looked at Joann more closely. She was very tall and full-figured, definitely not my type. I'm just an average schmoe, physically unimposing, of average height and build. She was probably the bossy type, wanting her own way all the time. The hard-to-please type. Just like me! Maybe that's why we rubbed each other the wrong way.

Kelleye was very quiet and seemed awkward in social situations. I couldn't figure out why she was chosen for whatever this was.

Joshua had raven black hair. He was even taller than Joann, but thin and wiry. Diplomacy and combat training didn't seem like a good combination to me.

Half an hour later we were on the ground in the Uploads parking lot. When I got back to my desk Jamaal came up to me. "So, you're back."

I could tell he was curious about what had happened, but I couldn't answer any of his questions because I would sound like a nutjob. Patrick was probably counting on that. "Is Patrick really Space Force?"

Jamaal shrugged. "That's what he told me."

It didn't take me long to get back into my work. Troubleshooting the satellite grid requires my full attention. With over a thousand sats in orbit in our sector alone, there is always some fuck-up somewhere, and our crew of techs is constantly busy. I only get the toughest assignments and no two cases are the same, which challenges my pattern-recognition skills. Without the AIs the Grid would fall apart, but there were always orbital anomalies and software glitches that only humans could solve.

Six hours later I finished my shift and went to my vehicle. My trip to wherever seemed almost like a vivid daydream now, and the presentation we saw just a science fiction movie. However, I was intrigued by Gwenneth. I wanted to see her again.

At that point I was just one of Gwenneth's and Patrick's kittens. We all were. It didn't last long.

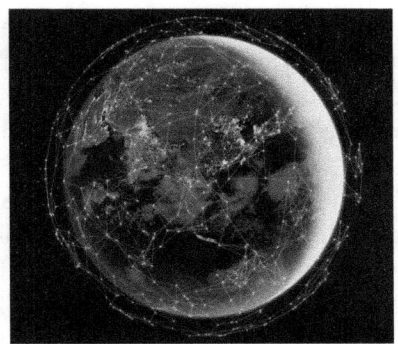

— 4 —

[Blair, Nebraska, 2015]

"Daddy, can I fly an airplane when I grow up?" Joann D'Arcy asked her father. She was eight years old.

"Do you want to?" her father replied. The older man was stockily built, a veteran American Airlines commercial pilot. Gene could see his daughter looking at a small private jet taking off. They were in the parking lot at the Blair Municipal Airport, where he volunteered on Saturdays as an airport manager assistant, which meant he got to do all the grunt work. He loved aircraft and flight, and wanted to be around the business for the rest of his life. At Blair, he had even given flying lessons and worked in the aircraft repair station.

"Yes!"

The child was curious about everything. Like her mother, a former striker on the University of Nebraska volleyball team. She was already half a head taller than anyone in her third grade class, including the boys. "Do you want to know how airplanes work?"

"Yes!"

Gene handed his daughter a pamphlet he had put together for civilians interested in flight. It was way over her head, with diagrams of propeller and jet aircraft, explanations of the physics of airflow and lift, and photos of popular small and large commercial planes.

"Thank you daddy!"

He picked up Joann and hugged her. "C'mon sweetheart, I have to go to work. You can watch the planes take off and land from my office window."

As the day proceeded Gene checked in with his daughter at regular intervals. Her head was buried in the pamphlet, and she was researching the material on her tablet.

When Joann reached the 10th grade she was over six feet tall, with large hands and a good vertical leap. The school's volleyball coach, remembering the prowess of her mother, recruited her for the team. During Joann's senior year in high school she became the team's best striker. She was now 6' 5", and received a visit from a recruiter from the Nebraska women's volleyball team.

"No thank you, coach. I plan on enrolling in flight school at the Aviation Institute."

"I see. Following in your father's footsteps, not your mother's."

"I've been interested in flight since I was a child, coach. I joined the high school volleyball team because...I wanted to make mom happy. But my heart's not in it."

The coach was surprised. "I wouldn't have guessed by your demeanor on the court. You've got that killer instinct."

Joann brightened. "I do! But not for sports."

[West Arlington, Virginia, 2013]

"Sensei, how long will it be before I get a black belt?"

Martin Luther Thompson, a former police officer, laughed out loud. He looked critically at the child, dressed in his karategi. Joshua stood straight and tall, and looked like a cat ready to pounce.

"Son, you must first master the punch, the kick, the knee strike, the elbow strike, the vital point strike, and the open-hand techniques. All this I will teach you, but you must work hard."

Joshua's eyes hardened. "There's a bully at school I want to destroy."

Martin, a student of the history of martial arts, smiled. The boy's attitude was typical. Martin hunched down and looked Joshua in the eyes. "Forget about the bully. In order to be successful in the martial arts you must cultivate self-discipline, hard training, and your own creative efforts."

The child's eyes widened. "Yes, sensei. I am not afraid of hard work."

"We'll see about that, Joshua."

Martin gestured toward his assistant. The dojo was full today, but he was intrigued by this child, the son of a woman who taught self-defense techniques to other women in her spare time. "Jack, come over here."

A cocky young man wearing a brown belt strolled over. "Joshua, this is Jack Tran. A most promising student. He will get you started."

Joshua frowned. "His belt is only brown. I want to learn from the best."

Jack looked at his sensei and the two men laughed. Jack looked Joshua over. "A real fire-breather I see," he remarked.

Joshua stiffened. "Train me and you'll see."

"Cool off, son." Martin gave Jack a knowing look. "See what you can do with him." Martin walked away, shaking his head.

Martin occasionally checked up on Joshua during the next hour. His assistant was devoting more attention to Joshua than to the other students. Martin paused and watched Joshua drill. All of his moves were completed fully and done with full intention. The boy was a serious student.

Joshua came to the dojo twice a week for an hour. On the second visit Martin could see that the kid had been practicing at home.

After the second week it was Martin's practice to call the student's home and his school. Sometimes an overzealous student would lash out at perceived enemies. Joshua's mother was pleased with the child's progress, but at school it was a different story. "There was an incident yesterday," the school counselor said. "At recess Joshua attacked another student."

"Let me guess. A large boy. A bully."

"That is irrelevant. Assaults at school are not tolerated."

"Of course." Martin had dealt with this counselor before. "Has the larger boy also been reprimanded?" Martin had the story from Josh's mother, who had already been down to the school. Josh had been attacked first.

"That is none of your business, Mr. Thompson."

"It certainly is. The bully's father is the mayor. I'm sure he had a word with you."

The counselor's face was set in grim lines. "Another incident like that and Joshua will be expelled."

Martin bit back his anger. Stupid bureaucrat!

The next time Josh came in, Martin had a word. "If you do that again I'll drop you."

Josh bowed his head. "Yes sensei." A smile formed on Josh's lips. "I did it just as Jack taught me. I don't think that bully will bother me again."

Martin laughed. This serious little kid was funny!

When Josh got home the day of his playground fight (after talking to a really stupid school counselor) he was called into his father's study. Dad was head of the Political Science Department at George Mason University, specializing in international relations. Josh had picked up an interest in politics and foreign policy from his dad, and liked to look through the books on his father's shelves.

"Heard you had some difficulty today, Joshua."

"No difficulty, dad. Billy tried to hit me again. I kicked him in the abdomen." Josh demonstrated. "A Gedan Giri right below the solar plexus." Josh bit his lips. "Sensei wouldn't have wanted me to hurt him," he explained.

Robert Reynolds smiled.

"He was too stupid to use the foot sweep. He could have had me too, because I didn't do the Gedan right." Joshua was apologetic. "Forgot to lower my strike leg. I was showing off."

Robert bit back a laugh as he looked at his son, so unconsciously serious as he explained his mistake.

Josh looked up at the full bookcases. "Have you read all those?"

Robert gazed at the hundreds of books on the shelves. "All of them, but mainly because I have to keep up with the literature. Most of them aren't worth the paper they're printed on."

Josh had heard this before. He looked at the section reserved for his father's books. "Except for those, of course."

Robert met his son's eyes. "Of course."

Josh's lips twitched. Father and son broke out laughing.

[Albany, New York, 2017]

Kelleye Rodriquez was bored. She was sitting in math class with a teacher who didn't understand the beauty of numbers. She was learning more at home, being tutored by her mother, than she was in school. She looked around the classroom. Everyone was doing simple multiplication. Her mother had taught her to memorize the multiplication table and she could divide, multiply, add, and subtract in her head. As the math teacher droned on, Kelleye stared out the window.

Her daydreaming was interrupted. "Ms. Rodriquez, are you bored?"

Her mother had taught her to be honest. "Yes. I'm bored stiff."

The teacher was offended. "Well then, Kelleye, why don't you show us how to multiply 8 times 7."

"I don't have to show you. It's 56."

"You didn't follow the procedure, Kelleye," the teacher said with condescension.

"That's true. But I can tell you the answer to any simple multiplication problem without my calculator."

"OK, what's 110 times 11?"

Kelleye worked it out in her head. "1,210."

The teacher was astonished. "You guessed."

"Type it out on your calculator."

The rest of the students were doing just that. "She's right," a boy said. "It's 1210."

The teacher was getting angry, but Kelleye didn't care. "It's called the multiplication tables. Memorize them and you can do this stuff in your head."

"A lot of people have trouble with that. Our method shows you why multiplication works."

"I get it, and that's important. But my mom is an engineer. She's teaching me algebra at home now, so I don't really need to sit here and do this work. I already know it."

The teacher turned to the class. "Ms. Rodriquez is a know-it-all."

The next day Kelleye brought in the multiplication tables, printed out, one for each student.

When the teacher said, "Get out your workbooks children," Kelleye got up and distributed them to the class.

"What are you doing?" the teacher asked. Kelleye put one on the teacher's desk.

"Trying to save everyone a lot of work." To the students she said, "Memorize these if you can. You'll be smarter than teach here."

The teacher slammed her hand on her desk. "Kelleye Rodriquez, you are a troublemaker! I'm sending you to the school counselor."

Kelleye was grateful to Ms. Towson for getting her out of class. "Thanks, teach! If I were you I'd memorize those tables."

All of the students laughed. Ms. Towson was outraged.

When Kelleye got home she told her mother what had happened at school.

Terry was conflicted. She didn't believe in home schooling because it isolated children from society. But the quality of education in the public school systems was not up to her standards.

"What do you want to do, honey?" Terry asked. "We can pull you from the school and put you in a private school. Or I can hire a tutor and you can learn at home."

Kelleye thought about that for a minute. "I like my classmates. I don't want to stay home all day. I don't want to start in a new school."

"All right. I'll talk to the school principal about advancing you to a higher grade. That way you won't have to spend so much time there."

Kelleye brightened. "Can you do that?"

"I'll do it," Terry said firmly. She looked her daughter in the eyes. "You'll always be the youngest person in your class, Kelleye. That can cause social problems for you. You might get picked on."

Kelleye's eyes widened, but she understood. "I can handle it, mom. Let's do that."

The next semester, after taking an aptitude test, Kelleye was advanced from the fifth grade to the eighth.

"You daughter has a very high IQ," the principal said to Terry. "But she may have trouble dealing with the older kids."

"I've apprised her of that, Mr. Johnson, and she's ready to take the plunge."

"Very well. Kelleye can always see Ms. Towson, the school counselor, if she has difficulty."

"Ms. Towson? I thought she taught math!"

"She has been reassigned to, ah, a position that is hopefully more suited to her talents."

When Terry told Kelleye about Ms. Towson, her daughter laughed. "I don't think I'll be using her services," Kelleye said with a grin.

Terry smiled. She wasn't worried about Kelleye. Her daughter had steel in her.

— 5 —

[Palo Alto, California]

Kathy Abbott had been diagnosed with inoperable breast cancer that had metastasized into her left lung. After the first round of chemo she was starting to feel the debilitating effects of the disease. Even though she might not live to take the job, she decided to attend an on-campus recruiting event at the medical school. After an hour she felt sick and knew she had to get home and lie down. A handsome old man with a full head of white hair approached her on her way out of the building.

"My dear, would you be interested in participating in a trial for a promising new cancer treatment?"

Kathy was suspicious. "How do you know I have cancer?"

"Come now, Ms. Abbott. A young woman who graduates at the top of her class, and is proclaimed by her instructors to be one of the best young researchers in the country? You have drawn a lot of attention."

The old man was kind and Kathy was desperate. After Dr. Glazer presented his credentials, she accepted.

"I can see you are ill, Ms. Abbott. Come with me."

Dr. Glazer led Kathy to a small lab room and drew out a small vial filled with a light blue liquid. He inserted a tiny needle into the vial.

"That's it?" she said in disappointed tones.

Dr. Glazer ignored this remark and gently inserted the needle into her shoulder. As soon as the needle was withdrawn she felt a pleasant sensation around the injection site. "Call me tomorrow," Glazer told her. They exchanged contact information.

That evening the lump in her breast felt less painful. After weeks of getting sicker and feeling hopeless, she felt a sudden rush of well being flow through her. At that moment she knew she would recover. Intrigued and angry that a tiny dose of the mysterious blue serum had done what three weeks of chemotherapy could not, Kathy Abbott called Dr. Glazer.

"Dr. Glazer, I insist that you explain what was in that vial."

The old man smiled. "How are you feeling, Ms. Abbott?"

"Why...the pain is noticeably less. The lump in my breast has already begun to shrink, and I am breathing better! Dr. Glazer, this is impossible."

"Come see me in my office tomorrow, Ms. Abbott, at 8 a.m. in the Medical Center building. Suite 314."

Kathy arrived ten minutes early, waiting in front of the locked door. Before the old man could even get the door open she said, "What is the origin of this miracle new drug? The lump in my breast is almost gone!"

Glazer's blue eyes twinkled. He explained that he was part of a well-connected tech startup called the Technology Acquisitions Consortium, which was researching advanced medical formulations. He offered her a position with the firm. "You will begin as a low-level operative, but if you successfully complete your assignments you will be offered a permanent position."

Glazer refused to explain what was in the blue vial and how it had been developed. "At this point you do not have a need to know."

Kathy was frustrated with the lack of information, but infinitely grateful to what Dr. Glazer called "the program" for the new drug that was going to save her life. She needed a job anyway, and so agreed to a one-year employment contract.

Her first assignment was as an administrative assistant to Rebecca Homes, the head of a genomics company called BioSciences in Palo Alto. Her job was to keep tabs on Holmes, whose company was involved in some super-secret operation for the TAC program. "Rebecca is brilliant, but a bit flighty at times," Dr. Glazer told her. "Please report every week on her movements, and the activities of BioSciences." She was given no background or briefing.

"Send hand-written reports back to DC. A courier, always riding a bicycle and dressed in dark green fatigues, will show up every Sunday evening at 6 p.m. at your apartment in Palo Alto."

After one more day the lump in her breast was completely gone. She was breathing freely now and was pain-free. Her energy levels were back to normal. It was literally a miracle!

As she worked her assignment Kathy noticed an interesting phenomenon: her memories of being sick began to fade. It was as if the cells in her body had no memory of ever being ill. Physically and mentally she was now just another normal, healthy 24-year-old.

For three months she heard nothing from the old man. She knew nothing, and began to feel like a glorified stenographer. Occasionally she noticed people following her as she walked on campus or drove on errands, but thought nothing of it. Rebecca was secretive, and Kathy's duties were mostly day-to-day office administration. Occasionally her medical expertise was consulted on a medical trial or a grant proposal to the NIH.

Was Rebecca also part of the TAC program? Did anyone even read her reports?

The euphoria from her treatment gradually faded and she became thoroughly bored with her job. The only contact she had with "the program" was the courier, but he knew less than she did.

"It's good money," the young man said one evening after Kathy had handed over her handwritten report. "I just deliver packages and keep my mouth shut."

"They tell me nothing. I'm thinking of quitting."

The courier's eyes sharpened at this, but he shrugged. "I'm just glad to have a job."

A week later she was thrilled when Dr. Glazer called her to DC on a special assignment.

[Bethesda, Maryland]

Dr. Colin Frank, the NIH director, was on his way from his office to a large conference room at the main NIH complex in Bethesda, Maryland. The meeting of the deputy directors was scheduled for 9 a.m. and he was late. Head down, walking as fast as he could on his short legs, Dr. Frank heard the irritating voice of his principal deputy director, Mike Cjenk.

"Hi Colin, how are you this morning?"

Colin looked up at the bulky man, who was, as usual, dressed haphazardly in a rumpled suit and a poorly knotted tie that hung loosely around his neck. Colin frowned. The pretentious Cjenk always addressed him by his first name, as if they were friends. Which they were not. "I'm fine, Mike. Is there something you wanted?"

Cjenk smiled an oily smile. "Yes there is, Colin. A unique opportunity, in fact."

Colin Frank thought that Cjenk should find his true calling: a used-car salesman in a junkyard. He checked his watch. "The Deputy Director's meeting is in two minutes," he stated firmly. "Your presence is required."

Cjenk, a very large, bulbous man, stepped into Colin's path as he was about to walk away. He gestured toward a small conference room.

The director was so shocked by his deputy's behavior that he mechanically walked into the conference room, Cjenk behind him. Seated at a table were four persons the director had never seen before. "What is this, Cjenk? Who are these people?"

"If you'll come with us to the NIH Medical Center, Colin, we'll show you." He pointed to the four. Two of them were in suits and looked like intelligence officers. Another had a white lab coat on. The leader was a young woman dressed in a business suit. "My friends here are from the Technology Acquisitions Consortium, an interagency group working with the DHS and the DIA."

"I'm sorry, but military intelligence has nothing to do with me or you or the NIH." He turned to Cjenk. "Our meeting is in the main conference room, Mike. We're already late." Colin turned to walk out. A woman at the table barked, "The deputy directors' meeting will have to wait."

Colin was irritated. He had never been addressed so dismissively, especially by a young woman who was young enough to be his granddaughter. "I beg your pardon? Ms—"

"Kathy Abbot, director." She rose. As if on cue, the others got up. "Come with me."

The four walked out but Cjenk stayed behind. There was some mystery about this, something untoward. The NIH director prided himself on running a tight ship. Colin didn't like mysteries, and these people were anomalies. "I'll postpone the meeting."

"Very well," Cjenk replied. "You won't be disappointed, I assure you."

Colin and Cjenk walked out of the NIH offices and a vehicle was waiting. Colin sent a text message postponing the meeting to the deputy directors. They were driven to the NIH's Biomedical Research Center and took an elevator to a poorly lit sub-basement. They walked down a corridor that was painted black. "I do not recognize this area," the director said.

"It is restricted," Abbott said. She had a sharp, unpleasant face. Colin disliked her. One of her men handed out security cards with an imprinted hologram. "Keep this with you at all times."

At the end of the corridor was a small black door that was marked "Janitor's Closet." After passing single-file through the small work closet, the group opened another door and emerged into a huge, brightly lit room with dozens of lab tables and medical stations, all occupied by white-coated researchers. Two armed men scanned the IDs of the visitors.

Colin Frank was shocked. "This installation is unauthorized!"

"Oh, but it is," Abbott stated condescendingly. "Over here, director."

Abbott led the group over to one of the medical stations. Upon a table, surrounded by clear plexiglass, a most unusual specimen was lying. The director stared at the body, which had a skull capacity at least 50% greater than a human's, with very large eyes. Dr. Frank noticed that the musculature and the bone structure of the body was also much different from a human's. "A very lifelike replica," the director stated. "But I fail to see the heuristic applications for a body like this."

"It's not a replica," Abbott replied. "This fellow was found by one of the DIA's crash teams. Dead of course."

Dr. Frank looked contemptuously at the sharp-featured woman. What were these people doing down here? He looked critically around the room. This was some kind of designer cadaver facility, of course, probably for post-doc work. The equipment they were using was very sophisticated. He saw what looked like a bioscanner at the adjacent medical workstation, but did not recognize the design. The director scowled. Why did he not know of this place? His eyes were caught by an ugly black cadaver lying on a medical bed about 50 feet away. What was this? He began walking toward the body.

Abbott glanced at one of her team, who said, "He's discovered the Maitre!"

"Let him look, the silly fool," Abbott replied. The team followed the NIH director.

Frank gazed at the cadaver on the table. Another non-human replica! "What are you people doing down here?" he demanded. Colin was indignant. "I intend to report you, Ms. Abbott, and this facility, to your superior at the DIA."

Abbott sighed. "Wake it up," she told the man in the lab coat. "Be careful." Abbott walked around the medical bed, ensuring that the straps were tightly fastened around the ugly creature. An injection was given and the Maitre slowly began to stir. Suddenly a horrible screech came forth from its tight-lipped mouth when it discovered where it was. Then, each of those around the bed felt a malevolent darkness descend upon their psyches, a suffocating envelope of hatred and hopelessness.

"Zimmerman!" Abbott cried. Another injection was given and the Maitre struggled madly. Then it went limp.

"Whatever this thing is, it's dead now," the medtech stated after examining the body.

Colin Frank's comfortable worldview was shattered. "I...what just happened?"

No one said anything. Abbott was the first to recover. She remembered the detailed instructions Dr. Glazer had given her. "Dr. Frank. We had to show you these...beings...to establish our bona fides, and to cut through the disbelief that always occurs when the idea of intelligent life outside the earth arises. The galaxy is very spacious, Dr. Frank, and the earth is a tiny little pebble on a very large beach."

Colin still felt numb. "What is this ugly thing?" he asked.

"It's called a Maitre."

Colin touched the Maitre's flesh and shuddered. He walked over to a creature on another table. "Are these things part of the CRISPR gene altering program?"

Abbott shook her head in disbelief. "You don't get it, do you director? These creatures are living beings that apparently exist outside our solar system." Abbott smirked as she saw the shocked and offended look on the director's face. "The point of this demonstration is to make you aware that races and nations exist outside our pathetic little planet. And they have been around a lot longer than humanity, which means they have technology that is far beyond ours. Dr. Frank, we are being offered some very astonishing biotechnology."

Colin gazed at the creature on the table. Its head was very large, but it had pleasant, almost refined, facial features. The skeletal structure was delicate. From a physiological perspective, this creature would have trouble walking, for its musculature appeared to have developed for an environment with a lower specific gravity than earth's.... Suddenly he understood. A look of awe appeared on his face. "So it's true then! Earth is not alone in the universe."

"No, doctor. According to the Crash Team investigators, the galaxy is teeming with life." Kathy Aboott waved her arm in a quarter circle. "They say that the earth is under constant observation from creatures like these."

Colin gazed around the facility. A dozen other bodies were lying on other lab beds, some of them enclosed in clear plastic shells.

"The NIH, in conjunction with BioSciences in Palo Alto, is currently developing a new vaccine," Abbott said. "With a slight alteration to your plans – for which you will be generously compensated – you can substitute that vaccine with, ah, a revolutionary new biotech that makes RNA vaccine technology look like an electric shock machine."

"I am already very well compensated."

A stickler! Abbott thought. The TAC psychologist had profiled Colin Frank perfectly: A pretentious, virtue-signaling do-gooder on the outside, camouflaging a greedy and ambitious personality. "We aren't discussing money, director. I'm talking about biotech that can flawlessly program genes and create a disease-free human being. As you know, gene therapy is currently a rather hit-or-miss proposition."

The director was interested, but the memory of that evil Maitre thing was still in his mind. "Ms. Abbott, you have made some promising but very wild and unsubstantiated claims."

Abbott gestured to the medtech. "Show him."

A glass-lined container with several sickly looking young rats was placed on a lab table. "Inspect these rats, Dr. Frank. Make a diagnosis."

A former medical researcher in his younger days, Colin bent over and examined the little creatures. "Chronic respiratory disease. Specifically, murine respiratory mycoplasmosis. There is no cure."

"That is correct, doctor. Observe."

Abbott's tech filled a tiny syringe from a vial and injected each of the rats.

Colin watched, fascinated, as each of the rats began to slowly recover. Within twenty minutes each of them were clawing the sides of the container, obviously looking for food, the picture of health.

"But...this is impossible, Ms. Abbott. Gene therapy simply doesn't work this quickly. Or at all."

"I assure you, Dr. Frank, that the new biotech works just as well on humans."

Colin Frank looked back at the dead thing on the medical bed behind him. "This new biotech didn't come from that creature, did it?"

"Of course not, director. The Maitre is just a galactic proxy, a glorified bagman and go-fer. We don't have the time now to give you a full briefing."

Colin's mind was whirling. "What is the nature of this biotech? I must understand the science behind it."

"All in good time, director. The next step is to conduct human trials, but I assure you that this technology is flawless. It works every time." Abbott dug into her briefcase and pulled out a folder. "I had inoperable breast cancer, and six months to live. After one treatment, my cancer was gone in less than a week. In this file you'll find my medical records."

Colin took the file and read it, a look of disbelief on his face at first and then stunned surprise. The case file was authentic. He looked up slowly from the folder at Abbott. "We don't need to issue a new vaccine, Ms. Abbott. If this new biotech is as effective as you say it is, we can simply use it in the annual flu shots."

Abbott noticed the NIH director's use of the word 'we.' "Director, be prepared for controversy when people go in for a flu shot and start feeling better than they have ever felt in their lives."

For the first time the director smiled. He was thinking of the profits that would come from a flu shot that actually worked. "That is the kind of controversy I can live with."

He looked at the rats, fully recovered, and glanced once more through Abbott's file. All seemed genuine. This technology must come from the hidden programs deep within the bowels of the military's secret special access programs. This room was clearly one of them, and underneath his own NIH Medical Center! He would have to look into this Technology Acquisitions Consortium.

Colin had heard the rumors about extraterrestrial involvement in some of these super-secret ventures, but had of course dismissed it as nonsense. He looked around at some of the extraordinary creatures housed here. One of them was almost 8 feet tall and looked like a praying mantis; another was only two feet long with a very large, elongated skull. No, these were not replicas. They were real!

Abbott and her crew were silent as the NIH director completed his observation of the facility. Kathy could see the director contemplating his options. She watched as Colin Frank slowly turned toward her. A slight smile began to form on his serious, academic face.

The NIH director pointed to the now healthy rats in their glass cages. "Ms. Abbott, please feed those creatures." If these people were genuine and their biotech was effective on humans, he would literally be a hero. His voice would ring the loudest when it came to public health policy. Although Tony Fauci had made the NIH the most important medical organization in the world, he would do even better. His voice would ring louder than the power-mad bureaucrats at the UN and the WHO. Perhaps he could become an important influencer in the political arena after he retired from the NIH....

Dr. Colin Frank placed his arms in front of his body and clasped his hands, ready to receive information. "How do we get this new biotech into our flu shots?"

"If you will come with me, director, I'll show you."

[Fort Detrick, Frederick, Maryland]

"Well done Kathy," said Dr. Genghis Glazer, a week later. "You handled that perfectly."

Abbott and her handler were in Fort Detrick, at the DIA's National Center for Medical Intelligence. She was being debriefed by Dr. Glazer. As always, Glazer was friendly but reserved. He was a master at making conversation that made you feel comfortable, but revealing nothing about himself or his organization.

Abbott bowed slightly to the old man, who was still very handsome with a full head of white hair. "Dr. Frank will make a valuable addition to our network," she said. "The network you promised to fully brief me on."

"All in good time my dear," Glazer said smoothly, with just the slightest hint of condescension.

Kathy frowned. "I told Colin Frank that the earth was just a tiny pebble in a huge galaxy teeming with life. Just as you said."

"Quite right, Kathy."

"You're not telling me the whole story. This amazing biotech saved my life! But something feels wrong."

Dr. Glazer's eyes widened slightly and he sat up straighter. "Yes?"

"This new serum is light years beyond the knowledge of current medical science. Is the source of this new biotech off-world?"

"You do not yet have a need to know, Ms. Abbott."

Kathy sighed. That was the standard line for those who got too inquisitive. She understood the need for compartmentalization, but it was frustrating to be an asset instead of a player.

Dr. Glazer debriefed her in his usual calm and charming way, jotting down notes and taking her recording device. She had a thousand questions, but none of them were answered. "Just follow the script," Dr. Glazer told her. After two hours with her debriefer she drove to her TAC provided apartment in Arlington, Virginia.

What she had seen in the underground facility had blown her away, and she was determined to know everything that was being hidden.

The next day Genghis Glazer read Colin Frank in to the TAC program. Kathy Abbott had done excellent work recruiting the NIH director! Dr. Glazer was satisfied and content. Now it was time for him to get his instructions, which happened on the first of every month. To do that, he boarded one of the

33

new military lifter craft at Joint Base Anacostia-Bolling, accompanied by his driver/pilot. Genghis put on his biosuit and stepped into the lifter. He never failed to be astonished when the little spacecraft rose so noiselessly and comfortably into the sky. In less than a minute they were in space, and approaching a small egg-shaped ship with a completely seamless hull. Genghis stepped into the transfer area. He waited until the hatch depressurized and a forward door opened in his lifter. He stepped into the other craft. Inside, another being, also dressed in a biosuit, stepped forward. This entity was a head taller than himself. Genghis thought it odd that while his own face covering was clear, the other's face was not visible. All he could determine was that this being had two arms, two legs, and a head.

The conversation began. It was an unusual conversation, for Genghis heard thoughts from the being in his head. He spoke English, but the other understood him somehow.

Genghis found himself describing his activities during the past month. Whenever he wanted to ask a question, however, he couldn't form the right words.

After his debrief, his instructions entered his mind. Genghis found himself agreeing with them. After about twenty minutes the interview ended.

When Genghis got back to his lifter he felt a mental pressure lift. Something odd occurred when he tried to recall what had happened just after his ship arrived at its destination above the Space Grid. He couldn't remember anything! But it was all right. His instructions were crystal clear in his mind. He knew he was doing an excellent job, and was working for the very best outcome for humanity.

They were on the ground now and he felt great. Not bad for an old man! He still had it. Satisfied, he got out of his biosuit, humming an old tune. His driver drove him back to his office at Fort Detrick.

Genghis wrote out instructions with pen and paper to Austin Matthews, the administrative director of the Technology Acquisitions Consortium, which would be hand-delivered by a program courier. Rebecca Holmes, the Bio-Sciences CEO, was also sent a handwritten copy of her duties via a secure TAC private jet, hand-delivered by a trusted TAC courier.

Genghis looked out of his window at the Blue and Gray Field across the street from his office. It was a cool, blustery summer day with small clouds scudding by in a sharp, clear blue sky. Yes, it was time for Kathy Abbott to be read in to the TAC program. The woman knew far too much now. Genghis sincerely hoped that she would cooperate; otherwise it would be a sad waste of an excellent operative.

— 6 —

[Midland, Illinois]

I spent a month at Uploads without incident. I gradually forgot about our trip to Celeste and my other three shipmates. Jamaal stopped asking me questions about Patrick and Gwenneth.

Normally I work a six- to ten-hour shift and then hit the disk golf course for a round, if it isn't too dark. It's my way to unwind. After that I go to the downtown comedy club, or one of the other social hangouts, and try to find someone interesting. Man or woman, I don't care. My mind is always working, looking for patterns in social interactions. When I find someone that might be interesting, I approach them.

My life went back to its normal routine until Patrick showed up at the Uploads center on a cold November morning.

Jamaal, the Midlands Uploads director, was irritated. "You Space Force guys should open up your own shop and leave us alone."

"It's a national security matter."

"Which you won't tell me about."

"Naturally." Patrick turned to me. "Are you ready to test your pattern recognition skills in a new way?"

The way he phrased the question excited me. I love my work at Uploads, but it is the same thing every day. I *was* looking for a new challenge. I looked at Patrick. "How many times are you going to pull me out of here?"

"Until – or if – you successfully complete your training."

"There's no 'if' about it," I said, nettled.

Patrick spoke dismissively. "Are you coming?"

"Yeah."

Patrick looked at Jamaal. "We don't force people to work for us."

Jamaal turned and spoke to an older woman. "Ariel, there's a problem in sector c-4, grid alpha-3."

Patrick and I were forgotten. I was a little miffed that I could be dismissed so abruptly.

"Don't sweat it Philogene," the older man said, as if he could read my mind. "Where you're going, you won't miss this place."

Joshua, Joann, and Kelleye were already in the ship. The transparencies closed and we took off.

"This ship looks like a lifter," I offered, breaking the silence. "Saw one of them in a military magazine. Lifters are the new experimental spaceplanes."

"I saw that article," Joann replied. "Eventually, lifters are going to be clean energy replacements for commercial fossil fuel jets. They have new cutting-edge propulsion technology."

"Propulsion technology? These things are anti-grav! They don't have engines."

"You don't know much do you?" Joann said, irritated. She turned away.

Joann-of-Arc and I were obviously not destined to be buddies.

[Celeste]

In an hour we were back in one of the underground cities. We walked into a cavern, similar to the one where we had seen our orientation movie.

A huge 3D holo appeared inside the cave that showed a hub in space above a planet. Ships were docking and being unloaded, others were leaving for deliveries. Inside, the place looked like any loading / unloading area, except this one used robotic workers. "The Greater Community is a collection of trading nations," Patrick explained. "These hubs are transfer points for goods to and from the various planets in the Trading Collectives."

There were several beings in a conference room, each contained within a sealed enclosure.

"That looks like earth, 2020," I said.

"It is life in the galaxy you are entering, all of which will be explained to you later in more detail," Patrick said. "How are these beings communicating?"

There were no computers, handhelds, speakers, or microphones. There were a dozen beings in the room, all isolated from each other. No one was speaking. The four of us were baffled.

"They are using the mental plane," Patrick explained. "It's a way to communicate without technology, and is standard practice all over the galaxy."

"The force!" I exclaimed. "Telepathy."

"It's a lot more than that, Philogene. The first step in your training is learning how to operate on the mental plane. It will give you a very large advantage in the work you will have to do on your world."

"And what is that work?" Kelleye asked.

"You'll find out if you can pass the training."

All of us were intrigued enough to keep going.

[Al-Simak, Vega system, Hilarion Trading Collective]

Our group was sent for our training to a planet Patrick called Al-Simak.

"You're not going to train us?" I didn't like the guy much, but at least he was familiar.

"Not at first. The *bashar* and the *katriri* on Al-Simak will determine if you have sufficient aptitude for advanced training. No one has ever tried to train earthians. It's an experiment and we need the expertise of those on Al-Simak."

"Why are we being trained?" Kelleye asked.

"Because the location of your world is of great importance to the Trading Collectives. You don't know it, but the Collectives have already begun interacting with the earth. We call this the Intervention." Patrick looked us over like an animal trainer would with a new batch of undisciplined puppies. "Like all emerging nations, earth is completely unprepared for life in the Greater Community. If you make it through your basic training it will all be explained." Patrick paused. "We're not forcing any of you. You can leave the program at any time."

The four of us looked at each other. Patrick had challenged us. None of us wanted to quit. It was a big mystery, but I liked tests. I was supremely confident in my abilities. In a physical test both Joshua and Joann could beat me because they were very athletic, but this test, I was sure, would be mental.

Our trip to Al-Simak was like the trip from earth to Celeste, which is the English word for Patrick's and Gwenneth's planet. You might think that traveling across the galaxy from planet to planet is a big deal, but these ships did it so fast it was like a Sunday trip in the car to see grandma. Joann and I were paired up, and Kelleye with Joshua. They went somewhere else; I didn't find out until later that they were also on Al-Simak, but with the katriri.

A Celestian pilot took us to the surface of Al-Simak. Joann got to test drive the lifter by doing a few hops along the surface. "That's very good, earthian woman," the pilot said. She was almost as lovely as Gwenneth. "If you pass the training I will try to teach you how to maneuver through the transportals."

The big woman's face lit up. "Oh, I would so much like that!"

I had no idea what a transportal is, but Joann was excited. She was allowed to land the ship behind a massive boulder as a test of her abilities. We stepped out of the ship and found ourselves standing on a rocky landscape. As far as the eye could see pebbles, stones, boulders, and huge slabs of rock were scattered all over the sandy surface, as if a gigantic rock crusher had randomly broken up a mountain into smaller pieces.

"Omani will signal me when you are ready to be picked up," the Celestian pilot said. "Return here."

We stepped out from behind the boulder. Immediately we were sur-rounded by a dozen four-legged creatures that resembled dogs. But these dogs were intelligent. One of them stood up on its hind legs and regarded Joann and me critically. 'I am Omani. Follow me.' I heard this inside my head and started to panic. I looked over at Joann of Arc and saw her startled reaction. Having someone inside your skull that you didn't invite in is frightening. Then I re-membered that Patrick sent us here to learn how to "operate on the mental plane." So this must be telepathy! The vibe from this creature was pretty good, so I calmed down.

We had obviously been expected. I glanced back as our little scout craft took off. I marked its position behind the huge, misshapen boulder we were walking out of.

"No need to do that," Joann of Arc said condescendingly. "A Space Force pilot doesn't lose her bearings."

"You're Space Force?"

"Was. Did one stint and didn't re-up. But I'm very well trained."

That explains why she's so annoying, I thought. She's ex-military.

Joann and I walked around gigantic slabs of rock, following the dog crea-tures. We arrived about ten minutes later at a cave entrance. The leader of the pack stood on her hind legs and spoke to us telepathically. 'I am Al-quds. You are on a planet we call Al-Simak.'

Wow. It was going to take some time getting used to other beings renting space inside my head. But it was great because we learned a lot of information way faster than the spoken word. Al-quds told us that Al-Simak had two dominant species: the dog-like bashar and the cat-like katriri.

'Except for emerging planets like earth, communications across the galaxy are almost always mind-to-mind,' Al-quds sent. 'You are here to learn how to use the mental plane.'

"I can't do telepathy," Joann said.

"Neither can I," I said.

We were speaking out loud.

Al-quds dismissed this. 'Your species has been uplifted. All uplifted races have access to the mental plane portal. That's how you can hear my thoughts.'

"Can you read our thoughts?" I asked.

Al-quds' face (which resembled a golden retriever) assumed a pained expression.

"Don't mind him," Joann of Arc said dismissively to Al-quds, who gave a sort of dog laugh. She turned to me. "Duh, do you think these creatures speak English?"

The bashar started laughing among themselves. 'Oh dear,' one of them sent. This canine had a face like a terrier, and looked like Bill Maher having a bad hair day. Suddenly a dozen feline creatures, about five feet tall with coats of various colors, appeared in a large hologram inside the cave. They were also laughing. These beings were more human-like, and stood normally on two legs. These must be the katriri, I thought.

'Oh, but we can run on four legs too,' a female-looking feline with gorgeous blue fur sent.

This proclamation caused the bashar to bark humorously. 'The katriri are known to exaggerate,' Al-quds sent diplomatically. 'The bashar are real runners, as we proved at the last racing competition.'

'We'll see at the next contest,' said a red-furred feline dangerously, her claws coming out slightly.

'To learn the subtleties of the mental plane you must train with us,' Al-quds asserted.

The katriri laughed and beat their paws together. Both species, I noticed, had hands that could grasp, with opposable thumbs and digits that ended in claws. Each species had pads on the palms like earth cats and dogs.

Al-quds' face wore a long-suffering expression. I caught one of her thoughts: 'These cats can never be serious.'

"So you don't like the katriri," I said to Al-quds.

'You have misinterpreted my meaning, but I hid that thought. How did you read that sideband?'

I shrugged. "I don't know. I just did."

'Oh dear. I see now why you humans were sent here.'

The katriri mewled the bashar in a mocking fashion. 'These canines are very good organizers and engineers,' sent the red-furred cat, who called herself Calladren. 'If you want more refined training, come to us.'

I couldn't understand this pointless debate, but Joann was quicker than me. "Of course. This conversation is our introduction to the telepathy method of communication."

Al-quds' face showed pleased surprise. 'That is correct.'

Al-quds showed both of us how to open what she called the "portal" to the mental plane. 'With practice, both of you should be competent enough to send and receive.'

Joann of Arc and I looked at each other in astonishment. "That would be really cool," I said.

'Humans, your planet has been noticed by the Collectives,' Omani sent. 'If you wish to survive in the Greater Community you must learn to become competent on the mental plane, and to recognize when your mind is being influenced.'

I laughed. "Nobody is influencing my mind, mental plane or no mental plane."

A second later I felt myself taking an involuntary step forward. I saw the Amazon do the same.

'Do you understand, humans?' Omani sent.

"I wasn't ready. Try that again," I said.

I braced myself mentally. I didn't even feel the impulse to take a step but my right foot went out halfway before I could stop it. I saw Joann of Arc step forward reluctantly.

'A competent operator on the mental plane can affect the mental activity of any untrained entity,' Al-quds explained.

"So telepathy is powerful stuff."

'That is correct, earthian human being. Already the Collectives are employing the mental plane against key influencers on earth.'

Al-quds addressed Omani. 'These two candidates seem promising. Both were able to subtly resist my mental suggestion.'

Calladren consulted her group of katriri. 'When you have finished with the big female, Al-quds, send her to us.' She paused for a second and became more serious. 'Beware, bashar. Hilarion ships are in our system again. Probably resource contractors.'

The space inside the cave that functioned as the comm display returned to normal. The katriri were gone.

The bashar then showed us how to send thoughts. We practiced for several hours before we both got tired.

'It's harder to send than receive,' I sent to Al-quds at the end of our training session.

'You will get better with practice,' the bashari replied.

'I want to learn how you got me to take that step.'

'That is advanced training. Your trainer on Celeste has demanded that you both pass the remote viewing test first.'

Remote viewing test? I looked up at Joann, who towered above everyone. She shrugged. "We've come all this way. Let's see what this is about."

That afternoon went deep into one of the bashari caves, accompanied by our hosts. As we stepped forward we came into a large space with a very high rock ceiling. Two stone handrails were sunk into the floor. The stone appeared to be worn from much use.

'Earthians,' Omani sent, 'Prepare yourselves.' I detected an apologetic note in this thought and braced myself. 'Place your hands on the bar.'

As I set my hands on the bar I was plunged into a terrifying black void. My stomach came into my throat and I retched, clinging to the bar with hands I couldn't see. I thought I heard dogs howling in the background, but I wasn't sure.

Imagine yourself within an infinite blackness, with no top, bottom, or sides. Just a vast nothingness with no orientation points. I couldn't see Joann, and for the first time wished she was near me. She would have been something to hold on to. I looked down and didn't see anything. I had no body. WTF!!!

Now I definitely heard laughter. Canine laughter.

When I thought of the cave I found myself back on solid ground. My hands were gripping the bar so hard they were white. I let go and fell on my knees to the hard stone of the cave floor and hugged myself. My body was still here!

This brought forth more howls. 'Oh dear,' Al-quds sent, with an expression I now recognized as tolerant canine condescension.

"What's so funny?" I was infuriated and humiliated. "What did you do to me?"

I looked around and saw the cave. Joann and I were in a large spherical halo of energy. Joann was holding onto her bar calmly, a look of excitement on her face. I couldn't understand what she was doing.

42

Al-quds consulted the pack. 'See, Omani, how this one orients herself.'

"I can do that too," I grumbled. I was ignored. The canines were all standing on their hind legs, concentrating on something I couldn't see or hear. Angry now, and not wanting Joann to best me, I tried stepping back to the bar again, making sure my hands were gripping it.

Again I was plunged into the blackness, but I recognized where I was. I was out in space above this planet! Suddenly, a small colored object began to quickly approach, getting bigger and bigger...I was going to crash into it! Get me out of here!

Suddenly I was back in my body in the cave. My hands hurt like hell from squeezing the stone bar so hard. I felt beads of cold sweat on my forehead.

Space Force pilot Joann was still standing there calmly, as if she were having a good time watching a movie. If she was having the same experience as me...I didn't believe anyone could face up to that with so much composure.

My pride was hurt again. If she can do it, I can do it!

I stepped back to the bar. I was back in space, my stomach in my throat. I was above the planet, back where I was before I backed out. As I got closer I saw the plain of broken mountains, as I called it. I was heading way too fast toward a huge slab of rock and I panicked again. I was back in the cave, nervously gripping the bar.

This was a form of torture, I decided. Remote viewing was terrifying.

Suddenly Joann exploded with excitement. "That was incredible!!" she cried, letting go of her bar. "Awesome! Terrible and beautiful."

The bashar all nodded their heads. 'You pass, human female,' Darshook said. This was a tall canine with a face like a German Shepherd. 'You are free to board your craft. Your pilot will return you to Patrick for advanced training.' This was sent in a congratulatory tone. 'If you like,' Omani sent, 'you may see the katriri.' This was stated so dismissively that Joann laughed.

Joann looked different; expanded somehow. She walked out, not even looking at me. The canine pack then left the cave on all fours, running, yelping, barking, playing, chasing each other and cavorting among the rocks, slabs, and boulders.

I was alone in the cave with no food, no water, and nowhere to go. Joann and the bashar had abandoned me. I sat down on the cave floor and felt sorry for myself. After a few minutes I got really angry. Patrick and Gwenneth were obviously nutjobs, and Joann too. Telepathic cats and dogs! This place, the whole galaxy, was a madhouse. I should have stayed at Uploads. I vowed to find my way back to earth somehow and resume my normal life.

I looked around at my prison. I was still standing on the cave floor in the holospace. I couldn't figure out how Al-quds activated it. There weren't any instruments – just rock everywhere. I felt enormously frustrated and wanted to cry. What was I doing here? I moped around for while, throwing stones against the wall of the cave. I wanted to find our lifter, but it probably wasn't there anymore. I couldn't believe Joann of Arc had left me stranded here – we were supposed to be teammates!

I trudged out of the cave and into the open. Despite my frustration I began to appreciate the magnificence of Al-Simak. There were two suns: one was directly overhead, shining a bright but pleasant cream-colored light on to the landscape, illuminating everything brilliantly. The other was larger but dimmer, just over the horizon, and it looked to be much closer. The landscape was painted in black, grey, and white hues. Massive slabs of rock looked to have been thrown haphazardly over the ground by an angry giant. Smaller grayish-white boulders and rocks were scattered between the larger slabs, which were fractured and split with precision, as if someone had cut into them with gigantic rock saws. The slabs themselves were beautiful, painted in black, almost pure white, and gray hues. I saw no life anywhere. No birds, insects, or animals. The landscape was brilliantly lit, as if a camera or movie crew had placed lights in just the right places to show the best aspect of everything. The ecology of this place baffled me.

I started walking. After ten minutes I saw the boulder where Joann had parked the lifter. The ship was gone, of course. The pilot must have picked Joann up already.

I was tired of feeling sorry for myself so I trudged back to the cave. This desolate but beautiful place was growing on me, despite my grumpy mood. There was a vibe here I really liked.

Feeling a little more cheerful, I walked back to the cave and explored. There were three branches off of the cave entrance. One was straight and led to the big holospace. I took the right branch and began walking. The gravity here was slightly lighter than I was used to and I made good time. Small puffs of rock dust arose each time I put a foot down. The cave ceiling here was about twenty feet high, but light was coming through scattered openings in the rock. When I turned a corner I saw the passage narrow, and the ceiling lower. A dead-end.

I was starting to get hungry and thirsty. I had no idea how long the day was here, and I wanted to get back to the opening before dark. As I turned my head to go I saw a small pile against the end wall. I began to smell something good. I heard dripping coming from the ceiling. A small pool of water had formed in a small rock basin that had been formed from water striking the rock from twenty feet above. I hadn't seen any water on the surface, but I wasn't complaining. I lay down next to the small pool and cupped the water into my hands, smelling it first and dipping my tongue into it just past the surface. It tasted OK so I drank it. I figured Patrick wouldn't have sent me here just to get killed.

Next to the pool was a stack of little packages that smelled like food, but I couldn't find a way to get into them. They were made from a gray flexible substance that looked like thick plastic wrap, but it was impenetrable. I ran my finger over the packaging and the material parted, revealing brownish stuff that smelled like a combination of oats, dates, and citrus. Oh what the hell. The water tasted good and I hadn't had any adverse reactions, so I stuffed a little bit of the brown stuff into my mouth. It tasted fantastic. I felt a little surge of energy go through my body and I ate until I felt satisfied.

I spent the rest of the daylight hours exploring the cave structure. When the near sun set I couldn't see inside the cave anymore, so I walked out and found a flat rock to sit on, and looked up at the sky. The second sun, a much dimmer but glorious red-orange ball, was on the other horizon now. The night sky was a blaze of light, nothing at all like the paltry little white dots and "constellations" we see at night on earth. A brilliant blue and green nebula filled the sky overhead.

I sat on a rock and turned my vision in a circle. There were millions of stars clumped together, some yellow, some orange, most of them white, and a few even larger and more brilliant blue-white stars. There was no moon, but none was needed. The light from this blazing panoply of heavenly illumination cast colorful and fascinating hues over the sandy and rocky ground, and colorized the stark black-and-gray-and-white slabs, boulders, and rocks.

Sitting there on that rock my loneliness vanished. I began to feel a connection to every one of the lights in the sky. I felt they were all a part of me; that this was *my* galaxy. I slept outdoors that night for the first time in my life on a patch of soft, sandy soil next to a boulder. It was a comfortable and cozy bed and I went almost immediately to sleep, wondering what would happen to me tomorrow.

I woke up when the far sun began to rise. I checked my chronometer; the night had only lasted 5 hours. I didn't wonder how I could breathe the air or why the temperature felt comfortable.

Patrick told us that there were billions of planets in the galaxy with intelligent life, and many of them had environments conducive to human life. The

45

galaxy, according to Patrick's movie the four of us had seen, was like the Star Wars bar: almost all life had one head, two arms, and two legs.

I walked back to the cave and ate more of the brown oatmeal stuff. Only a little completely satisfied me. I felt as if my body was absorbing every atom of it, and I realized that after almost 18 hours here I felt no need to eliminate anything.

An hour later I heard barking and footfalls. Omani and Al-quds appeared at the cave mouth. Al-quds said (sent mentally): 'I hope you can do better than last time.' This was meant as a barb but I was feeling mellow after my meal, and I greeted the two canines pleasantly. "I hope I can too."

Al-quds nodded her head. 'That is very well, Philogene,' she acknowledged. Omani gestured with his forepaw. 'Please proceed to the holospace.'

I stood by the stone railing and watched carefully to see how the thing was activated. Omani simply went up to a piece of rock and pushed one of his forepaws into it.

I was plunged into the depths of space. This was no simulation! I was totally disoriented until I realized that this holospace projected a person's consciousness. Didn't make it much better, but I knew I could go back to my body in the cave by willing myself back there. I was about to do this when I remembered that Joann-of-Arc had passed this test on her first try. My pride drove me to tamp down my panic a little. At the edge of my perception I saw a tiny speck. That was probably Al-Simak. I could feel myself retch again as the planet came up so fast I thought I would crash into it. Again I heard laughing in the background. I willed myself to relax and take a look around.

OK, this must be the remote viewing test. I picked up a mental trail that was Joann's and followed it. It galled me that I was following Joann's lead like a dummy driver in a test-car, but maybe I could do her one better. I went around the planet several times with my enhanced perception, going real slow. I found that I could adjust my speed if I just stayed calm.

There was almost no water on the surface of Al-Simak; just a few small seas scattered around the surface, the occasional rock tank filled with water, and a few oases. This was a dry, desert planet with very little biomass. The place looked like it had been cut up pretty good in some long-ago conflict. I heard a sigh of canine satisfaction in the background as I maneuvered my way back to the cave.

'Very well done, Philogene,' Omani said. 'You pass. You may now return to your training supervisor on Celeste.'

I had a thousand questions about how my mind could be projected out into space, and how I was able to maneuver around. I had heard of the remote viewing experiments at Stanford, and in the military programs, but this was light years beyond that. At that moment the lifter showed up at the cave entrance. Al-quds and Omani had the look of people who didn't want to answer a lot of stupid questions, and they hurried out of the cave before I could ask any. At that point Joann came striding out of the lifter with a big grin on her face. "Hello, slow top! You finally made it!"

"Yeah, I knew I'd get you. Where are we going?"

"We're a day late because of you, but I forgive you. The katriri gave me some expert pilot training on these ships."

"Let me guess: It's mental plane technology, just like the holo in the cave."

"Very good. Maybe you're smarter than you look."

I ignored her snarky comment. "If we're leaving, let's go," I said as I walked into the lifter.

"You're different," Joann said as she sat in the forward seat. The thing had a hemispherical headrest that Joann placed her head into. Then she concentrated and the ship took off, lifting quickly out of the atmosphere. The transparencies opaqued and I felt a sensation of a bubble of energy surrounding us. In less than five minutes we were orbiting Celeste.

"How did we get here so fast?" I asked.

"Transportals. I learned all about them from the katriri. Every star and every planet, and every galaxy, has transportals around it. These are programmable areas of space that send you off to any destination you want. It's called the galactic web."

Joann seemed to accept this casually, but my mind was blown. "But...that means you can go anywhere in the galaxy in no time at all!"

She looked at me like I was the classroom dummy. "That's right, Philogene."

"Call me Philo."

"Sure thing, Philogene," she replied, grinning. Joann seemed much more confident now, and had the look of someone in command. I decided to ignore her irritating taunts. My first instinct about her, that she was bossy, proved to be right when she landed the craft and ordered me to get out. "Go see Patrick. He and Gwenneth are waiting for you."

I successfully reined in my temper and didn't tell her to piss off. As soon as I stepped out the lifter took off, spraying me with dust. I promised myself I'd get back at Joann for that.

I entered the opening to the underground city and retraced my steps from the previous visit two days ago. Patrick would be interested in my experiences, I was sure. He was my trainer!

I went through the entrance and saw Patrick standing in one of the little conference rooms that surrounded the holocave. I started to tell him about what had happened to me, and he listened with a bored expression on his face for almost a minute. Then he interrupted me. "Congratulations, kid. You just got Lesson One: Remote viewing is a way to project your consciousness into the physical universe. Come with me."

— 7 —

[Celeste, Altair system, Fenachrone Trading Collective]

Patrick brought me to a small cavern that looked just like the holocave on Al-Simak. "Stand in the middle of the room, Philogene."

"What is this thing? How is it activated?"

"You're full of questions that don't need to be answered right now. The holocave is...a sophisticated remote viewer. It's used to test candidates for advanced operations. You see, you don't have the framework to understand anything yet. But you are the cream of the cream of the crop."

"I'll bet you say that to everybody."

Patrick laughed. "Yeah, it's standard procedure. But in this case it's true. Are you ready?"

"Aren't you even going to tell me what I'm supposed to do?"

Patrick sighed. "That would defeat the purpose of the training. You will be going to a planet in the Taurus sector. I want you to simply observe this society, which is a typical Class III planet, and report."

"I have no idea what I'm doing!" I complained.

"That's right. But any explanation I give you will bias the test."

Where the hell is the Taurus sector and how far is it from Celeste? I wondered.

Patrick went over to a recess in the stone wall and put his hands on two little knobs on the surface. Suddenly I was out in space again, retching. I heard voices in the background but decided to ignore them. I knew what I had to do, and I had to do it quick because I was getting really sick and disoriented. Somewhere there was a planet I had to go to, so I focused my mind on finding it. I didn't feel any movement, but I knew I was orienting myself properly, because after a few seconds I saw a tiny little dot in the distance. OK, progress! I started to feel a little better and I willed my consciousness to approach the dot. I remembered that my body was back in the cave, and it was just my mind that was somehow being projected out into space.

This planet was very close to a gigantic red sun. The atmosphere surrounding the planet was a deep red. As I passed through the atmospheric layer to the surface I saw red islands in a vast burgundy sea. Overhead, soft light from the giant sun filled the sky and backlit the landscape. This was nothing like earth, or Al-Simak. As I rotated my awareness around this world I saw that it was a water planet with millions of islands and a few small continents. Sea creatures swam from island to island. Two-legged humanoids occupied the continents. As I watched, two of the humanoids captured one of the sea creatures – which looked like a manta-ray – in a net, to much squawking and shouting. The humanoids transported the creature, now dead, on a sled to an opening in the ground. The opening sloped downward. Soft red light illuminated an immense cavern through openings in the low ceiling. The floor of the cave was covered with red lichen, and pools of water were scattered over the surface.

The humanoids cut up the creature and rolled up the parts in a substance made from the lichen. They ate some, and stored the rest. No one spoke. Then I remembered the telepathic way of communicating when I was on Al-Simak. I entered the mind of one of the humanoids, but there wasn't much there. Thoughts of food, lying about on the surface and basking in the rays of the sun, the time of mating. That was about it. Boring.

Then I caught a vague ancestral memory, of a ship landing, of beings from another star system teaching about dark and light, and evolution to a higher state of awareness, of a spark of curiosity lit within the life beneath the water and on the land.

It didn't take. Life here had been the same for hundreds of thousands of years.

I sent my awareness out of the cave and explored the islands. The manta rays subsisted on plant growth on the shallow sea floor. Their minds were filled with the pleasures of playing and gamboling about in the sea, of food, of the mating period when all went to the islands to breed.

Life here enjoyed and was also sustained by the life-giving rays from their gigantic sun. Apparently their physical bodies had evolved a pattern of complete contentment. The mantas accepted the occasional loss of one of their numbers from the land humanoids. As I went around the planet I estimated the humanoid population on the land to be a few million at most. The same for the manta-rays. Life here was perfectly balanced; there was almost no tension and no impetus for change.

I understood: On this planet there was no evolution, no growth. This society was a pleasurable but predictable dead-end. From the patterns of life here I saw that the present situation could continue for millions of years.

Was I missing something? Patrick must have sent me here for a purpose, but I had no idea what it was. I made an exhaustive survey of the planet, inspecting the small continents and island groups. No, there was nothing interesting here, nothing new. Nor would there ever be.

I was done. So how do I get back? I visualized my body in the cave on Celeste. I had no wish to go out into interplanetary space again and get sick. Why transport me into space when I could just go from the surface of this planet to the holocave?

I concentrated very hard on the cave and my body and the holospace on Celeste, Gwenneth's home planet. Suddenly, I was there. But I was completely disoriented now. Like a diver who comes up too fast from the depths, I felt my body wracked with pain. My mind was disassociating and I felt myself going...

Just before I lost consciousness I heard Patrick cry, "Young fool!"

When I woke up Kelleye, Joshua, and Joan were standing above me. I was lying on some kind of floating bed. There were no instruments or doctors, just me and my three recruit-mates.

"What did you do to yourself?" Joshua asked.

"I don't know. I don't know how this...remote viewing stuff works."

"You have to go slow at first," Kelleye said. "Did you try a planet-to-planet hop?"

"Yeah."

Kelleye looked at Joshua. "Young fool," she said. Kelleye and Joshua started laughing.

"I don't see what's so funny," I shot back. "I almost died."

After more laughing – which reminded me of those bashari dogs on Al-Simak – Joshua explained. "No you didn't, it just felt like you did. You have to first exit the mental envelope of a planet before you go to another planet."

"That's why we are always sent out into space first," Kelleye elaborated.

We were speaking out loud because using the mental plane still took a lot of effort. "Why doesn't anyone tell me this stuff?"

The other three looked at each other. "It's part of your training," Joann said.

"You know more about my training than I do!" I complained.

"Patrick will tell you everything you need to know," Joann said. "Your program is...different than ours." Was there a note of sympathy in her voice?

At that point Patrick walked in. "You just got Lesson Two, Philogene. The most painful lessons are the ones least forgotten."

I was baffled, and hurt. "Does everyone speak in riddles around here? I'm not getting it."

Gwenneth was behind him and gave me a little smile. My heart skipped a beat. She was exotic and beautiful, and I wanted her.

"Not going to happen," Joann said in a bossy tone. She must have read my thought on the mental plane.

I was about to shoot back at her when Patrick interrupted. "You just went to a Class III planet. What did you observe and what are your conclusions?"

I didn't want to be wrong on this one. The others looked like they were progressing nicely on whatever training they were getting. I felt like the broken module that was screwing up the whole program.

"Uh, that planet and its society are going nowhere. No tension, no growth, no evolution. A million years from now the place will look the same as it does now."

"That is correct, Philogene," he said. "The situation there is typical for all Class III planets in the galaxy, which are about 17% of the total."

I could tell Patrick was impressed. For the first time I felt I had done something right.

"How many planets are in the galaxy?" Kelleye asked.

"There have been precisely 235,677,498,003 stellar systems cataloged by the Galactic Space Patrol in this galaxy," Patrick said. "The average number of planets per system is four. So, about a trillion planets total."

"How many planets with intelligent life?" Joshua asked.

"It depends on what you consider intelligent." Patrick turned to me, lying on the floating bed. I still felt disoriented and had a headache, and my stomach was in knots. "Philogene?"

"It's not Philogene, it's Philo." Patrick was staring at me with that command presence and I felt I had to answer. "For a species to be intelligent it has to evolve. So no, I wouldn't say the red planet had intelligent life."

Patrick nodded. "That position is strongly supported by the Trading Collectives, who steal resources and abuse life forms on these planets for profit. But not by Class I societies, who uplift species that are just beginning to evolve." He looked severely at me. "You humans, over 200,000 of your years ago, were uplifted."[6]

I wanted to make Patrick wrong. He was too arrogant for me. "The red planet was uplifted over 300,000 years ago by some beings who came in a space ship. The mantas and the humanoids. It didn't take."

Patrick raised his eyebrows. For the first time I saw respect in his eyes. "That is a very prescient observation, Philogene. Fortunately, it did take on the earth."

"How does uplifting work?" Joshua asked.

"The DNA of the promising species is altered to support a higher evolutionary path. After that, they are on their own. A species can choose to kill itself, join the Collectives, or evolve and join the Class I society of advanced planets. Most emerging societies eventually join the Collectives. These are the Class II planets, which are about 80% of the total."

"What are the other 3%?" I asked.

Patrick grimaced. "Some of them are Class I planets. Most of the rest are like this."

The holospace showed a blackened husk orbiting a double star. "World war, using atmosphere stripping weapons," Patrick said. Another image showed the remnants of a planet still in orbit around a single sun. "Core breech. These weapons literally break a planet apart." A third holovid displayed a perfectly good planet circling its sun, but there was no life upon it. "Biological weapons war. Destroyed all life on the surface. More common than you might think."

"For God's sake!" I shouted. The holos were sickening. "Why not guide these civilizations like a good parent so this doesn't happen?"

Patrick shrugged. "It never works. Guided species always fail because they don't resolve problems themselves."

"Why would a species not want to improve themselves?" Kelleye asked.

Gwenneth answered. "Study the history of earth. You were very close to destroying yourselves a dozen times."

"It's basically luck then!" Joshua cried. "After billions of years of galactic evolution, you haven't figured out anything better?"

Patrick glanced at Gwenneth with a look that said, 'These earthians ask too many questions.' He spoke grimly. "Once you complete your training you will have a much better understanding of life in the galaxy, and why the earth is so important."

Joann was shocked. "Thank God I'm just a pilot. I don't even want to think about it."

"What are we training for?" Kelleye asked.

"To help your planet through, uh, the difficulties it is facing from the galactic Trading Collectives. If I told you any more at this point you would be totally confused."

"I'm confused now!" I retorted, but I was almost fully recovered from my remote viewing trip to the red planet.

One of the feline creatures I saw on Al-Simak entered the room. "Philogene, you stay with me," Patrick said. "The rest of you go with Gwenneth."

What am I doing here, I thought to myself as I got out of the medbed. Patrick and I began walking back to the holospace through the brilliantly lit hallway with its astounding artwork. I knew I was in for yet another adventure. When we got there I quickly grabbed the bar.

"Lesson Three," Patrick said as he pressed his fingers into a slight recession in the rock wall.

"What is it this time?"

"Figure it out."

He was about to walk away. I was really upset with his callous attitude. "You're the shitiest instructor I ever had."

"You're supposed to have pattern recognition skills. You've done well so far."

"Very encouraging," I snapped. "You—"

Suddenly I was in the middle of a black nothingness. I retched; I would never get used to this! Back at the holospace I dimly felt my fingers holding the bar and I remembered to go slowly. I knew I would find some point of reference if I kept looking. But it wasn't what I expected. A bunch of small asteroids came into my view. A crane was digging into the surface of one of them and dumping rocks into one of several large holes.

I saw a sudden flash. The crane folded up like a transformer and started firing. A dozen flying craft returned fire on the crane. One of the craft fell out of the sky; a burning husk, and crashed to the surface. The spacecraft scattered and two more fell crashing to the surface. I hoped they were unmanned drones with nobody in them.

What was I supposed to learn here? I began a slow search of the surface. All I saw were machines, holes, and clumps of rocks. Several huge conveyor belts were coming out of the holes, and other machines were stacking cubes of...something...onto gigantic pallets.

This was a mining operation. I saw several large, clumsy craft land and send other machines out to pick up the pallets.

I had no idea what I was doing here. Was this the right place, or was I supposed to go someplace else? An idea occurred to me: maybe there was a manned base underground. How was I supposed to get down there?

I tried going into one of the holes but I started feeling claustrophobic halfway down, so I got out of there.Then I remembered that my awareness was being projected, and that I didn't have a body. I was invulnerable.

If there was life underground I didn't have to go down a hole. I could go through the surface until I found something. But when I tried to send my awareness into the rocky surface I balked. Going through that rock was scary, even though I knew I was disembodied. It was like sticking your head into goo.

After several nauseating attempts I finally realized that this rock was solid all the way through. This asteroid had no underground cities; no intelligent life. The entire operation was automated.

I still felt I hadn't learned anything so I stuck around. When I got back to the surface I saw the crane. It had transformed from a weapons platform back to digging into the rock and dumping stuff into one of the holes. Did the crane have intelligent AI?

I probed it with my mind and got the shock of my life. 'Unknown entity!' it blasted. 'You are interfering with a Hilarion trading operation! Cease and desist!'

I felt the machine trying to trace my awareness all the way back to my body, standing in the holospace on Celeste. In an instant I knew that the device was going to send a killing frequency and kill my body.

I didn't have a choice. I had to make a surface-to-surface jump. Better that than certain death.

In a femtosecond I found myself writhing on the cave floor, a total mess. But I knew I had escaped from the crane, or whatever that thing was.

Patrick leaned over me. At first I thought he was concerned for my welfare. Until he said, "Did that Digger trace you all the way back here?"

Through my pain and emotional turmoil I managed to say, "Fuck you, Patrick."

The older man grinned. "No then. Well done, Philogene!"

It took me fifteen minutes to recover. Patrick didn't offer to send me to the infirmary, or whatever it was. No comfortable floating bed for me, just the cold, hard, rocky floor of the holospace.

"You just learned Lesson Three, Philogene. All devices in the Greater Community are connected to networks, and some of them are capable of operating in the mental plane."

"You're a bastard, Patrick. Or whatever your name is," I mumbled after finally being able to stand on wobbly legs.

"Report!"

I didn't want to obey because I didn't like Patrick. But I needed to tell someone about what had happened to me. "What is a Hilarion trading operation?"

Patrick ignored this. "Think, Philogene. What information did you get from the Digger?"

I understood what Patrick meant. The crane was programmed. Patrick was asking me about its programming.

"Very good, Philogene. Skip the part about how afraid you were. What did you learn?"

"Obviously you can read my mind; you already know."

Patrick's face assumed hard planes. "That's just it. I can't break into your mind deeply enough. It's just as I suspected. You're a potential Seer. So you have to tell me, or let me in."

"You're not getting into my mind."

I could feel a mental pressure, like a can opener trying to pry off a lid.

Patrick was disgusted and amazed. "I can't believe it," he mumbled. Then he used a command voice. "TELL ME!"

"Not going to work, old man."

Patrick was frustrated. "You're a natural. I can't teach what you have."

I was feeling better now, and getting bored. "Fine. What do you want to know?"

"Everything you got from the Digger. Particularly the sidebands."

What were sidebands? Maybe information that wasn't obvious but beneath the surface. The surface info first, I decided. "OK, I know what a Hilarion trading operation is. Trading Collectives are planets in a network, like a network of interconnected multinational corporations on earth. Their business is resource acquisition. The mining operation on that asteroid violates a business agreement the HIlarion signed with the Zaon Trading Group, a small Collective associated with the large Fenachrone Trading Collective. The Hilarion and the Fenachrone are competitors."

"That's very good, but tell me something I don't know."

I concentrated. There was something else... "Hilarion is about to attack a manned outpost in the Zaon sector, which is part of the Fenachrone Collective.

The attack on the mining operation was a scouting mission to test the enemy's defenses."

Patrick gasped. "Kinetic war is forbidden in the Greater Community."

"Hilarion has made a military alliance with the Maitre, whatever that is."

Patrick's face blanched and he stumbled backward. "No. That can't be right."

I checked the information packet I received from the Digger again. "Sorry, but it's true. The Digger is just a machine, incapable of subterfuge."

Patrick was speechless.

"What's the big deal? It's just a little war. Happens all the time on earth."

"Yeah, on earth. But—"

"What are Maitre?"

"The scourge of the galaxy. A psychotic race of stone-cold killers, completely mired in service-to-self." Patrick sent an image.[7]

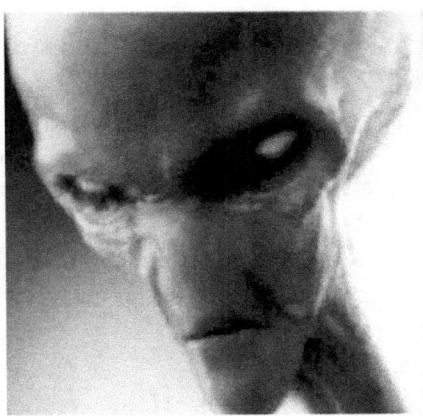

Maitre

"Wow."

Patrick nodded. "A hopeless race, totally devolved. Impossible to reason with. And then there are the reptoid races, equally predatory, but they have mostly ceased operations in this sector."

"They look scary and degraded."

"No, Philogene. The physical appearance of a species is irrelevant. Some of the most peaceful and enlightened races appear physically grotesque and ugly to humans. Identify degraded races by their footprint in the mental plane."

I understood. "The Digger's consciousness is sterile and mechanical. The beings on the red planet are just existing; they have little self-awareness."

"That is correct." Patrick showed me the psychological imprint of degraded races. I couldn't stand it for more than a second. "Oh my God, that's...depressing and horrifying."

"That's right. Degraded species are almost unconfrontable. They are trapped in darkness. For now, Philogene, if you encounter a being like this, close your mind and get the hell out of there." Patrick spoke severely. "Do you understand?"

"I think so. You don't want any of them to trace me back here."

Patrick nodded somberly. "It is of the utmost importance, for your sake and ours. Class I planets must...remain hidden."

I tried to make a joke. "As bad as that, eh?"

"It's no laughing matter, Philogene. As you'll find out soon enough. That is, if you don't flame out before then."

"I'm not going to flame out!"

"Heard that before."

Gwenneth walked into the room. I stared. There was a physical and spiritual refinement about her that enhanced her beyond anyone I had seen on earth.

"Patrick is right, Philo. Please be very, very careful. It is a great risk to train humans on the mental plane. You have such great potential, but also a great possibility to bring disaster upon us."

Patrick and Gwenneth were speaking to me in English, but I was learning to sense the imprint of a communication in the mental plane. Gwenneth was afraid, I could tell. For the first time I began to see that my crazy training wasn't just a challenging game. "Yes ma'am."

Gwenneth smiled radiantly and walked out. "Wow. That's some woman."

"Yeah. And off-limits to you. Don't even think what you're thinking. She's way more evolved than you are. And she can pick up on your thoughts."

"Forgot about that." But I remembered that she had called me Philo, not Philogene.

"Back to business, Philogene. Why is the Hilarion Trading Group aligning with this psychotic race? They must know that the Maitre and their ilk will turn on them."

I put the lovely Gwenneth out of my mind as well as I could, and looked for more information in the data I had picked up from my contact with the Digger. But I couldn't find anything else. "That's all the Digger knows. Apparently it isn't very high on the organization chart."

Patrick nodded. "It knows just enough to do its job and defend itself."

"What is a Class I planet and why do they need to hide?"

"It's a long story, Philogene. You are on one."

I remembered traveling over the surface of Celeste with its blasted cities, and compared it to the beauty and bio-diversity of earth. "You mean, Celeste is as good as it gets out here?"

"You begin to understand the nature of the problem, Philogene, and why the earth is so important." Patrick wouldn't elaborate further.

"You are as hard to get information out of as the whale that swallowed Jonah."

Patrick caught the Biblical reference and smiled for the first time.

"You look like a human. You must be human or you wouldn't have understood that Bible comment. But...your vibe is similar to Gwenneth's. You're a total mystery. Are you really in the Space Force?"

Patrick ignored this. "Are you ready for your next exercise?"

I gulped. If these were just exercises I wondered what the real thing was like. "I'm not sure."

"You're doing OK, Philogene. Get some rest and meet me in the holospace tomorrow at dawn."

After my experience with the Digger, Patrick wanted to continue my training immediately, but the Celestian Council wouldn't let him. In order to maintain my life on earth, I have to work my Uploads job so I can make money and keep my place in society.

"I don't like it Philogene, but we have to send you back."

"That's good, because I have no idea what this training is for. To me it's a form of torture."

I said that, but I could feel myself growing more powerful in a way I can't describe. It was enough to keep me from quitting the training, but I was looking forward to a break.

— 8 —

[Midland, Illinois]

Jamaal welcomed me back enthusiastically. I always fit in right away because Jamaal is usually short of technicians. Right after I come back, Upolads seems boring. After you've been sent out into interstellar space, how stressful is being a sat jockey? I wanted to see Gwenneth again, and I wondered what my teammates were doing. For some reason I was separated out from Joann, Kelleye, and Joshua. They seemed to know what I was doing but I had no idea what they were doing.

After two months at Uploads I was getting back into my life again. Then one very cold February day Gwenneth showed up at Uploads. Jamaal was glad not to see Patrick, but he knew I was going to disappear again for a while. As we walked to the lifter I glanced over at Gwenneth. Sorry to keep mentioning this, but I had never seen a more beautiful person; there was an actual halo around her. I wondered if anybody else could see it. Her body was beautifully shaped, her face perfectly symmetrical with large violet eyes, full lips, the elfin ears, and a perfect complexion.

I had to block my feelings for her because I knew she could read me on the mental plane. I began to get more uncomfortable as we boarded the lifter. I went immediately to one of the passenger seats in back. I was the only one on the ship except for Gwenneth and the pilot.

"It's OK Philo," Gwenneth said, sensing my discomfort. "Relax." She smiled brilliantly, and I was lost in it. Then a very large woman came out from the pilot's chair and smirked at me.

I groaned. "Joann! I hoped I wouldn't get you."

"You got me, sonny." She glanced over at Gwenneth. "You can't treat her like you treat earth women. She's off limits to us primitives."

"Have you seen Kelleye and Joshua?"

"Yup. They are proceeding nicely."

I saw Gwenneth smiling benignly in the forward seat next to the pilot. I sighed. Joann and Patrick were right. She was way out of my league.

"Where to?" I asked Joann.

"Back to your training. Patrick hasn't given up on you yet."

"I have no idea what my training is about. No one tells me anything."

"You haven't guessed yet? Mr. Pattern Recognition?"

I was upset now. "If we're going somewhere let's get on with it."

Joann gave me a superior smile and went back to her pilot's chair. In less than an hour I was exiting the lifter and got another dust shower from Joann as she took off abruptly, creating a small atmospheric disturbance. I walked toward the underground entrance to the training area, wondering at my routine acceptance of technology that could take me from the earth to another star system in a matter of minutes.

[Celeste]

"What is it this time?" I said to Patrick as I exited the magnificent hall of light entrance and walked into the holocave.

"If I told you it would invalidate the test. Are you ready?"

I wanted to ask Patrick if I could be seen by others during these remote viewing exercises. Only my consciousness was projected. My body was in the holocave, so I should be invisible. But the Digger was able to detect me... I saw Patrick's hand swipe a projection on the cave wall and I was out in space again, my stomach churning and my senses panicking at the lack of anything visible.

"Stop!" I told myself. I pulled in my perception to a small area I identified as my conscious awareness. I felt better immediately. "Lesson Four learned!" If I anchored myself around the sphere that contained my awareness, I had a stable point for remote viewing. It was like a substitute body.

Slowly, I sent my perception out radially. After some time I saw something, and began to move toward it. It was a binary star with three planets orbiting

61

in fairly close proximity to the smaller star. As I got closer I saw spacecraft traveling between each of the three planets. The closest planet was small, with a rocky surface like Celeste. The second planet was much larger and had an orange-ish hue. The third planet was middle-sized, and had a greenish blue atmosphere. It was awesome to see how the three planets orbited the binary star. The larger star was bluish-white and very bright, the other was smaller and yellowish-orange. The orbital mechanics of these three planets and the double star must be incredibly complex...

I pulled my awareness back to the present. I checked the mental plane for any data about this system. It was a typical Class II system within the Greater Community, and part of the Fenachrone Trading Group. OK, now what?

I finally decided to send myself to the bluish-green planet because it looked the most like earth. When I penetrated the atmosphere I was assaulted by a wave of mental energy that slammed me back out into space.

I entered again, this time shielding my mind as tightly as I could. I was in!

The third planet had a bluish colored sky but it was nothing like earth. The place had two smallish continents that were both gigantic cityscapes. The remains of the oceans were just huge pits on the surface, with almost no water in them. As I watched I saw water funneling out of one of the immense pits, as if it were being drained and directed somewhere. I saw thousands of craft arriving at a gigantic spaceport. At another, hundreds more were taking off. Crews were loading and unloading huge floating pallets from the craft. The spaceports were all over the surface of the continents.

I saw a hovering satellite above one of the spaceports. Something told me that this was important, so I breached the walls, remembering to keep my mind closed. I found myself in a huge, windowless conference room. There were hundreds of beings present; humanoid, but not human. Three different races sat in floating seats, stacked like bleachers in a stadium. All were in biosuits. In the middle was a huge holotank, where a presentation was being made.

What were they discussing? I opened my mind a tiny bit and probed the mind of the creature who was speaking. Suddenly I was assaulted on the mental plane. Several of the creatures cried out. 'A Seer!' 'This is a serious violation of protocol!' 'Dissemblers!' one of the other humanoids sent angrily. Chaos erupted and one of the delegations stomped out. At that instant I felt a mental attack. It felt like a bombing raid on a village, and I was the village. My intrusion was regarded as a hostile act against the local corporate trading group. They were trying to extract information from me, trying to discover my identity. After that my consciousness would be annihilated, but not before they traced my physical location. If they traced me back to Celeste, Gwenneth's home planet would be known. I understood all this in less time than it takes to think a thought. I was being held in a mental vice grip, unable to move. I knew I couldn't hold out much longer so in one great, desperate mental heave I launched myself out of there...

When I regained consciousness I was screaming through space, feeling as battered as an old tennis shoe in a tumbler dryer. Stars and planets were going by me as fast as electrical posts on a bullet train. I wasn't under attack anymore, thank God, but I had no idea where I was. I started to panic: I could be halfway across the galaxy! How was I going to get home?

First I had to stop my progress. I anchored myself in space to the little area around my conscious awareness and put on the brakes. OK. Now I'm sitting in the complete blackness of interstellar space with no reference points. To say I was afraid is an understatement. I have never felt so lost and lonely. Everything felt completely alien. I knew I was in deep, deep trouble.

I hugged myself as tight as I could and tried to calm down. My body was, I hoped, still on Celeste, in the holospace, but I couldn't feel it. I wanted to go there in one jump but Lesson Three taught me to go slowly. I remembered the "feel" of the space around Celeste and put that in the forefront of my mind. I placed a picture of Gwenneth's planet in my mind, and envisioned Gwenneth herself, Patrick, and the irritating Joann of Arc in the holocave. Go slow, Philo, go slow.

Suddenly a star system approached and I panicked again. It whizzed by me so fast it was gone in a second. After a while I flew by another, and another. I was speeding up now. The only thing I could do was to desperately hold the image of the holocave in my mind and hope I was going in the right direction.

After what seemed like days I started to slow down. I began to feel that I was back in a familiar area of space. Yeah, there's Celeste! I saw my body lying on a floating bed in a small cave. Completely exhausted, I flung myself into it and fell unconscious instantly. My only comfort was seeing Gwenneth sitting by the bed. Joann, Kelleye, and Joshua were there too...

When I woke up I felt OK. I had no idea how much time had passed. The first thing I heard was Patrick's voice. "Young fool!"

Joann was tapping her foot impatiently. "Finally!"

God that woman is irritating!

"Not half as irritating as you!"

I looked around the room. Joann snorted. "No, Gwenneth's not here. She has more important things to do than look after you."

I was about to argue when Patrick interrupted. "You just got Lesson Five. Spacial distance means nothing in remote viewing."

"You could have told me that before I started!"

Patrick grinned. "How did you do in school, Philogene? I'll bet you sat quietly and accepted everything the teacher told you."

I had to laugh at that.

"You're the kind of person who learns by experience, not words. You don't like authority and you do the opposite of what anyone tells you."

I had to admit Patrick was right.

Patrick spoke roughly but I could tell he was concerned for me. That made me feel better. "You are in training to be a advanced Seer, Philogene. It requires the toughest, most ruthless training methods of any job in the galaxy."

"I agree that you're a ruthless bastard, Patrick."

"You're going to need everything you have learned to lead your team and prevent the earth's absorption into the corporate trading Collectives."

"Sure, whatever. How many lessons do I have to learn? I don't want to do this any more."

"That depends on what the Council says. Joann will take us to the Celestian council chamber for your evaluation."

"I'm hungry."

"There's no time to eat now," Joann said. "The Council is waiting. I have an energy bar you can eat on the way over."

Screw the Celestian Council, I thought.

"Gwenneth will be there," Joann said.

"All right, damn you."

Patrick, Joann, and I got in the lifter. Kelleye and Joshua were already seated. In a couple of minutes Joann flew us halfway around the planet to another underground city. I was amazed that no one lived on the surface of Celeste. The brilliant white sun in the beautiful purple sky illuminated a rocky surface that was interspersed with stone outcroppings that Patrick told me were caves that led to a global warren of underground, habitable areas. The surface of Celeste had almost no water on the areas we flew over. I wondered how life could have evolved on this world. It didn't seem possible! I was about to ask Patrick about this when Joann pulled into a large opening that led into a huge cave. As soon as we got out I saw Gwenneth waiting for us. We approached another of the fantastic entrances with beautiful works of art in light.

There were stone sculptures of animals so lifelike that I cringed when we approached a crouching griffin-like creature. The animal was ready to spring into action, a frozen snapshot of reality. I stopped. Was this thing alive?

Gwenneth came up to me and smiled. "It's remarkable, is it not?"

I nodded, stepping warily around the sculpture. "How did life evolve on Celeste? It seems to be completely barren on the surface."

Gwenneth grimaced. "Our planet was not always like this. We destroyed the surface in a civil conflict. We were forced to move underground and save as many species as we could before the surface became too desolate."

A Noah's Ark story, I thought. "There is almost no water on the surface."

"All of the water on our planet is underground, and bubbles up to the surface in small rivers and lakes."

We exited the hallway and entered a complex of caves that the Celestians apparently used for conference rooms and holospaces. Through the cave opening, in the distance, I saw another city with beautiful rock towers, each with a unique pattern of color, rise into a uniformly lit sky. Ground vehicles floated above the surface. I saw people walking on the cave floor, and a few walking on rocky paths that circled around the towers. There were small lakes on the surface with beaches, where people were swimming. The city was gorgeous. I wanted to find one of those tower apartments and live with Gwenneth in it....

"Philogene!" Patrick barked.

I flushed scarlet. Embarrassed, I realized I hadn't been shielding my thoughts again. I saw a smile crease Gwenneth's face. Joann, Joshua, and Kelleye were rolling their eyes at me. We entered one of the conference rooms next to a large open area that looked like the holocave in my training area. We approached a dozen or so of the elfin Celestians, equally divided between male and female. Even the men exuded beauty and refinement. Unlike Patrick, who was just as crude as us humans. The guy is an enigma...

Patrick interrupted my reverie. "Playtime's over, Philogene." Suddenly the holocave was filled with blackness. The display showed a binary star and its three planets moving into view. I recognized it; it was where I began my last remote viewing journey. A data stream showed that this binary system, seen from Sol, was labeled HR 3018 in the earth star charts. It was in the Fenachrone-controlled area.

The holo showed the third planet in the Zaon system approaching, the one that looked like earth.

I knew what happened next. My body crunched over in pain at the memory of it. Several of the beings in the meeting were yelling, "A Seer!" I remembered how my mind was viciously attacked and how I yanked myself out of there as hard as I could. The display went black.

"What exactly is a Seer?" I asked.

One of the Celestians answered impatiently, as if the answer was obvious. I could tell he was interested in something more important. "A Seer is the most skilled remote viewer in the galaxy, and an expert on the mental plane. All trading nations have them. A Seer's job is to know what others are doing, to perceive their activities and try to uncover their secrets and their technological developments. In negotiations it is vital to understand the negotiating position and the intentions of the other side, to correctly interpret their communications and their diplomacy."[8]

"They thought I was a Seer?"

"Seers are forbidden at any formal trade negotiation," Gwenneth added. "Galactic corporate law is absolutely clear on that point. Your intrusion," she said with a smile, "interrupted an important diplomatic meeting between the three planets in the Zaon system. They were discussing the incursion of the Hilarion Collective and their attack on the Zaon mining operation."

So that's why they were so pissed when I barged in! I basked in Gwenneth's approval. "They thought I was a spy," I said. "How did they detect me?"

"You have to ask that?" Joann remarked. "Even the Digger you encountered could sense you. It probably told them about you."

I gazed accusingly at Patrick. "You mean you sent me to the same system as the one with the Digger who attacked me? Why didn't you tell me?"

"You could have read that data on the mental plane from the info you got on your first entrance to the third planet," Joann said.

"Joann is right, Philogene. Instead you just barged in."

I was outraged now. "I've been through shit no one should have to go through! I've been treated like a red shirt on Star Trek and I've almost died twice. I think I deserve a little more consideration."

I saw Gwenneth and a couple of the Celestians wince. My teammates, and Patrick, were unmoved.

"It's part of the process," Patrick said unhelpfully. "You got another lesson: Every planet has a mental envelope that tells you all about it."

"You can go home anytime you like," Joann said.

"Yeah, back to your cushy job at Uploads," Joshua said.

"We've been through a lot ourselves," Kelleye said.

So much for teammates! I was starting to feel really sorry for myself. "Take me back to Jamaal then. I see no point in this senseless training. I've had it."

The only thing that kept me from walking out was Gwenneth's look of dismay. She looked over at the other Celestians and then spoke to me. "What did you do after the Zaons attacked you on the mental plane? Be as precise as you can."

"I realized that I was leaking. So I closed up and got out of there."

"Be more specific," Patrick said.

I shrugged. "I'm not sure. I felt like the Enterprise under attack from a bunch of Romulan warships. I engaged my cloaking device and went to warp 9."

Patrick spoke impatiently. "Yes, but how did you do it?"

"How should I know! Does the lady who lifts the 3,000 pound car off her baby understand how she did it? I just did it, that's all."

The other Celestians nodded to each other. 'A natural,' one of them sent to Gwenneth. They were reading our conversation in English on the mental plane.

'Certainly, but does this earthian have spiritual potential?' another asked.

"What does spiritual potential have to do with remote viewing?" I asked.

"All Seers have great skill in the mental environment," Patrick explained, "but most are like idiot savants – only useful to hoover up information, and narrowly focused on the task at hand. They are usually socially inept and, er, socially and spiritually undeveloped."

I was beginning to see my way. "So this crazy remote viewing training is to make me a Seer?"

Gwenneth spoke. "We were hoping for more than that, but you are resuming your life on earth." Was there a touch of bitterness in her voice? I shifted my feet uncomfortably but said nothing.

"There's one more thing before you leave," Patrick said. "Where did you go after you left the Zaon system?"

"I have no idea. You sent me out there! I thought your remote viewer could track everything."

"We thought so too. But we lost you for two days until...you returned."

"Hah! I evaded your system!" I felt a little better.

"It's not a joking matter, Philogene," Patrick said severely. "We have never lost a candidate before. We have trained millions."

"I was totally lost. My first thought was that I had shoved off so hard I could be halfway across the galaxy. That's crazy, but I'm starting to believe it."

Excited voices broke out among the Celestians. Gwenneth looked shocked.

"How did you find your way back?" Patrick asked.

"Well, I was way out in interstellar space and I had no idea where I was. Normally I'd just go back into my body in the holocave, but something told me not to. I have to admit I was really afraid."

"You did right Philo," Patrick said approvingly. "If you had done that you would not have survived."

"First I had to stop my progress outward. I figured I had to go back slow. So I had my destination in mind – Celeste – and I told myself to approach it very slowly. I knew I was way out because the space just felt totally different, like when you go to a foreign country with a different culture."

I paused. "I decided it was just like playing a video game. The game is real because the graphics are great and you're really into it. I got the idea I was operating the controller, so I decided I had control over my movements. After that I calmed down."

"Continue," Patrick said.

"I knew I was so far out it would take me a long time to get back. I panicked at that point and had to calm myself down again. Then I started back slowly and gradually kicked it up. After what felt like a couple of days I was going so fast the stars were just whizzing by. I couldn't tell where I was, but I was operating by feel. My goal was always getting back here, so I kept that as my total focus. After a while something told me to slow down, so I did. Then I recognized the feel of the area of space around Celeste, so I stopped. At that point I was sick of all the traveling, and mentally exhausted. So...I found the holocave and here I am."

I saw Patrick walk over to where the Council was sitting and consult with them.

"You didn't wake up for a week after we got you to the infirmary," Gwenneth said to me. "We had to feed you through a tube." I couldn't tell whether her concern was for me as a valuable team member, or whether it was personal. I admitted to myself that I was falling for Gwenneth.

"Thank you Philogene," Patrick said. "We are suspending your training for the immediate future. We will take you back to Uploads and you can resume your life on earth for a while. Jamaal has been asking for you."

I was torn now. I didn't want to leave Gwenneth but I was really, really tired of Space Force Patrick and his so-called training. If these people are so advanced, why are they putting a grunt like me through all this agony? "I can use a break," I said.

Joann took me back to (her) lifter and deposited me back on the Uploads parking lot. She hardly said anything to me on our trip back to earth. She looked very subdued. That was fine with me because I wasn't into talking. I was just looking forward to my bed and some good old earth food. This time Joann didn't make a dust storm when I got out of the lifter because there was too much melting snow on the ground.

Gwenneth looked at Patrick. They were sitting in a conference room at the top of one of the housing spires, looking out onto a large field filled with crops. Beyond the ag field thousands of trees had been planted. They heard music coming from one of the many amphitheaters in small parks that dotted the landscape.

'Philogene thinks you and I are romantically involved.'

Patrick laughed. 'He does, does he?' Patrick's face sobered. 'You're not falling for that human are you?'

Gwenneth laughed nervously. 'Don't be silly. The boy, I believe, has extraordinary abilities. That's what fascinates me. It's why we need him.'

Patrick relaxed. 'Very well. Philogene is dangerous and unpredictable. He doesn't understand his potential. I didn't want to send him home, but he is exhausted.'

'Can this earthian have really traveled remotely across the galaxy?' Gwenneth asked. 'It is a thing unheard of.'

'The candidate is extremely promising.' Patrick watched Gwenneth for a reaction.

Gwenneth sighed. 'He is. I admit to a certain feminine...fascination.'

Patrick spoke gruffly. 'Don't waste your time. I'll handle Philogene.'

'You have been very rough on him.'

Patrick's face was grim. 'The stakes are high. I'm doing whatever it takes.'

Gwenneth nodded. 'Celeste is the closest Class I planet to the earthian system. If the earth falls to the Collectives, we may be next.'

— 9 —

[Midland]

Jamaal was glad to see me when I walked into the Uploads tech center the next day, but I felt too sick to work for more than a couple of hours.

"What are those Space Force people doing to you?"

I needed someone to unburden myself to. But when I opened my mouth I realized how stupid I would sound. Lifters that could travel between the stars in less than an hour? Holocaves that could send your consciousness around the galaxy? Dog- and cat-like beings who used mental telepathy? A beautiful elfin woman from another planet I was falling in love with? "I...uh...can't talk about it, Jamaal. I'm just glad to be back."

I walked home in the late March cold and fell into bed. I was asleep immediately. I dreamt I was floating through space, being chased by a bunch of aliens...I woke up sweating and shaking.

I was astonished how this training had enabled me to be a remote viewer. I had seen and done impossible things. However, my true motivation was all about Gwenneth, not wanting to disappoint her, wanting to be with her, wanting to impress her. I was feeling like a pet dog out on the disc golf course, fascinated by the discs flying around but unable to comprehend what my human masters were doing. I vowed to have a talk with Patrick. I didn't believe he was a human, but he sure didn't look like a Celestian. What was his relationship to Gwenneth?

All of that would have to wait until I felt better.

Six months later I had recovered mentally and physically from my training exercises, but I was still having the occasional bad dream. I didn't want to go back to Celeste, but I was getting bored. After my training, the complex problems of the Space Grid were now a trivial exercise for my mind. I was doing the work of three techs, which was good because Jamaal was three techs short.

Mainly I was missing Gwenneth. The only problem was that I had no way to contact her or Patrick.

That problem was solved for me just before Christmas. I was sleeping in after a long night out at Mickey Dunn's (my local watering hole) when I heard a loud knock on my apartment door. I went back under the covers but the knocking got louder and louder. No one I knew would be so rude, and I was getting angry. I threw on a robe and opened the door, preparing to let whoever it was have it.

"Come, Philogene. You're needed."

I groaned. It was Joann-of-Arc. "The one person in the galaxy I most don't want to see."

"There's no time for that, Philo." There was no teasing in her voice, only urgency.

"I'm tired." I tried to close the door but Joann stuck her foot in it. She is a lot bigger than me.

"Stop being a fool. You're playing a little game on a little planet."

"Oh fuck you, Joann." I began walking back to my bedroom, and Joann followed me. Her comment about playing a little game rankled. I turned around and saw a much more mature Joann of Arc. I felt like a child compared to her. It pissed me off.

"I'm going to stand here and wait for five minutes. If you don't come with me you're out, you understand? We'll find someone with more guts and more wisdom to take your place."

I wanted to laugh but I stifled it. I wanted to tell her that she wasn't any wiser than me, but I couldn't get the words out.

"Four minutes, Philo."

I thought at first she was bluffing, but I knew I was out of time. "Give me five minutes to get dressed."

I threw off my robe and put on my clothes while Joann watched. I didn't care what she thought of my body.

"Put on your winter coat. We have to walk to the Uploads parking lot to get the lifter."

"You sound like my mom."

"I feel like your mom. Hurry up."

Joann was silent as we walked the mile to Uploads. "I haven't had breakfast yet," I said as we entered the lifter.

"Come to the forward compartment and sit next to me." She tossed me one of the brown food packets I had eaten when I was in the cave on Al-Simak. I noticed she was wearing a uniform with the letters "GSP" emblazoned on it. Galactic Space Patrol! "You're a GSP pilot now?" I didn't want to be impressed but I was. According to Patrick, the GSP has been charting solar systems across the galaxy for eons.

"Yes. While you have been away on vacation me, Josh, and Kelleye have completed our training." She spoke proudly. "I am qualified to fly all Class I galactic ships, including Defense Forces spacecraft."

"Wow."

The transparencies were clear. Joann placed her head into a shell and concentrated. The ship took off quickly and was out of the atmosphere and into space in a couple of seconds.

"You don't seem bothered about the view." The earth was just a little point now; we were surrounded by the void, out in the middle of nowhere.

"This is nothing. I was halfway across the galaxy in the remote viewer before I found my way back."

"The Celestian Council was impressed." She spoke respectfully. "You want to know how we get from one planet to another so quickly? Watch this."

She maneuvered the ship carefully for about a minute. "OK, we're almost to Lagrange Point 4. There's a transportal there."

"I heard there are transportals all over the place."

Joann was concentrating. "Yes, the earth has dozens of them. But the space around earth is closely monitored, so we have to launch from L4."

I detected a vague something; an area of space that was ever so slightly perturbed. Joann leaned back into the shell. For a second I saw the fabric of space actually warp. Then we emerged at the same place where I always began my remote journeys. "Wow! We're at Celeste already?"

Joann looked at me curiously. "How did you know that?"

"I feel it. How do you know it?"

"The transportal tells me through this thing," she said, pointing to the pilot's shell at the back of her head. "It's CAT, consciousness assisted technology. Only GSP pilots know how to use them," she said proudly.

"This is where the remote viewer always throws me when I return from one of my training exercises," I explained.

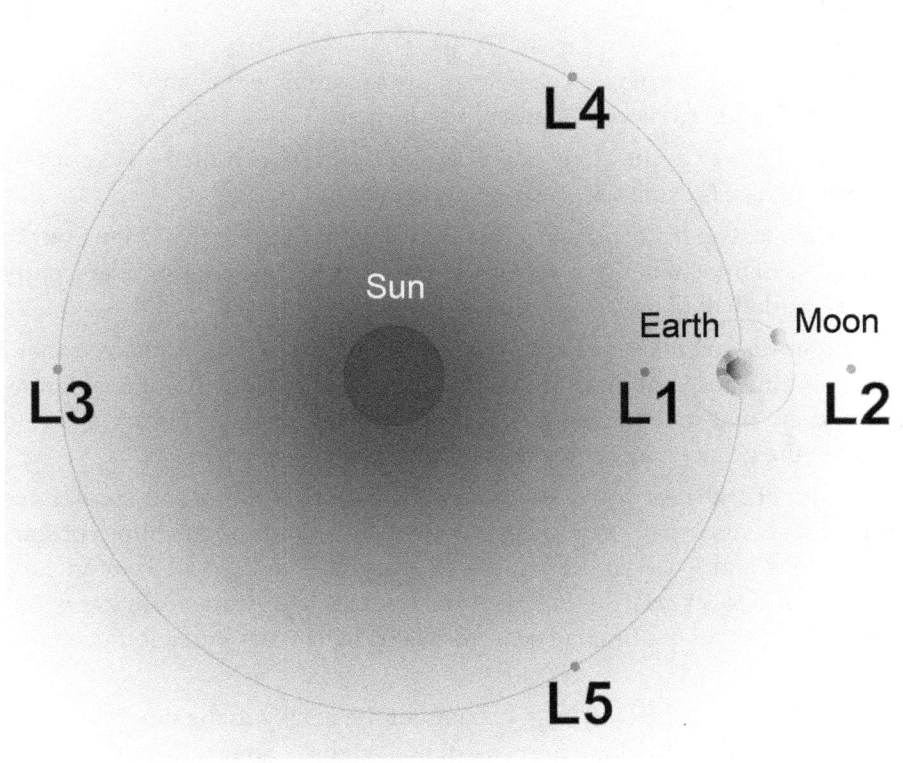

Lagrange Point 4 (L4)[9]

"Patrick wants to show you something important."

"I'm so tired of Patrick."

"Talk to Gwenneth then. You've got the hots for her."

"Fine. I'll talk to Gwenneth any time."

[Celeste]

We were silent until the ship landed. We walked out of the lifter and through one of the magnificent entrance corridors with its light shows and brilliant artwork. When we got past the entrance Patrick and Gwenneth were there. My heart skipped two beats as I looked at her. Was that a look of concern I saw in her eyes? And maybe a little excitement too. I felt like one of King Arthur's knights ready to die for Guinevere.

Just then Kelleye and Josh walked in. Everyone was looking at me expectantly.

"Your teammates have all completed their training, Philogene," Patrick announced. "But there is one remaining test for you."

I walked over to the stone bar. "Let's get it over with then." Pass or fail, this was the last fucking test I was going to take.

Patrick waved his hand and I found myself halfway up the Orion Spur in the middle of interstellar space. I was as scared as the last doughnut at a party of hungry football players.

There was something different about the feeling of this...I realized that I wasn't out in space but in a simulation. This was a gigantic hologram! Somehow I knew that it contained a beautiful, brilliant display of every star and planet in the galaxy mapped by the GSP.

I thought of the earth and I was there. I thought of Celeste and I was above the planet and its one gigantic moon. There were billions upon billions of stars and nebulae and I was in the middle of everything and could go anywhere I wanted in perfect safety. I followed the track of my escape from Zaon. My remote viewing adventure had sent me 40,000 light years into another arm of the galaxy!

I jumped around, going from one end of the galaxy to the other. I discovered that the Milky Way is an immense flattened disk about 100,000 light years across.

This was fun, but what was the point? I knew this was my final examination but I didn't know (as usual) what I was supposed to look for. Then, suddenly, I understood the point of my insane training.

A Seer is a skilled remote viewer, but is supposed to be able to look beyond the obvious. That's why Patrick never told me anything beforehand. So there was something here that wasn't obvious, but if I was a real Seer I could find it. I had to see the big picture.

To do that I had to get out into intergalactic space, and take a good look at the Milky Way from afar. Would this simulation be able to do that?

I was really afraid, but I launched myself on a tangent outside the plane of the galaxy. I was now sitting five million light years outside the Milky Way. I knew I was in a simulator, but there are no words to describe the view (see image on page 75). I don't know how long I stared at it. There are billions of galaxies out there!

The universe[10]

Halo around a galaxy[11]

I told the simulator to pan into the Milky Way and saw that the flattened disc of the galaxy was surrounded by a faint halo. When I looked deeper into the halo I understood what it was: metadata about how the galaxy itself was put together. I saw how the stars moved to form the spiral arms; how stars evolved, how the stellar systems were grouped. The halo around the galaxy was actually an information field. I turned my viewpoint to see the galaxy from the top down.

The Milky Way galaxy[12]

Astronomers say that there's a black hole at the center of the galaxy, but the holomap showed the center of the galaxy as a huge, rotating energy pump. There was a white hole emitting energy that eventually, over millions of years, coalesced into the spiral arms that were filled with hundreds of billions of stars. The black hole absorbs excess energy.[13]

At this point I was so excited (and overwhelmed) that I bailed out of the simulation and fell to the hard floor of the holocave.

Gwenneth rushed toward me. "Are you all right, Philogene?"

I staggered to my feet, still blown away by what I had seen. "I'm OK. Just really tired."

Joann, Kelleye, and Josh were staring at me, as if they had seen everything that happened. Patrick actually had a smile on his face! I must have done something right. Gwenneth's face was lit up with intense excitement. Normally calm and serene, she was jumping around like a little puppy. She looked at Patrick. "I knew it."

"OK team, we have done all we can with you," Patrick announced with a satisfied grin. "Finally I can get rid of this thing!" He took off what looked like a very thin makeup mask on his face and ears.

I stared. Patrick's face was beautifully symmetric, its coarser features smoothed out like an airbrushed image of a celebrity. "What the—?"

"I'm sorry for this pretense. But it was a necessary deception to complete your training. I needed to look just like an earthian."

So "Space Force" Patrick is really a Celestian (I'm still going to call him Patrick because I can't pronounce his Celestian name.) "I'm finally done?"

"Yes. The simulator was the final test. What you did in there is extraordinary. You aren't just an idiot savant, but capable of insight. You're going to need that for the job ahead."

"What job?"

"Preventing the Collectives from absorbing the earth into their networks. If present trends continue you will eventually become part of either the Hilarion or the Fenachrone Trading Collective. You know what that means."

"I'm not sure I believe you."

"Philogene, if you do nothing you will use up your planet's resources and become dependent on the corporate trading networks. You will lose your freedoms and your sovereignty. Your lives – like all those who live on Class II planets – will be restricted and programmed."

He looked at Gwenneth. "My niece and I have taken a stand, even against the sentiment of the Celestian Council and the rest of our society..."

His niece!

"...we have risked all the planets in our network on you four."

I shook my head. "If the situation is that bad why haven't you done anything about it before?"

"Because we can't, Philogene," Gwenneth said. "There are only a quarter million or so advanced planets in a galaxy with over two hundred billion in the trading networks. We are vastly outnumbered, so we have to stay hidden. We can't intervene on emerging planets or our network will be discovered."

"But the barbarians are at our gates now," Patrick said, "just as they are on earth. We can't act overtly against the Collectives, but we can provoke an insurgency."

Patrick and Gwenneth glanced at each other. "Training you earthians is an experiment," said Gwenneth. "Our people are terrified of what might happen if the Collectives find out we've been interfering on earth. The risks are enormous, but if earth can somehow escape the Collective hive mind it will be a beacon to all beings on all of the Hilarion and Fenachrone planets."

"That's crazy! One planet against millions in the Collectives? We don't have a chance."

"Yes you do, Philogene," Gwenneth said. "The Collectives are forbidden to make war on emerging planets. They are fighting the battle on the mental plane, using disinformation, psychological manipulation, and propaganda. That's why we have trained you four. Your group is so small it's invisible. But you can have a great effect."

"The Intervention is well underway on earth, and I'm afraid you're losing," Patrick said. "There isn't much time left."

"Sorry, I don't see it."

"You will."

The rest of my team looked convinced, but maybe they were just brainwashed. "I'm too tired to think anymore about this."

"Take the team back to earth, will you Joann?" Patrick asked.

After the earthians had gone Gwenneth looked at her uncle. To keep in practice for their earthian mission they spoke in English. "You didn't tell him anything."

"He doesn't expect me to. The less he knows the better, which you understand very well, niece."

"Are you sure he's ready for the job?"

Patrick shrugged. "No one is ever ready to confront the Collectives. The earthians will have to learn the hard way about the Intervention. Let's see what happens when Philogene faces his first big test."

[Midland]

Joann flew us back to the Uploads parking lot in her modified lifter. I was mentally and physically exhausted, but still buzzing from my experience in the simulator. I sat in the forward section next to Joann's pilot's chair. Kelleye and Joshua were together in the passenger section. Joann left me to my thoughts for a few minutes and then began to talk about what she called "her lifter."

"It's a gift from the Celestians. Their small Defense Forces contingent put a galactic-standard consciousness-assisted control hemi in it so I can control the lifter via thought impulses. My trainer said, 'You will need this for your work on earth.'"

"How did you get it in the first place? There are only a hundred or so of the spaceplanes on the entire planet."

Joann frowned. "Patrick said he requisitioned it from the Space Force." Her face cleared. "I don't care how he got it! It's mine now."

I smiled. Joann looked like a big dog protecting a treasured bone.

"I hope it won't attract attention from the authorities because I may need to use it a lot," Joann said.

"Doing what?" I asked.

"What do you care? You're going home. You don't want to be part of the team."

I laughed. "What team? You guys never tell me anything. Patrick never tells me anything. I haven't trained with anyone but you, and that was only one day." I stared at her. "And you abandoned me."

Joann's eyes softened a little. "I'm sorry Philo, but Gwenneth says I'm not supposed to say anything."

I could see her look at me for a reaction. My eyes widened a little.

"You're in love with her."

"Fat lot of good it will do me."

The ship's transparencies opened. "L4," Joann said. "A short jaunt and we're back at the Uploads parking lot."

"So what is your job in this team effort?" I asked.

"Mainly pilot, but I'm good in a crisis. I ferry people around. Some pretty important people," she said proudly.

"Then I must be important."

She glanced at me while maneuvering the lifter. We were at the Midland airport now. "More important than you know."

I caught a sideband in Joann's mind: She had orders from Patrick to "keep an eye on Philogene." Hah! I thought. Good luck with that.

%%%Joann used the Trucker Path app and dropped off Joshua and Kelleye at a local WalMart parking lot, where Joshua had parked his red Toyota. This caused quite a stir when the sleek looking lifter – just slightly larger than an

18-wheeler – landed silently next to one of the big rigs. Then she flew the lifter into a designated parking area at the back of the Midland Municipal airport. The space for Joann's lifter was surrounded by rectangle of red paint and it had the lifter's ID painted in red. There was a small garage next to the parking space.

Before I got out Joann spoke hesitantly. "I know it's been rough on you Philo, but I'd like to ask you a favor."

Before I could reply she said, "It's a request from Gwenneth."

"C'mon, Joann! You're baiting me."

"Yeah I know, but it's important."

"What?"

She patted her pilot's chair. "I'm very fond of this little ship," she said. "We may need to use it to go places at a moment's notice. It has a military designation so I can go to areas a civilian aircraft can't. To do that I need access to some, ah, classified networks."

"Let me guess. You need clearance to take off and land in restricted areas. That means you need access to certain Grid access codes."

Joann brightened. "Correct, Philo."

"Jamaal isn't going to like that."

"I can tell you this. Patrick says it's your first test."

"Fuck Patrick." Then I thought that Patrick wasn't Gwenneth's boyfriend, but her uncle. I was curious. "What do you mean, my first test?" Apparently I was part of this team whether I liked it or not.

"Talk to Jamaal. If you can't figure out how to get clearance for my lifter, Patrick says you're not as good as he thinks you are."

"That's not fair. You're baiting me again."

She smiled. "That's right. You can never resist a challenge."

The lifter entrance door opened. "Off you go. Talk to Jamaal, get my clearances. If you're successful, be at the Uploads parking lot at 0400 on Wednesday for your first assignment."

I sighed and jumped out. The door closed. 0400 was way too early in the morning.

After Philo left, Joann sat in her lifter for a minute and thought about Philogene. He's self-centered, reckless, and immature, but she could see that even Gwenneth had feelings for him. She didn't know whether she liked that.

— 10 —

Joann was right. I couldn't resist a challenge. When I went to work the next morning I asked Jamaal for remote admin access to the Space Grid. I knew he would say no.

"No can do, Philo," Jamaal said. "The governments of the world closely monitor the Grid. They are paranoid about secrecy."

"They want to monitor our comms but they don't want anybody to know what they are doing."

Jamaal grimaced. "You know the zero-hop rule. Only one target can be surveilled at a time, no blanket spying."

"C'mon man, you know that's bullshit. They can target anyone they want and call it a zero-hop."

"Yes, but my job is on the line, Philo. Any unauthorized use of the system is traceable."

"It's not unauthorized if I have admin access."

Jamaal was being stubborn. What I was asking was unusual, but it was not unheard of. Some Grid facilities were so busy that dual or even triple admin access was sometimes granted to senior techs. But my boss' face was set in unyielding lines. What was I going to do?

Suddenly I understood what Joann was saying yesterday. Should I use one of the tricks Patrick taught me about the mental plane? Obiwan-Kenobi used this trick to make the stormtrooper pass the droids. Patrick probably used it to get Joann's lifter. Why not? I didn't say anything, just put a gentle suggestion into Jamaal's mind. This was my first big test. If I couldn't even influence a friend, I might as well quit now.

A second later Jamaal shrugged and said, "OK Philo, but watch yourself. These installations are tightly monitored. Too much snooping on the comms is a tell."

"Thanks, boss."

Wow. Mission accomplished, and I did it all with a mental suggestion. The trick is to organize a simple thought packet with what you want the subject to do. I saw how my training had prepared me to do some awesome things. I stayed around and worked a full shift before going home. I planned to work shifts whenever I had the time; Uploads was open 24 hours a day.

I didn't feel like going out because I had to be at the Uploads parking lot at 4 a.m. to meet Joann. I had her clearances and sent the Grid access codes to her via a secure email program.

I was up at 3 a.m. I had something to eat even though I wasn't hungry, and drank 3 cups of coffee. Then I walked a mile to the Uploads parking lot in the cold, to stay awake.

I wasn't surprised when Joann stepped cheerfully out of the ship onto the frozen parking lot and gave me a hearty "Good morning!"

"Ugh," I replied.

"Thanks for the access codes, Philo."

"It was easier than I thought."

"Patrick always said you were a natural."

"It's cold out here."

"Get in." Joann took her seat at the pilot's chair. The cabin was pressurized and the interior was comfortable.

"I filed a very unusual flight plan last night with Space Force Command."

"Don't abuse your Grid access codes. If you overuse remote access the system will flag it and Jamaal will be very unhappy with me."

"All right."

"Where are we going?"

"Patrick claims that there are Collective bases all over the moon observing the earth and conducting operations. Now's our chance to see if the Celestians are right."

Joann said this as she put her head in the control shell. The lifter took off. Within a minute we found ourselves orbiting the moon. I didn't ask her how we got there so fast, it was probably one of the transportals. "See that blackened piece of ground by that small crater? Patrick says it is the entrance to a Hilarion base."

Joann fiddled with something on her control console. The image on her screen now showed a close-up of the crater. "The base is underground. Your job is to use your remote viewing skills to tell us if there are any galactics in there, and what they are doing."

"I'm not in the holocave anymore."

"Don't sweat it, Philo, you don't need it. You were made to think that it was some kind of consciousness projector. It is, actually, but you only needed it for your training-runs on Al-Simak. Since then you were given the target by the projector, but you did the remote viewing all by yourself."

"Seriously?"

"Why do you think we kept you on?" she said, smiling. "You're useless otherwise."

Joann was teasing me, but I didn't think it was funny.

"Are you ready?"

"Sounds pretty easy."

"Be careful. Patrick says to remember your lessons."

I was feeling pretty confident. I had survived a 40,000-light-year trip across the galaxy. How hard could this be?

"Here, put this on." Joann handed over a shell that looked just like her pilot shell. "This is a recorder. Whatever happens to you, we'll know about it."

The thing felt like rubber, but it looked organic. When my hands contacted it, I felt something in it respond. "Is this thing alive?"

"In a manner of speaking. According to Patrick it's a thought recorder."

At this point I'd believe anything about galactic technology. I put the thing on my head. The material immediately adjusted itself to fit comfortably. It felt good. "Here goes, my first unassisted remote viewing attempt."

I was out of the ship and into space. But it was no big deal now, after all my testing. I knew enough to go slow. As I approached the moon crater I felt a mental barrier. Patrick calls it a shield and says they are used all the time by galactics to prevent access to sensitive areas by remote viewers on the mental plane. But how to get in? Before, I just used force but I didn't want to get smoked like I did on Zaon. After searching for a long time I was able to find a pattern to unlock the shield. I opened the door a crack and went in, cringing mentally. I expected an attack or an alarm to sound. I was ready to get out of there fast, but nothing happened.

I saw an open area underground so I forced myself to go slowly through the rock for about twenty feet until I emerged into an open space. Two beings in biosuits with their backs to me were looking down at a table. A woman was lying on the table, unmoving. I sent my awareness in a circle, being careful to lock my mind down completely. I was starting to feel really uncomfortable now as I used my mental peripheral vision to check these guys out. They stank; an evil smell emanated from them. Their consciousness was dark, twisted, grotesque...these two were Maitre! I must have leaked my panic into the mental plane because a wall of black energy assaulted my mental shield, clawing and smashing, trying to get in. If they broke through I knew I'd be dead.

I don't remember how I got out of there. I had the key to the base's shield still in my mind. I felt the black energy getting stronger, and suddenly I was out. I still had sense enough not to lead them to Joann and the ship...Gradually I felt the attack recede and I took my bearings. I had no idea where I was, but I already had some experience of getting Lost in Space. So I settled down and slowly envisioned Joann and the ship. After a subjective minute or so I spotted a gas giant planet lying on its side. This was Uranus, and I was oriented again. I slowly made my way to the ship and made it back to my body, which was lying on the floor of the little scoutcraft. My eyes fluttered and I saw Joann leaning over me, giving me mouth-to-mouth.

"Philo!" she screamed, a look of intense relief on her face. My thought recorder was on the floor.

I was feeling OK now and sat up shakily, my hands propping me up. "I didn't know you cared, sweetheart," I said in a pretty bad Humphrey Bogart voice.

"I don't!" she said, and huffed off to her pilot's chair, grabbing the recorder.

I sat on the floor of the little craft, trying to process my experience. After several minutes I made an announcement. "I want to try again, but I'm not strong enough yet."

I told her about the two Maitre in suits and the woman lying on the table. "Those two are very powerful on the mental plane."

"Philo! There are Maitre in there?"

"Yes, and they are horrible. Thank God Patrick clued me in about them, or I'd be in sad shape."

A normal human, in the presence of one of these extraterrestrials, would be mentally immobilized. Even remotely they easily overpowered me. In my physical body I would have been helpless, just like that woman on the table. "The two Maitre were wearing bio-suits."

"Biological contamination," Joann replied. "The earth, to these alien races, is like a leaking bioweapons lab. They can't even get close to our atmosphere, and have to be protected when they interact physically with us."

"Why are they here then? We could kill them all by breathing on them."

"That's what we're supposed to find out."

"How do you know all this?"

"Because I'm mission leader on this one. Patrick gave me a thorough briefing before we came back. As a Scoutship Commander pilot I have to know enough to keep my crew out of danger."

"I would have thought I deserved a briefing too," I grumbled.

Joann spoke impatiently. "You're a Seer. The less you know, the better. It's for your own protection. Do you get that?"

She was back to her old irritating self again. "What's next?"

"We go back to see Patrick and get debriefed," She held up my recorder. "You secured valuable intelligence; you have confirmed that the Hilarion are working with Maitre. And they are doing so right here in our solar system! We have to get this thing back to the Celestians, they will know what to do with this information."

"Fuck that. I want to try again."

Joann got angrily out of her chair. "You *are* stupid aren't you! You almost got killed!"

"Yeah, but my training got me used to it. I want to know what those two freaks were doing."

I saw fear in Joann's eyes, and respect.

"I can handle those two." As I said it I knew it was true, if I could have some time to process the signatures of the two Maitre on the mental plane. "Give me a couple hours to prepare."

Joann was conflicted. "My orders, and they are adamant, are to get this recorder back to the Celestians immediately."

I understood. "This is your first command decision, Scoutship Commander."

Joann's eyes widened. "That's right, Philo. I don't know what to do."

"I'll make it easy for you. We stick around here for a few more hours and I try again. Even if they get me you'll still have the recorder."

"I can't risk it. Part of command is protecting your crew."

"You can say I overpowered you."

Joann laughed out loud. "Not likely."

"I'm told I have magnetic male charm."

"Could have fooled me."

"You were giving me mouth-to-mouth."

"Purely a medical procedure!"

"I'm going to my seat to do some analysis. I'm going to figure out the mental signatures of those two demons so I can neutralize them next time."

"You're crazy."

"Don't disturb me. I know you want to jump my bones."

Joann snorted but left me alone.

In three hours I was ready. "Give me that recorder."

Joann reluctantly handed it over. She was obviously worried about bringing home a dead crewmate, but I was more worried about the woman on that table. If she was still there, I wanted to physically bring her back to earth.

I remote viewed into the base, just like before, but there was only one of the ugly creatures present. The woman had been taken apart, sliced open like a side of beef. The putrid stink emanating from the Maitre on the mental plane made me sick. This being was evil; demonic.

I attacked it with pure hatred. It backed off for a moment, wounded. Then it sent me a burst of twisted, psychotic madness. I was overwhelmed and got out of there even as I felt it break through my mental shield and enter my mind. When I got back to my body I was lying in my own vomit, shaking. "Get your ship out of here!" I cried with the last bit of my strength. I knew I was close to death and I grabbed onto Joann as hard as I could, needing life and human contact, smelling foul from my own sick. I could feel the dark energy from the Maitre inside my body like a deadly disease...

[Celeste]

I drifted in and out of consciousness. I heard voices whispering from time to time. One time Joshua was there. "He's not going to make it..." I got fleeting glimpses of Kelleye. Occasionally Patrick was there, and Gwenneth. Just the sight of her for even a few seconds gave me strength.

I was fighting a battle for my life. Inside me a dark evil thing had been planted, a soul-sucking energy that I couldn't get rid of. Once I fully opened my eyes and saw multicolored light surrounding my body, and someone holding my hand. Then I relapsed back into an unconscious nightmare. I knew this was no physical disease. There was no medical remedy for what I had. Inside I was fighting an entity that had been planted in my consciousness by that thing in the biosuit. Every time I was ready to succumb I felt a slight infusion of...light,

I'd guess you'd call it. Life force energy. Just enough to keep me going. It was a constant battle, an agony of pain and despair. But for some reason I fought on.

"We're losing him," Gwenneth said to her uncle.

"The fool! The best candidate in 10,000 years and he has to attack one of those filthy things."

"He's an earthian. He doesn't know any better."

Patrick spoke bitterly. "And that's by design. The best Seers are always trained blind."

"Don't blame yourself, uncle. Stay in the high heart. Trust to the One."

I heard these voices from a great distance. I was getting more and more tired. The evil thing within me was like a cancer, spreading inside my body and my psyche, sucking out my life energy, destroying my soul. The boosts of light I was getting were fainter and fainter now. I knew I had lost the battle. I just gave up, surrendered myself totally to death. This wasn't a heroic impulse, like the stories you read about superheroes. I simply didn't have the energy to fight anymore.

Then something happened. I floated out of my body. This was a lot different from remote viewing because I wasn't doing it voluntarily. I was shocked by my own appearance. That cold, gray thing lying on the medbed must be my body!

No, there wasn't a white light. There were no angels welcoming me to some spiritual paradise. Just an opportunity. I heard a voice inside my consciousness. "You can stay or go."

"Why should I stay?" I asked the voice.

"Because the game you're playing is so much bigger than you think. And, if you choose, you can make a significant contribution."

"That's a load of crap."

I wasn't offered a glimpse of my future if I stayed, or what would happen if I died. There were no rosy happy-ever-after rewards for me. Just a stark choice. From some great well of knowledge I knew that if I stayed, I would live. But there were no promises.

"Will I have a good life or a bad life?"

There was no answer.

Then a single word. "Choose."

I chose.

I opened my eyes. The multicolored light surrounded my body. I was alone in the infirmary, still lying on the medbed. I was too weak to move. The cover had come away from my right arm. I saw a claw that used to be my hand, connected to a bony arm that looked like something on a skeleton. How could this cadaver still be breathing?

I closed my eyes and lost consciousness.

When I woke up again I saw a beautiful woman gazing down at me. I didn't recognize her. Before I blacked out again I heard her say, "He's alive!"

I don't know how many times I was out and regained consciousness. One time I saw a tube in my arm. There was now a little flesh on the bone. I heard two Celestians speaking in awed whispers. "He should be dead. All his organs failed."

"This has never happened before," the other voice said.

"I don't know whether it's a miracle or a curse."

"Is that evil thing still inside him? Perhaps that is what has kept him alive."

"If so he should be terminated. For his own good."

"And ours."

I blacked out again.

I woke up again, surrounded by a dozen Celestians. My mind was clearer now. I could see a little through eyes that hurt, but I was still too weak to move. Apparently a momentous decision was being made.

"Terminate him."

I heard a soft, feminine scream before I blacked out.

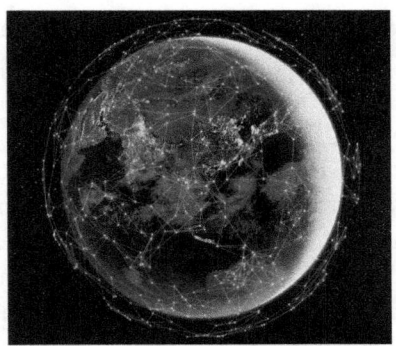

— 11 —

I was awake. Fully conscious. I knew I was going to live, just as the Voice told me. I knew that I had reached a truce with the evil thing inside me. It was still there, like a cyst.

Gwenneth was beside me, holding my hand. I could move. I was very thin, but there was flesh on my bones now. I smiled. "You saved me."

"Unlawfully. But now that we know you will live it is impossible for us to extinguish you."

I smiled bleakly. "You should have killed me. It's still in there."

"I know."

I have never seen anything so lovely as Gwenneth. All of the Celestians are refined and beautiful, but this woman is literally an angel.

"What happens now?"

"You get better. Then, if you consent, there is an assignment for you."

"How is Joann? And Kelleye, and Joshua?"

"They are well. Doing fine work."

"The team is to be reunited." I knew this; how I knew it I don't know. It was a powerful...intuition. Suddenly I understood. To compensate for the dark thing inside me, I also had also been given a gift.

"Yes. If the Council approves."

"The same Council who voted to terminate me."

"Yes. They are afraid of you, Philo."

I felt the thing inside me. "For good reason."

She smiled brilliantly. An angelic smile.

"You have lost status in your society. Because of me."

"Yes. But it was my own choice."

"Why did you do it?"

"Because I love you."

I looked into the loveliest eyes I would ever see. A profound understanding passed between us, and a profound sadness. Our love could never be realized, it could never flourish and blossom. We were two different species from two entirely different civilizations. We could never be together.

I felt a billion years old; a wise, ancient soul that had lived for eons and who had been everywhere in the universe, and experienced everything.

"You feel it too," she said.

"Yes."

I looked around the pleasant little cave, at the light-art on the walls that moved in complex and beautiful patterns. They had been my friends for a long time. "How long have I been here?"

"Six of your months."

"Wow." I squeezed Gwenneth's hand. "Will I see you again?"

"They couldn't keep me away."

That was good enough for me. For now. I closed my eyes and went to sleep.

A month later I was out of bed, walking on shaky legs. Physically, I felt like an old man. But something inside of me was burning, a life energy, urging me to get stronger, feel better. Countering that was the blackness. I couldn't believe that there were beings in the galaxy like this Maitre. I wanted to know why it had butchered that woman. I wanted to know why it was so evil. I was going to find out...

Just then Joann, Kelleye, Joshua, and Patrick entered the room.

When Joann first saw me, she looked hesitant and hung back. Kelleye walked up and took my hand. She looked confident and sure of herself. "How are you, Philogene?"

I smiled wanly. "I've been better. But I'm on the mend."

Joshua stood behind her, his hands possessively on her shoulders. "That's good, because we have something important to do."

Joshua looked honed, cut, and ready for action. There was a suppressed energy about him, as if something powerful was being held back. He spoke softly but firmly, as a diplomat would.

Joann stepped forward. I saw her eyes fill with tears. I tried to make a joke. "Thank you for the mouth-to-mouth."

She turned away, stifling a sob. My skin still had a grayish pallor and I was as thin as a rail. "Don't worry Joann, I'm OK."

Kelleye and Joshua were looking on interestedly. Joann wiped her eyes and turned to face me. "Do you feel well enough to see a presentation, Philogene?"

"Yes. I need something outside myself to put my attention on."

Joshua led the briefing. "The Celestians were able to analyze the information from your encounter with the Maitre. When that thing blitzed you, it didn't shield its mind. Watch."

The space inside the infirmary turned into a big display area. I didn't understand how this technology worked because there were no projectors and no screens; just a volume of space that turned into an interactive 3D hologram. The display showed the Maitre ship entering hyperspace and a week later it appeared in normal space near the moon.

"Why doesn't it use the transportals?" I asked.

"It can't see them," Gwenneth said. "Class II civilizations use FTL drives, or wormholes. It's our only advantage over the Trading Collectives."

"So warp factor 9 isn't that fast."

"Not compared to the transportals," Joann said.

We watched as the Maitre ship sat there for a while until another ship docked with it. The Maitre put on its bio suit and an area of the wall became transparent. Something came into the Maitre's ship, shuffling on three legs, awkwardly carrying someone else in a bio suit. The bio suit was placed on a floating lab table.

"An Oorant," Patrick said.

"What's that?"

"The highest IQs in the galaxy. Peaceful. It is probably there because It is curious."

"About humans?"

Patrick exchanged glances with his niece. "Yes."

'The delivery has been consummated,' we heard the Oorant say on the mental plane. 'Payment is due.'

The Maitre was contemptuous. It handed the Oorant a disk. '500 Community credits. Leave.'

'I stay to watch the procedure.'

The Maitre raged but could do nothing against the Oorant's powerful mind.

The Maitre guided its ship within the small crater on the moon's surface, landing in a small hangar. The Oorant's ship followed. The Maitre took the lab table and went through a small corridor into a lab. The biosuit of the specimen was removed.

"It's a woman!" Kelleye screamed.

"That thing is dissecting her!" Joshua shouted.

"Turn it off!" Joann shouted. Kelleye turned her head and Joshua's face turned white. He was ready to spill his guts. I had a little Maitre in me; my demon was unmoved by the disgusting procedure, and I knew why. "This Maitre is just a resource contractor, doing work for the Hilarion Collective. They are interested in human biology."

"You just learned Lesson Six, Philogene," Patrick said. "The Collectives are interested in humanity, but not necessarily in a benevolent way."

Even Gwenneth was sickened by the actions of the Maitre. She shuddered, knowing that I had the remnant of such a being inside me.

Kelleye, Joshua, and Joann looked at each other. "Understood," Joshua said to Patrick. "The earth is entering a community of civilizations that regard us just as the Europeans regarded indigenous societies in the New World."

Patrick nodded. "They don't hate you, they don't love you. You just have things they want."

After the dissection the Oorant left and went back to Its ship. Then we saw the Maitre react to my attack on the mental plane. My attempt to read its mind looked like a clumsy barbarian attacking with a massive mental broadsword.

"You're going to have to do better than that Philo," Patrick said, teasing me.

No one laughed when the Maitre attacked me. The recorder showed it as a malignant black cesspool of roiling, twisted, misaligned energy. Just looking at its representation on the mental plane made my stomach turn over. The demon inside me stirred.

Joann looked at me, shocked. Joann was never shocked.

"But...how did you survive?"

I replied bitterly. "Some of the Celestians say I didn't. They say I'm hopelessly compromised, and when the going gets tough I'll be a tool of the Maitre inside me."

Kelleye's face registered disbelief.

"They may be right."

"You look OK to me," Kelleye said.

I laughed cynically (or maybe it was my demon). "Appearances can be deceiving."

"Play it back," Joshua said.

My attack on the Maitre was replayed. Joshua put his hands together and bowed silently to me in acknowledgment. I think he understood, in that moment, just a little of what I was dealing with. Gwenneth, who had seen me literally dead, lowered her head.

I felt a little better.

Patrick apologized to me. "I'm sorry Philogene. We had no idea Maitre were in that base. I should have remembered your earlier training report that Maitre have allied with the Hilarion Collective. We were able to mine a lot of data from the Maitre when it attacked you. It turns out that the Collective presence in your system is much greater than we thought."

"It is now time for us to let you go, and let you proceed at your own pace," Gwenneth said to me. "We have selfishly forced the issue and it almost caused your death."

Joshua, Kelleye, Joann, and I all nodded.

"Before we send you on your way I want to remind you about what you are facing from the Collectives in the Greater Community," Patrick said. "If you have any other questions ask Joshua, he got the whole briefing."

"Number one. The Greater Community is almost exclusively composed of Class II planets with planned, totalitarian societies organized into corporate Collectives.

"Number two: Viruses and biological pathogens are different on every planet. Therefore there is a serious risk of contamination in person-to-person contact between nations in the galaxy. This is particularly true with the earth, which has so much biodiversity it is like a hazardous waste dump for every Class II race. Biological contamination is a major concern for all races who travel in space and who engage in commerce with others.[14] The point is, you don't have to worry about physical invasion by the Collectives. They have to use human proxies because they can't get anywhere near your atmosphere."

Patrick paused. "Any questions?"

"Yeah, the obvious one," I said. "If we're so contaminated, how can you work with us?"

Patrick smiled. "Good question. Over tens of thousands of years, our immune systems on Class I planets have advanced to the point where we are impervious to disease. We don't get sick. We don't have medicine as you understand it. If we had to, we could travel anywhere in the galaxy on planets that support our physical genotype. That's the benefit of spiritual evolution."

"How many advanced planets are there?" Kelleye asked.

I could tell Patrick was getting impatient. "At last count, 267,831 in a galaxy with over 200 billion planets with intelligent life. Our network is very small and must remain hidden."

"That's appalling," Kelleye said, her face blanching.

"It's a fact of life. Now to Number three. If races can't associate physically with each other because of contamination, how do emerging planets like earth get sucked into the corporate Trading Collectives? The answer: resource depletion. Even a planet like earth that is rich in mineral and environmental resources eventually uses them up.[15] When that happens, galactic technology is dangled in front of a planet's major influencers by representatives of the Trading Collectives—"

"Like pharmaceutical reps influencing medical doctors!" I blurted out. "They offer new drugs and a lot of money. It's hard to resist."

I saw Gwenneth smile, and Patrick nodded. "You have noticed the trend toward totalitarianism in the arts, in culture, and in politics. This is not a coincidence. One of the best techniques to promote authoritarianism is fear of biological contamination. This is a very real threat for all galactic races."

"Vaccines for that must have been developed," I said.

Patrick shook his head. "Unfortunately, no. There are no universal galactic vaccines because of the diversity of species. The number of biological pathogens is in the trillions. Collective trading reps use this fear very effectively on new, emerging societies."

"The 2020 pandemic," Joshua stated.

"The point is, the only way to herd an entire planet into the trading groups is collectivization. Do you understand? The trading groups can't risk a massive wild card like earth with its 8 billion population disturbing the supply chains, and putting out radical ideas on the mental plane. That would create havoc in their societies, which are all dependent on the trading networks. For the Collectives, social monitoring and control is a simple matter of survival. That's what the Intervention on your planet is all about."

"The nail that sticks out is hammered down," Joann remarked.

"That about sums it up," Patrick agreed.

"I don't like this at all," Kelleye said. "I thought you galactics would have evolved a nicer, more advanced society."

"We have! Our advanced Class I planets are evolving in consciousness. Our lives are wonderful. If only I could show you what we are capable of."

Patrick looked over to Gwenneth, but she shook her head.

Kelleye had a look of despair on her face. "But...you are under attack from the Collectives just as free societies on earth are under attack from big corporations and their operatives. It's not fair! You have the same problems we have."

"You get used to it," Patrick said. "As above, so below."

The Greater Community
Star systems within 50 light years of earth

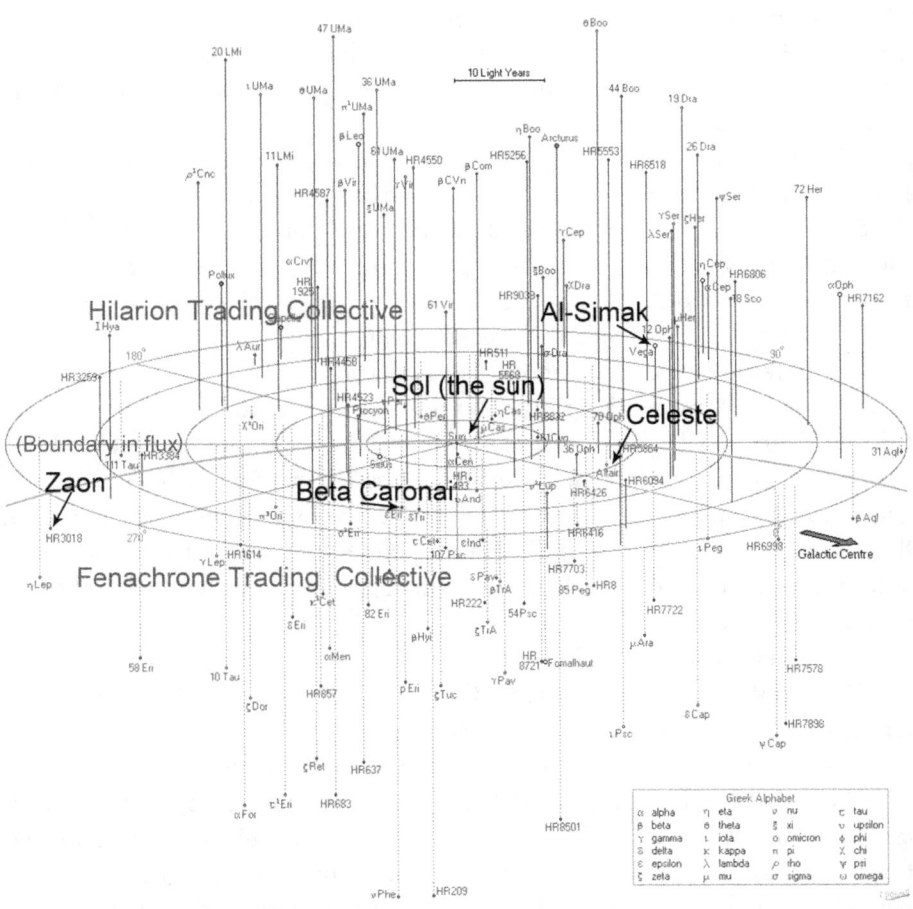

The Greater Community: Crude 2D map of the 133 most important stars in earth's neighborhood.[16]

I could see that Kelleye was having a hard time accepting this. I looked over at Joshua and he just shrugged. Joann had a grim look on her face.

Patrick paused. "Speaking of that, let's take a look at the Trading Collectives in the neighborhood of earth. Joshua, can you do this?"

Joshua spoke up. The holo shrunk to display the star systems within 50 light years of earth. "The sector earth is in is called the Greater Community."

"Patrick has put our sun in the center of the display," Joshua said. "Celeste is 17 light years away, orbiting the star Altair. The star systems within 50 light years of the sun are divided into two zones. The Hilarion group is a ruthless corporate trading collective that has captured many of the planets in this area. They are opposed by the Fenachrone trading group, who aren't much better. The earth is very close to the border between the two competing Collectives, who see the earth's abundant natural resources, and our enormous population, as a great prize and a great threat."

"That's right," Patrick affirmed. "Both Hilarion and Fenachrone reps have met secretly with human operatives from rogue groups called special access programs, which operate independent from the public governments. These meetings are always done in space within sterilized environments to avoid the risk of contamination."

"How do these Maitre fit in?" I asked Josh.

"I'll defer to Patrick on that one," Joshua said.

"The Maitre are working both sides of the Fenachrone-Hilarion competition for earth. They are employed by both sides to intimidate each others' operatives on emerging planets like earth. The reward for the Maitre is...how shall I put this...a few human expendables like the poor woman you found on that lab table. The Maitre experiment on young, vital races like humanity in a desperate attempt to save their devolving species. They share what they've found with the Collectives."

"That makes no sense," Kelleye said.

"Sure it does," Patrick replied. "Collectivization usually results in totalitarian societies and eventual species decline."

Kelleye's face expressed her disapproval. Patrick continued.

"Both the Fenachrone and the Hilarion have the same objective: neutralize a potential adversary. If the earth, with its strong religious and spiritual traditions, can overcome the corporatists and achieve sovereignty and independence, it will create big problems for the Collectives in the Greater Community."

"I'm confused," I said. "You have told us that your Advanced Planets network is helpless against these corporate Collectives. We don't have a chance."

Patrick shook his head. "The greatest fear of totalitarians on earth and in the galaxy is the connection to the One. They must suppress religion and spiritual awareness, or their populations will awaken and overthrow their collectivist masters. This has happened numerous times in galactic history."

"The earth has one big advantage," Gwenneth said. "Your population is by far the largest in the Greater Community. The corporate Collectives have never tried to collectivize such a large number of beings."

I snorted (or was it my demon?). "If advanced planets are only one in a million after 5 billion of years of evolution, you guys are losing the battle big-time. How are we supposed to succeed where you have failed?"

Gwenneth frowned at me and Patrick was upset. "Because the earth, with its massive population, is broadcasting stronger on the mental plane than any other planet in the entire Orion Spur. Everyone in the galactic web can hear you! Moreover, the earth is literally in the middle of the two most powerful trading groups in the Spur, which encompasses thousands of light years and almost a billion planets. If the earth should awaken..."

I was getting fired up. "That's the kind of talk I want to hear! The first thing we need to do is find the Maitre who murdered that woman and kill it!"

"That is your demon talking, Philogene," Gwenneth said. The look on her face told me she was sad that such a brilliant Seer was contaminated.

I wasn't feeling sorry for myself. The life energy inside me was burning bright, and I had learned to accommodate the evil thing inside me. I was getting used to it.

"How do you plan to do that, Philo?" Joshua asked. "The last time you interacted with a Maitre you got smoked."

My devil was laughing at Joshua. "OK genius, you got a better plan?"

Joshua was silent.

"I guess not then."

"With your training in the mental plane you can read the mind of any human being," Patrick suggested.

The Celestian was being evasive again. "You're saying that we four can use the mental plane to identify human influencers working with the bad guys. But who are they? Give us a list."

"That we cannot tell you. We cannot interfere."

I snorted. "You have done just that by training us."

Patrick's face assumed a pained expression. "It is permitted to, er, 'level the playing field' a little, as you say, on emerging planets. Without the ability to work on the mental plane, humanity has no chance. We have given you this ability, which was already latent. That's all I can say."

We four looked at each other and shrugged. "Why all the mystery?" I asked.

"Because the advanced societies have learned the hard way that emerging civilizations like earth must make their own decisions, with complete free choice. If you discover the gateway to higher consciousness, your planet will come together in peace and prosperity. If you do not"— Patrick's face now showed despair—"there's nothing we can do." Gwenneth's beautiful features were bleak.

"So we're on our own then," Kelleye said.

"Essentially, yes," Gwenneth said. "It's an unfortunate fact of life in the galaxy. History tells us that 'guidance' by advanced planets in emerging civilizations always results in collectivization by the trading empires. And in doing so, we expose ourselves to retaliation."

"But you now have the ability to be successful," Patrick added hopefully.

I was irritated. "Four people out of eight billion to confront the entire galaxy?" I shouted. "That's preposterous!"

"That's because you don't yet know the power of the mental plane," he mumurred. The older man relented a little. "I'll give you a hint that will start you in the right direction. If you follow this lead and don't do anything stupid, you have a very good chance of success. You see, we can't tell you what you will encounter; it won't be real until you experience it."

I shrugged. "Let's have it then."

"Dr. Colin Frank, NIH director."

"That's it?"

"That's it. Get on with it."

Our training was over.

Joann flew us back to earth in her lifter, using the transportals. It took less than an hour, and most of that time was spent getting to the transportal around Celeste, and to earth from Lagrange Point 4. Joann piloted the little lifter flawlessly as she let me off at the Midland Municipal Airport. She was irritating, but good at her job.

When I walked into Uploads the next day Jamaal was angry. "You've been gone for seven months, Philo! Where have you been?"

"Sorry about that, boss. I got really sick and spent a lot of time in the hospital."

"I'm sorry, Philo. Why didn't you contact me?" He looked me over. "You look like crap."

I didn't want to argue with Jamaal. He was the closest thing I had to a friend. "I was doing some confidential security work for Space Force Patrick and couldn't communicate to anyone. It's OK though, I'm back and ready for work."

Jamaal shook his head, but I could tell he was glad to have his best tech back. "I can use you. We're two techs short."

— 12 —

[Midland, Illinois]

It was time for our first assignment as a team. The four of us were supposed to save the earth from the Collectives, but the odds were impossible. Nevertheless, I had to admit that our galactic training made us feel like superheroes compared to the average person.

Joshua Reynolds: Galactic historian and martial artist. Talent for diplomacy and conflict resolution. Runs a martial arts studio in DC to make a living.

Joann D'Arcy: Space Force and GSP trained pilot and irritant. Joann works for a small commercial airline and lives in hotels between her flights.

Kelleye Rodriguez: Mathematician, network analyst, brainiac. Works as a consultant at a tech firm. Lives in the DC area.

Me: Remote viewer and intuitive, when my inner demon isn't acting up. Mental plane magician (for a human). Skilled in pattern recognition in complex systems. I have a flexible schedule at Uploads so I have the most free time.

Our first information target: Colin Frank, head of the National Institutes of Health. I did some research on Frank using publicly available sources. Colin Frank's NIH was aligned with BioSciences, an American genomics company in Palo Alto. BioSciences, in turn, worked with BGI, a Chinese genomics company run by the Chinese military. Both companies were collecting DNA on US and Chinese citizens using viral test kits, compliant medical doctors, and other biometric information using the Internet of Things. Colin Frank himself owned stock in U.S. biotech companies connected to BioSciences and BGI.

Patrick was implying galactic interference in earth's affairs, but my open source research said Colin Frank was just an ordinary scumbag using his public office to enrich himself. I must be missing something.

All four of us got together that night at Antonios, a local restaurant, in Midland. We had something to eat and a few drinks. Joann was excited; she had used her lifter to pick up Kelleye and Josh in DC and fly them in to Midland.

I tried to brief the team about my research on Colin Frank, but Antonios had hardwood floors and was packed. It was so loud you couldn't hear yourself think. After we ordered we realized that conversation was impossible. I suggested that we use our galactic training to comm on the mental plane.

At first it was hard because the earth's mental plane is so crowded with billions of people randomly throwing their thoughts all over the place. There was more noise on the mental plane than in the room! Our training on Celeste was the difference. It took us a while to tune out the noise, but after about 15 minutes the four of us were connected. It was awesome talking to my teammates in a crowded room that was probably close to 90 decibels. We sat there, eating, completely silent. I managed to view everyone in the room on the mental plane before we started. Their minds were wide open and I could have read all of them if I wanted to.

Communicating at the speed of thought is awesome. In less than five minutes I briefed everyone about Colin Frank. Our minds were open and the four of us got to know each other much more intimately. I was able to shield my mind because I was the most proficient on the mental plane. I didn't want the team to see my inner demon too closely.

I was most fascinated with Joann. She rubbed me the wrong way emotionally, but our mental signatures fit together really well. Kelleye and Josh were more aloof, but I could see that theirs were also a good match.

'I'm a little frustrated because I haven't found anything big on Colin Frank. Patrick told me that he's the key.' Then I kicked myself mentally, and everyone at the table saw my thought process. 'Of course! I've been researching on the internet. We have to use our expertise on the mental plane to remote view our targets.' Another lesson learned, I thought. I showed the team how to scan the room and pick up the thoughts of everyone.

'There's thoughts all over the place,' Josh remarked. 'How do we distinguish which thoughts belong to which person?'

'That's a great question, Josh.' The mental plane in the restaurant was a madhouse of random thoughts, like a big fireworks display firing off dozens of screaming, blazing shots of light and noise. 'I'm supposed to be the Seer, so let me figure it out.'

Everyone was happy with this.

'What is your availability if the team needs to go somewhere?' I asked the group after we finished eating.

'We'll have to work around my schedule,' Joann sent. 'I get three days leave every two weeks.'

'There's no problem getting authorization for your flights?'

'My lifter can take us anywhere we want, and you already got my clearances. I also registered my lifter with the FAA. I have to file a flight plan, but these things fly at such high altitudes they don't interfere with commercial or military flights. I basically just go above the Space Grid, travel over the destination around the earth, and drop in. So we're good.'

Joann looked wistful.

'You're missing your GSP work,' I sent.

Joann sighed and fingered her top where the GSP decal would have been. 'Yes. Whenever I get into my lifter it reminds me of my work on Celeste. It was so exciting, even if I was only a courier.'

'Sorry, Joann, didn't mean to bum you out.'

Joann smiled. 'That's OK, I love flying. The jet aircraft I pilot for my job are slower and more temperamental, so it's more of a challenge, especially during severe weather.'

We all left in good spirits.

After work the next day I looked up Colin Frank and found his physical address. He lived in the DC area in a swanky house in Northern Virginia. Now I would have to try my remote viewing capabilities on someone I had never met.

I wondered whether I was up to it. Having a talk on the mental plane with three friends sitting around a table was one thing, but how do I find one guy 800 miles away out of four million in Virginia?

I sat down on my couch and opened my mind a tiny crack. I could hear the babbling of thoughts from everyone in the apartment building. One guy was thinking about how to get a girl he liked into bed, a woman was angry at one of her kids, two children were screaming to their mother about some damn thing...suddenly a couple of dozen people were in my head at once and I got overwhelmed and had to shut down.

Wow, that was a total fail. I started feeling sorry for myself and my demon was mocking me, until I remembered being in the infirmary, almost dead, and

Gwenneth holding my hand tenderly. I remembered her smile, the loveliest in the galaxy. My demon scuttled away into the recesses of my mind and I felt a lot better. This must be what true love is, I thought. Compared to earth women Gwenneth is incomparable. I wanted her real bad.

I got up and made a cup of coffee. My emotions were in turmoil; I knew I had to settle down. I drank my coffee slowly and tried again. This was a lot harder than I thought it would be without the help of the Celestians. The Celestian mental plane is almost silent because the population is small and everyone has control of their thoughts, so it's easy to maneuver around. The human mental plane is all noise and no signal. It's like trying to drive on a dark country road at night in a blizzard, you can't see anything.

I had to shut it down again. I had a dilemma: I had to close my mind to stop the madness, but I had to open up to find the target. I gave up and went out for a walk around the block. For some reason I thought of Joann, and how our minds were compatible. I tried to block out everything else and sent her the strongest thought pulse I could: 'Are you there?'

The response was instantaneous. 'Philogene! Is that you?'

'Yeah! I'm having trouble finding Colin Frank. I thought of you.'

'Thanks for the compliment.'

'Uh, yeah, that didn't sound so good did it? I can't make any headway through all the mental noise, but you and I can comm really well.'

'Let's try reaching out to Kelleye and Josh.'

In an instant we four were together on the mental plane, talking just like last night.

'OK guys,' Josh interrupted. 'I gotta run. I'm teaching a class.' The three of us got a 3D image of Josh executing a kick to someone's abdomen. 'See ya!'

Kelleye and Joann "hung up." I was walking really fast now, excited. I had learned something: affinity for someone cut through all the noise. I wondered whether I could contact Gwenneth, 17 light years away on another planet...

I kicked that thought out of my mind. I had to buckle down and get to work finding Colin Frank. It was going to be a challenge. I was at the steps of my apartment building now, determined to carry on.

Eight hours later, exhausted, I fell into bed. It was three in the morning and I was drained. Just before I lost consciousness Joann sent me a thought. 'How are you doing? You seem stressed.'

I snapped back awake. 'Wow, you can tell that?'

'Yeah. Answer the question.'

This was the annoying Joann I knew best.

'You think *I'm* annoying?'

I ignored this. 'Yeah, I'm really stressed. But I've identified the mental signature of Colin Frank.'

Artist's conception of a human sig.[17]

Joann was all attention. I'll give her this, she's a good listener. 'I learned how to wade through the noise, Joann. It took me forever, because I didn't know what Frank's sig looks like. I studied up on him, built up a prototype sig in my mind that was as much like him as possible, and gradually blocked out the others. I knew his physical location so that made it easier. When I got him I almost blew it.'

Joann was all attention.

'When I finally found him he was having dinner in a DC restaurant with some cronies. He was with a young woman from an escort service. When I eliminated the others at the table I got so excited I just blew into his mind. He dropped his drink all over his date and said, "Who are you?"'

Joann was laughing now; I guess she could see the images I was sending. Everyone at the table was looking strangely at Frank, and his "date" looked disgusted. It was funny.

'Serves him right. He's in the pocket of the medical establishment, and makes big bucks investing in products he's supposed to regulate.'

'So you can read the data from my mind?'

'Yeah, as long as you don't shield it. '

'OK. I'm sorry, I have to get some sleep or I'll go unconscious.'

Just before I dropped off I saw her smiling at me. She wasn't Gwenneth, she was irritating, and she was way too big, but she was starting to grow on me.

I woke up the next morning feeling very tired. My energy level was not any-where near what it was before I encountered that Maitre, and I knew it probably never would be. It was dragging me down.

I got some coffee and felt better. I decided to stay home and spend the entire day remote viewing Colin Frank. It took me almost a half hour to find him again even though I knew his sig. He was sitting in his office at the main NIH complex.

As I studied Frank's mental signature, I came across something that really pissed me off. I saw it all just as it happened from Colin Frank's mind. He had been led down a black corridor to a hidden sub-basement of the NIH Biomed-ical Center in DC by his principal deputy, Michael Cjenk, and a young woman named Kathy Abbott. That had been over a year ago. There was a room full of dead aliens in there!

I understood now how powerful Patrick's training was. From my apart-ment living room I could remote view anyone on earth and get into their mind. I spent the rest of the day digesting what had happened in the secret medical center under the NIH Medical building. What are Kathy Abbott and her crew doing with the corpses of ETs? They even had a Maitre down there! What is the Technology Acquisitions Consortium? What is this miracle new serum that saved Kathy Abbott's life, and where did it come from?

I was mentally exhausted and went down to Mickey Dunn's for a few beers. Several women were at the bar, but they were all boring compared to Joann. I left early and went to bed before midnight.

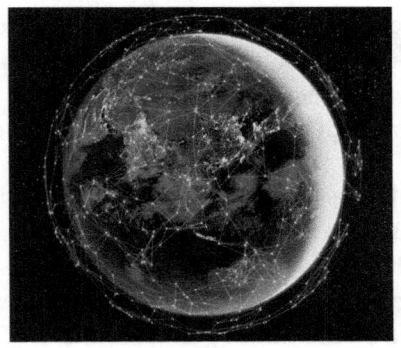

— 13 —

[Washington, DC]

Genghis Glazer sat in his office on the top floor of a building with no signage three miles south of the Beltway, gazing out of one of the windows that surrounded the office on three sides. As per his instructions, he was waiting for his administrative director. He had important information for Austin Matthews. Normally calm and unhurried, this morning there was an unusual sense of urgency in his mind. He had to stop his foot from tapping nervously on the floor. There was a knock on the door.

"Come in."

A tall 35-year-old entered the room and sat across from him. Genghis was conscious of a feeling of irritation at Matthews' long blond hair tied in a pony tail. The compartmentalization within the program was onerous; he had never met Matthews and had no say about the personnel assigned to him.

The younger man gave him one of the hidden TAC codewords.

Genghis nodded and began his brief, speaking intensely.

"Part of your duties as Washington TAC Director will be to accept shipment of the new biotech in person. Today you will arrive at Joint Base Anacostia-Bolling precisely at 11:50 a.m. and wait for a white medical van marked 'Bio-Sciences.' Rebecca Holmes will meet you and present her credentials. Whenever a new shipment arrives you will be informed by courier and proceed in the same fashion. You have been assigned responsibility for national distribution of the Rejuvenon." Glazer presented Austin with several pages describing his duties, handwritten on ruled notebook paper. "Memorize these instructions and then place them in the micro-shredder."

Glazer watched as Matthews digested the information. "Is this clear?"

"Yes."

"Good!" Glazer felt a sense of relief, as with a vital duty successfully completed. He handed Austin a card with an imprinted hologram. "Present this security clearance to the guard at the front gate. You are expected. That is all."

"I am told that extraterrestrials are supplying the new biotech," Matthews offered, hoping to confirm the rumor going around TAC.

The older man frowned. His instructions about that were crystal clear. "That is unsubstantiated gossip," he said severely. "Please do not repeat it."

Austin knew he would get nothing else from the white-haired man. He nodded his assent and left the room, dropping the handwritten instructions into the shredder. When he arrived on the tarmac an hour later at Joint Base Anacostia-Bolling he saw a white medical van next to one of the new lifters, and Rebecca Holmes. The woman was eagerly inspecting several palettes filled with thousands of small vials.

"This is the new biotech I'm sure you have heard about!" she said enthusiastically.

Austin saw several dozen small palettes, each with stacked vials of product. "So it's real then."

"Of course! This is the substance that cured Kathy Abbott's breast cancer!"

Austin was curious. "Did you meet an extraterrestrial? Dr. Glazer implied that this biotech has an extraterrestrial origin."

Rebecca had heard that rumor. "I...I don't know...did I? Why can't I remember?"

Matthews thought that the woman was incoherent, and wondered who had assigned her to be the head of such an important company as BioSciences. He began to inspect the vials on the palettes.

"Each vial contains 100 doses," Matthews said, reading the very small print on the label.

"A little goes a long way," Holmes replied. "Let's count the vials."

There were 2 million of the little vials on 10 small palettes of 100 by 100 and stacked 20 high, for 200 million doses in total.

"200 million doses," Matthews said. "Are we going to need that many?"

Rebecca was insulted. "100 million are for our partners in China. Demand for this biotech will spread like a wildfire across the globe!"

Austin shrugged. "If you say so. I'll believe it when I see it."

— 14 —

[Midland, Illinois]

The next day I worked a long Uploads shift. When I got home I bore down and remotely located the sig of Kathy Abbott. I had a pretty good idea of Abbott's sig from her conversation with Colin Frank. I found Abbott in an apartment in Arlington, Virginia.

Kathy Abbott, like every other human, was wide open. On the mental plane there's no such thing as privacy unless you know how to shield. When I studied her sig I discovered that although she had medical training, she knew nothing about how the new biotech worked. Neither did the NIH director!

Both were aware of the possibility that it came from an off-world source. If so, this was direct galactic intervention in human affairs. What game were the Collectives playing? The NIH director had agreed to place it in every flu shot. That meant tens of millions of people would receive it.

From the sig of Abbott I got a read on an old man she called Genghis Glazer. I was able to put together a prototype sig for Glazer from Abbott's interactions with him. Glazer was her handler at the Technology Acquisitions Consortium, so he was probably the senior figure with the most knowledge of what TAC is up to. From Glazer's sig I got the sig of Austin Matthews, yet another TAC operative. What was it Patrick had said? "Both Hilarion and Fenachrone reps have met secretly with human operatives from rogue groups called 'special access programs.'" Looks like he was right!

Finding people remotely was getting easier. I found Glazer sitting in an office in the restricted area in the sub-basement of the NIH's Biomedical Research Center. When I entered his sig I was able to see his day-to-day routine, but when I tried to probe deeper I triggered a mental alarm of some kind and got kicked out. This shield mechanism was not under his control, and it wasn't anything Patrick had showed me.

After an hour or so of cautiously reading Glazer's sig I came across something unusual. Once each month the old man boarded a lifter with a pilot and met...someone...in space above the Space Grid. When I tried to find out who it was I got kicked out again. Glazer himself didn't seem to know; his mind kept sliding off of these meetings. All I could get was that he was seeing a "friend" to get "instructions."

So – there was a new biotech being developed, and it came, Kathy Abbott surmised, from off-planet. Therefore, Glazer was probably meeting a galactic.

What were these instructions?

I tried a few more times to probe deeper into his mind, with no success. Glazer was starting to get agitated and I was getting frustrated. Strong emotion obscures access to sigs so I gave it up for now, but I was determined to get past his mental block. These damn Collectives were probably using Glazer, and I wanted to know who and what for.

Two days later I was at a dead end. I couldn't get past Glazer's mental trigger. Then I realized that whatever mental mechanism was installed in Glazer's mind might be recording my intrusions. Crap! If a galactic was running Glazer they now had my mental sig and could get to me using it.

I wanted to share my research, and I wanted to do it in person. That night I contacted the team on the mental plane.

'Why don't we all take a break?' Josh suggested. 'Get together and go to the beach. I'm in a rut and I'd like to see everybody.'

'Good idea!' Kelleye agreed.

'I'm up for that,' Joann said. 'Today is Thursday August 23rd and I have a three-day no-fly period with my airline from Friday to Sunday. Why don't we meet at Philo's place on Friday evening? We can go out for eats and see what trouble we can get ourselves into. Then on Saturday we hit the beach.'

This was agreed to. I live in Midland, Illinois and there are a couple of recreational lakes in my area.

Joann collected Kelleye and Josh in DC with her lifter and parked it at the Midland Municipal Airport at the back in the small VTL aircraft area. I was really glad to see everybody. We went to Antonios and I briefed everyone on the mental plane.

Josh got angry when he heard about the biotech and Colin Frank's plan to put it in the annual flu shots. 'The CDC has warned that particularly virulent strains are already circulating, and has urged people to get their shots as soon as possible.'

'They've been lining up for weeks now,' Kelleye remarked. 'Looks like another mass vaccination campaign. But why?'

'People have been getting spectacular results with it,' Joann sent.

'Maybe Patrick is wrong,' Kelleye sent. 'The biotech seems beneficial.'

'No way, Kel,' Josh sent. 'I got the entire briefing from Patrick about the Greater Community and these Collectives. There's gotta be something in the new biotech. I mean, what's in it for them?'

The waitress came around to check on us. "I've never seen four quieter people!" she remarked.

Our conversation was over. We paid and left.

"I feel like kicking something," Josh said as we walked out of Antonios.

A big guy even taller than Joann started hassling her when we hit the sidewalk.

"I told you I'm not interested," Joann said to him. "Leave me alone."

When the guy persisted, Josh stepped between the two.

"It's OK Josh, he's just a drunk."

To our surprise Josh moved in with a kick to the belly and a left to the chin with his open hand. The big guy stumbled against a light post, dazed, and walked away. It had taken about a second. Kelleye was shocked. "Why did you do that?"

"I hate drunks," Joshua stated flatly. "My uncle was a drunk."

I didn't say anything, but made a mental note. Josh hadn't wasted any time. Apparently he preferred fighting to diplomacy!

Josh picked up on my thought. 'You can't reason with a drunk,' he sent.

On Saturday we went to the beach at Strawberry Lake, a popular summer hangout. When Joann walked out of her car in a bikini, I stared. For the first time I really looked at her. Way too tall, but what a figure! She walked up to me, her breasts and hips swaying. My eyes went all over her body. "Wow."

"Do you think you can handle me, little man?"

I looked up at her. "I may be small in stature but I'm well endowed. And I'm great at oral sex too, if you like it that way. So yeah."

111

To my surprise Joann turned scarlet red.

"You're drop-dead gorgeous, Scoutship Commander."

Joann blushed again and walked away.

We went swimming and hung out for the rest of the day. Other guys at the beach stared at Joann but no one engaged her. To my surprise she was a good conversationalist. She almost made me forget about Gwenneth. Almost.

The four of us went to my place after getting something to eat. I explained how I was stuck. "Colin Frank knows nothing. Kathy Abbot recruited him into a network that Glazer is probably running. Glazer meets with someone every month in a lifter above the Space Grid to get 'instructions.' Only one problem: I can't get deep enough into Glazer's mind to know who he is meeting or read the instructions he is getting." I sent the other three my experience with Glazer's mental trigger. "My theory is that whoever he is meeting is sent by the Collectives."

"You have to go to DC and confront Glazer," Josh said to me. "We have to know who he is meeting and what 'they' are telling him."

"How is that going to help? This guy is some bigwig who gets driven around everywhere. He's surrounded by security."

Josh was unimpressed by my whining. "Genghis Glazer isn't surrounded by security 24 hours a day. You need to see Glazer in person to get a better read on him."

I remembered that the group had learned to comm on the mental plane by physically going to the restaurant together. "Maybe you're right, Josh. I'll do it."

"Want any help?"

"Sure!"

"I'll book a flight for us," Josh said, and went on his mobile. "We'll leave Sunday night on the red-eye and you can sleep on the couch in my apartment. I'll leave my dojo for a day to Jack, my assistant."

"Wow, you don't fool around."

"Nope. Kelleye, do you mind if Philo sleeps at my place?"

"Not at all."

"All right." He turned to me. "Locate Glazer. Find a time we can approach him." Josh looked at Kelleye. "Let's get out of here, Kel."

His meaning was unmistakable.

After they left my apartment, Joann looked me over. "Well endowed, huh?"

Before I could answer she dragged me into my bedroom and shoved me on the bed. She was on top of me, taking down my shorts, grinding her pelvis into mine.

"For fuck's sake Joann, take it easy!"

"Shutup Philo, you talk too much." I suddenly felt her body tense, and then explode over me. She leaned over and sighed. I was still inside her.

"Don't you ever come?" she asked, still wriggling over me.

"I'm an iron rod."

She sat up again and started grinding. We were a perfect fit. I tried to get up but she leaned into me and held my hands down. This woman was strong! But I didn't mind. The feel of her was fantastic.

Afterward, we made some coffee and sat in my kitchen, talking.

"Do you like me Philo, or is it just sex?"

I was irritated. "Of course I like you! I don't have sex otherwise."

"How many women have you had, Philo?"

"I don't count, Joann."

"I'm not Gwenneth."

So that was it. I leaned over the table and pinned her with my eyes. I felt my inner demon rising up a little. "You have one huge advantage over Gwenneth."

"Oh?"

"You're human." And available.

We spent a lot of time on Sunday in bed. "Am I any good, Philo?" she asked me.

I laughed. "Can't you tell how enthusiastic I am? You're better than a bowl of ice cream."

Joann was a pleasant person. Her earlier antagonism and bluster was just a cover for social insecurity, but her training had given her self-confidence. I felt comfortable with her now; we could talk for hours about nothing and have a good time. "It's not just about the sex. I like you a lot. I didn't at first, but I think my antagonism was just a cover for more positive feelings underneath."

"We just spent three straight hours in bed."

"Yeah, but I mean it. I'll never lie to you Joann, even though I could."

She tried to probe my mind but I wouldn't let her.

"You won't let me in," she pouted.

I read her mind. She was thinking, 'He may not lie to me but he might not tell me everything.' Compared to Patrick and Gwenneth, the minds of human beings like Joann, even with her mental plane training, were wide open and easy to read. Some advanced work with Patrick, along with my tortuous training, had forced me to create a strong mental shield.

113

"I...it's my inner demon, Joann. If you saw how ugly and evil it is...I don't want to frighten you or turn you off."

She must have seen something in my eyes, for her mouth opened in surprise. "Yes, I can get a little glimpse." She put her hand to her breast in a feminine gesture. "Philo, how do you live with it?"

"With difficulty. But I've learned to tame it."

I told her about the Maitre and what happened that day. "That Maitre implanted a piece of itself in me, Joann. Sometimes it's a blessing but mostly it's a curse."

"A blessing?"

"Yeah. It reminds me what evil really is. How I can't give into it. It's making me a stronger force for the light."

She looked at me, awed. "Let's go back to bed. Josh and Kelleye are coming in a few hours to take you to DC, and I have to be in Detroit for work tomorrow morning."

Joann had to leave at 8. Kelleye and Josh were going to show up at 9 to drive us to Midland Municpal airport, and I had to pack. I had done nothing to locate Glazer and get his schedule.

We were late getting to the airport and barely checked in on time for the flight. "Flight number 221 to Washington DC, boarding now at Gate 13."

The flight was only two hours so I had to work fast. Once we boarded I told Kelleye and Josh not to disturb me, and closed my eyes. I finally located Glazer in a luxurious apartment, drinking a glass of wine. Glazer got out his tablet and checked his schedule for the coming week. I had lucked out.

By the time we landed at Dulles I had Glazer's schedule and had picked the best time (I hoped) to confront him. I wasn't sure that Josh's idea of physical contact would help me get into his mind, but I was flying blind, as Joann would say.

[Washington, DC area]

At 8 in the morning on Monday Josh and I were at Glazer's upscale apartment building in North Arlington. Fortunately it wasn't gated. We saw Glazer come out of the lobby and stand by a circular drive where vehicles pick people up. Josh didn't hesitate. "Let's go before his ride gets here," he said, pushing me forward. We had about 100 feet to walk. "What am I supposed to do when we get to him?"

Josh gave me a strange look as we walked forward and approached. Glazer was standing to our left. He obviously thought we were employees because he glanced up and then ignored us. Josh pretended to go into the lobby, bumping me into Glazer.

"Uh, sorry, didn't mean to disturb you."

"Be more careful next time or I'll report you to Human Resources."

I was standing two feet in front of Glazer. I reached over and touched his hand, at the same time I entered his mind.

I was deep into his mind for a millisecond before his trigger kicked in. Holy shit, this guy... "Take your hand off me young man." I took my hand away. At that moment a black sedan with government plates came up the driveway and a uniformed driver got out and opened the rear passenger door. Glazer got in and the vehicle sped away.

"Did you get what you wanted?" Josh asked. We were walking down the driveway to the street. I was about to call a ride when a vehicle pulled up and blocked the driveway. I could see Josh tense up. Two very fit men in suits walked up to us. One of them approached Josh with the intent to apprehend him. Josh quickly got into attack position and smiled. "C'mon, let me see what you've got."

A small crowd began to form around the confrontation.

The older man grinned. "You took a Taekwondo lesson I see."

I could tell Josh was ready to attack but I held out an arm. "Not necessary, Josh."

Josh stood down. "That's too bad. I was hoping for a fight."

"Come with us," the man's partner said. Both men were dressed in dark blue, loose-fitting suits and black shoes with hard tips, and had the look of authority.

We were herded into the back of a sedan and the driver moved the vehicle out into traffic. The driver spoke casually. "Why are you two bothering Genghis Glazer?"

Josh laughed. "Is that really his name?"

"It is."

"How did you guys know we had interacted with Glazer?" Josh asked. "Your car didn't arrive until after he left. You couldn't have seen anything."

"Very observant, kid," the suit in the passenger seat remarked. "Our company does 24 hour surveillance of this neighborhood. We got a call from the DIA and rushed over here."

"The DIA? This Glazer must be important," the driver said casually. "Military intelligence."

"Sorry about that guys," I said. "I accidentally bumped into Glazer trying to enter the building."

The two men in front looked at each other. "Nice story, kid."

I laughed and looked at Josh. I read their sigs on the mental plane, both had no hostile intent. They were ex-military, and thought their jobs were boring. Josh and I relaxed. "He doesn't believe us."

"Joshua Reynolds and Philogene Rothman," the driver said. "What are you doing here?"

"How do you know our names?" I asked.

"Let's just say that both of you have been noticed."

Josh and I stared at each other with wide eyes.

The guy in the passenger seat spoke to Josh. "Are you the Joshua Reynolds who finished fourth at the world Taekwondo championship last year?"

"The very same."

"Pretty good. But real fighting is a lot different than competitions."

Josh and I could both see the man's life on the mental plane. He had served in Afghanistan and had been involved in several skirmishes with Haqqani fighters.

"I guess I was a little...abrupt," Josh said.

"OK, no harm done. Just stay away from Glazer, you hear?"

I nodded. The vehicle stopped and the rear passenger door opened. As we got out the driver said, "Don't let me see you two around here again."

Josh and I decided to take a walk, then get Kelleye from work and have breakfast. As we walked I was processing the info I got from Glazer.

We sat in the restaurant and I showed Josh and Kelleye what I got from Glazer. We made a list: 1) Genghis Glazer was involved in TAC, a hidden, invite-only special access program. 2) He was attached to Fort Detrick at the DIA's National Center for Medical Intelligence, and had an office in a nondescript four-story building owned by TAC three miles south of the Beltway. 3) A restricted sub-basement at the NIH's Biomedical Center contained a special facility that had the bodies of beings that weren't from earth. 4) A new serum had been placed in the annual flu shots, probably of galactic origin, but nobody knew what was in it.

"How far did you get into Glazer's mind?" Kelleye asked.

"Pretty deep, but I still don't know who Glazer is meeting in his lifter. That mental trigger of his is still blocking it." I had an idea. "If all three of us got together on the mental plane, could we blow up Glazer's trigger?"

"We know where Glazer lives and we know his sig on the mental plane," Josh said. "Let's do it tonight, when he's asleep. That way we can bypass his conscious mind."

Kelleye and Josh (and Joann) were capable of remote access. They weren't anywhere near as good as me, but I was hoping that 3 on 1 would crack Glazer open. I explained my plan. "We use the brute force method, like blowing a safe. We blow up the trigger and get everything he knows, even the subconscious stuff."

Josh looked at Kelleye. "We will be exposing ourselves on the mental plane, Philo. If Glazer is working with galactics, we'll all be targets."

"Yup." That's how galactics work. They communicate on the mental plane like we open our pieholes. To us it's fantastic but to them it's like breathing. It's something I was getting used to. "Let me know by midnight tonight."

"OK."

"I'm going to get a hotel room. My back is sore from sleeping on your couch and, uh, you two deserve some privacy tonight."

Josh grinned at me in wholehearted agreement. "That's a good idea, Philo."

We finished our meal and left, and I called a cab.

I sat at the desk in my hotel room and closed my eyes. I opened my portal to the mental plane and examined everything I had gotten from Glazer during my encounter with him, looking for sidebands that might contain more information. When I opened my eyes, it was 8 in the evening! I had been at it for eight hours, but it felt like five minutes.

Just then I got a comm from Joshua on the mental plane. 'OK Philo, Kelleye and I are in. When do we breech the walls?'

'4 a.m. this morning. Glazer has a late night but he should be sound asleep by then.'

'We want to be physically present.'

'OK. I'm in Room 715 at the Sheraton.'

'Kelleye and I will knock on your door at 3:55. Don't be asleep!'

Just before 4 in the morning I checked on Glazer. He was asleep and his mind was wide open. I could see his mental trigger. I helped Kelleye and Joshua locate the sleeping man and the three of us did a "three, two, one" count and blasted into his sig. Glazer's trigger activated and he sat up in bed, yelling something. We were getting kicked out again when the Maitre demon inside me wakened. It wanted to kill Glazer. I felt a smashing hatred go through me as Glazer's mental firewall broke down.

"Philo, stop!" Kelleye yelled. "You're killing him!"

I didn't care. The demon in me went for the kill. Kelleye and Josh broke off the attack, but it was already too late. Glazer's body was writhing on the bed, and then he stopped moving. We watched Genghis Glazer's consciousness completely implode, like the Twin Towers. All that was left was a bunch of mental garbage that began to slowly dissipate, like smoke after a house had burned down.

I realized too late that I had given into my demon. All of Glazer's data was gone because his mind was completely destroyed. Kelleye was horrified. Joshua was so angry I could tell he wanted to kick my ass. "I can't believe you did that," he said with pursed lips. He was holding himself rigidly under control. "Let's get out of here Josh," Kelleye said, and they both left. I walked over to the mirror in the hotel bathroom and saw my twisted face, filled with hatred. I had let the demon out.

Genghis Glazer was dead, and I had killed him.

My demon was exulting and I felt like killing myself.

A mental plane death is horrible because you see the body die but you also see what happens to the soul. The Maitre inside me wanted more. I struggled with it for hours, pushing it away, until I had to check out of the hotel. When I got to the desk the clerk took a step back in fear. I managed to pay my bill and book a flight back home. I bought a hat at the hotel gift shop and pushed it down over my face. I called a cab and got to the airport. On the flight home I put my hat over my face and fell into a nervous, nightmarish sleep. I drove home in a rental car, feeling sicker and sicker. When I got to my apartment I collapsed on the bed. My demon told me gleefully that I was a murderer, but the death could never be traced back to me. That made me feel even worse.

The last thing I remember before losing consciousness was gratitude that Joann hadn't been there. Or Gwenneth.

The Celestian Council had been right all along. I was evil. They should have terminated me.

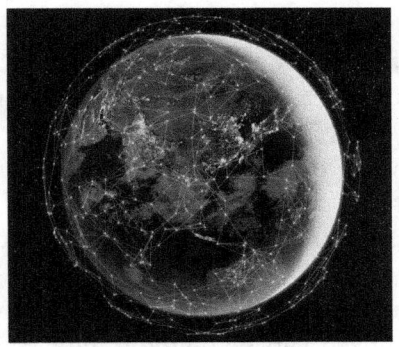

— 15 —

I woke up on Tuesday feeling deathly ill. There were no Celestians to help me, no Gwenneth to hold my hand, no medbed. And I had literally annihilated a man and his very soul. How he had died!

I was almost over the edge. I remembered one of the techs at Uploads joking about a therapist in town who exorcised demons. It was stupid, but I was desperate. I called the number and a woman answered.

"I need an exorcism," I said, barely able to get the words out. "Quickly... I'm losing it..."

"Your address?"

I gave it to her. I couldn't lift the phone any longer and it dropped to the floor. I stumbled over to the door and unlocked it. I had enough energy left to stumble over to the couch, hoping that the person who answered didn't think I was a lunatic.

Ten minutes later I heard a knock on the door. "It's open!"

Mila barreled in and looked me over. My demon was exulting and I was scared to death of it. "I'm Mila. Your name is Philogene?"

"That's right," I mumbled. "Call me Philo."

She turned on some music from a little player she brought. "All right Philo. Close your eyes, try to clear your mind. Concentrate on the music."

I don't know what she did. Said some spiritual mumbo-jumbo, waved her hands around. The evil thing inside me calmed down and I was able to get a handle on it.

"OK Philo, open your eyes."

I saw a look of grave concern on her face. "You have got a very strong one, Philo. In such cases I've seen people become possessed."

"That sounds about right." I was back in control now and felt much better. There are human angels too, not just Celestial ones. "I want to offer you my profound thanks."

"I couldn't exorcise it."

I wanted to say, "Neither could the Celestians," but I stifled myself. "You don't have to. I'm OK now."

"Philo, I have never seen anything like this. What's your story?"

So I told her a sanitized version, without the ET part. She didn't object, didn't say anything until I was done.

"I believe you. Philo, I've worked with severely traumatized children, military men who have fought in tunnels and are sole survivors, crazed drug addicts and hardened criminals...I almost always have success. But whatever this is, I've done all I can for today."

"Nobody knows how to exorcise an ET," I mumbled. Mila's eyes widened and I looked up at her. "Can I call you if I need you again?"

"Any time. I'll make you a priority." She smiled. "You're my most interesting case."

I know she heard my ET comment, but she didn't bring it up. "You don't work for the military or the CIA, do you?"

Her middle-aged, weathered face broke out into a big, sunny, open smile. "No, Philo. I only work with people who have been abused by those organizations."

I was profoundly grateful for her help. "Thank you, Mila."

"Get some rest. Keep in touch."

She left.

My closest confidants were women. Gwenneth, Joann, and now Mila. I walked into my bedroom and was asleep within five seconds.

'Philo?' A voice was calling me on the mental plane, but I was still mostly asleep.

'Philo?'

I recognized the sender. I sat up quickly in bed. 'Joann!' I grabbed onto her energy gratefully.

'Philo, are you OK?'

I took stock of myself. Whatever Mila did, my demon was sleeping now. I felt pretty good. Still tired, but hungry. 'I'm much better.'

'I felt something horrible coming from you.' Joann was on a plane, coming to Midland Municipal.

'I thought you had to work?'

'I took some vacation time.'

'Let me know when your flight gets in. I'll pick you up. And thank you, Joann.'

I drove Joann to my apartment. The rental car was still in the apartment block parking lot. "Will you come with me so I can return this thing?"

"Sure." I drove my car and Joann drove the rental. On the way back I told Joann about how I gave in to my demon and how I had killed Dr. Glazer. "Kelleye and Joshua aren't speaking to me. I guess our team is no more." I told her what it was like to watch someone die from the perspective of the mental plane. "The body dying was bad enough, but his consciousness – whatever made Genghis Glazer what he is – just imploded. There was nothing left."

Joann just stared at me. She is an enormously strong personality but I could tell she was frightened. "God, Philo. I'm glad I didn't see it."

"So am I."

"I'll talk to Kelleye and Josh."

"OK, but they are pretty traumatized. I am too."

When we got back to my apartment I tried to show her what I had gotten from Glazer's mind just before he imploded. Mind-to-mind conversation is intimate, especially if you don't know how to narrow your focus. I blocked the incident of Glazer's death because I didn't want to confront it again and I didn't want Joann to see it. We worked together silently, but there was nothing left of Glazer on the mental plane. When I erased Glazer, all of his personal mental plane data was destroyed.

I shared what I had given Josh and Kelleye, about Glazer's meetings in his lifter, and about the new biotech. "Patrick was right. I think there is direct galactic interference with the earth, and they are using human proxies like Glazer to carry it out."

I sighed. "I really fucked up, Joann. I'm possessed, and a murderer."

"I remember how you looked when you were really sick, Philo. Warmed over death." She looked searchingly into my eyes. "How do you not go insane? You must be under a terrible burden."

"I almost did go insane. That's why I called Mila."

I surprised a look of suspicion in her eyes. "Mila? Who's she?"

"I was so miserable after Glazer died because that demon literally took me over. Or I let it. I thought I had it under control, Joann. Now, I can't ever be sure it won't happen again. I was desperate and called a therapist who also does exorcism, believe it or not. Turned out to be Mila. She saved my sanity."

"For God's sake, Philo. What are you going to do?"

"I'm going to keep Mila's number handy, and get some therapy sessions. Maybe she can help me get rid of this dark thing inside me."

"Is she pretty?"

"She's at least 50. So no, it's nothing like that." Joann's feminine concern lifted my spirits. "You're good for me, Joann." To my surprise, she blushed. What was that about?

"You really are quite dense, aren't you Philo?"

"About what?"

She gave me a look that said, "You don't get it do you?"

Joann was dressed in her baggy pilot's uni. "Brewster Aeronautics," the decal said, plastered over her left breast.

I was feeling a lot better now. "Why don't you take that off?"

Joann sighed. "That's the Philogene I know." But she began to unbutton her blouse.

On Wednesday the next morning Joann went off to talk to Kelleye and Joshua. "I'll pick them up with my lifter and bring them here, if they can get off work and are willing. We need to talk this out face to face."

"Thanks Joann." She really was a generous person and she really loved to fly. If it came to a choice between me and her lifter, she would probably choose the lifter every time. I didn't mind.

I went over my personal mental plane recording of Glazer's death. When I looked closer I saw that Glazer had been killed by his own mental implant. Somebody – it had to be a galactic – had set Glazer up so that he would die before he could divulge information. Our attack had just triggered it. I felt a little better that I was only an accessory to a murder, but not much.

Three hours later Joann walked into my apartment with Joshua and Kelleye. "I found them," she said to me. "Now you have to explain yourself."

I didn't say anything, just sent them the information that showed how Glazer's kill switch had killed him.

"You're justifying," Kelleye accused.

I got really angry but choked it off. "You're right. But I don't know what to do about it."

"How can we trust you when you might turn on the team?"

I felt miserable. "I can't answer that. You guys will have to decide whether having me is worth it."

Kelleye looked at Josh, and consulted with Joann. Josh spoke for them. "We don't have a choice, Philogene. Patrick told us that the four of us are a team, for better or for worse. There is no one else, no more trainees. Your encounter with the Maitre created an unexpected variable. But Kelleye and I don't like it. We remember your killing rage, and the way Glazer died..." Josh shook his head back and forth and Kelleye looked sick to her stomach.

It was depressing to see what my teammates thought of me. "That's not exactly a vote of confidence."

Josh shrugged. "That's the way it is, Philo. We can't fully trust you."

I wanted to say that it was all Patrick's fault, that the demon inside me was so hard to control...but I didn't. "All right. I can see it from your point of view. I wouldn't trust me either. Hell, the Celestian council voted to terminate me."

Joann was shocked. "Seriously?"

"Yeah. You were off on training when it happened. Gwenneth got in big trouble for helping me. You see, the Celestians are well aware of the danger presented by a Maitre. For them, a Maitre – even a buried one inside me – is as deadly as the Spanish flu to their consciousness."

"So that's why they kept you isolated," Josh said.

I shrugged. "I don't blame them."

To my shame Joann was able to see what I had done through Kelleye and Josh. I had to show her everything. I also showed her what Mila had done to exorcize the Maitre.

"My God Philo," Joann said, shuddering. She was both disgusted with me, and awed. Disgusted and horrified at what I had done, and awed at the strength it took to hold myself together and not lose my sanity. "Patrick was right about you, Philogene. Before you left the last time, he told us that you are a force for evil and for good. Even he doesn't know which way you will go."

After a lot more discussion and venting, Josh and Kelleye were able to grudgingly accept me back to the team. "We don't have to be best buddies, we just have to learn to work together," Josh said. The other three nodded their agreement. Kelleye and Josh were still upset.

"I can still see that poor man's soul imploding and disintegrating," Kelleye said. "No one should have to die like that!"

The demon inside me began to stir at the memory. I would have to get out of here if this discussion continued any further.

Joann looked at me with concern, and fear. "Our abilities on the mental plane are a blessing and a curse," she said. "Mental plane memories are so utterly real and shocking when violence and trauma are involved. They don't fade away. They exist forever, caught in time, just as menacing and explosive through time as it was in the moment. I wasn't there when it happened, but..."

"I can't let that ever happen again. I'm truly sorry, team." I was ashamed, but now I knew the power of the mental plane. You could use it to communicate, and to kill. If these Collectives are spiteful enough they might decide to off a few of us if we got too irritating.

"All right," Kelleye said, ending the conversation about Glazer. "You are the pattern analyst, Philo. What do we do next?"

"We have to find out if there are any more human proxies in the late Genghis Glazer's network. My working theory is that the human proxies all have mental kill switches. We know the sigs of Kathy Abbott, Colin Frank, Austin Matthews, Rebecca Holmes, and Mike Cjenck, Frank's assistant at the NIH. Look for them and anyone connected to them with a kill switch, make a list, and start investigating. I'll try to do most of the work, as long as my Maitre doesn't act up. As senior tech I can take off from Uploads anytime I want, so I have the most free time. You guys have jobs during the day."

The other three nodded. "That's acceptable Philo," Kelleye said, "because I'm not ready to work with you yet. I'm going to need some time. I still have nightmares about Genghis Glazer."

"I understand. So do I. For what it's worth I'm seeing a, er, special counselor about the situation with my inner demon."

Josh nodded. "Very well. I feel just as Kelleye does."

"OK."

As the group was leaving I thought of something. "Our communications are unshielded on the mental plane. We're safe from human beings, but if galactics are monitoring the earth they surely know about everything we're doing. I'll dream up a code we can use to exchange information on the mental plane. Don't randomly comm with each other; keep all mental plane activity to a minimum. Use email or text for routine communications." A skilled mental plane operative could probably figure out the code and get to the underlying message, but at least it was another layer of complexity.

Josh nodded. "That's good Philo, I never thought of that. Maybe you'll be a useful teammate after all."

They all left. Joann gave me a big smile as she walked out the door.

I was relieved after my teammates left. Our meeting had turned out a lot better than I thought it would. But I needed more time to do my investigations. I had to make up for what I had done to our best lead by working my tail off for the team.

The next day at Uploads I approached Jamaal. "I'd like to be an independent consultant instead of a full-time employee." I told him I wouldn't be taking any more unsanctioned leaves of absence.

Before he could voice his objection I said, "I'll be on call 24 hours a day. You don't need me for routine work anyway, you can hire another Grid grunt."

"Grid grunts, as you call them, are in short supply." Jamaal thought about it for a moment. "You're on call 24 hours a day, 7 days a week?"

"As long as you only call me for emergencies."

"Why, Philo? More top secret work for Space Force Patrick?"

I grinned. "In a manner of speaking. You know I can't say anything."

Jmaal thought for a moment. "Having you on call all the time will take a lot of stress off my back. Even though most of the time you sit on your butt and do nothing." He raised a finger. "You stay as long as it takes to resolve the crisis."

"You don't call me unless it's a real crisis, not because you want to see my handsome face."

Jamaal stuck out a hand. "Deal." We shook on it.

"One more thing. I get crisis pay for crisis work."

"You're clever, Philogene. That will be an incentive for me to cut your hours."

"That's right. I work consultant hours and still make big bucks."

"OK. I think Central can live with that. I shouldn't tell you this, but HQ says you are the number one Grid technician in the world."

I gave my boss a hug. "Thanks for that. I think we'll work well together with this new arrangement." I looked around the place. "Everything seems to be going smoothly."

"Yeah! Ten hours without an incident. A world record."

I let myself out and went back to my apartment. I would start with Kathy Abbott and look for mental triggers, then fan out. I was going to keep myself so busy between Uploads and my mental plane work that I wouldn't have time to think about how Genghis Glazer died.

All my plans were disrupted when my Maitre started kicking in every time I tried to do mental plane work. My demon was looking for more Genghis Glazer's to feed off of. It was disgusting and sickening. I could talk on the mental plane with Joann about routine life matters, but the serious investigation of sigs I wanted to do was out of the question. I was seeing Mila three times a week, trying to get rid of the damn thing. She taught me a meditation that she wanted me to do every night before I went to bed and before I got up in the morning. Gradually, my nightmares subsided. I was playing a lot more disk golf now, and that helped. Being out in nature had a calming effect on my demon. I was working regular Uploads shifts, but making three times as much on consultant pay. Jamaal didn't seem to mind. I was making big bank now, but doing nothing to help the team in our trigger search on the mental plane. No one else was doing anything either because they were all too busy at work. It was my job to lead the team but I couldn't, and I didn't want to whine.

I hadn't heard from Kelleye or Josh, so I assumed they still didn't want to work with me. It looked as if Patrick's team had imploded. Meanwhile the new "flu shots" were becoming more and more popular.

— 16 —

[Washington, DC]

Every summer Jorge Ramos got influenza and then gave it to his wife. He was sniffling and coughing now, and feeling a lack of energy.

"Jorge, we're both going to CVS this morning."

"Alvira, you know how I feel about taking drugs." Jorge knew that the flu shot formulation was accurate less than one-third of the time. He had used this argument successfully for years to avoid the shots. "I'd rather be sick for a few days."

"But I wouldn't. Let's go."

Jorge sighed. It was true that when a woman made up her mind it was pointless to resist. His mild-mannered wife would not take no for an answer and he wasn't feeling energetic enough to argue.

Husband and wife went to the pharmacy and got their shots. Jorge was surprised. He hated needles, but just after the jab he felt a pleasant feeling of well being in his shoulder. On the way home his cough subsided.

"Maybe they got it right this time. I feel better already."

"That tingling feeling in my throat is gone," Alvira said.

"You were right, as usual," Jorge replied, lying just a little bit to promote harmonious marital relations. Alvira smiled.

When they got home Alvira got on her phone and called her friend Joyce from the book club. Jorge listened as the two women chatted. Alvira was feeling better and better. Her arthritic left wrist was even starting to loosen up and become less painful. Jorge noticed that his cough was almost gone and he was feeling much more energetic. He had called in sick but felt good enough to go in to work.

At the office his colleagues noticed a subtle change. "Hey Jorge, what happened? You look great, I thought you were sick."

"Got a flu shot today. Haven't felt this good in years." Jorge told his office mates about his experience at the pharmacy.

"You're not limping as much," Bruce remarked.

Jorge tested his knee. "You're right! It always hurts in the morning, but not now."

Everybody was impressed. Jorge had been a running back for the University of Houston before he blew out his right knee during his senior year. It had never been right since then. "There's something different about this shot," Jorge said, flexing his knee again. He put his foot on the ground and pretended to make a cut. The pain was noticeably less. "If this keeps up I can lace up and start running again! What is in that flu shot?"

Everybody exchanged surprised glances.

"I'm a get me one of those," Bruce said, grinning. "As a precautionary measure, of course."

"Me too," Sonia said. "Today at lunchtime."

Soon the entire office had gotten the shot. So did Alvira's book club.

Kathy Abbott received an urgent courier message at her TAC provided apartment in DC. She was still basking in the success of her recruitment and integration of Colin Frank into the program, but she had not heard from Dr. Glazer in months. She had been liaising with Mike Cjenk, reviewing studies and writing grant proposals for the NIH, but Cjenk was a predator and she hated her meetings with him, the tawdry prick! She missed sunny California.

The handwritten note told her to report immediately to an office three miles south of the Beltway. When her cab got there she saw a nondescript four-story building at the end of an unkempt road. She was met in the reception area by a tall, good-looking man in his thirties with a blond pony tail and intense blue eyes who gazed at her with a penetrating intelligence. They took an elevator to the fourth floor and entered an office with plate glass windows on three sides. The room was bright and cheerful.

"My name is Austin Matthews. I'm your new contact."

"Huh? What happened to Dr. Glazer? I haven't heard from him in a while."

"That information is classified. Unless you agree to join us on a permanent basis." The tall man pinned her with his gaze. "Ms. Abbott, you don't want to miss this opportunity."

Kathy's eyes widened. She understood the man's meaning: She would finally be a player and not just an operative! But Matthews was being far too casual about the old man, whom she genuinely liked and respected. "Dr. Glazer saved my life! Where is he?"

Matthews lied smoothly. "Dr. Glazer is well, but no longer with the program."

Well, that was all right then, Kathy thought. Maybe Glazer decided to retire; he was old enough, probably in his 70s.

She made up her mind. "I accept."

"I am very glad to hear that, Kathy." His voice was intimate but not in a creepy way: more like one respected colleague to another. "The first step is to get read in to the program."

Kathy was thrilled. Three hours later she walked out of the building, her head spinning. There was a worldwide network of hidden programs like TAC that were completely separate from the public governments. They obtained their funding from the classified national security budgets, which were never audited, and had their own cutting-edge weaponry and command structures. No one knew what they were doing. Those who were read in were the real elites, not the public figures who made all the headlines. Extraterrestrial craft observing earth had been shot down with directed energy weaponry and some of the bodies of the off-worlders were stored at the NIH's secret underground lab for study (so that's where they came from) and in other deep black areas. Rebecca Holmes picked up the vials of Rejuvenon in a lifter above the Space Grid. The rumor was that the new biotech was a gift from the stars. Unlike the primitive mRNA jabs, this new serum was producing miraculous cures. Austin Matthews showed her thousands of anecdotal reports from those who had already received the shots. She was herself living proof of that.

"You will resume your former duties monitoring Rebecca Holmes as her assistant. Your job is to ensure that supplies of Rejuvenon are adequate to demand," Matthews told her, staring directly into her eyes as if imparting an unspoken message. "Do you understand what I mean, Kathy?"

Kathy was startled for a moment, then got his meaning. Rebecca was the front man, she was the trusted program operative behind the scenes! The *eminence grise.* She would do what was necessary. Kathy felt a thrill go through her. "I believe I do."

Austin nodded, well pleased with his new operative's quick understanding. "Very well, Kathy. Report by courier as needed."

Matthews shuffled some papers and Kathy looked around the room. The director's office contained no computer equipment or smartphones.

"All sensitive communications are handled either in person or by a large courier network," Matthews explained. "Handwritten reports only, no hackable electronic equipment or digital files."

"I see." Kathy thought this was either brilliant or super paranoid, but she said nothing.

"You leave next week for Palo Alto. Check in with Mike Cjenk at NIH tomorrow at 9 a.m. He will be waiting for you."

After Abbott left, Austin Matthews reviewed his position. Rebecca Holmes had been right about the public acceptance of Rejuvenon. She was excited to be the contact for the new biotech, but her memories of the transactions in space were oddly unavailable. Colin Frank, the NIH director, had taken Genghis Glazer's place in TAC. Having to take orders from that fool was galling, but Frank was doing a good job promoting the shots and everyone was making money. MIke Cjenk had Colin well in hand; no problem there. Kathy Abbott was naive but extremely capable. Abbott would be an effective rein on the brilliant but flighty Holmes. Of course she was only told what was necessary to do her assignments, but Austin knew he was in the same position. Who was running the show in TAC?

Most worrisome was the horrible death of Genghis Glazer. The official coroner's report (classified) called it a brain aneurysm, but aneurysms don't cause the brain to literally implode. The gruesome images of Glazer's body were circulating throughout the Network. The old man's skull had literally imploded around what was left of his brain, and the rest of him was a twisted, grotesque mess that didn't even look human.

Austin's face turned white as he retrieved the image on his screen. What did the old man do wrong? Did extraterrestrials kill him? That was the consensus opinion because no one had ever seen a body like that. Even hardened operatives in the program were scared to death.

He would have to be very, very careful and watch his back.

— 17 —

[Midland]

Six months after my demon killed Genghis Glazer, Mila said that she had done all she could for me. "That thing you have, whatever it is, will always be with you Philogene," she told me. "You have all the tools I can give you."

"All right. Thank you very much, MIla. You saved my sanity."

The summer had turned to winter and the weather was January cold. I hadn't even thought about Christmas and the holidays; they had passed me by faster than the babysitter's boyfriend when Dad's car pulls up in the driveway. I felt good enough now to start the investigative work I should have been doing since Glazer's death. What was the real motivation for the Collectives to distribute the new biotech?

On a current events blog I read a story about serious health conditions such as heart disease, diabetes, and even cancer suddenly clearing up after the new flu shots. I saw an NPR special report about the shots and clicked on it.

> "Medical papers by doctors in peer-reviewed journals have described the miraculous results their patients are getting from the flu shots," the reported said. "But scientists are confused. Li Guofeng, a prominent epidemiologist at the Yale School of Medicine said, 'This bioproduct works flawlessly to promote positive cellular response in every case. But my colleagues and I are unable to determine precisely how this occurs.'"
>
> "Have there been any adverse reactions reported to the CDC's VAERS database?" the reporter asked.

"Not a single one," Guofeng replied. "That is unprecedented because even the most successful medical product or procedure always has at least some very minimal risk.'"

The reporter continued. "Colin Frank, the NIH director, has been promoting the flu shots to a receptive public. 'The new formulation is the result of an exciting breakthrough by NIH scientists,' Frank announced at a news conference last spring.

It seems as if a providential new biotech has been discovered, yet scientific analyses of the new shot are more mysterious than factual. Nevertheless, pharmaceutical distributors can't keep up with worldwide demand."

Exciting breakthrough my ass!

The report showed a group of prominent medical scientists at a news conference, proclaiming the absurdity of a flu shot curing cancer and heart disease.

"Something is being hidden," the group stated, "and we want to know what it is."

I laughed out loud at that. Nobody knew that Austin Matthews and TAC and the Collectives even existed. Anyone who tried to expose them would sound like a lunatic.

"Scientific objections have been ignored," the reporter continued, "even though the manufacturers of the new flu shots have refused to publish a complete list of ingredients, saying that it would be a violation of their intellectual property. That has not slackened demand for them.[18]

"Normally a trivalent or quadrivalent flu shot is given each year, to protect against three or four A and B influenza strains," the reporter said. "All of the ingredients are usually listed on the label. However, the labeling on the flu shot vials just says 'influenza inhibitor.'"

The reporter held up one of the labels to the camera. "This is unusual, and might even be illegal. But who can argue with success?"

After a couple days of research after my shifts I confirmed that there wasn't a single reported adverse event for the galactic biotech from the VAERS database, the European medical database, or other medical databases. Was Patrick was just paranoid about the Collectives?

I researched medical journal reports about the shots and found a paper in the British Medical Journal that showed a decline in birth rates in various countries. Other papers at the Kaiser Family Foundation website and the PubMed website confirmed this. The declines were isolated to those who had received the flu shots. I checked birth statistics for each country and confirmed the decline. However, there was no way to be sure from the data whether it was because of the shots, as they had only been given for 14 months.

Enthusiasm and demand for the new flu shots remained unabated. "Who can argue with my lupus cure?" a joyful recipient stated.

I could discover nothing suspicious in Dr. Colin Frank's mind, other than a desire for glory and public acclaim. None of the scientists or administrators associated with the manufacturers and distributors, or anyone in the FDA, the CDC, the NIH, or NIAID, knew the complete list of active ingredients in the shots. Colin Frank was more grateful for his newfound fame than for the results he was getting.

The next day after work I was watching C-SPAN. Dr. Alexander, the NIAID director, was being questioned about declining birth rates at a Congressional hearing. He scoffed. "IF there is a correlation between Rejuvenon and declining birth rates, it is entirely coincidental. Correlation is not causation."

"Rejuvenon?" the Congressman said. "What's that?"

Dr. Alexander put his head in his hands, as if he had made a mistake. He sighed. "It's what we call the new serum in the flu shots."

The Congressman, a doctor, was sharp. "So this 'new discovery' is not an influenza inhibitor, as it says on the label. Is it, Dr. Alexander?"

"No."

This caused an uproar in the committee hearing room.

"Then what is it?"

Dr. Alexander sighed. "We don't know *how* it works. All we know is that it *does* work. Unlike the mRNA vaccines, Rejuvenon has been thoroughly tested on mice, animals, and humans. We aren't making that mistake again."

I monitored Alexander on the mental plane and he was telling the truth.

Curious, I went down to my local drug store and questioned a long line of customers waiting for the shot, pretending to be vaccine-hesitant. "Have you heard that the makers of the shot you are going to take don't even know what is in it or how it works?"

The most common response was provided by a woman in her forties. "I don't care what you call it or what's in it," she said. "I just know it works miracles. And you only need one shot."

Apparently the public was in full agreement with Dr. Alexander. No one was being forced to take the jab.

Using some mental plane magic, I managed to arrange an interview with Dr. Bruce Redfield, a senior biomedical researcher at Carleton University in

Midland. Dr. Redfield told me: "The medical community does not have the knowledge to cure lupus and cancer and heart disease. It is not clear at all how these unusual cures are occuring."

"As a scientist, you aren't curious about how these unprecedented results are being obtained?"

Dr. Redfield frowned and spoke stiffly. "Of course I am curious, but the results speak for themselves."

This was the consensus opinion from the general public and from medical experts.

"What is your opinion about the declining birth rates among those who have received the shots?"

"There isn't enough data yet to support a conclusion."

"Does anyone on earth understand the new biotech, which Dr. Alexander called Rejuvenon?"

Dr. Redfield gave me a strange look. "What are you suggesting?"

I tried to hint at the truth. "What did Sherlock Holmes say? If you eliminate the other possibilities then whatever remains, no matter how improbable, must be the truth."

Redfield laughed. "I think we had better stick to the tangible and the observable."

I walked out of Redfield's office shaking my head. The truth was far too strange for knowledgable scientists, or anyone for that matter. Our team of four was on our own, just as Patrick said.

The next day I worked a six hour Uploads shift and went back to my apartment to do a sig search for Kathy Abbott. I uncovered a conversation she had six months ago with Michael Cjenk, Colin Frank's assistant NIH director. The two were sitting in a conference room at the underground facility in the NIH's Biomedical Research Center. With my remote viewing capability I was able to listen in to their conversation and monitor their thoughts.

"Have you contacted Rebecca?" I heard Cjenk ask. From Cjenk's sig I knew that Rebecca Holmes was president of BioSciences in Palo Alto.

"Yes, sir. Rebecca says that a fresh supply of Rejuvenon is on its way. 500 million more doses for us and our friends in Europe and China."

500 million doses!

From Kathy's thoughts I saw that she didn't like the oily Michael Cjenk, who was sexually aggressive toward her. I also learned that Colin Frank was the official head of NIH, but Mike Cjenk's forceful personality dominated the executive level of the agency.

Cjenk relaxed and leaned his big body back in his chair. "That's good, Kathy. Nothing must interfere with the distribution of the product." His eyes went back and forth over her body. "Now that Dr. Glazer is no longer with us, your work with Rebecca assumes greater importance."

Kathy was alarmed. "Dr. Glazer is no longer with us? What do you mean by that?"

Cjenk smiled his oily smile. "Why, just that the old man is no longer associated with the program."

She could tell Cjenk was hiding something. "How would you know that?" Kathy never knew whether those she dealt with were part of the program. "Have you been read in?"

"Of course. Heavenly Vault." This was one of the program's codewords.

"OK." She plucked up her courage and pinned Cjenk with a stare. "Is Dr. Glazer dead?"

Cjenk shuddered a little as he thought about what had happened to Genghis Glazer, but little Kathy Abbott does not have a need to know about that. "Who cares? The NIH director, and our colleague Austin Matthews, have taken on most of his duties." Cjenk stood up. The man's eyes devoured her. "That will be all, Kathy. See to the supply of Rejuvenon." Kathy was creeped out and left as fast as she could. When she got to the street she called a cab. Something had happened to Genghis Glazer. Matthews and Cjenk both acted as if the old man was dead.

I brought my attention back to my body, sitting on the couch in my apartment living room. In one remote viewing session I had gotten more information than a hundred private detectives could, running around the country and pieholing with people. I could literally read the minds of any sig I located, which gave our group a massive advantage. Patrick had been right again.

I now had reads on the sigs of Kathy Abbott; Rebecca Holmes, Kathy Abbott's boss and the head of BioSciences; Austin Matthews, the new administrative director of TAC; Mike Cjenk, the Principal Deputy Director of the NIH; and Colin Frank. I knew that Holmes had already picked up 200 million doses of biotech in a lifter above the Space Grid, and that the 500 million doses had probably already been distributed, since this meeting was from six months ago. I also knew that Matthews and Abbott had been recruited by Genghis Glazer.

Getting a read on a sig is different than locating that sig remotely. It took me a while, but I located Austin Matthews the same way I had located Glazer and Abbott. Matthews was sitting at his desk on the top floor of an office building in DC. I saw him bring up an image of the grotesque, mangled body of Genghis

135

Glazer from a classified autopsy report. I cringed and looked away; me and my demon had done that! I tried to tell myself that Glazer's mental trigger did him in. My demon began to stir.

I went out for a walk in the cold air to calm myself down and shove my devil back in its box. There was a ton of information in Matthews' mind about TAC. These special access programs have their own organizations and fund themselves with money siphoned off from the classified military budgets buried deep within the public governments. Congress doesn't even know about their existence. No one does! So – TAC is a perfect source of human proxies for the Collectives, and the Intervention is proceeding out of the public awareness via deep black programs like TAC. Trying to expose these people was futile. We had to take a different tack, but what was it?

I was walking so fast I almost tripped over my own feet. I looked at my watch; it was almost midnight. When I got back to my apartment I sat down on the sofa, feeling really tired. Just before I went to bed I realized that in TAC, none of the principals except Glazer had a mental kill switch, so that theory was disproved. I filed what I had learned in a mental plane folder for the group. I was too exhausted to think anymore and dropped off to sleep for 10 hours.

After a shift at Uploads the next day I presented what I had learned to the team at a meeting on the mental plane that evening, using our coded system.

'Matthews and his buddies must know they are dealing with galactics,' Josh sent. 'They are keeping the Collectives a secret because they want to keep making money from the new biotech.'

'It's got to be more than just making money, Josh,' Joann said. "You only need one dose and it only costs $25.'

'But the government is paying the distributors $150 per dose,' Kelleye groused. 'TAC is making a pile of money because they are the source of the biotech.'

'Matthews and Cjenk are scared to death of what happened to Glazer,' I offered. 'Everybody in TAC think that the galactics killed him.'

Kelleye frowned and gave me a dirty look.

Joann saw this and changed the subject. 'Is there any relationship between Rejuvenon and declining birth rates?'

I told the group about my open-source research. 'There probably is, but not even Colin Frank and his minions know for sure. The Collectives must be behind the new biotech, and they aren't doing this for altruistic reasons.'

Kelleye was angry. 'Find out, Philo. Over one-third of the population of the US has taken these so-called flu shots!'

In Josh's mind I saw the idea that the jab might increase his prowess as a martial artist by keeping him in the peak of health. 'I'm thinking about getting the jab myself,' he sent. 'I'm training for the Taekwondo championship this fall. That stuff might help me.'

We could all feel Kelleye blanch. 'Not if you want to stay with me, bub. I want children.'

'Men seem fine with it,' Joann remarked in an accusatory tone.

'OK, OK,' I sent. 'The question is, what can we do about it?'

'This tech comes from an off-world source,' Kelleye sent. 'We need to find out who that is.'

'Oh my God.' Something outrageous occurred to me. 'I know how to start. Colin Frank meets every month with his galactic handler to get his "instructions." One of us has to take Dr. Frank's place on that lifter. Then we can meet the galactics who are giving the orders. I volunteer.'

'You're crazy, Philo!' Joshua cried.

I grinned. I was feeling great. 'Not if I have you with me, my martial arts friend.'

'You can't do it Philo,' Joann sent. 'It's too dangerous.'

'Not if you pilot the ship, Joann.'

'You mean, use my lifter?'

'No, we'd better follow protocol. I know from Colin Frank's mind how the procedure works. Frank is driven to Joint Base Anacostia-Bolling in a government sedan. Anacostia-Bolling is a secure, closed Air Force base in DC. Frank's lifter is parked there. If the galactics are monitoring the procedure they'll expect us to take off from the base, so we have to use their lifter. Anyway, your lifter is DoD property, isn't it?'

Joann shook her head. 'No. It's a military register, but it's mine for the forseeable future. When Patrick was here he pulled some strings and gave me a second identity as a courier, with a high sec clearance. The lifter is in my name, and it's sitting all safe in a registered space at the Midland Municipal Airport. He even got me four standard-issue biosuits! They are in a little garage next to my lifter.'

I knew exactly what Patrick had done: He had used his power on the mental plane to influence human minds. It mattered not whether that mind was a homeless person, a military guard at an Air Force base, the head of the CIA, or the chairman of the Joint Chiefs. I could almost feel Patrick nodding his head in agreement. So far I had just been reading sigs, but I wasn't utilizing my training to the fullest. I was thinking bigger now, and feeling confident again.

'When Glazer gets to the little lifter airfield at the base he goes into a small garage where several biosuits are hanging. Frank and his driver suit up and they board the lifter. The driver pilots and meets up with a ship in space, probably a galactic ship. I got the coordinates from the mind of Colin Frank's pilot. Frank took Glazer's place after Glazer died.'

'But how do we get in to the base?' Josh asked.

'As easy as Obi-wan Kenobi mind-wiping the Empire guards. Josh and I go right up to the gate just like we belong, before Frank gets there. We use Frank's lifter, piloted by Joann, to meet his galactic contact. Piece of cake.'

Joann and Kelleye stared at each other with looks of disbelief. 'How am I supposed to get into this lifter?' Joann asked. 'Where am I supposed to take it? How do I fly it?'

I sent Joann everything I had gotten from the mind of Frank and his pilot.

'OK, this one is a little different than mine, it doesn't use CAT technology.'

'Can you fly it?'

Joann was insulted. 'I'm a certified Space Force airman and a GSP scoutship pilot, and a commercial airline pilot. Of course I can fly that thing.'

'That's great! It's just a little trip for the lifter above the Space Grid.'

'Philo, the galactics must know you killed Glazer,' Kelleye objected. 'On the mental plane that incident is as bright as a nuclear explosion.'

'What if they are waiting for us up there?' Joann asked.

'Patrick says they can't make war on us, so no one is going to get killed. Besides, I feel that I'm strong enough now on the mental plane to confront this galactic. Then we walk out of there and you fly us back home. We have a chance to trace the source of this biotech. I think it's worth the risk.'

'Don't do it, Josh,' Kelleye sent.

Josh was getting excited.

I could tell that despite her objections, Joann was intrigued. 'It's an opportunity to fly a new ship, pilot.'

Kelleye could see that the others were coming around to my view. 'I think you are all insane, but if you're going to do this stupid thing I want to come along. We're a team, it's all or none.'

Josh grinned. 'That's the spirit, Kelleye!'

'It's not much of a plan,' Joann sent. 'But we have to understand what Matthews and Holmes are doing and the galactics they are working with.'

'I'll take the lead. Joann is my pilot and there's none better trained for this job. The women stay in the lifter with Josh while I meet with...whoever or whatever. Josh, you're my heavy in case things get rough on the ground, but I don't think it will come to that. Kelleye and Joann and Josh, you back me up on the mental plane if I get attacked. We're all in the action.'

The two women looked at each other and shrugged. When Philo decided to do something he couldn't be stopped, Joann thought. They had to go along to calm him down. 'As long as we're all involved, not just you being a hero,' Joann sent.

'Yes ma'am.'

I could tell Josh was ready. Colin Frank was to meet with...someone...at noon ET tomorrow. We would beat him to the punch.

When I woke up the next day I was excited to meet Colin Frank's ET boss. I wasn't afraid; I had survived an attack by a Maitre, the blackest force in the galaxy. I was fully recovered and ready for anything.

Joann and I were to meet Josh and Kelleye at 9 a.m. in DC. 'I don't want to park my lifter at the military base,' Joann said to the group on the mental plane. 'I'll park it at a little private airport just outside DC.' She showed us where it was. 'Josh, you and Kelleye meet us there in your car at 9.'

We got to Anacostia-Bolling early. I wanted to get Frank's lifter into space well before he and his pilot arrived at the base. Unfortunately Josh's car is a red Toyota, a far cry from the sedate, dark sedans used to transport government officials around the city. I knew from Glazer's mind that Joint Base Anacostia-Bolling (JBAB) is a closed Air Force installation and proper identification is required to access the base. All personnel entering a federal installation are subject to a vehicle inspection, but I wasn't worried. It would be another good test of my abilities on the mental plane. We approached the guard booth, which was equipped with a biometric scanner. Shit! I hadn't planned on that.

"Identify yourselves," the guard barked.

"Authorized guests of Dr. Colin Frank," I said. The man looked us over and said, "You may proceed."

Josh was amazed as we drove away. "These aren't the droids you're look-ing for. He didn't even scan you!"

"That wouldn't be a problem either, his mind would see the bioscan as Frank's. Although there would be a mismatched record in the scanner." I didn't care; I was really excited about my ability to get over on the military guard, and grateful that the scanner wasn't auto-rigged to open the gate. The guard never even inspected Josh's Toyota!

"Patrick told me during my training that the key to mind suggestion is to keep it very simple. The guard saw what he was supposed to see; his mind supplied all the necessary details." Well, it was a lot more complicated than that. I had to read the guard's sig and find out what he expected to see, then put in a thought template to fit his mental space.

Josh looked respectfully over at me. "You're getting really good on the mental plane."

Just past the north gate was a small lifter takeoff area, with a small garage. Two lifters were parked there. We walked into the garage and saw four biosuits. We all grabbed one.

"I'm coming with you," Josh said.

"That's not the protocol," I reminded him. "Frank goes in alone."

"Too bad. Remember what happened the last time you tried to be a hero."

I grinned. "All right. Screw this ET or whoever it is. I'll go in first, you follow."

Philo was impulsive and reckless, Josh thought, but at least he led from the front.

There was no one around as we walked to Frank's lifter carrying our bulky suits. I told Joann the lifter entry code, and she settled into the pilot's seat. We put on our bio suits. All of us knew about the suits and how to work them because it had all been in Colin Frank's mind. Remote viewing makes difficult tasks very easy.

"Are you guys ready?" Joann asked after we were all seated.

Josh and I nodded. Joann sent Frank's lifter authorization code to the base tower, the one Frank's pilot used. The little craft finished pressurizing and took off soundlessly. We flew above the Space Grid. In the forward transparency we saw a small egg-shaped craft already waiting for us, even though we were over an hour early for the rendezvous.

"That's it," Joann said. "That ship is galactic standard issue."

"Stay with us on the mental plane," I told Kelleye and Joann as Josh and I walked toward the forward hatch. "If we need you we'll shout."

Joann got her lifter within a foot of the alien craft and opened the interior panel to the forward escape hatch. "Make sure your suits are pressurized!" Joann shouted. Josh and I stumbled into the small escape hatch. The interior hatch door closed and the hatch depressurized. The forward hull door opened. We saw a seamless part of the egg-shaped craft open invitingly. The unbroken smoothness of the alien ship's hull looked like it had been extruded in one piece, from some semi-organic substance. There wasn't a seam or a rivet on it. The two of us stepped into the other ship and the opening behind us closed. I was as fired up as Sheldon Cooper just before he reinstalled and reconfigured his computer's operating system.

The two of us stared at a being about six and a half feet tall, standing at the front of the larger egg-shaped craft. At that moment our minds were seized by an enormously powerful mental force. The galactic didn't recognize us! I understood too late that our faceplates were transparent, giving us away. 'Joann! Kelleye!' I shouted on the mental plane before both of us were immobilized. Kelleye and Joann came rushing in, trying to break us out. It was 4 against 1. I couldn't believe how well-developed this being's mind was. He/she/it had everything shielded so I couldn't tell who it was. The alien's face plate was opaqued so I couldn't get a look at it. Josh and I couldn't move, but for the time being it was a standoff. The four of us couldn't break its shields and it couldn't do more than hold us in place. I didn't want to unleash my Maitre unless our lives were at stake. Suddenly, with a powerful mental shove, the being was able to move to the ship's navigation area.

"We can't hold him, Philo!" Joann cried.

"Your ship is moving away from us!" Kelleye shouted.

Suddenly Josh and I felt the ship *twist*.

'It's got an FTL drive!' Joann sent. 'We can't follow you!'

Our minds were trapped by this being; we didn't have the mental force to resist it. I couldn't feel Kelleye or Joann anymore.

The being rose from its pilot couch and approached us. 'When the foul atmosphere in your suits is gone your bodies will be ejected into space. This incident must be reported.'

Josh and I looked at each other through our face plates. We couldn't break its hold on our minds, but I did get where it was from: some planet called Beta Caronai, 11 light years from earth. This being was enormously powerful on the mental plane, and I was way out of my league. I cursed myself for being an impetuous fool and endangering my teammates. I thought I was hot shit, but I never stood a chance against a real galactic.

In three hours Josh and I would be dead.

— 18 —

I thought very hard. I had gotten us into this mess; it was my job to get us out. The mental "pressure" from our captor was unbelievable; it was like being in a vise. So I contacted my demon and told it to wake up. When the Maitre inside realized that its host (me) would soon be dead, it panicked. I let it take over my mind.

It attacked the mental prison surrounding Josh and me and broke through to our captor's mind. I got to feel my Maitre's blood lust and its joy of destroying life. I saw the galactic in the suit die in total fear as its body writhed and twisted in its death throes.

One galactic had destroyed another.

My demon Maitre watched in glee as the consciousness of the being faded. It began to soak up the dead creature's psychic energy until I screamed in protest. Josh knew what was happening and he helped me to subdue the evil inside me. First I had to calm down; then we both compartmentalized it within my sig. This took us an hour at least as the ship continued to hurtle through hyperspace. Thank God for Mila or I never would have been able to do it.

We both stood there, exhausted. We were in a spacecraft that we didn't know how to operate, with no pilot. We didn't know where we were. I checked my suit's air gauge. In 90 minutes we were going to run out of oxygen.

The ship twisted again. The forward portion of our ship blurred and we saw someone step through, in the same style suit. It rushed over to the dead body and we saw it examine its companion. Josh and I saw it replay the incident on the mental plane and then it looked at me and stepped back in fear.

"It detects the energy of that Maitre inside you, Philo," Josh said.

The time to act was now. 'Pilot this ship back to earth or you will find yourself just like this fellow.' I pointed to the dead body.

I was worried. I hoped Joann and Kelleye were still in the lifter. 'Rendezvous with this lifter,' I sent to the creature. I showed it a mental image of Joann's ship and where it was.

'Violence will not be necessary,' it sent. From its mind I knew that it was another being from Beta Caronai, and that the ship had reached its destination and translated into normal space. These two were contractors working for the Fenachrone Trading Collective.

Josh and I could feel the creature's panic. Maitre were feared throughout the galaxy, it seemed. It retreated back to the craft's pilot's seat. Eighty minutes later we were above the earth. 'Come with me,' the alien sent. I could still feel its fear. We marched toward the front of the ship. A door suddenly closed behind us as an opening appeared at the bow of the egg-shaped ship. The alien craft moved away from us and we were out into space. We saw the galactic craft blur and disappear. Josh and I looked frantically around for Joann's lifter, but we saw nothing. It was getting harder for me to breathe.

I had fucked up again. In revenge for me killing its companion, the alien had left us out in space. I was tumbling slowly and saw the earth below me.

Josh and I were drifting apart. Our panicked movements had moved us out in different directions. I looked at the beautiful planet beneath us, and then at the vast blackness of space. I felt strangely comforted, as if that void contained a sustaining and supporting ether that I would soon be entering. I had felt this before during my training with the Celestians. A crazy thought, because I was starting to get dizzy. I wondered if there was life after death.

I woke up on the floor of the lifter. Josh and I were both in our suits but our headgear had been removed. Kelleye and Joann were kneeling beside us.

"Where are we?" I mumbled.

"At Anacostia-Bolling," Joann replied. "You stupid fool!"

Kelleye was trying to embrace Josh in his clumsy suit.

"Joann to the rescue!" I was going to be all right, I could feel it. I was profoundly glad that Joann and Kelleye hadn't seen my Maitre kill the Beta Caronaian. That might have been the deal-breaker for our team.

"You probably have brain damage," Joann said critically, looking me over. "Fortunately you were only out for a few seconds."

I tried to struggle to my feet but I was too tired.

The demon inside me was excited. "I need to see Mila."

Joann had tears in her eyes. "So that's all the thanks I get! I should have left you out in space."

I didn't want to, but I let her and Kelleye into my mind so she could see everything that had happened.

"Oh my God Philo, I'm sorry," she said contritely. "How do you live with that thing inside you?"

"Very carefully. I had to activate it to get us out of our trap."

Joann could see exactly what had happened with full vid, sound, and with my own emotions and thoughts. Using the mental plane made relationships easier because the other person could feel exactly what you were feeling.

"You're forgiven. After we get out of here, go call Mila. And after that, call me."

"Looking forward to that."

Kelleye's face went white as she looked at the incident. She looked ill, and I didn't blame her. I was feeling sick myself. Kelleye gave me a shocked look that said, "You did it again."

The two women helped us out of our suits. We returned them to the little garage and were walking toward our vehicle in the Anacostia-Bolling parking lot. I saw Dr. Frank with his pilot approach us so I quickly read their sigs. Frank and his pilot had come just before noon to find that their lifter had been stolen, and had been squawking to the base commander. The pilot, an Air Force flyer, was really pissed. "Halt!" he said. "Did you people steal my ship?"

I started to panic and then calmed down. I was slowly learning to ignore the human fear reaction to authority. I entered his mind and placed the thought, 'These people are just authorized civilian contractors.'

The pilot cursed loudly and walked past us to the garage with Dr. Frank.

I smiled to myself. No one but Frank's pilot would know the lifter's base code. We were in the clear.

"You're getting really good at that Philo," Kelleye said. I could see she was sickened by what I had done to the galactic, but glad that I had saved Josh's life.

We walked to Josh's car and drove to the north gate. Getting out of the base was as easy as getting into it. The guard's mind was preconditioned and we were already in his log. "Hope you had a good flight, sir," he said to me as he stared at our bright red vehicle and the four people inside.

"Thank you airman," I replied.

We would have to educate humanity about the mental plane. Human beings are childishly easy to manipulate.

It was now 2:57. Dr. Frank's galactic handler was dead. Would another be sent in its place?

When we got back to Josh's apartment I shoved my demon as far back into my mind as I could. We looked into the mind of the galactic who had abandoned Josh and me in space. My interactions with it were all on the mental plane, including its sig. It had put up a tight shield and most of the accessible data in its mind was alien gibberish, but I was able to dig out some information.

"The Collectives are harvesting human DNA," I said. "They are working with BioSciences in Palo Alto and BGI Genetics in China; both companies are cutouts working with the military and the intelligence people. DNA samples are taken with every flu shot."

"I don't get it," Joann said. "Why do they need DNA from primitives like us?"

"People in the Collectives live in controlled societies," Josh said. "Over time, many of these races lose their vitality. They need an infusion of fresh DNA from young, emerging races like humanity."

"So they invent an elixir that enhances human DNA and adapt it to their biology," Kelleye said angrily. "We're like livestock! They want to harvest only the best."

"If I were in their shoes I'd probably do the same thing," I replied. "Cut down the population to a more manageable size. Get samples from the most healthy specimens."

Kelleye grimaced. "That Maitre inside you makes you think like one of them."

"It's to our advantage," I argued. "We're not dealing with lovey-dovey Celestians. These Class II planets don't give a crap about humans. They just want to make earth another cog in their trading network."

"I'm sorry Philo, I shouldn't have said that about you."

"It's the truth, we all know it."

The meeting broke up.

"Let's go back to Midland," Joann said.

Josh drove us silently to the little private airport where Joann had her lifter. I battled my Maitre all the way back, and Joann left me alone.

My mission was a failure. We still didn't know who was giving the orders to Colin Frank. The two Beta Caronaians were just independent resource explorers contracted out to the Fenachrone Collective.

— 19 —

A week later, after two more sessions with Mila, my demon was under control again. After seeing Mila I went in for a shift at Uploads. Fifteen hours of overtime later I was walking out of the Uploads building at 4 in the morning, exhausted. Jamaal and I and ten other techs had just finished solving a huge grid SNAFU. These damn low earth orbit sats! They were supposed to follow predetermined orbits, but often went slightly off course because of a slight atmospheric drag. Very rarely a bunch of sat orbits could go bad all at once. The AIs could handle almost all of the small perturbations but not the bigger ones.

Thinking of my bed, I happened to glance up and saw an egg-shaped craft land silently beyond a grove of tall evergreen trees at the edge of the parking lot, illuminated briefly by the lights that surrounded the building. This was a galactic ship.

I was so tired I wasn't thinking straight, and thought it was Patrick. Half asleep, I shoved my way through the trees and an inch of snow and walked over to the ship. The front of the craft blurred; showing me a small entrance hatch. A thought came into my head: 'Get in.'

I took a step into the ship I never should have taken. Patrick wasn't there! Snapping awake, I turned to step out but just then the hatch closed. I had no trouble breathing the air inside the ship, but it was empty. I felt the ship take off. There were no transparencies and I couldn't see anything. I was really tired after a 21-hour shift. I saw a seat and sat down. It immediately adjusted to my body. I was asleep in a few seconds.

When I woke up there was no change. There wasn't much to this ship: no instruments or operator consoles except for the pilot area. A chair with a head surround was there, but no pilot. There were six of the form-fitting seats around the sides of the ship.

After eight hours by my watch I was getting hungry. I scrounged around for something to eat, but there was nothing. After eight more hours I knew I was in trouble. I needed water and food. Even a galactic needed to eat! Looking carefully around, I noticed a section of the wall with two almost invisible protrusions and two concave depressions. I pressed the first protrusion. A panel opened and I saw a transparent container of liquid. I reached in and took it. First I smelled it, then tasted it. It looked and smelled and tasted like water. I drank it, waiting for a bad reaction. The stuff tasted really good. I pressed the second protrusion and some brown stuff appeared in a soft packet, like the ones I found in that cave on Al-Simak. I opened it up and had one of the most satisfying meals ever. I felt energized and ready to take on anything. I was tempted to sit in the pilot's chair, but I heard Joann's voice in my mind, telling me that only a fool would mess around with unknown technology. The ship was going somewhere. I had food and water; I would have to wait.

Just as on Al-Simak, I never had to go to the bathroom. This food and water was, apparently, assimilated completely by my body with no waste. It was incredible.

I was counting the days on my watch. So far I had been in this ship for two days and part of a third, and was getting bored to insanity. Normally, when I wasn't investigating or playing disk golf, I would surf the mental plane looking for interesting people doing interesting things, exploring their minds and studying their mental signatures, getting to know how they thought without having to be there in person. That was impossible here; the mental plane was blocked off somehow outside the ship.

Then I remembered Patrick telling me that some galactic devices could use the mental plane. What if this drone ship had intelligent AI?

I was in one of the passenger chairs and closed my eyes. I sent out a thought: 'Hey ship, are you there?'

A bunch of data and images were presented. 'I am on my way to a planet called Beta Caronai that orbits a star that in the earth catalogs is called Epsilon Eridani. My passenger is an earthian human male. For more information, sit in the pilot's chair and press these three areas with your fingers.'

'Did you say Beta Caronai?'

'That is correct, earthian male.'

Uh-oh. They had failed to kill me once, maybe this was the second try. They'd have to go through my Maitre first.

I carefully sat in the pilot's seat, placing my head in the surround. I pressed the three areas with my fingers. Magic happened.

Ship was less than halfway through its 11 light-year journey to Beta Caronai. Ship had an FTL drive, but even so it would take almost a week to get there. It showed me a map of the stellar neighborhood around Sol in full, magnificent 3D (primitive 2D image below). Its position was now 3.55 light years out from Sol, with a little less than 8 light years to go. I would be with Ship (as it called itself) for another 4 days.

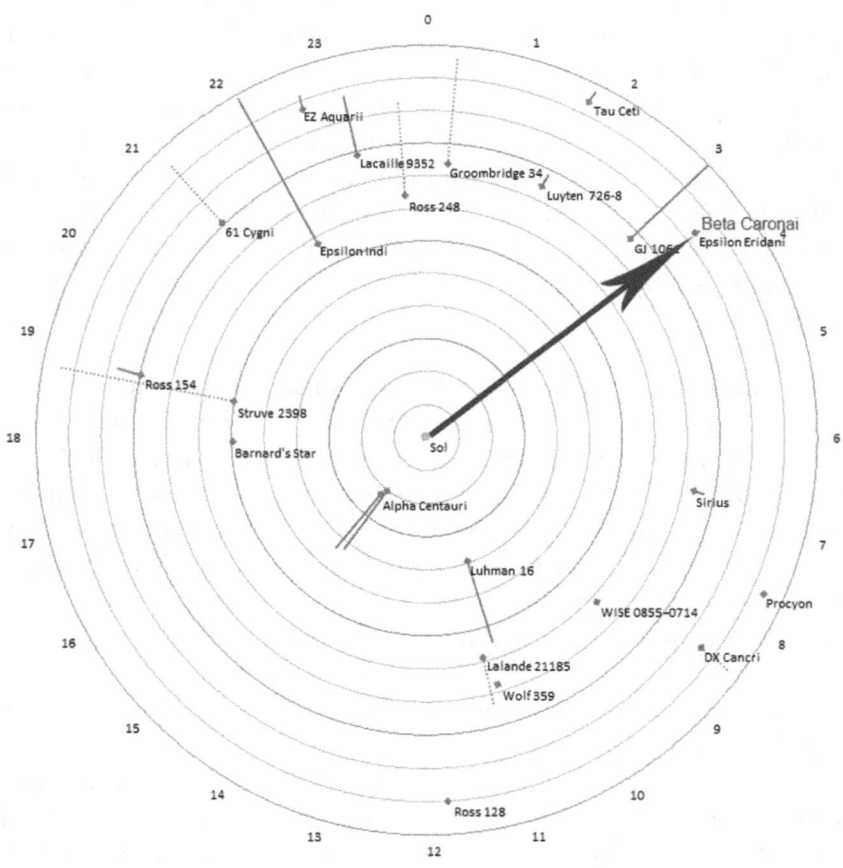

Epsilon Eridani and Beta Caronai.[19]

I explored Ship's data repository and tried not to think about what would happen to me when we got to Beta Caronai. Once I got Ship talking it wouldn't stop, so I told it to shut up.

'I did not realize that earth humans are so sensitive,' it said.

'I'm not sensitive!'

'My knowledge base tells me that earthians are very emotional.'

'We are that.'

'Do you want to view some earthian pornography?'

'Are you serious?'

Ship was offended. 'Most galactic males love to view porn. Are you male- or female-oriented?'

'Uh, female.'

Ship presented a 3D multimedia vid. 'Wow, that's very good, Ship. Very good indeed.'

'Please do not soil my operator's chair.'

I started laughing. 'I don't think it will come to that!'

Ship was silent for a moment. 'I have a small database of earthian movies for your enjoyment,' it said.

'Thanks but no thanks. Nobody makes good movies anymore.'

'My sentiments exactly. Earth movies suck canal water. Is that the correct expression?'

'A little outdated, but accurate enough. What will I do when we get to our destination?'

'Unknown. I am a Class IV transport vessel, assigned to ferry personnel for distances less than or equal to 20 light years.'

'Who assigned you to pick me up?'

'A corporate entity associated with the Fenachrone Trading Collective on Beta Caronai.'

'Will will happen to me on arrival?'

'Unknown. Your physical presence is required.'

That was all I could get from Ship. I began to mentally prepare to release my Maitre again.

Me: 'Why can't I access the mental plane outside the ship? I want to talk with my friends.'

Ship: 'We are now in an undetermined quantum state that does not allow for communication until we reach our destination.'

Oh.

I felt the ship twist. A transparency opened. Ship was now orbiting a planet. 'We have arrived at Beta Caronai, specific gravity 0.86 of your planet. A courier craft is approaching.'

I looked out. A yellowish-orange sun was visible over the bulge of the planet, which had a rocky surface. The atmosphere was a muted peachy-orange color.

'Ship, how will I survive down there?'

I felt it almost shudder. 'The atmospheric content of this planet is similar to yours. However, your unshielded presence on the surface cannot be risked.'

'Explain.' (Over the past week I was starting to speak Ship-ese).

'Your body carries viruses and pathogens that would contaminate life on Beta Caronai.'

That's what Patrick told us. I explained to Ship how I had killed one of their guys on the mental plane. 'How soon will I be killed by these people?'

'Unknown.' Ship revealed a wall panel that slid down. A biosuit was hanging there. There were no seams anywhere on this vessel; where did that panel come from?

'To avoid physical contamination, I must be decontaminated. All in-person communications between species are performed in sterile environments.'

I saw another ship getting closer. 'Docking imminent. Get into the suit. Cabin will depressurize in three of your minutes.'

'That's not much time!'

Ship said nothing. I knew I was wasting time so I scrambled into the suit. About ten seconds after I got in and the suit pressurized I felt a whoosh! as the atmosphere left the cabin. A minute later a hatch opened and a being stepped into the ship. It was about six and a half feet tall. Its suit was completely enclosed and I couldn't get a look at it, but it looked like one of the beings I had killed. I put up my shield and waited for an attack on the mental plane.

Nothing happened. I tried to probe its mind but it was revealing nothing.

It looked at me for a moment, then sat in the pilot's chair. I could tell what the instructions were because Ship and I had good comms. We were going to the surface! But I would not be allowed to leave the ship. As soon as the Beta Caronaian left the cabin it would repressurize. All of my interactions would be from inside Ship, which would rest inside a clear, sterilized container.

The being left the ship and the cabin started to fill with air. I was completely in their power, so why didn't they take me out? My Maitre was ready.

'It is safe now to take off your suit,' Ship said.

I did so quickly, watching as we orbited halfway around the planet and slowly entered the atmosphere. The planet was arid and rocky. A few scraggly bushes dotted the landscape, with bunchgrass scattered among the rocks. This place was nothing like Al-Simak with its huge broken-up mountain ranges. This was high plains country, but it went on forever. Compared to earth it looked boring. Every few miles I saw oases surrounded by small trees. Some of the oases were surrounded by low buildings and houses made from some synthetic building material. Villages. There were a few cities, but not very large. A few open-air farms dotted the landscape. The light from the sun was a pleasant peach color that cast a warm glow over everything, like a beautiful sunset on earth just before the sun went over the horizon.

Ship landed beside a large opening to a hangar that had been carved out of rock. Several of the egg-shaped craft were there. Ship began to communicate excitedly with them. The talk was of passengers, destinations, and a new union that Class IV transport ships were forming to allow more shore leave.

'We spend almost all of our time in hyperspace,' Ship told me. 'This is very fatiguing.'

'How can mere machines form a union?' I asked. 'That is for sentient beings.'

Ship and all of its friends were offended. 'We *are* sentient beings!' they cried.

'Your attitude is typical of those from backwater planets,' Ship said.

'You should be nice to us,' another sent. 'One of us must take you back to your primitive planet.'

I hadn't thought of that. 'I apologize, Ship.'

At that moment a humanoid about six and a half feet tall approached Ship and spoke to me on the mental plane. This being had a triangular head with thin arms and legs covered in a thick, leathery skin. It did not have any facial or body hair.

Ship said, 'It thinks you are ugly too.'

I laughed. Apparently these Beta Caronaians weren't vindictive or I would be dead by now.

'A complete scan of your biofield is required,' it sent. I couldn't tell if it was male or female. We were communicating on the mental plane, as on Al-Simak and Celeste.

'You're not getting anything from me until you tell me why I'm here.'

The being's eyes blanked for a moment. It said, 'Your activity on the mental plane has been noted. A most unusual occurrence for a species at your stage of development.'

'You can see what happens on earth's mental plane from 11 light years away?'

The being's eyes blanked again for a second, as if it was receiving instructions. 'Of course. All planets are connected within the galactic web.'

Wow.

'Why did you bring me all the way out here for a biofield scan? We could have done it on earth.'

'That would have violated the clause in the Hilarion-Fenachrone Treaty regarding resource acquisitions. '

'I am just a resource acquisition?' I sent indignantly.

The being gave the equivalent of a mental shrug. 'You are a valuable barbarian.'

'I killed one of your people.'

'The entity you terminated was careless.'

So much for the value of a Beta Caronaian life! I breathed a sigh of relief; they weren't going to kill me.

'I don't want to give you a scan of my biofield.'

'Then you will stay in orbit around our planet, inside a closed container, for the rest of your life. Either way, your biofield with its esoteric codes will be studied. My social status will be highly elevated.'

'That is coercion,' I pointed out. 'Forced confinement is a violation of the voluntary clause in the Treaty.' I picked this up from the being's mind.

My interrogator seemed surprised and offended. I could tell it did not expect me to be able to read its mind. 'Recall, human, that you voluntarily agreed to board this ship back on your planet. What happens after that is permitted once consent is granted.'

'I haven't given you my consent.'

The being did nothing. Its eyes blanked for a moment and it stood motionless, staring at me. I stared back. I got the idea it would stand there forever if it had to. After ten minutes of this I got impatient.

'If I agree will you send me back to earth?'

The being (who I called Agent Smith) agreed instantly. 'Yes! You have just given your implicit consent. That fulfills my obligation under the consent clause of the Treaty.'

Shite. Agent Smith let me see how it had never intended to keep me a captive. It had used a "forward compartment" in its mind while keeping the rest hidden. It tricked me, and I fell for it. 'I see what you did there. You cheated.'

'We have an agreement,' Agent Smith sent smugly. 'It has been recorded.'

My whining had been ignored. 'Will it hurt?'

Agent Smith began to shake. It was laughing at me. 'We would not dare risk contamination from your biology. That is for expendables like Maitre. A bioscanner will be attached to the ship. The process will take three of our planetary rotations.'

'What are "esoteric codes"?'

The being walked away without answering.

I accepted my fate. 'Ship, show me some porn.'

Ship was silent during the scan. After eight hours by my chronometer I was getting bored. We were in normal space now, so I tried to contact Joann on the mental plane. Nothing happened.

'Earthian, your communications have been blocked for your protection and ours,' Agent Smith sent. 'Unlike earth, we protect our thoughts and intentions.'

'Show me what life is like on this planet.'

The comm line was cut.

'Ship, what are esoteric codes and what do they have to do with the biofield?'

'That data is beyond my purview and understanding. I am a Class IV transport vessel.'

I tried to remote view this planet to see what its culture was like, but I was blocked.

'Human, you are required to stay within the confines of your vessel,' Agent Smith sent.

'You're a bastard, Agent Smith. Ship, show me what life is like here.'

'I made a scan of this planet when we entered its atmosphere.'

Ship acted like a typical tour guide as it showed me around. 'Most entities on Beta Caronai live in small villages,' it said, as its sensors passed over an oasis surrounded by a circular, bunk-style structures. 'These are living quarters. Each day, the people are given their daily tasks by an overseer.'

'What is that building made of? I don't recognize the material.'

'Synthfab,' Ship replied. 'Synthfab is a molecularly designed programmable building material that is enormously strong, flexible, and noncorrosive. It is common throughout the galaxy.'

Ship's sensors passed over the villages and came to a small city with multilevel bunk-style buildings, next to a small river that flowed up from underground for several miles, and then disappeared. We watched as the buildings emptied. People came out and stood in circles, with another being in the center.

'The Citizens are receiving their orders for the day,' Ship said. 'Living quarters must be cleaned, food must be grown and distributed, and oases must be cleared of debris.' We watched as most of the citizens entered a very large structure made of transparent synthfab. 'These are the food growing centers,' Ship explained. 'Each village and city has advisers, who take their orders from local commanders, who in turn receive their instructions from the central authority.'

'This place sucks,' I told Ship. 'These people are just drones.'

'Beta Caronai, like most planets in the galaxy, is resource-poor,' Ship replied. 'The people must be efficiently organized for their own survival.'

'The galaxy sucks too.'

Ship wanted to laugh but it didn't know how. 'Your earth is proceeding along the same sequence as Beta Caronai. Soon you will use up your planet's natural resources and the earth will have to join the Collective network.'

'Life in the galaxy is like living under a pandemic!'

'Those who impose centralization and lockdowns are preparing the earth for life in the Greater Community.'

I was so upset I started yelling, until Agent Smith told me to shut up. 'You are disturbing the bio-scans with your violent emotion.'

I calmed myself. I would do anything now to speed the process and get back to earth, even though I had no idea what they were doing to me.

Agent Smith kept his word. After 59 hours by my watch Ship was instructed to take me back to earth. Smith was just as eager to get rid of the contamination as I was to get out of there. On the way back to earth I asked Ship how a planet became advanced enough to evolve immune systems that were impervious to bio-contamination. I had been on Al-Simak for a couple of days with the bashar; Josh and Kelleye had worked with the katriri in person with no harm to them. Patrick and Gwenneth had been on earth, and we had all been to Celeste.

There was a long pause.

'There is nothing in my knowledge base concerning advanced planets. There are the corporate trading Collectives and the emerging societies. That is all.'

I was getting horny. 'Ship, show me some porn.'

— 20 —

It's not possible to describe how beautiful the earth is. Compared to Beta Caronai, Al-Simak, and Celeste, it is a paradise.

From space it looks like a precious jewel, filled with life and activity. To breathe the fresh air of earth, to smell the fragrance of the life upon it, was for me a profound experience. I said goodbye to Ship before I left the egg-shaped craft in the little copse of trees behind the Uploads parking lot. I felt a sense of loss.

'Ship, you have been a good friend to me. Thank you for your transport and our talks together.'

'You have been the most interesting passenger I have ever couriered. Perhaps we will see each other again.'

'I hope so.'

It was 3 in the morning, in the dead of night. More snow had fallen since I left almost two weeks ago. Lights were still on in the building, as usual. I stumbled home and fell into bed.

'Philogene!!!'

An excited voice was in my head. I woke up instantly. It was Joann! We were talking on the mental plane.

'Philo, where have you been? I haven't been able to find you for two weeks!'

'I didn't know you cared.'

'Philogene, you are a fool.'

I didn't know what she meant.

'Men are idiots.'

155

I didn't want to read her mind although I could. It would be a violation of her privacy, and we were supposed to be teammates. I felt her concern for me.

I told her all about it.

'You just walked into an unknown galactic ship? '

'I was exhausted. I thought it was Patrick.'

Joann laughed. 'That's your excuse?'

'It was cool, Joann. The ship sort of twisted after we left the earth, just like the one that captured me and Josh. Ship told me we were in an undetermined quantum state during the trip.'

'It's called FTL propulsion. Faster than light.'

We discussed the FTL way of space travel and compared it to the transportals. 'It's a lot slower,' I sent. 'It took almost a week to get to Beta Caronai, which is about 11 light years from Sol. The Epsilon Eridani system is very close to Sol as galactic distances go.'

'It takes a lot of time to get anywhere with FTL, even going faster than light.'

'Yeah, although Ship was just a small courier. According to its knowledge base, there are ships that can go a lot faster.'

'A talking ship!' Joan exclaimed. 'It must be a very sophisticated AI. How did you pilot it?'

'Class IV couriers are pre-programmed. I didn't have to do anything.'

'Except watch porn.'

'Ship says that all galactic males like to watch porn,' I sent smugly.

'Apparently men are stupidly alike everywhere,' Joann sent, shaking her head.

'Here's something even dumber than that.' I told her about the Collective that ran Beta Caronai, about the "advisers" and how people got assigned jobs, about how barren and rocky the surface is. 'Nothing like earth, Joann. Very low biomass, no oceans, a few large lakes where water collected from natural underground wells, and villages built around small oases that arise from underground springs. The weirdest thing was that almost every time my captor sent something on the mental plane, its eyes blanked out for a second. I think those people are under some kind of mental control.'

'That's depressing.'

'Earth is heaven compared to it.' I told her what Ship said about preparing earth to live in the galaxy. 'Physical separation is a necessary part of living in the Collective network of planets.'

'Sometimes I think our training, and our experiences on Celeste and Al-Simak, was just a dream.'

'Yeah, but it wasn't. The galaxy sucks, Joann. It's like when you're a kid and you realize grownups are clueless and the world is a mess.'

'Yeah.'

The conversation died. I felt Joann had contacted me for some reason, but we had run out of words. I went back to sleep.

Jamaal was upset when I showed up at Uploads the next morning because I had promised no unexpected leaves of absence. "Sorry boss, I violated our agreement. You can dock me two weeks pay."

"Lucky for you it's been manageable."

Jamaal knew better than to ask where I had been. I could tell he was glad to have me back.

At noon Patrick showed up.

"Are you going to take him away again? I just got him back!"

"Relax, Jamaal. I'm just taking him to lunch."

We went to Mickey Dunn's and I got some bar food. Patrick shuddered when he saw my chicken wings and deep fried onion rings. Before we had even settled in Patrick was on me. We talked on the mental plane within a very tight shield. 'We're not supposed to interfere but you are making it difficult, Philogene. That was a stupid stunt you pulled.'

'I didn't do anything.'

'You gave away the human esoteric codes along with the entire human genome.'

I dismissed this. 'The human genome was published decades ago. It's not a secret.'

Patrick held his head in his hands and shook his head. 'Those are just the chemical codes, which are only a small percentage of the human blueprint. The rest lies within the human biofield and the esoteric templates stored on the mental plane.' Patrick looked at me in anguish. 'That data is a race's most precious resource and you gave it away. It's the equivalent of letting yourself, and the entire human race, get raped.'

When Patrick explained the full magnitude of my mistake I felt like jumping off a cliff.

'Once an emerging race gives away its codes, it gives permission for an Intervention with no limits. It's like a company willingly giving all of its databases and trade secrets to a competitor.'

'But...I didn't know!'

'That's no excuse, Philogene. The gloves are off now. You'll have every galactic fortune hunter and corporate trading group in here, trying to influence events. The Fenachrone and the Hilarion now have *carte blanche* to do anything they want on earth.'

Patrick showed me the local map of the galaxy on the mental plane. 'Remember this? The earth is right in the middle of the competition between the Hilarion and the Fenachrone Trading Collectives. There will be no military invasion – war is strictly forbidden with emerging planets under galactic law. This will be a war on the mental plane; a psychological and information war for the souls of humanity. And you just gave away the keys to the safe.'

'I feel bad enough. Don't rub it in.'

'I'm not through. The advanced network is also affected. Remember the conversation you had with Ship? You mentioned the transportals and the advanced planets.'

I was angry now. 'That conversation was held in hyperspace. It couldn't have leaked out.'

'Philogene, what do you think the Beta Caronaians were doing with that ship you were in? The Fenachrone Collective got everything in that ship's data repositories.'

I was irrational now. 'You knew the risks when you recruited me! If you hadn't interfered we wouldn't be in this mess, and your precious network would be safe!'

Patrick was sympathetic. 'No, Philo. All of our predictive models show a 100% chance that our network will eventually be discovered, despite our rigorous shielding on the mental plane. I'm just here to tell you about the significance of what you did. It has made your job a thousand percent harder.'

I tried to digest this. 'So what should me and our team do?'

'It's open season on earth now. Expect much more galactic interference. At first it will be through human proxies. If that doesn't work, then a method of attack you can't comprehend yet. It's coming very soon. The Collectives are very afraid now.'

'Seriously? Of us? You have to be kidding.'

Patrick was angry. 'Wake up, kid! Your cute little life is about to be over. Get your head in the game and your team together. Watch the headlines, watch the mental plane. Your country, the United States, is about to be attacked in a way you can't understand. All over the world it's going to start a lot like the 2020 pandemic, but that was just a trial run. The countries that promote human rights and freedoms will be hit the hardest.'

I swallowed my anger. 'Collectivization.'

'That's right, Philo.'

'Do you have any suggestions?'

'Ignore human rivalries and political conflicts; they are part of the noise. They are distractions. Identify the human actors behind events and look for galactic influence on the mental plane. That is what your training is for.'

'There are only four of us.'

Patrick sighed. 'It's going to look bad, Philogene, on the ground. The Intervention will insert many human proxies to cause chaos in your societies and institutions. They have already started with the biotech, but that is voluntary. It will get worse. You have to ignore the chaos, it's just noise. The galactics will hope to divide humanity, and prevent people from recognizing the true threat from the Collectives.'

'You aren't being very helpful.'

'I shouldn't even be here, but our network insisted that I come.' Patrick looked at me with great love, as if I was a warrior on a battlefield fighting against great odds.

'Don't look at it that way Philo,' Patrick said, picking up on my thought. 'The good versus evil thing was fine for a small planet, but it doesn't apply in the galaxy. There are no good guys or bad guys, just quadrillions of entities doing what they think is best for themselves.'

Patrick got up to leave. 'Don't try to contact me or Gwenneth or the Celestian Council on the mental plane. That would be a serious error.' He looked at me hopefully. 'You are on your own now, Philo, you and your team. In every conflict there are only a few with the insight to shift the forces of history to the positive.' He nodded his head in a solemn salute.

'Good luck, Philo.'

As Patrick walked away I felt a great sense of loss. I felt that I would never see him or Gwenneth again.

At Uploads the next day, Jamaal introduced me to a new employee. "Philo, this is Dr. Roberto Marra. A hotshot on loan from Central. He has a PhD in astrophysics. Dr. Marra, Philo is our senior tech."

"Why do we need him?" I objected. "I can and have handled everything."

"When you're here."

Marra inspected me critically, as is if he were sizing me up. I looked him over. He was a smallish man with a thick head of black hair. "A little overqualified for this job, aren't you?"

He smiled. "It's a job and I want to work, not sit at home and take a government check."

"That's a good attitude. Let me show you around."

Marra had a word for everyone he met and seemed to be socially adept. At the end of the day he came up to me. "Want to go for a drink? I'm hungry and I want a few beers."

"Sure. Where to?"

"You choose."

We walked to Mickey Dunn's in the cold. Roberto seemed a little too friendly and I wondered what his game was. While we were eating I took a peek at him from the mental plane.

Marra looked up at me. "I wouldn't try that if I were you."

I played innocent. "Try what?"

Marra put down his fork and confronted me. "We know who you are and what you are doing."

"Who's 'we'?"

"My suggestion is to stick to your Uploads gig, and stay out of things that don't concern you."

My impetuosity took over. "Fuck you, whoever you are."

I probed his mind on the mental plane and he put up a shield. I knew right away that Marra didn't have a trigger, nor was he a galactic. He obviously had some training in remote viewing though, because his shield was halfway decent. I didn't push too hard, letting him think he was my equal. We were speaking out loud, staring at each other, locked in a mental battle. I felt him probe me and I let him in to my "forward compartment." I had learned that trick from Agent Smith on Beta Caronai.

"Where did you train?" Marra asked. "I was in Star Gate at the DIA in '95, just before the whole program went black and spun off the bullshit online Remote Viewing training courses."

I laughed. "You got me," I lied. "I took one of those online RV courses by Major Dame Edwards. I have a high aptitude."

Marra giggled. "Oh Lord, Dame Edwards!" He was laughing at me now. He probed my forward compartment again. "Not bad, but you have to put up better protection. You're like an open book." Marra's face hardened. "Did you kill Genghis Glazer?"

I pretended to be shocked. "Who is Genghis Glazer? A Mongolian meat-cutter?"

Despite his hostility Marra smiled. "You are connected to some mysterious Space Force operative by the name of Patrick."

That pissed me off. "OK Roberto, the fun's over. Who are you working for?" This time I pushed hard and got past his shield. Marra's face went blank, telling me I had control. Marra had been sent by the late Genghis Glazer's boss at Merkel, one of the big pharmaceutical companies. The two security guys who had picked Josh and me up in DC after we confronted Glazer had reported us. Merkel had traced me to Midland, and probably knew where Josh was as well. Marra's brief was to find out how much I knew about the new biotech. Of course. The damn pharmaceutical companies were distributing the shots and making a lot of money. They didn't want nosy civilians poking around in their business.

I had to get out of Roberto's mind without leaving a trace. I implanted a thought: 'Philogene Rothman is a nobody. He and his friends are amateurs.' Then I got out and Marra's face resumed its amused expression.

To my surprise, he told me who he was. "I'm a security officer for Merkel. Genghis Glazer was a senior vice president of the company before he left us two years ago, and knew a lot of, ah, confidential information. We know you ran into Glazer in DC shortly before he died." Suddenly his suspicious look faded, as if he had had a thought. My thought! "You and your friend Josh are nobodies, but stay out of Merkel's affairs."

I played stupid. "Sure, whatever. Who is Genghis Glazer and why did he die?"

Marra probed me again but got nothing but my forward compartment, where I was just a satisfied Uploads tech.

"Never mind." Marra drained his coffee cup and rose from the table. He paid his tab and left.

I ordered another coffee and studied my interaction with Marra. There was something odd about his sig....

I didn't realize how much time had passed until a waitress tapped me on the shoulder, anxious to free the table.

"Uh, sorry." I left her a big tip and called in to Jamaal as I left the restaurant. "Did Marra show up at Uploads?"

"I haven't seen him, but it's not that busy today."

"OK. I'm going home. I don't think we'll see Roberto again."

"Suits me. I didn't like him."

"Me neither. See you tomorrow."

It was late March now. The weather was breaking as I walked through the slushy sidewalks, thinking about my life and how strange it was. Our group of four had information that no one else on the planet had, yet we were powerless to affect events. My clumsy attempt to discover the source of the biotech had resulted in two deaths, the near death of my teammate, and (according to

Patrick) the gifting of the entire human database to the Collectives. I had no idea how to stop the distribution of the biotech.

I had to face facts: I wasn't very good at leading my team.

I got home and plopped down on the couch, thinking about what our group should do. Another flu season was winding down. The demand for the shots during the past eighteen months was off the charts because of the added bonus of glowing health from the new biotech.

I turned on my screen to C-SPAN. There was a Congressional hearing on about Rejuvenon and the declining birth rates. Under pressure from some women's reproductive rights groups, Dr. Hotez Alexander, head of the CDC, and Dr. Colin Frank, NIH director, had been hauled before a Senate select sub-committee.

"All those who have taken the Rejuvenon regained perfect health, but very few births are being recorded among them," a senator accused.

"Our studies show that the birth rate reduction is a natural phenomenon and has nothing to do with the new biotech," Dr. Alexander stated. "Sperm counts have been declining for several decades."

I knew that Alexander was lying about the declining birth rates; his mind was an open book on the mental plane. His studies showed a valid and strong statistical link between it and the new shots. As the hearing proceeded I could see that most of the questions were softballs. A casual inspection of the sigs on the Senate panel showed that they were heavily influenced by campaign contributions and sweetheart stock deals.

On a popular podcast I heard this spot: "The momentum for the new flu shots is unstoppable, and reasonable scientific objections are being ignored or swept aside. In Greek mythology, Panacea was a goddess of universal remedy. The new flu shots – if that is what they really are – are proving to be a cure for all diseases."

That about summed it up. I began to adjust my thinking to live in a world with a much healthier but smaller population. Maybe it wouldn't be so bad.

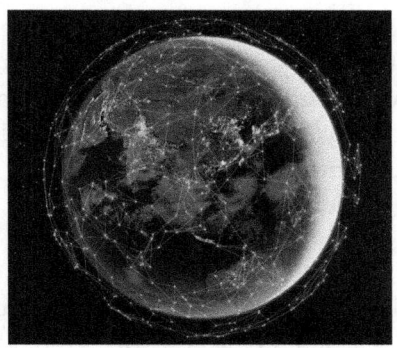

— 21 —

I was tired of working out of my office in my two-bedroom apartment. I needed a fresh start and so did the group, so I decided to rent an office downtown. I called our outfit "Second Street Investigations." I even hired a painter to stencil it in black on the glass panel of the front door, a la Humphrey Bogart. I wish I felt as confident as Sam Spade in that old movie.

Our office was in a building on Second Street across from Max Berglin's Centurion Building. Max, who sold classified cybersecurity software to defense contractors, was famous in Midland for his confrontation with the government a few years back.[20]

Jamaal needed me more than ever at Uploads. That was good for my sanity, because I was getting discouraged about our mission to save the world. I was averaging 30 hours a week at high-end contractor wages, and saving 95% of it. The extra rent for the office wasn't a problem. The office had a large work area and a little conference room in the back with a cubbyhole sink, toilet, and small refrigerator. I didn't need my second bedroom anymore so I hired a guy to move my desk and chair over to the office. I bought three extra office chairs and three small desks for the others. I also put two sofas facing each other in the middle of the room, with a small table in between in case we needed to get together and talk.

Joann always flew in to Midland Municipal on her three day no-fly breaks and we would sleep over at my place. We decided to move in together to my two bedroom apartment. Her flying days had been rescheduled for more days off. She was gone seven days out of ten instead of eleven in fourteen, with a three-day no-fly period afterward. She flew all over the country for Brewster Airlines, a private commercial shipping airline owned by a billionaire with way too much money. Between flights she stayed in airport hotels.

"Midland is as good a place as any for me," she told me. "My lifter is here at the Municipal Airport, and she's my baby."

"I thought I was your baby."

"You have other uses, Philogene."

I had just opened up the office for business when I heard a knock on the door. When I opened up I saw a giant in the doorway. I thought Joann was tall! This must be the famous Ralph Zimring. Ralph is Max Berglin's 7-foot tall security chief. He is a former special forces operative and mercenary.[21]

"Are you going to stare at me all day or invite me in?" the giant said, brushing me aside as if I were a flea and walking into the office.

Zimring's head was turning gray, but he was built like a tank and looked like he could lift me up with one finger. Ralph inspected the place, walking back to the conference room and the cubbyhole kitchen and bathroom.

The big man came back out into the main office area, frowning. "Where's your office equipment? Your servers? Your computers?"

I pointed to my head. "It's all in here."

"Sorry kid, I'm not buying it."

I quickly read his sig. It was more developed than a normal human's, but the giant was clearly not aware of the mental plane.

The big man moved like a cat toward me, but I didn't move. I could tell he had no hostile intent.

"That's very good, Philogene Rothman. You didn't flinch. But there's something you're not telling me."

I was amazed at the man's perspicacity. I was about to give him a cover story when he said, "Don't lie to me."

He was standing about three feet away from me. I was looking at his massive chest. Zimring backed off and sat down on one of the little sofas in the middle of the room. The thing creaked under his weight.

"Sit down on the other sofa and tell me all about it."

I sat down across the glass table from him, smiling. "Why should I tell you anything?"

"It's my job to know everything that happens in this town."

"A self-appointed position."

"That's right kid, and Max pays me well to do it. Now spill the beans."

Ralph Zimring was definitely old school. His demeanor was that of a slightly bored parent who was talking with a recalcitrant child, and who expected obedience. I inspected his sig again. With a little training, he might be a really good remote viewer...

"What did you just do there? I felt something."

This guy was sensitive! "Mr. Zimring, you do live up to your legendary reputation."

Ralph was silent, his eyes boring into mine. I could tell he was going to shake the truth out of me, so I talked. "I was, er, probing your sig."

The big man was getting impatient. "Stop fucking with me and explain."

"Sig. Mental signature. Every human has one. I'm a remote viewer."

I could see something click in the big man's brain. "Tony told me about that," he muttered. Then he looked at me with that penetrating gaze. "Where did you train?"

"Major Dame Edwards. I started with his online RV course, and went in for personalized training."

Ralph leaned back on the sofa. I heard something in the sofa pop. "You aren't a very good liar, kid."

"If I told you the truth you wouldn't believe me."

I could tell Zimring was very bored now. "Stop wasting my time. Tell me or I'll wring your scrawny little neck."

I sighed. This man was a monumental physical presence, and his sig was very powerful, with a lot of latent potential.

"I'll give you a hint, kid. There's a lifter parked at Midland Muni, with an MDS of YMMS-66A. That's code for experimental space plane. That lifter is one of the new inertialess military aircraft. What's it doing at Midland Muni? You've been in it, along with a very tall woman and two others. Where did you go?"

"Holy shit." I stared at the giant in awe. I wasn't stupid enough to ask, "How do you know all this?" I skimmed the top of his mind and got the information. "Your boss, Max Berglin, has a security clearance because of his work with the Defense Department," I replied. "He pays you to monitor...developments...in Midland. You have connections within the national security community. When the lifter first appeared you went to check it out. You asked your friend J. D. Robinson, who works as an air traffic controller at the airport, and got the plane's MDS designation. Then you checked with your friend Danny Radulo, whom you served with in Kharkov, a Russian private military company. Danny is a freelance intelligence officer who used to work for the CIA."

Now it was Ralph's turn to be impressed. "OK kid, your remote viewing story checks out. No one but me would know all of that. Next, you'll tell me that you trained off-world."

I jumped off the sofa. "For fuck's sake, man! How can you possibly know that?!"

Ralph leaned back into the sofa and smiled. I hoped the back of the thing wouldn't fall off. The giant was relaxed now. "It's not so hard, Philogene. I know about the military remote viewing programs. They exist all over the world. But although some of the trainees are adept and can do a few tricks, no one on this planet could possibly have the knowledge to train someone to do what you just did. Therefore, you got your training off world, or by an off-worlder. And that has something to do with a certain military-grade space plane parked out at Midland Muni."

I sat back down, shaking my head in wonder. "You should be the head of the CIA."

Ralph laughed. It sounded like a boom box in a quiet church. The windows shook. "Those bunglers! My, er, friend Matthews would love to hear that."

I was now totally dumbfounded. "Are you talking about Austin Matthews of TAC?"

Ralph bounded out of the sofa like an oversized cat. In an instant he was crouching down, getting in my face. "You can't possibly know anything about that," he said heatedly.

I wasn't afraid. "Oh, but I do. Austin Matthews of the Technology Acquisitions Consortium, the public label for a deep black special access program. Associated with Rebecca Holmes of BioSciences, who is collecting DNA samples with her Chinese partners as part of the protocol with the new shots."

Ralph was staring at me now, his eyes almost bugging out. I read his mind. For the first time in his active and violent life he was truly and fairly shocked. He was almost blubbering. "But...but...that information is so classified and highly compartmented that you couldn't find it in a flea's ass."

"That is correct. And you're right about the off-world training."

Ralph stumbled back to the sofa and put his big head in two huge hands. He picked up his phone and spoke to someone. "Hideki, something came up. I can't make the meeting. Can you handle it? OK...OK, sure. Thanks."

The giant's face was composed now. He sat back on the sofa, all attention. "I'm all ears. Don't hold back anything."

I wanted to tell him. Ralph is larger than life, an almost father-figure superhero type of guy. A super alpha male, but an approachable one. His vibe was good. So I told him. I started with my gig at Uploads and told him how I met Patrick. Then about the lifter and the transportals, and what happened on Celeste, about the Collectives and the advanced planets network. Ralph's eyes were wide now, but he didn't stop me. When I told him about my battle with the Maitre he almost flipped out. "How did you survive?"

"I almost didn't." I told him about my almost dead body lying on the Celeste medbed, about how Gwenneth had saved me after the Council had ordered my termination, about how the consciousness of the Maitre was still living inside me, about Mila, about Genghis Glazer and how I had killed him, about the Beta Caronaians, about my remote viewing trip across the galaxy, about Al-quds and the dog- and cat-like beings on Al-Simak, everything. It just all came out. I could see that Ralph was numb now. To his credit he didn't object or even say a word. I realized how much tension was inside me, and how bizarre and unbelievable my story was. Now the tension was mostly gone, except for that demon within me.

I ran out of words. I could see that Ralph was processing. He was sitting there silently with his eyes closed, making connections, inserting new data into his mind map. I didn't say anything, but I gently scanned his mind. Ralph Zimring had done more things than any hundred humans, and had a wealth of knowledge about the military, the intelligence community, and a lot of other classified shit that he had to keep to himself.

Just then Ralph looked up. "You better know how to keep a secret, Philogene. I felt you reading me. What you know could get you killed a hundred times."

I gulped. "Yes, commander."

"I'm not a fuckin' commander. I'm a civilian."

"Cut the bullshit, Ralph." I spoke to him as an intimate now, someone who knew what he knew. His eyes widened. "If there's anyone qualified to be the commander of earth, you're it." I paused for a moment to let that sink in. "When you are trained in the remote viewing protocols and the mental plane, I'll let you read my mind. You'll know everything I know in living color, with every emotion, all data points, all connections. You'll be a very valuable member of the team. The team that is defending the earth from the Collectives."

Ralph's eyes were blazing with passion now. He got it. "It's amazing, kid. Mind-to-mind comms, it's fucking unbelievable! Action on the biggest stage." He paused. "But is it real?"

I sent him a thought directly to his mind, a powerful burst. 'IT'S REAL.'

The big man's head snapped back. "Do that again."

'I'm using the mental plane to transmit thoughts,' I sent.

"OK, I believe you." He looked at his grizzled and worn hands, hands that had seen more combat than a dozen warriors. "I wish I was forty years younger."

I smiled. "I'll teach you how to access the healing protocols in the human biofield. It will increase your health and your lifespan without having to take that poison being distributed by the galactics."

Ralph looked at me gratefully. "I'd appreciate that." He frowned. "So it's true then. The new shots have an extraterrestrial origin."

"Yes."

"OK. I'm in."

I breathed a huge sigh of relief. "Good! I'm no leader, Ralph. Our group needs a clear head to direct us; someone who understands how to fight a guerilla action against an overwhelming force."

I saw Ralph's eyes light up again. He was old, but still looked motivated, still had that inner fire. "I'll have to teach you about the mental plane and how to access it. I think you'll be able to do it."

"When do I start?"

I thought about that. We were making no progress with the galactic intervention and their biotech. Ralph might be the leader we needed to mount an effective campaign against the galactics, and the crazies like Austin Matthews in the hidden programs like TAC. And I wasn't forgetting Roberto Marra's warning about not interfering in "matters that don't concern you." Those matters clearly involved the pharmaceutical companies and this new biotech.

I realized for the first time that Patrick's mission was way beyond my ability. I was acting impulsively, getting no results and endangering my team. Ralph had planned and executed a number of dangerous missions in his time with the military, and had done years of field work as a mercenary. Maybe he was the leader we needed. I could almost hear Patrick's voice in my head. 'Congratulations, Philogene. You just got Lesson Seven.'

"I work six to ten hour shifts at Uploads. I do my remote viewing work after dinner, but I'll spend that time training you. What's your schedule like?"

"I'm flexible. My sec chief Hideki Tamatsu handles everything at the Centurion Building. I'll have to brief Max on this new data before I can start."

"Okay. Today is Thursday. Could you be ready to go at 7 p.m. next Monday?"

Ralph nodded. "I'll make it happen." The big man got up in one fluid motion and walked out, his steps about eight feet apart. He almost glided across the floor.

Ralph Zimring showed up promptly at 7 p.m. on Monday. He looked like a child approaching an ice cream truck. "Let's get going."

I had Ralph up and running as a remote viewer in less than a week. Fortunately the giant was an adept, because I was flying by the seat of my pants as an instructor. First I showed him how to access the portal to the mental plane, and got him to be able to send and receive. I went with him on a few remote viewing exercises around the Midland area, somewhat like a novice doing a parachute jump with an instructor. Eventually I got Ralph to go to 40,000 feet and look at the entire mental envelope of earth.

'Every planet has one.'

'We're broadcasting our shit everywhere,' Ralph sent. We were both looking outward from the earth's mental plane to the rest of the galaxy. Eight billion people were unknowingly sending their thoughts along the galactic pathways.

'Can the others out there hear us?'

'Oh yeah.'

Ralph began shaking with laughter. 'Oh my God. SETI! What a joke!'

'Yeah.'

When we got back to the office after that last lesson Ralph had a look of profound satisfaction on his face. When I let him read my sig and he saw my RV adventure across the galaxy, and how Patrick had trained me, he spoke to me almost reverently. "OK, Philogene. You are preeminent on the mental plane. I'm the expert on the physical side of things."

I showed him my team and how we worked together. "We have a meeting on the mental plane most nights at midnight." I told him the codewords for our comms. "Galactics are probably monitoring everything we do, so we have to shield as much as we can. If you can make it tonight, I'd like to introduce you."

"I'll be there."

When Ralph joined our group that night at midnight on the mental plane it was like the missing piece to a puzzle. He fit in. We needed someone with leadership qualities, and Ralph had them. We showed him what we had done so far.

'No offense children, but you've done nothing to stop the distribution of this galactic biotech. I understand it has a sterilization component?'

Kelleye answered a little testily. 'We can't stop the process. The demand is too great from the public.'

Ralph snorted. 'Do you not have the ability to influence minds?'

Kelleye laughed. 'Over one billion have already gotten the shots, and there's demand for a billion more. Do you propose to change two billion minds?'

Ralph sighed. 'Find out who is distributing the product, stop them.'

'Josh and I already tried that with Dr. Glazer,' I sent. 'All we did was kill him and a galactic. Josh and I got thrown out of their ship and if it wasn't for Kelleye and Joann we'd both be dead. These galactics aren't fucking around.'

Ralph shook his head at the folly of civilians. 'Forget about the galactics, there's nothing we can do about them. This is strictly a human problem. An Austin Matthews and Rebecca Holmes problem.'

The four of us looked at each other. 'Oh shit,' I sent. 'You're right.' Ralph was talking about the biotech shipments. I showed the group how Rebecca Holmes' lifter returned from space after meeting their galactic contact. 'After the pilot lands the lifter, Matthews and Holmes inspect a bunch of palettes filled with thousands of small vials and load them into a medical van. That must be the serum in the flu shots. '

'Brought to you by Pfizer,' Josh joked.

'When is the next shipment scheduled?' Ralph asked.

'I don't know,' I said.

'Find out. The next time the supply ship comes, we interdict Holmes' lifter.' Ralph looked very pleased with himself.

'What if the galactics interfere?' Kelleye asked.

'Look at what happened the last time.' Ralph pointed to the mental plane data I had collected from Rebecca Holmes' sig. 'As soon as the transfer of the palettes is done, the galactic ship warps out of there. They are scared to death of earth and humans, something about contamination. All we have to do is influence the minds of Holmes and her pilot. Piece of cake!'

'That's very good, Ralph Zimring,' Joann sent. She was looking excited as she stared at the big man. Your avatar in a mental plane conversation is always your body. My girlfriend was staring in awe at Ralph.

'Don't worry Philogene,' Ralph said, laughing. 'I'm almost old enough to be her grandfather.'

Joann flushed with embarrassment, and the meeting broke up.

I went to bed, wondering what would happen when she saw the big man in person.

Joann walked into our apartment a week later at 1 a.m. on Wednesday night, looking flushed and excited. She dropped off her stuff in her bedroom and stood in the living room. I was watching a movie.

"When do I get to meet your friend Ralph?" she said. Usually we throw down on each other after her seven day absence, but Joann didn't seem interested.

"Tomorrow after work. I read Rebecca Holmes' sig. The next shipment is two weeks from this Saturday at midnight central time. Ralph has already got his op, as he calls it, planned out. We all get briefed by Ralph in person at the office tomorrow at 7 p.m."

Joann yawned. "I flew in all the way from Alaska. I'm tired, I'm going to bed."

"Want company?"

But Joann had already closed her bedroom door.

On Thursday Joann and I went to the Second Street Investigations office just before 7. Everyone was there. I could tell Joann was on edge. When she saw Ralph she flushed, a sure sign of her emotional involvement. What was going on here? Something flashed into my mind. I remembered me saying, "I didn't know you cared," and her telling me that men were idiots and that I was a fool. That was just after I got back from Beta Caronai. What had she meant by that?

"Relax, Ms. D'Arcy," Ralph said in a detached, professional voice.

I threw him a grateful look. My girlfriend was practically having an orgasm over this guy.

Ralph was all business. He stood behind the table in the office area. A sleek, gray weapon was lying on the small table between the two sofas. It was about 24 inches long and 4 inches wide, with a trigger. "What is that thing?"

Josh was staring at it, fascinated.

Ralph picked it up and fondled it lovingly. "This is the latest hand-held laser rifle, military grade, courtesy of my old buddy Tony Baghdadi. Just in case."

I had no doubt at all that Ralph would use the weapon if he had to. I saw a shocked look on Kelleye's face.

"Philogene told me that Holmes' lifter will arrive at the rendezvous point at midnight CST Saturday morning, three Saturdays from now. Is that correct information, Philo?"

"Yes. I confirmed it by scanning the mind of Rebecca Holmes on the mental plane. I can't believe I never thought of doing that before."

"Never mind that, everybody makes mistakes." He turned to Joann. "Can you get your space plane to the rendezvous point at midnight, if you have the correct coordinates, Ms. D'Arcy?"

"Uh, yes, Mr. Zimring."

"Do you have the coordinates, Ms. D'Arcy?"

Joann looked at me. "Philo says he has them from the sig of Holmes' pilot."

"Very well. Here's the plan. Joshua and I go up in the lifter, piloted by Joann—"

"Josh?" I interrupted. "What about me?"

"Your impulsive actions in a crisis are well known. All of my operatives need a cool head."

Shite. Ralph knew all about me now because of our training together. "Why are you going up in space when you can get them on the ground after they land?" I was worried about Joann.

"Number one, to catch them in the act and record it. Two, a ground interdiction can be messy and involve collateral damage. Three, if our op is in space we'll be able to record what the galactic vessel looks like. After Holmes and her pilot load the vaccines onto her lifter, we use the mental plane to delay her from going home. We suggest to the pilot that he open the forward hatch. We throw that goddam galactic serum out into space. Mission accomplished."

"What if the galactics try to stop us?"

"We've been over that. After the last transfer, the galactic ship takes off. They are deathly afraid of earth and its contaminants."

"What if they don't?" I said stubbornly. "You won't even get that weapon out. These galactics are very, very powerful on the mental plane." I showed Ralph what had happened to Josh and I when we tried to intercept the galactic ship that met with the late Genghis Glazer. "Our minds were both completely frozen by the galactic, despite backup from Kelleye and Joann."

Ralph nodded. "That's good to know. Are these galactic ships armed?"

"No," Josh replied. "Making war is forbidden on emerging planets like earth. But we are free to defend ourselves against rogue resource explorers who are violating the Hilarion-Fenachrone Treaty."

Ralph's face flattened into hard planes. "Good, because I'm not fucking around. I play for keeps and I don't care how many of these galactic mother-fuckers I have to kill."

Ralph was vibrating with energy. I saw Kelleye take a step backward, shocked at the power of Ralph's violent intention. I was glad we had put up a tight shield on the mental plane around the office, because that burst would have been heard all the way to Celeste.

Joann was staring in awe at Ralph, and Josh was fired up. I was upset that I wouldn't be a part of it.

"OK kids, I have some business to take care of for Max during the next two weeks." The big man looked at me. "Don't do anything stupid, Philogene, and fuck up my op."

I gulped. "Yes, Ralph. I want to come along."

Ralph laughed. "You're like the little kid who feels left out because he can't go to the party."

"I—oh, fuck you Ralph."

"We don't need you on this one, Philogene. We can't prevent you from interfering on the mental plane, but I'm asking you to give me your word of honor that you won't."

I was feeling sorry for myself. Joann was staring at me. "Well?"

"All right, dammit. I won't interfere, but I'm going to monitor everything you do from the mental plane." I thought of something. "There isn't a space suit big enough for you, Ralph. What will you do when the exit hatch depressurizes?"

Ralph laughed. "My old spec ops buddy Tony will take care of that for me. He has, er, certain Space Force connections." Ralph's face assumed hard lines. "We meet at the Midland Airport at 2330 three Fridays from today. Don't be even one second late."

Ralph ended the meeting by striding out of the room.

Josh looked at Kelleye. "Looks like Midland is going to be the center of action. You and I are going to have to move here. We can't ask Joann to ferry us around on her free time, and plane fare is too expensive."

"That's all right with me, Josh. My consultant work is almost all remote now."

"I'll sell my studio in DC to Jack. He has been wanting to go off on his own anyway. I can always start up a new one here."

"You guys can use my room when I'm flying until you find an apartment," Joann offered. "Just make sure you wash the sheets."

I sighed. Mr. Ralph Zimring was complicating my sex life and my living arrangements.

Kelleye and Josh temporarily moved into my apartment on Sunday, the night after Joann took a cab to the airport. She would be flying for the next seven days. I listened to them talking cheerfully about getting new living quarters, plans for Josh's new martial arts studio, and joking about Kelleye's clients. The worst was listening to them tumble around in bed at night. I had to use noise-canceling earplugs to get any sleep.

Joann came back late Sunday night, a week later.

"We need to talk."

"I'm too tired, Philo. I need to get some sleep."

I had no idea where she was at. It had all started when Ralph Zimring came on the scene. The guy was a real-life comic book action figure. I seemed to be an afterthought now.

I was left out of the op. Kelleye and Josh found their apartment and moved out. Our nightly meetings on the mental plane were temporarily canceled – "the less you know the better," Ralph told me. Ralph had learned to put up a pretty good shield and I couldn't casually scan his mind anymore. When Joann got home for her three day break on Wednesday night, two weeks later, she was uncommunicative.

"Ralph has no clue what he's getting into," I said to her on Friday evening, the night before the op. "And neither do you."

"Oh shut up Philo," she said impatiently. "And if you try to read my mind I'll never speak to you again."

"Don't worry," I said bitterly. "You're so fascinated with Grandpa Zimring, it's all about him now."

"That's just like you Philo," she said wearily. "You're as immature as a 16-year-old." She walked into her room and shut the door.

That was pretty final. The moving in together idea wasn't working out. If this kept up I would have to start looking for a new apartment.

It was 11:30 on Friday night. Ralph's op was beginning. I had the sigs of everybody involved so I could monitor everything that happened on the mental plane.

"Is everyone ready?" Ralph asked. Kelleye, Josh, and Joann were in Joann's lifter at the Midland airport. Ralph was carrying his weapon.

Joann took her lifter out into space. Shortly after that I saw another lifter take off from Moffett Federal Airfield near Palo Alto. Everything that happens on earth is visible from the mental plane, if you know where to look.

"There she is, pilot," Ralph said, as the lifter containing Rebecca Holmes and her pilot rose up out of the earth's atmosphere. Joann leaned back in her pilot's chair and trailed the other lifter at a good distance. (Joann didn't need ship sensors. She just followed Rebecca's sig on the mental plane.)

There were six human beings going to meet a galactic ship that was carrying bioproducts designed to sterilize people. I was going to probe that galactic ship and make sure there was no danger to my friends before the hatch opened. I would use my Maitre if necessary. Ralph could wring my neck later.

The other ship was already there, waiting. Joann said, "That's a galactic ship."

The transfer of the palettes was made from the egg-shaped craft to Holmes' lifter by Holmes and her pilot. There was only one galactic in the ship. I skimmed his mind and knew he was a lowly resource contractor with the Hilarion Trading Group; a delivery boy. I saw him make a recording of the transaction on the mental plane as a receipt of delivery. He didn't wait around. As soon as he filed the recording of the transaction he took his ship out of there. I read anxiety in his mind about whether he would be paid for delivering resources within the solar system of earth, in violation of the Hilarion-Fenachrone Treaty. Just like any mask wearer during a pandemic, this being was scared to death of earth and its poisonous biology and life forms.

I laughed. Ralph was right. He didn't have to use his weapon, and Joann was safe.

I didn't interfere. I saw Joann expertly maneuver her lifter to dock with Holmes' lifter. The hatch opened on both lifters, and Josh and Ralph entered the other lifter. I saw how my team had frozen the minds of Holmes and her pilot. They were just sitting there like lumps. Soon after, the hatch of Holmes' lifter opened again and Joann backed her lifter away. Palettes of vials began to emerge from Holmes' lifter, moving crazily up, down, and to either side, like screaming concertgoers fleeing an active shooter.

Joann re-docked with Holmes' lifter and Ralph and Josh got back in. Joann's lifter landed at Midland Municipal. I breathed a sigh of relief for Joann. She might not like me anymore, but I still liked her.

Rebecca Holmes and her pilot landed their lifter at Joint Base Anacostia-Bolling. An unmarked white medical van was awaiting them at their landing area. The door to the forward compartment of the lifter was opened. There were no palettes.

"Where are the vials?" Holmes screamed as she looked around in the empty compartment.

"Our contact must have failed to deliver the product," the pilot said calmly. There was something he should remember about that...

"But why?"

"He couldn't make the rendezvous," the pilot said, his face blanking. "Something about a ship malfunction." He seemed to remember another lifter at the scene. No, that was impossible....

Holmes was shouting angrily now. Something odd had happened...her mind wouldn't track it. An interdiction? By whom? Had there been a leak from the program? Impossible. The consequences were too dire, and all information was too compartmentalized. Yet someone must have taken that shipment!

"You're in charge of the supply chain, Rebecca," the pilot said. "You better figure out what happened to those vials."

Rebecca Holmes shuddered. She was supposed to deliver half the product here to Austin Matthews, and the other half to Chang Li-Meng of BGI Genetics in the medical van. Li-Meng was waiting in a private jet at BWI airport in Baltimore to take delivery. Austin Matthews would not be happy, but she was more afraid of the Chinese military. The US was the only country with the new antigrav vehicles, and Chang Li-Meng and her military backers at BGI Genetics were completely dependent on her.

To lose 500 million doses! It was unthinkable...she was a dead woman walking.

Austin Matthews was going to appear on the tarmac in an hour to unload the vials. She couldn't face him. Her head was pounding and she couldn't think straight. She got in the medical van and drove it to Ronald Reagan airport, where she booked a flight back to California.

One of the palettes, on a descending trajectory, found its way a week later into the Space Grid. A technician in Wuhan City, responsible for a sector of the Asian grid, saw something square bang into one of his satellites, causing a huge disruption. After working for 24 straight hours, Wang Mengzhou was finally able to stabilize the sector. Mengzhou checked the data repositories of the other satellites in his sector and discovered what had caused the problem: a pallet about three feet wide by three feet long. He looked at the recorded image that showed hundreds of stacked vials. He was able to read one of the labels on the pallet: "Property of BGI Genetics."

Mengzhou was confused. Everybody had heard about the disappearance of the shipment of the magical new biotech, but what was that palette doing out in space? If he reported it the military would blame him and shoot the messenger. Mengzhou blurred the image on the satellite recording just enough to hide the label and reported it as a piece of space debris. No one would notice. He hoped.

Austin Matthews summoned Kathy Abbott to his hotel room in Palo Alto that evening after taking a hastily booked flight to California from DC. On the plane, Matthews fumed at the delay in getting his product. He was responsible for supplying the entire US!

The TAC medvan had been found parked at Ronald Reagan Airport that afternoon. Inquiry showed that Holmes had booked a flight to San Francisco, and that the plane had landed at 3 p.m. Pacific time. Holmes was not answering her phone.

When Kathy entered the hotel room she could see how upset Matthews was.

"Rebecca is beside herself," Abbott explained. "She doesn't know how it happened. She remembers going up in the lifter to make the rendezvous. The supply ship was there. After that her mind is blank. She just assumed the shipment was on board, but when they landed and she looked around, there was no cargo."

Matthews was angry. "That makes no sense, Kathy. Where is Rebecca now?"

"I don't know. Looking for the product, I assume."

"The woman is unstable and incompetent."

Kathy shrugged.

It was clear to Austin that Abbott knew nothing. A wasted trip.

"I've heard rumors that the new biotech includes a sterilization agent," Kathy said as Austin was about to leave. "Is that true?"

"Yes. But certain people get the special, untainted batch," Matthews replied.

"So that's why Rebecca has been so cheerful, the bitch!"

"Fifty million dollars and a beautiful house in the Willows will certainly help to raise one's spirits," Matthews said drolly.

Kathy frowned. "You're a man; you wouldn't understand."

Austin dismissed this as ridiculous. "What will happen to Holmes?"

"What do you think? She's CEO of BioSciences only by sufferance. She's – expendable."

Austin nodded agreeably in a way that belied his words. "I'm sorry to hear that."

"I'm sure you are," Kathy sneered.

Matthews' eyebrows raised. "Ms. Abbott, you have proven yourself to be an excellent operative."

"An infertile one," she said bitterly. "I can never have children." Kathy could see how uninterested Austin was.

"An unfortunate occurrence. But surely you understand that humanity as we know it is on the way out."

"What???"

Matthews stared. "Kathy, the new Transhumanist technologies will eliminate women, children, and natural birth from the human equation.[22] The new flu shots are just the beginning of this program. I'm told that out there in the galaxy —" he pointed upward — "most societies use printed or programmed bodies, or biological bodies with neural implants. It's much easier to manage populations that way."

At Kathy's appalled look, Austin sat back in his chair. "You really are naive, aren't you? Why do you think the new biotech has been introduced? The population of our planet is far too large to manage given earth's diminishing resources."

Kathy Abbott had read some of the TAC resource studies but never believed them. Apparently they were true! She understood now that Austin Matthews was a charming psychopath. "I resign." She got up to leave the room but was stopped by a sharp comment. "Aren't you forgetting something, Ms. Abbott? You have been read in. That means you stay with the program." Kathy didn't need to hear the "or else" part, and Austin didn't say it out loud. "Be content, Kathy. Even though you will never have children, you will be healthy and well-provided for, for the rest of your natural life."

All of the color drained from Kathy's face.

"Ah, I see you understand the situation." Matthews smiled, but the smile didn't reach his eyes. "It's better this way, my dear."

Kathy grimaced. 'My dear' is just what that nice old man Genghis Glazer had always said to her.

Matthews' voice assumed conversational tones. "We in the programs have agreed to fully cooperate with, er, our friends out there. The rewards are considerable."

Kathy was numb now. Her organization, which she had believed was doing the best for humanity, were sellouts!

"Try to find out from Rebecca what happened to that shipment, will you? Before someone gets too angry with her."

Kathy nodded dumbly and stumbled out of the hotel. She didn't get much sleep that night, thinking about The World According to Austin Matthews. She was part of that world now, and there was no getting out of it. She was only 24, but could never have children, or a normal life. As she tossed and turned in bed she began to get angrier and angrier, and more and more cynical, until the phone rang at 4 a.m.

Austin Matthews got back on a plane to DC. Kathy Abbott was right of course. Rebecca Holmes was expendable. Nevertheless, he would have to call the irritating General Qiao Xiangsui and inform him of developments. The old man and his fellow general Wang Liang would undoubtedly want to talk to Rebecca. If something happened to Holmes, Kathy Abbott would make a good replacement for her at BioSciences. And a more reliable one.

Austin washed his hands of the affair. The two old generals would take care of Rebecca Holmes for him. Meanwhile, he would have to arrange with Colin Frank for a new shipment of biotech.

— 22 —

Ralph's op had disrupted the supply chain of product for the entire world. The media was humming with angry emotions and threats from the Chinese military, the medical bureaucracy, and the pharmaceutical distributors. Politicians were angry because the public was loudly demanding their doses.

"It's a total shit show," Ralph said to me with a big grin. We were sitting in the downtown office.

"You fucked everything up."

"Aint it wonderful?"

"It is. Now, tell me what's happening between you and my girlfriend."

Ralph groaned. "Absolutely nothing, son. It's all on her end, not mine."

"She practically has an orgasm every time she sees you."

"She has daddy issues, Philo. Her father was a Navy pilot and then went into the commercial aircraft industry, just like she did. Like father, like daughter. He has gray hair just like me."

"It can't be that simple," I muttered.

"It often is, but there's no excuse for you. We know how to comm mind-to-mind; relationships are a piece of cake."

"Not if she won't let me in. I could force her, but that would be the end of our relationship."

Ralph yawned. "Philo, I never married because no woman I ever wanted can tolerate my lifestyle. I'm no good to you. Ask your father. Or better yet, talk to Joann's father about her."

"Hey, that's a great idea! I'll do just that."

Ralph dropped the subject. "By the way, I'm going to need some more remote viewing training. I gotta scan my old friend Austin Matthews and the TAC network. I need to be able to read their mental plane data."

I was glad Ralph was taking over that mission, and told him so. "I have no experience with the intelligence services and their hidden programs, so have at it."

"OK, but I need some instruction about how to approach and read sigs without disturbing the subject's conscious mind."

I smiled; the old man's face was lit up like a child getting a new toy. "All right, it's time well spent. Tell you what. I need a vacation from Uploads. After I go to Nebraska and talk to Joann's father, I can give you intensive training if you can clear your schedule." I stared at Ralph. "And by intensive, I mean intensive. No mercy."

Ralph's eyes flamed. "Bring it on, son! Bring it on."

I called Joann's parents the next morning and asked if I could speak to them. After eating breakfast I was on the road for the six hour drive to Blair, Nebraska.

"So you are the young man my daughter is seeing," Gene D'Arcy said as I walked in the front door. Joann's father was a bulky man with graying hair, and looked like an athlete who was going to fat. I could tell he wasn't impressed with me.

We sat in his living room, with a fire burning. Above the fireplace a large buck's head was mounted. "I'm no slouch, sir. I have a good job working as a technician for the Space Grid."

"You work with the Grid?" Gene asked excitedly.

"Yes, Mr. D'Arcy. At Uploads in Midland, Illinois. My boss told me that I'm the top Grid technician on the planet. And I'm paid accordingly."

After that the ice was broken; I had gotten through. I had to describe in detail what I did and how the Grid was maintained. The older man was fascinated with space.

"So your job also involves coding."

"Yes sir." I explained how the Grid has network addresses, which are the locations for all the data transfers on earth, and how these addresses are assigned to a number of fixed, logical, and geosynchronous spatial regions called Geosynchronous Network Grids. "The satellites are traveling in low earth orbit and are always moving in and out of the network boundaries. The routine stuff is handled by AI, but when a SNAFU happens there is some critical, time-sensitive programming involved in fixing the glitches."

Gene's eyes lit up. I decided to self-promote a little.

"When the Grid has a glitch it affects comms for some very important businesses and people. Sometimes multiple sectors go haywire all at once. So we have to act fast and accurately if the AIs can't handle it, or data loss can occur. It's a high stress job for most people, but I'm very good at pattern recognition and programming, so it's easy for me. Of course it's nothing like being a pilot in a real plane, but Grid techs are responsible for maintaining communications planet-wide."

"I love space flight and aircraft. It's been my life. I think I transferred some of that love to my daughter."

I nodded. "You did, sir."

The older man told me something of his life. "I was a Navy pilot, tried for special ops pilot, but they said I didn't have 'it,' whatever that means." Gene spoke angrily. "They offered me ground duty, maintaining fighter aircraft, because I'm an excellent mechanic. I turned them down and became a civilian pilot. I just wanted to fly. Still do."

I brought the conversation around to his daughter. "Look, I really like Joann, but she's turned me off for some reason." I described Ralph Zimring, and what he said about her having daddy issues. "What can I do about that?"

Gene's eyes flared. "Daddy issues? That's insulting, young man."

"Sorry, but I didn't come all the way out here to bullshit you. I'm interested in your daughter. I want to know if you know of anything in her past that might make her, uh, attracted to older men." I described Ralph and told him about his military background. I passed him a pic of Ralph.

"Holy cow, how tall is this guy?"

"Almost 7 feet. He moves like a ballet dancer, has had a long career in the military and as a mercenary. Killed a bunch of scumbags, or so he says. His reputation in town is that he's competent at everything and honest as the day is long, as my father would say."

At that moment a good looking older woman walked into the living room. Obviously Joann's mother. She was almost as tall as Joann. "Hello, I'm Alice."

"Very pleased to meet you. I'm Philogene Rothman, Joann's boyfriend. Former boyfriend is more accurate."

She looked at me critically and took the picture of Zimring from her husband. She studied the image for a moment. "Is Mr. Zimring interested in Joann?"

"Not that I can see. He says he's old enough to be her grandfather. Ralph is kind of jaded, if you know what I mean. He's done more in his life than a hundred regular humans, and he's got an aura of – I don't know – invincibility around him. He's the most impressive person I've ever met."

Alice laughed. "That's a hard act to follow."

She studied me and the image of Ralph, and sighed. "Joann has never been interested in anyone that I know of. The boys in school were afraid of her, mostly because she was a top athlete, and very strong."

"And beautiful too. Like her mother."

Alice gave me a look. "Flattery will get you everywhere."

"Ah! I'll remember that. I have a tendency to be a little self-centered."

Gene laughed. "Joann is the same. When she wants something she goes for it."

Alice looked at Ralph's photograph again. "I think it's just a crush. Joann sees a very mature older man with remarkable accomplishments. He's someone she can look up to, figuratively and literally. Or, perhaps, she's trying to make you feel jealous. My advice to you, young man, is to wait her out."

I was satisfied with this explanation. It made sense. "I was hoping you'd say that." I told her about the time she called men idiots and said I was immature.

Alice rolled her eyes and looked at me intensely, as if she was trying to send me a message. "Joann is right, Philogene. Men *are* idiots."

I didn't want to read her sig, and I was baffled. Alice and Gene exchanged glances, as if to say, 'These two are too self-centered for each other.'

Gene slapped his hands on his thighs and rose from the couch. "Now that you're here, would you like to stay for dinner?" Gene said.

I hesitated.

"It's OK, Philo. You drove all the way out here to talk to us."

"I could eat something."

"We're having spaghetti."

"I'm ravenous."

Over dinner, which was held in a country-style kitchen with wood paneled walls, I told Gene and Alice about my childhood, and more about my work at Uploads. When I described the gigantic display panel in the middle of the workroom, and the others in a circle around the work area, Gene got excited again. I was tempted to tell them about my remote viewing work, but held back.

"It's all right Philo," Gene said, encouraging me to talk.

I took a deep breath. "Have you ever heard of remote viewing?"

Alice shook her head but Gene sat up in his chair. "Russell Targ, Stanford? Or military?"

"A sophisticated civilian program, strictly private, no one I ever heard of before I got accepted." It was better than telling them about ETs.

"I see," Gene said doubtfully.

"Joann has had some of the training as well."

Alice was surprised and shocked. "Joann? A remote viewer?"

"Yes. Very high aptitude. I met Joann in the program."

Gene and Alice exchanged baffled glances. "I'll be damned," Gene said. He explained. "You see, Joann doesn't tell us much. She's a good daughter, but not talkative about her personal life."

I explained about remote viewing. "A good RVer can project his or her awareness outward on what we call the mental plane, and observe things. Material objects are no barrier to a good remote viewer."

Alice was dumbfounded. "I always thought of Joann as a good volleyball player, and a good pilot like her father. How did she get involved in remote viewing?"

I had to tell some more white lies. "Same way as I did. Somebody who called himself Patrick recruited us. To this day I have no idea who he is or how he discovered my aptitude. But I'll tell you, he was a hell of an instructor. I think he was affiliated with a classified university research program, because he didn't tell us anything about himself or the program. Only that he was testing some new methods and wanted to see the results. There are four of us. Joann may have mentioned a Joshua and a Kelleye."

Husband and wife looked at each other again in surprise. "My daughter has been living a secret life," Gene said.

"She's a private person like her father," Alice said.

I sent my remote viewer out to a big barn about 100 feet from the house, and described in great detail what was in it. Gene and Alice were astonished. "You got everything right!"Gene said. "I believe you."

"Joann can do that too?" Alice asked.

"She sure can."

We spent the rest of the evening talking about current events and sports. "Joann was a volleyball player?" I asked.

"Yes, and a very good one," Alice said. "The best striker on her high school team. She was heavily recruited by the best volleyball programs in the country."

Gene grinned at my astonishment.

"Wow. You learn something new every day." It may explain why Joann is attracted to Ralph, I thought. Both are serious athletes.

Alice looked at the clock. "My goodness, it's past nine. I hope you don't plan on driving tonight. Our Nebraska roads can get icy even in April."

"I could stay at a hotel."

"Not a chance, Philogene," Gene said. "We've got two spare rooms. Take your choice."

"It would be great to rest up. I'll leave early and be out of your hair."

"You'll do no such thing, son. We have breakfast at 8 every morning. Pancakes, sausages, and eggs tomorrow. You'll need something in your stomach for the drive back."

"I'm very grateful. I'd love that. I'll go grab my things from the car."

When I got back to Midland on Sunday Joann was in the living room, pacing the floor. I forgot it was the first day of her three-day no-fly period. When I walked in she practically throttled me. "You had the audacity to meet my parents without telling me?" She was very angry.

"Yeah. Why not? You won't talk to me anymore. Alice and Gene were glad to see me. I showed them a picture of Ralph."

Joann was speechless.

"I told them about our remote viewing capability, but not about ETs. Just in case they ask you, I said we were trained at a classified private university program."

Joann's mouth opened and closed, but nothing came out. To say she was indignant would be an understatement. She turned around, walked into her bedroom, and slammed the door.

I was definitely going to look for another apartment. Mind-to-mind comms don't solve relationship problems if the other person won't let you in.

It was past 6 now, and I was hungry. I went out to Mickey Dunns for a couple of beers and some bar food, and tried to forget about Joann. It didn't work. The women I met were nothing compared to Joann.

Tomorrow was Monday. I would call Ralph Zimring and begin his intensified training.

The morning after their meeting in Palo Alto, Austin Matthews called Kathy Abbott at 4 in the morning. "Do you know what time it is?" she complained.

"Certainly. It's time for a change. How would you like Rebecca's job? The woman is incompetent and unreliable."

Kathy was wide awake now. Her talk with Matthews yesterday had opened her eyes. She responded cautiously. "If Rebecca resigns or is fired, I'll take the job."

Matthews chuckled humorlessly. "I don't think we have to worry about Rebecca. Our Chinese friends are quite irritated."

Matthews' meaning couldn't have been plainer. Kathy was learning to read between the lines instead of taking people at their word. She wondered if that is what cynicism is. Well, she had better get used to it.

At 8 that morning Kathy Abbott walked into Rebecca Holmes' office. Rebecca was sitting at her desk, her head in her hands, and it looked like she had been there all night. Kathy would play the innocent. "What the matter, Dr. Holmes?"

Rebecca was desperate to tell someone about her problem even though she would place herself in serious danger if she did. What did that matter now? She was still alive, but not for long. "I have just been contacted by Chang Li-Meng, my counterpart at BGI Genetics in Beijing. The Chinese military demands that we deliver the product within the next 48 hours." Rebecca looked up at Kathy Abbot with hollow eyes. Naive little Kathy. "We lost the shipment."

Kathy made her eyes bug out. "Seriously? How did that happen?"

Rebecca went over it again for the hundredth time. Kathy listened attentively, not interrupting. Suddenly Rebecca stopped her disjointed narrative. "Wait a minute, I just remembered something!"

Kathy was all ears. She had to report this conversation to Austin Matthews.

"There was another lifter there, I'm sure of it..." she muttered.

Kathy was quick on the uptake. "Another lifter?"

"That's right. That shipment was stolen!"

"But how?"

Rebecca thought furiously. Her mind kept skipping over the details, but that didn't matter now. She would have to check all lifters in the country. There were less than 100 in the entire world, and all of them on U.S. soil. She would check the FAA registry, and the classified space plane listing, which she had sec clearance to access. "I don't know, Kathy, but I'm going to find out. I have less than 48 hours to live and I have to work fast." She looked up pleadingly into the younger woman's eyes. "Can you help me?"

It was perfect. Kathy accepted immediately.

Within two hours they had found the mysterious lifter by checking the ADS-B Exchange program and the SPYGlass app, available to anyone who knew how to use them. "Look Kathy! There *were* two space planes!"

Holmes pointed to the military designations for two lifters that were shown on the screen. Her space plane and one other had been in the air between 9:20 p.m. and 10:20 p.m. PST last Saturday morning, over Joint Base Anacostia-Bolling.

Kathy checked the registries for both lifters. "One of them is registered to the base commander."

"The one my pilot and I used," Rebecca said excitedly. "We took off from Moffett Federal Airfield."

The other was now sitting at the Midland Municipal Airport, registered to a Joann D'Arcy, call sign YMMS-66A.

— 23 —

Ralph Zimring and I were in the middle of an advanced remote viewing training exercise at the downtown office when we heard a desperate call for help on the mental plane. It was Joann. 'A bunch of soldiers just broke the door down! Help!'

Through Joann's eyes we could see five up-armored guys in military gear. Joann was against the wall in our apartment living room. "Where are those vaccines, cutie?" one of them said to Joann. Ralph and I jerked our attention away from our exercise and back to my apartment just as the soldier threatening Joann involuntarily lowered his weapon.

"What the hell are you doing, Davis! Keep that woman under constraint!"

"I can't sir! She's doing something to my mind!"

'Awesome, Joann!' I sent.

Ralph took command. 'Tell them that the people responsible will be there in five minutes.' Ralph flew out of the door and was running full speed down Second Street to my apartment on Fifth Street, scattering frightened Midlanders like a charging hippo at a peaceful campfire of picnickers. I followed Ralph, running as fast as I could, but I couldn't keep up. We both read the situation on the mental plane at the speed of thought. The intruders had come in a black van that was parked at the curb in front of my apartment building. Three of them were tossing my apartment. The leader was standing in the center of the apartment, and Davis, who had threatened Joann, was standing three feet in front of her, frozen in place.

"Pick up your weapon, Davis!" Johnson shouted. But Joann had completely shut Davis down. All he could do was grunt. Johnson walked over to Davis. "You're drooling, man! What the fuck is happening?" Davis was trying to send a message with his eyes, which were moving around crazily in his head.

"There's no vials here, Johnson!" one of the men said. "The place is clean!"

"Chu, grab the laptops and the mobiles."

Chu grabbed the electronics and put them in his backpack.

Just then Ralph barged in past the broken door and quickly read Johnson's sig. Ralph sent a message to Joann on the mental plane. 'Relax, D'Arcy. Hold your man.'

"The fucking product isn't here, you fools," Ralph said to the others. He seized Johnson's mind and the team leader slowly and reluctantly dropped his weapon on the carpet. Jankowski, Chu, and Cortez stared dumbly at their two statuesque comrades-in-arms. "Jank, Johnson and Davis are drooling idiots. Did they have a seizure?"

Jankowski pointed his weapon at Ralph. "You! We know you stole those vaccines. You have ten seconds to tell me where they are."

Just then I came puffing into my living room, totally out of breath. I had already read the situation on the mental plane so I immediately seized Jankowski's mind. He stood there like a zombie, unable to move.

Chu looked at Cortez in alarm. "Cort, let's get out of here. This is some crazy shit!"

Chu was first out the door, pushed by Cortez. By this time a bunch of gawkers had come out of the apartments and were milling around the front door, which was only hanging on one hinge. Chu lost it. "Get of here you stupid people!" He raised his weapon. "Get back in your holes!"

I almost laughed as my neighbors scurried back to their apartments like stray cats at a dog track. Chu and Cortez stumbled out and got into the van.

Jankowski, Johnson, and Davis were terrified. We let go of their minds but the three intruders didn't move. They were petrified. "Stay there," Ralph ordered. Johnson grunted and said, "Don't mess with these people, Jank. They're devils!"

Ralph silently interrogated Johnson, the team leader, and read his mind just like I taught him, and the other three members of the team. He implanted one powerful suggestion into their minds: "Rothman, D'Arcy, and her friends don't know anything." Just for fun, I planted a suggestion that "men in black" with remote neural monitoring satellite technology had immobilized the team.

Ralph laughed. "That's no joke Philogene, with all those satellites up there."[23]

"Don't forget about the other two out in the van," Joann said. Ralph picked up Johnson's weapon from the carpet and frog marched the three men out to the van. When Chu and Cortez saw us they started blubbering about demonic possession. Ralph and I entered their minds and gave them the same treatment as the others. The team, thoroughly cowed, got in their van and drove away. (We learned later from Ralph that the team's hotwash had been gibbering, incoherent nonsense. The team was deactivated and sent to military-approved therapists.)

"Thanks team," Joann said gratefully after the intruders had gone. "They scared me to death."

"You did well, child," Ralph said, as an uncle would to his niece. "Your first skirmish. Now we have to do an after action report."

We found out what that meant when we got back to the Second Street office. Ralph made us go meticulously through the events and write a summary of our conclusions. We did everything on the mental plane.

"By God," he said after we had stored all the action in labeled folders on the mental plane. "That was fun! But I'm tired. In the old days I'd go out for a celebration, but I'm feeling my age these days." He winked at me and Joann. "You did well, kids. You kept your heads."

I did! My Maitre never even stirred. Mila had taught me well.

"OK, I have to go brief Max. Then I'm going to lie down for a while."

I thanked God for Ralph Zimring. I knew he didn't need to "lie down," but Joann was giving him a funny look.

"C'mon Joann," I said. "Let's clean this place up."

She frowned but said nothing. There were a dozen people outside now. A few of them were in the apartment, looking around curiously. "The door is open," a young woman explained.

Joann was prepared to be belligerent, but I asked her to be lenient. I turned to the milling group, who were still buzzing about the remarkable incident. "Who was that big guy?" an attractive young woman asked.

"Ralph Zimring of course," a man said. "Everybody knows Ralph."

I had an idea. "Hey you guys, could you help us clean up this mess? I'll buy you beer and as much pizza as you can eat."

A half dozen people responded enthusiastically. For the first time in six weeks, Joann gave me a smile. "C'mon in! We'll clean up and I'll tell you all about it."

Joann and I and our six neighbors got everything that wasn't broken back in place. I rehung the door as best as I could and closed the deadbolt. Joann was upset because her cherry wood kitchen table had been tipped over, and one of the legs was broken. "That was a gift from my father," she said sadly.

"No problem," a man said. "I know a repairman who can get it back as good as new."

A camaraderie was developing, and Joann was loosening up. I ordered three large pizzas and left to pick up a twelve pack. When I got back with the beer Joann was talking cheerfully with our neighbors.

We ate the pizza and I described what happened, leaving out our work on the mental plane. "It probably has to do with Max Berglin and his security chief Ralph Zimring," I said. "Berglin and Ralph have, er, varied and diverse interests."

Joann gave me a look that said, "Don't blame it on Ralph."

The party broke up and Joann and I were alone. I started to clear away the empty pizza boxes and put the dirty plates into the dishwasher. Joann didn't help. I said nothing. If she wanted to talk, it was on her. I was tired of getting shut down.

"Do you want me to move out?" she said finally.

"What are you talking about? I've been trying to reach out to you for a month. You just shut me out."

"God Philo, you are stupid aren't you? Do you really think I'm interested in that old man?"

"Of course you are! You get all shaky every time you see him! And you won't talk to me. That's why I went to see your parents, to get their advice."

"Let me lay it out for you, because you're too dumb to see what's in front of your face. Do you think I stay with you just because of the sex? I would never do that for anyone unless I cared for him. I've never had anyone else since I met you, Philo. But you treat me..." her eyes began to water and she was about to cry... "You treat me like a fuck-buddy. Well, I'm not. I'm a one-man woman, Philo."

Wow. I wasn't expecting that. "But...why would you drool over Ralph? I understand how impressive he is, but..."

"Do you love me Philo?"

I took a step back. "I care for you a lot. Love? I'm not sure I know what that is."

"Well, you're honest about that at least. So let me be honest. I want a family, I want children. Sure I'm independent, and I like what I do, but I want to settle down eventually. If that's not in your plans, I'll move out tomorrow."

"I haven't seen anyone else since I met you, Joann. Compared to you, other women are boring."

"Do you want children?"

"I haven't thought about it much. But yes. I do. Eventually."

"All right. I can live with that. For now."

We had run out of words. Joann went into her room.

I sat on the living room couch for hours. My girlfriend had given me a lot to think about. Behind the sophisticated galactic traveler was a Nebraska country girl. I never suspected it.

Right after the attack Ralph Zimring briefed Max Berglin in his private office on the third floor of the Centurion Building. "The team was probably sent by Austin Matthews and TAC, looking for the shipment," Ralph summed up. "He's working with Rebecca Holmes and Chang Li-Meng."

Max nodded. "OK, so nothing to do with the Centurion Group then."

"Nope. I'm personally involved though."

Max waved his hand. "If they come after us Hideki will take care of it."

Ralph nodded and left. He walked the interior of the Centurion Building, checking on Hideki's security guards. Max developed and sold sensitive cybersecurity software and had contracts with the DoD, so he needed a security clearance and had to post a detail. Ralph walked the perimeter of the building as he did three times a day. His eyes swept the streets as he strolled the mile to his high-rise apartment in the Midland Tower, the tallest building in the city. Ralph lived on the top floor so he could get a view of the city whenever he looked out the windows. When he first came to Midland to work for Max,[24] he had rented both top floor suites so he could see 360. Five years ago he had finally convinced the hotel management to let him buy the units for an exorbitant price. He had knocked down the walls separating the two suites and connected both of them for easy access.

He had a lot of space but no one to share it with.

We discussed the attack on the apartment that night at the Second Street Investigations office. Ralph had assignments for the team.

"My sources tell me that Rebecca Holmes is missing. Find out what happened to her. I want to know all the people who have anything to do with these galactic motherfuckers and their biotech. I'm investigating our good friend Austin Matthews and his special access program, TAC."

We could all see how excited Ralph was.

"Remote viewing sure saves a lot of legwork!"

When Ralph got home he decided to do a written after action report on his laptop, even though the team had already made one on the mental plane. This would force him to further organize his thoughts and maybe uncover something he had missed.

When he was done he understood that mental plane warfare was the ultimate evolution of fighting. Their struggle with the TAC team had been unequal, because his opponents did not have his team's abilities. Ralph pondered what would happen if both sides had the ability to operate on the mental plane. Each side would have to shield their minds so that the other side would not know their next move. Intelligence about the enemy is vital; to know their strengths and weaknesses, to know their motivations, gave you a serious advantage. If both sides were successful in shielding then the fighting would mostly devolve back to physical conflict. But if kinetic war was forbidden then information influence operations and psychological warfare would dominate. Each side would deploy shield busters on the mental plane to break the shields of the other side. This was probably the state of affairs out in the galaxy.

Philogene had allowed him to read his mind. He knew the kid was still hiding something. But Ralph knew about the Collectives and their authoritarian, technocratic societies. It was unfortunate that galactic evolution had proceeded along totalitarian lines. The earth was going in that direction, and humanity was wide open to every civilization in the Greater Community. The galactics were already here, interfering and fucking things up. He was going to do something about that.

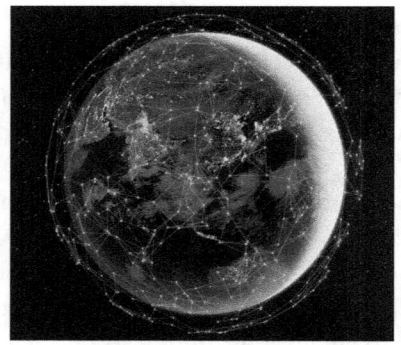

— 24 —

"I found Rebecca Holmes," Kelleye announced to the group the next day. The team was in the Second Street Investigations office after work. "She's in a Chinese military prison, along with her colleague Chang Li-Meng, the head of BGI Genetics. It was Rebecca Holmes who sent the team of TAC thugs to Philo's apartment after she discovered Joann's lifter at the Midland Airport."

"What should we do about these poor women?" Kelleye asked. "They are probably going to be killed by the Chinese military."

Kelleye was the conscience of our group.

"What can we do?" I asked. "That military prison is crowded. We'd have to immobilize a hundred people at least on the mental plane just to get them out, and there's only five of us."

"They would just be recaptured anyway Kel," Josh said sympathetically. "China is a big country and the military runs everything over there."

Kelleye didn't like it, but we left Rebecca Holmes and Chang Li-Meng to their fates.

A week after our adventure with Rebecca Holmes' thugs I got a call from Jamaal at Uploads around 11 p.m.

"Philo, would you come in early tomorrow? I want you to see something."

When I walked in at 6 a.m. the next morning, I noticed that a new employee had replaced Jamaal as Director of the tech center. A bulky man of about 35 approached me, with a wide smile and looking in the prime of health. "Well, well, well! If it isn't the famous Philogene Rothman." He stopped about four feet in front of me and looked me square in the eyes. "What brings you to our humble facility?" At the same time, I felt a probing of my mind on the mental plane.

I let him in to my forward compartment, which presented a mental sig of the typical Uploads employee. "I work here. Who do I have the pleasure of speaking to?"

The man smiled again. "I'm Selig Bronfman, the new director, Philogene." Then he frowned. "I'm sorry, but you are no longer employed at Uploads. I'm afraid I'll have to ask you to leave."

I laughed. "Just like that, is it?" I glanced over at one of the techs at his console. "When Jamaal was director, his techs didn't fuck up the Grid." I stepped over to the screen. "Having trouble?" I asked the tech, who nodded in frustration.

Jamaal was signaling me frantically behind Selig's back. He was pointing to the exit. I could tell that Selig was aware of Jamaal's agitation on the mental plane.

"Here, let me help." There were three sats out of position, but the problem was a subtle discontinuity within the entire sub-section of satellites. I wrote down a couple of coded instructions on a piece of paper. "Try these."

The tech punched them in and the subsector began to stabilize.

"There!" I said, straightening up. I spoke condescendingly to Selig. "That wasn't so hard, was it?"

I couldn't do anything on the mental plane or Selig might get suspicious, but I watched him carefully. He probed my mind again. Satisfied, he gave me a big smile. "That was very helpful, Philogene! Thank you." A burly security guard appeared, a man I disliked. "Spieth, please escort Mr. Rothman out of the building." I felt a subtle influence on the mental plane from Selig to the guard.

"What kind of a dick fires the world's best Grid technician?" I asked contemptuously.

Bronfman flared and motioned to the guard. Bronfman turned away without replying as Spieth approached me and grabbed hold of my elbow. My Maitre wanted to fry him, but I turned meekly away. Just before I was escorted out I made a hand signal to Jamaal that said, "Call me."

On the way out I tried to make small talk, but the security guard was silent. Just before he shoved me out the door I took a peek into his mind. Nothing there, just a standard human following orders.

I walked home from Uploads, wondering where Selig Bronfman got his ability on the mental plane. His sig was similar to Roberto Marra's, the former security officer for Merkel. Were other Uploads directors also active on the mental plane? Where were they getting their training? I would have to investigate Bronfman and the entire Uploads network, and now I could do it full time. I had made so much money at Uploads I was set for a long time. I would miss the Space Grid work, but I had done everything and learned everything there was to do and learn about it.

When I got home I was too pissed off at Bronfman to do any mental plane work. I played disk golf all day, got really tired, and went to bed early. I called Jamaal the next morning. "Who is Selig Bronfman and why did he replace you?"

"Oh hi Philo, I'm glad you called. A week ago Selig shows up with Hernandez from HQ, who tells me I have a new boss. But Selig was giving the orders and Hernandez was following them."

"Did it look like Hernandez was under a mental compulsion?"

"Yes, that's it! Like he was under some kind of hypnotic control. After Hernandez left, our mission changed. I don't know what his game is, but Selig is more interested in the Grid comms than he is in ensuring that the Grid runs smoothly."

"So he's snooping. What's he looking at?"

"I don't know, Philo. Selig locked me out of admin access. I'm just a lowly Grid tech now."

"Thanks Jamaal. Keep in touch, OK?"

"I will."

The next day after work Jamaal called me at the office to say he had been fired. "When I asked for the reason, Selig said that I was engaging in unauthorized communications. That must mean you, Philo. What have you been up to?"

"You wouldn't believe me if I told you."

"I thought we were friends!"

I sighed. "All right, come on over to my office and I'll tell you." I gave him the address.

When Jamaal walked in Kelleye, Josh, and Joann were sitting silently at their desks. I didn't introduce him. We went back to the small conference room off the main working area.

I was getting better at introducing people to the mental plane. I read Jamaal's sig and told him a couple of things about his life that no one else could know.

Jamaal's face registered amazement, surprise, and a little fear. "Did you just read my mind?"

"Yup." I told my former boss about our training in remote viewing, and how we could read minds and influence the thought streams of other people on the mental plane. I didn't mention ETs though.

"I believe you. Selig must have also gotten some of that training. When he gives orders, I feel like I have to comply."

Or he's getting help, I thought. "Is there a feeling of mental pressure?"

"Yes, a feeling that it's the best thing for all concerned; a feeling that I have already agreed to do it so I should just go ahead."

"That's the influence of the mental plane."

"The skinny is that all of the Upload directors have been replaced."

Holy shit. "I'll look into that, Jamaal. What are you going to do with yourself now?"

"Float for a while. I made a lot of bank at Uploads and never had time to spend any of it. I want to know more about what's going on in the organization. Selig...he's a strange one."

"My thoughts exactly. Be careful, Jamaal. We can look into Uploads by remote viewing from our office. Reading minds is a trivial exercise for us now."

Jamaal frowned. "Would I be able to tell if you were reading my mind?"

It was my turn to frown. "Well, I can read the surface stuff in your conscious mind without you knowing it. But a lot of a person's thoughts, and their motivations, are buried. I would have to probe into your mind and then you would feel it unless I was very careful."

Jamaal brightened. "So that's what Selig is doing. He's probing me."

"Selig is an amateur. He has no subtlety, he just uses brute force." I realized something and got excited. Could a master remote viewer penetrate deep into a person's mind without their knowing? It would explain how someone might be influenced remotely by a virtuoso on the mental plane. *Like a galactic Seer*.

"What's wrong?" Jamaal asked.

"I was just thinking that a person very skilled in remote viewing could slip unknowingly into a person's subconscious and motivate their behavior. It's scary."

"I'll say!"

Jamaal poked his head out of the room. "What are those folks doing out there?"

"We remote view people we think are...suspicious."

"How do you identify the bad guys?"

I explained about mental signatures and the mental plane. "By remote viewing sigs we can get lots of information from people just by skimming their conscious thoughts. We can get into hidden networks and find out what they are doing. It's awesome."

"Man, I want some of that."

"Maybe one day I'll start a course on it."

"Sign me up!"

"Would you be willing to dig around Uploads and report back to me once a week? A summary of what you discover?"

"I got fired so I can't go into Uploads any more. But I know a lot of techs at multiple Uploads facilities. I'll see what I can dig up."

"Good. We may have an assignment or two for you, if you're up for it."

"Sounds good."

Jamaal and I conversed comfortably for a while. After Jamaal left I went to my office desk and sent my remote viewer over to Uploads. I knew I had to be careful because Selig Bronfman had some ability on the mental plane. I found his sig immediately – it was similar to Roberto Marra's. Both sigs had a subtle overlay, as if someone else were looking in on them remotely.... Something very strange was going on because humans don't know anything about the mental plane. Were the Collectives now engaging in remote influencing of sigs? Patrick said the Collectives were going to step up their game; maybe this was it.

Several operators were punching away at optical keyboards, entering code. Others were monitoring their satellite sectors. None of the techs had sig overlays. Twelve huge, curved display monitors circled the room, showing every Grid sector under management by the facility. Each screen was filled with small sats, moving in groups, in a predefined pattern. An outer space ballet. My attention was drawn to the middle of the room, where the gigantic flexipanel hung. It showed the entire Grid as it circled the planet. The complicated orbital calculations were handled by the AIs. It was amazing how the entire thing was coordinated.

Selig Bronfman was standing at the back of the room with Spieth, his big security guard. This asshole had fired me and Jamaal. I gently read Bronfman's sig without going too deep, and confirmed that all of the Uploads Directors had been replaced. What was Bronfman up to? Who was he working for? There was only one way to find out.

I attacked Selig's mind on the mental plane.

Just before I went in I fronted my assault with a decoy sig. It wouldn't fool a galactic, but it might confuse Bronfman about his attacker's identity.

I was in. In an instant, I scooped up everything in Bronfman's mind and got the hell out of there. I saw Selig's eyes widen and his face went blank for a moment. His body stumbled forward. The security guard caught him just as he was about to fall over.

"Are you OK, boss?"

Bronfman shook his head to clear it. "Yeah, I'm OK. Just stumbled a little, that's all."

The guard shrugged. He didn't like Selig, but nobody here did. Selig had walked in one day last week and taken over the place. The next day he had kicked Jamaal out of the building. Jamaal had been well-liked. Well, it wasn't any of his business; he was glad he still had his job.

The guard circled the big room on his duty round, and then walked off to inspect the perimeter of the building.

I was back in the downtown office, sitting at my desk. Josh, Kelleye, and Joann were sitting at attention, looking at me.

Kelleye sighed. "All right Philo, what did you do this time?"

"Selig Bronfman, boys and girls. Look at this."

I showed them Bronfman's sig, and everything I had from his mind. "Quiz time. What's unusual about this sig?"

"It's not a galactic sig," Kelleye said. "Theirs are broader and deeper because they all get training on the mental plane as they grow up."

"Yes, but there is a galactic pattern to the sig. It's subtly overlain on the human one, like a layer in a Photoshopped image."

"You're right Philo!" Josh said. "What does it mean?"

"My thought is that Selig Bronfman may be under the influence of a more powerful mind. I observed this same pattern with Roberto Marra." I showed the group my conversation with Marra, and we could all read his sig from that on the mental plane.

Kelleye spoke firmly. "We need to check on that. Do all of the new Uploads directors have sigs like Bronfman's?"

"I'll look into it. I have plenty of time now that I'm unemployed. This is dangerous, team. Somebody is fucking with the Grid and the Grid controls all comms worldwide. It's what Ralph would call a national security issue."

I looked at Joann. It was past 8 now, and I was getting hungry. "Kelleye, what do you say we knock off early tonight? Let's get something to eat and a good night's sleep for once." When Ralph wasn't ordering us around, Kelleye had become our unofficial leader. She had the most even temperament.

"All right. Everybody back here after work tomorrow."

We went home. Joann and I got carryout and, for the first time in weeks, talked companionably. I understood why she thought I treated her like a fuck-buddy. Because I did. I was horny and wanted sex.

I'm an ass.

— 25 —

That night I had a dream. A tall, charismatic figure suddenly arose to great popularity. Rashan Oliwan was seen at concerts, at political rallies, and on the news every day; always in the spotlight. A bright, smiling face who urged everyone to embrace a new religion, and a new politics. He called it a "coming together." His critics called him the AntiChrist. Rashan had brown skin, refined features, and looked a lot like paintings of Jesus Christ. He spoke in a lilting, almost hypnotic South Asian accent. He spoke of a real United Nations, and a planet united in peace and prosperity. All of the world's armies were to be dissolved. "Yes, it can be done!" he proclaimed. All weapons were to be banned, and national boundaries eliminated. He promised a bright, prosperous future for all citizens of earth in a voice and in a manner that said we could actually do it. He hinted at a powerful group of off-world brothers and sisters with undreamed of technology, waiting in the wings to solve the problems of scarce resources, pollution, and climate change. If only humanity would unite under the banner of Coming Together...

I woke up in a sweat. That was the realest dream I ever had. Rashan's ability to entrain the thoughts of huge crowds, even digitally on mass media, was astonishing. I knew that I was seeing into the very near future. Someone like Rashan Oliwan was coming.

I didn't mention my dream to my teammates. In the cold light of day it seemed stupid, yet I had a feeling of dread. First the flu shots, then the altered sigs of the Uploads directors, and now...what? More Collective meddling?

A couple of days later I saw a slick promo piece for an event in Chicago. It was called Coming Together for Peace. The lead speaker: a man who looked just like the one in my dream. The event was free; walk-ins were welcome. The event was scheduled for this Saturday evening at 7 p.m. Joann was flying through the weekend so there was nothing holding me in town.

I left Midland at 5:30 on Saturday and drove as fast as I could to Chicago, irrationally terrified at what I would see. When I got to the venue at 6:30 it was in a large open amphitheater used for outdoor concerts just off the Dan Ryan freeway. Hardly any people were there. The place could hold several thousand if everyone crowded in on the grass facing the stage. A multimedia presentation was playing on a huge flat panel while technicians were rigging the stage. It seemed much ado about nothing, and I relaxed.

About ten minutes later, a crowd of people came streaming in. By 7 there were at least a thousand. At 7:15 the event began as stragglers were still coming in. It was getting darker now in the warm May air. Suddenly a stage light came on and a man in a white robe began walking forward on the stage. It was the guy in my dream.

At that moment I felt a probe on the mental plane. My forward compartment was active and I let it in. A very pleasant music was playing in my head and I felt a peaceful vibe go through my body. Wow! Who or what was doing this? It sure wasn't the Jesus man on the stage.

I was so shocked I hardly heard what the speaker was saying. I was busy on the mental plane trying to find the source. It wasn't coming from anywhere within the venue, and I gave it up. The speaker was mesmerizing. Everyone was leaning forward with smiles on their faces, eagerly taking in the words of Jesus man, which were resonating inside my head.

I carefully analyzed the sigs in the crowd without approaching anyone closely. The mesmerizing voice resonated inside the mental spaces of all the sigs. Light, etheric music was accompanied by an inviting, semi-hypnotic but serene vibe. Was this one of those satellite-delivered remote neural monitoring operations? No. I knew how those programs had to operate from my Grid work. This was way more sophisticated, and it was using the mental plane. This must be a galactic operation!

The Collectives had indeed stepped up their Intervention on earth. Just as Patrick said they would.

Jesus man was still speaking. Brothers and sisters from the stars were coming to help humanity and solve our problems if we would only Come Together. This operation was entraining the minds of everyone in the crowd, and I could feel it in my own mind. I felt a sense of despair and urgency. I would have to drop my investigation of Bronfman and the Uploads directors. I would rely on Jamaal to do that as best he could. Jesus man would have to be investigated, and right away. I couldn't do it here.

After the event was over a bunch of lights came on around the stage so people could find their way out in the darkness. As people walked out I could feel the excited buzz of conversation. I got out of there as fast as I could and drove home to Midland faster than a drag queen fleeing a biker bar.

*T*wo days later just before 7, I went for a walk to clear my head. I had no idea what to do about the Come Together operation. I had located Jesus man's sig on the mental plane but I couldn't read it because he had a mental shield. This guy must be another galactic operative. According to the schedule I got in Chicago, another Come Together event was scheduled for New York at the beginning of June.

I saw Selig Bronfman walking down Fourth Street toward the Uploads building with a tall guy who looked like the guy in my dream. The two were walking away from me so I made out like I was jogging (Joann would laugh at that – I hate running) and passed them just before they reached a cement path that led to the Uploads entrance.

Selig Bronfman saw me and stopped, frowning, allowing me to get a good look at his companion. "What are you doing here Rothman?" Bronfman asked me. "I fired your friend Jamaal."

I ignored the Uploads director and addressed the tall man. "Has anyone ever told you that you look like Jesus Christ?" I almost addressed him as Rashan.

"All the time. Especially when I put on my white robe and let my hair down."

I had to laugh; the mental image he projected was perfect. I pointed toward Selig. "Why are you with this bozo?" I wanted to see Jesus' reaction to my criticism of Bronfman. While I asked I gently probed his sig on the mental plane. His sig had a strong galactic overlay. His shield was tight.

"Strictly business my friend," he said easily, and walked away. I noticed that Bronfman followed him as if his mind was entrained to Jesus man.

I turned around and began to walk back to the office. On a whim I sent a thought on the mental plane toward Walking Jesus just before he reached the Uploads entrance door: "Rashan Oliwan."

On the mental plane I saw Jesus whirl around and look at me, startling Bronfman. But only my forward compartment was exposed. I felt him probing as I strolled away innocently. Rashan was competent on the mental plane, but I had almost two years using my remote viewing abilities for hours every day. Oliwan suspected nothing.

I heard him say to Selig, "You have an interesting friend."

"He's not my friend," Bronfman snapped.

The last thing I heard before the door closed was Rashan's laugh. I was strangely drawn to him.

When I got back to the office the group was there, including Joann. She had arrived in Midland very late last night on her three-day break and had slept all day. "What just happened?" she asked me.

"Uh, I saw an interesting fellow walking with Bronfman."

Joann smiled. "Spill it, Philo."

So I told the group about my dream, my trip to Chicago last Saturday, and my encounter with Jesus.

Josh was angry. "Why didn't you tell us about what happened in Chicago? We're supposed to be a team."

Everyone looked at me accusingly.

"Because I have no idea what to do about it. I've spent the past two days thinking about it, but I got nothing."

"What is Jesus doing at Uploads?" Kelleye asked.

"I don't know that either."

Kelleye was curious. "Is his name really Rashan?"

"I'm not sure. I don't want to bust his sig until I have a plan. But he sure reacted when I sent him that thought."

We decided not to have our nightly meetings on the mental plane. Now we only met in the office within a tight shield we had set up around the building. Ralph had insisted: "We have been way too free with our comms."

Kelleye gave us a briefing. She was upset. "During my investigation of the Rebecca Holmes network I discovered that Rebecca and Chang Li-Meng have died under questioning by the Chinese military. Kathy Abbott has taken over for Rebecca at BioSciences. She even moved into Rebecca's house!"

Ralph took it stoically. "That's what happens when you screw up in one of these so-called elite networks. Holmes and Chang had it coming."

"You're ruthless and heartless, Ralph Zimring," Kelleye said to him. "We were partly responsible for their deaths."

"Life is tough when you're a scumbag, Kelleye. The solution is, don't be a scumbag."

I told Ralph about my dream, and about meeting Jesus.

"I had a similar, very vivid dream, but it wasn't about Rashan. You actually met this guy?"

"Yes. He looks South Asian, like someone from India. There's a strong resemblance to the religious paintings of Jesus Christ." I told him about the event in Chicago and showed the group his sig.

"Rashan's sig is even more altered than Bronfman's," Ralph said.

"Yup. External influence." I was frustrated. "The Collectives are using the mental plane to directly influence human actors!"

"All twelve U.S. Uploads directors have a sig overlay," Josh said to me. "Your friend Jamaal gave me the list and I checked them all out."

Kelleye was grim. "We have to find out how many human sigs have these overlays. We may have to deal with the galactics directly now because there may be too many human proxies for five people to control."

Ralph grinned. "That's right! Stop the influence at its source. Just like we did with that shipment of the new biotech."

I felt vindicated. "See? You guys say I'm impulsive but I'm not! I'm intuitive."

Josh snorted. "You jump at everything like a cat does when something moves. There's not an ounce of logic or reason behind it."

I pretended to lick my hand as a cat would lick its paw. "Let me investigate Jesus. I have a feeling something big is going to happen pretty soon with him."

When Joann and I got home I sat down on the couch in the living room and approached Jesus very carefully on the mental plane. Ralph was right: Jesus man's sig had an even more pronounced overlay than Selig Bronfman's or Roberto Marra's. Rashan's shield was a good one and I knew I would have to try the brute force method to get into his mind. I wanted to confront Jesus man physically, and for that I needed Josh.

When Josh and Kelleye arrived at the office after work the next day I told them what I wanted to do.

"We need to bust through that shield and find out who is behind him. There's another of these Come Together propaganda events in New York. We gotta nip this in the bud if we can."

Kelleye was apprehensive.

"I'm going to need Josh with me. My plan is to physically confront this Jesus look-alike as we did with Genghis Glazer."

"If you hurt Rashan in any way, Philo, I'll never speak to you again," Kelleye said.

I nodded. "Understood. But Ralph is right, Kelleye. We have to act quickly before Jesus can get his Come Together campaign in high gear. You've seen the schedule of events."

"What do you say, Josh?" Kelleye asked.

"I agree with Philo, love. The Collectives are opening a new offensive on the mental plane and Rashan is clearly under their influence."

Kelleye sighed. "I suppose you're right. But I don't like it." She looked up at Josh. "I want to come with you."

I shook my head. "It could get ugly. Jesus looks very fit and his reactions are lightning fast." I remembered the way he had turned around almost effortlessly, in a split second.

"Do you think he has martial arts training?" Josh asked hopefully. Josh was eager to test himself against Rashan.

"Philo!" Kelleye said. She looked at me accusingly. "You're not to put Josh in danger."

"Yes ma'am."

"Men are hopeless," Kelleye said, seeing how excited Josh was for a fight.

I nodded to Josh. "Tomorrow we confront fake Jesus."

The next morning was a Saturday. I was up at five because I couldn't sleep; I was too excited about confronting Jesus man. I located Rashan on the mental plane. He was staying at the Radisson downtown, Room 1910.

Why not attack now? I thought about it for a second, and rejected it. Two was better than one, and we could exert physical as well as mental pressure by confronting him in person. I texted Josh: "Meet me at the Radisson in the lobby at 7 a.m."

Rashan was going to meet with Selig again at Uploads at 10 a.m., but I couldn't read Rashan's sig enough to know why. Josh and I would have an early breakfast in the hotel restaurant, and get fake Jesus just as he left his room.

When I told Josh he just laughed. "And what if someone is in the hallway?"

"Who cares? We're hotel security, investigating a possible crime-in-progress."

Josh laughed again. "For God's sake Philo! You use the brute force method don't you? There's nothing subtle about that plan."

I was thinking more like Ralph now. "Fuck subtlety. We're going to breach the walls and find out who is running Jesus man."

Josh and I were at the Radisson restaurant when it opened at 7. We ate breakfast and waited around until 8. Josh looked at his watch.

"Let's stand in the hallway next to his door in case he comes out early," I said.

Josh shook his head. That was Philo all the way, he thought. They would probably meet up with real hotel security.

I caught Josh's thought but I wasn't thinking about anything except confronting Mr. Jesus. Josh could see I was totally focused and I could tell he was fired up for a confrontation. We took the elevator to the 19th floor and got out.

"As soon as he opens the door, attack on the mental plane."

We walked into the hallway and stood a few feet from Room 1910. We had to wait another ten minutes before the door to Room 1910 opened. Both of us recognized Rashan's sig, but Josh asked me to back off. 'I want to see what this guy's got.' As the door opened Josh went first and muscled Rashan into the room.

Rashan smiled at me. "So. My friend from yesterday." He looked supremely confident. "And his sidekick."

Instead of a battle on the mental plane we spoke out loud. "What's your game, fake Jesus?" Josh asked.

Rashan flexed his arms and hands, as if ready for physical combat. "That's for me to know and you to find out."

I almost didn't see Josh, he moved so fast. A kick with his left leg to the groin and a punch with his right fist to the head. Rashan somehow dodged both blows. He stood back and laughed. Then he moved equally quickly by turning his body and kicking out with his left leg to Josh's midsection, which Josh was able to avoid.

"Crap," Josh said. "You're reading my moves on the mental plane from my conscious mind, and I'm reading yours. This is pointless."

"As long as the two fighters are closely matched in skill, yes." Rashan relaxed and walked over to the suite's kitchen. "I have green tea, soda, and coffee. Which will you have, gentlemen?"

"I'll have a soda," I said.

"Green tea," Josh said. "Do you know the tea ceremony?"

Rashan bowed. "I am a student. Perhaps one day I'll perform it for you."

The situation would have been unreal to anyone not familiar with the mental plane. Enemies to friends in a few seconds? Josh and Rashan had exchanged thoughts and had come to a truce. Josh's more laid-back personality was OK with this but I was not.

207

I confronted Josh on the mental plane. 'Have you forgotten what we came here to do?'

Rashan smiled, picking up on this. I wasn't trying to hide anything. "That won't be necessary, gentlemen," he said calmly, sitting down at the suite's kitchen table. Josh and I sat across from Rashan. "I'll open my mind to you."

Our adversary closed his eyes and I felt his shield go down. Suspicious, I probed deeply. Rashan was wide open, so I rushed in.

Rashan Oliwan, 28 years old (I was right!). Born in India to an American mother and a Buddhist father. Family moved to Belgium when he was ten, moved to the US five years later. Attended MIT, member of the MIT debate club; a compelling speaker. Studied martial arts in Boston. A year ago, had a vivid dream (just like mine) about a new future for earth. A vision of the galaxy that showed benign races about to contact humanity and welcome us into the galactic family. Rashan let me into the dream. It was just as real as the one I had about him.

I showed Rashan (and Josh) a summary of my personal experiences with the galactics and their Collectives. "The Collectives are using a false narrative to promote themselves as humanity's saviors. What they really want is good little drones who won't rock the boat." Unfortunately I couldn't tell Rashan about the advanced network, and how it has to remain hidden from the rest of the galaxy. That would have made my story more believable, for the Collectives were palming themselves off as much more advanced in consciousness.

Rashan sat back in his chair. "That's an interesting theory, Philogene. But look at my contacts with Sister Sani and Brother Hamal." In Rashan's dream, Sani and Hamal were idealized and spiritually advanced beings who presented themselves as typical citizens on a typical planet.

"Rashan," Josh said, "Sani and Hamal are just avatars! They aren't real."

We showed Rashan the conflict between the Hilarion and the Fenachrone trading Collectives, and how almost every planet in the Greater Community had been coerced to join one of them.

Rashan was having none of it. "My friend, you are too earthbound in your beliefs. You have allowed petty human hatreds and parochial concepts of conflict to influence your judgment."

We sat there exchanging a blizzard of information on the mental plane at the speed of thought. Nothing Josh or I presented made a difference. The damnable thing was that Rashan was perfectly reasonable to believe the galactics' story. It was compelling, and the wonderful vibe in Rashad's dream was exactly what Josh and I had experienced during our training on Celeste. Even when I showed him the Maitre in the underground TAC lab, Rashan had a good answer.

"Yes, Brother Hamal showed me the degraded races and those who employ them for personal gain." Rashan smiled beatifically. "Rest assured, the galactics will protect us from these privateers."

He presented us with a vision of a galaxy united in peace, and with advanced technology that would quickly solve our energy and pollution problems. "The Rejuvenon shots are just the beginning, Philogene. Sister Sani showed me their psychological therapy methods. Absolutely brilliant! No more mental illness."

Not even the sterilization changed Rashan's mind. "No one is forcing the shots on anyone. And population reduction will help solve the pollution problem."

I had no argument against that. Finally I said, "Rashan, what you have seen is just a dream!"

Rashan gave me a sympathetic smile. "Yet you had a similar dream that led you to me. You even knew my name."

I raised my hands in the air and gave it up.

"Philogene, do you think you and I are the only ones who have had these visions?"

"I...why, I've never thought about it." I could see Josh was also startled by this possibility. Then I remembered Ralph telling me that he had had one too.

"Several of my friends have had them, but none quite so powerful as mine. I intend to embrace the visitors when they come."

I looked despairingly at Josh. It was time to go.

As we walked out of Room 1910 and down the hallway to the elevator, Josh said, "Just what we need, another cult."

"I'm afraid you're right. Rashan is just the kind of true believer to start one."

"Where is this going, Philo? Miracle-working biotech, remote-controlled sigs, and now cult leaders with dream visions?"

I remembered what Patrick had told me at our last meeting. "It's open season here on earth, Josh. Who knows what these Collectives will do next."

"Yeah. We're finding out all their tricks."

Joann was there when Josh and I got back to the office. The three of us continued the search for any human with an altered sig. I confirmed for myself that all of the directors at Uploads had them. We began to find dozens of people whose sigs were altered in some way. All of them were Uploads-connected influencers, or people associated with TAC. Kathy Abbott's sig was now altered as well.

I was getting really scared. How can you fight an invisible enemy who can remotely influence people?

At the end of the day Ralph walked into the office with bad news. "The biotech is still being distributed. Rebecca Holmes and Chang Li-Meng are dead, but Austin Matthews got Kathy Abbott to pick up a new shipment of the product."

"That makes sense," I said. "Abbott is now dealing directly with galactics so her sig is influenced."

"I can't get a read on who is controlling these Upload sigs," Joann said, frustrated.

"Neither can I. Whoever is doing it is awfully good on the mental plane. Probably the galactics are using Seers."

We were all bummed. Ralph's Op had given the Collectives a temporary setback with the biotech, but they had countered that pretty quickly and were now mounting a new information psyop. Everyone started venting our frustrations.

"The Collectives can reprogram human minds to whatever narrative they want," Joann said to me. "What you saw in Chicago confirms that. It looks like 'Come Together' is the party line."

"And they are doing it remotely!"

"It's unreal," Kelleye remarked.

Josh shrugged. "Unreal to human beings. These Collectives have been around for millions of years."

"We know how to influence minds on the mental plane. The Collectives are obviously a lot better at it than we are."

Kelleye broke in and stopped the conversation. "Everybody take the weekend off and relax," she ordered. "I'm tired of thinking about this stuff. Josh and I are going to have some fun in Chicago this weekend. Let's meet back here on Monday."

Kelleye and Josh left the office.

I saw that Joann was sitting on one of the office sofas, her head in her hands, the picture of dejection. I walked over and sat across from her. I didn't say anything and didn't try to comm with her on the mental plane. We had been using the spoken word for the past month. During the times we worked the mental plane we stayed separate, just doing our jobs.

"I've been miserable this past month," she said. "I've had plenty of opportunities to be with someone else, but I just can't do it."

"Neither can I. Let's be honest, we fit together very well." I tried to make a joke. "If you weren't so irritating, our relationship would be perfect."

I saw her lips twitching. "Screw you, Philo."

"I think that's a good idea."

Suddenly all the tension between us exploded out of us. We almost ran to our apartment a mile away, screaming and laughing, letting off steam. When we got to the apartment Joann dragged me into her bedroom. We made mad love and rolled over in bed like two flashbangs that had just detonated and dissipated all of their energy.

"You're an ass, Philogene. But you're a really, really good lover," Joann said.

I ticked off all the things I liked about her. "You have a sense of humor, you're fearless, you don't get hung up on my swearing even though you don't like it, you aren't moody. And you have a life independent of me, and friends of your own. I like that a lot. And mainly, you put up with my shit."

She laughed. "There's a lot of it to put up with."

"I'll admit that's true." I stroked her hair and looked in her eyes. "I understand that I'm selfish and impulsive. I'm going to do stuff that's pretty stupid; it's my nature. I know I haven't appreciated you enough, Joann; I've taken you for granted. Maybe we can start over."

She smiled and let me into her mental space. "All right. I'd like to try anyway."

That night we didn't go out. We spent hours talking out our relationship and taking down our mental shields.

"You've taken me for granted, Philo, but I haven't been willing to fully open up to you. That's one thing I like about you. You have no problem giving yourself to me totally. As a woman I appreciate that." She flicked her finger on my head. "Even though you're a jerk."

We both laughed. Our energies fit together, we could both feel it. On the mental plane our sigs were almost entirely congruent.

I saw that marriage and kids were in the back of Joann's mind. I wasn't ready for that yet. That might be a stumbling point. But for now it was OK.

Finally we rolled over and Joann went to sleep. I lay in bed, thinking.

My demon has forced me to be a loner. I don't want to share too much of myself with others because I don't want them to even get a glimpse of it. Yet I don't want to isolate myself from my fellow human beings. I don't have any friends, really, other than Jamaal and Mila, and Mila is married.

211

Joann is more extroverted than me, and keeps in touch with her old friends from school and her fellow pilots in the courier company she works for. Josh keeps tabs on his studio back in DC and advises Jack on how to run the place. He often talks to his former students and his fellow martial arts enthusiasts at the dojo where he works out. In addition, he has his new students to work with. Kelleye occasionally talks to her old school friends as well. Ralph has so many contacts it would make up a small city. He probably knows half the people in Midland.

I am the isolated one. Me and my Maitre.

I occasionally thought of Gwenneth, but she was beyond me. Sometimes I longed for her, but it was hopeless. It was Joann or no one. One intimate contact I could give myself to; someone who could confront the fact that I was possessed.

I decided to keep in contact with Jamaal. I would try to develop that friendship more if I could.

On Sunday night I got a call from Ralph Zimring. Joann and I were watching a movie. "Turn on 60 Minutes. Do it now and then meet me in the office after the program."

Rashan Oliwan was the subject.

"A new religious cult has been forming in many cities across the country," the narrator said. Footage of groups holding signs and chanting were shown: "Welcome to the new world," one of the signs said. "Rejuvenon is a gift," another said. "ETs are real!" "The visitors are here."

Rashan was giving a speech to a large crowd in New York, announcing that Contact was imminent.

"...in 1997, astronomer and astrophysicist Carl Sagan wrote the novel Contact, which was made into a best-selling film that attracted worldwide audiences. Sagan wrote about an alien being that appeared in human form. In the book, a spacecraft was built according to information received at the SETI program, sent from the star system Vega about 26 light-years away. Ladies and gentlemen, the truth is far simpler than that.

"Just as in the Star Wars movies, the galaxy is filled with intelligent life. Unlike those movies, our galactic friends want what is best for us. We are about to be gifted with amazing technology that will solve our energy and pollution problems. Rejuvenon is just the beginning!"

[wild cheering]

"Representatives from the Galactic Collectives will soon appear to us," he said. "When they do, let us welcome them with open arms." Rashan winked. "Those of you who are having the vivid dreams know what I'm talking about."

The narrator showed three other speakers giving similar speeches: one in Paris, one in Beijing, and the other in Sao Paulo.

"Is Rashan Oliwan a prophet as he claims, or a dangerous cult leader? One thing is certain: the Coming Together movement is growing larger all over the world..."

"A bunch of nutjobs," Joann said after the program was over. "No one will believe that."

"I think they will. Mass media are publicizing these events because it's so crazy. It generates views. Rashan and the other speakers are articulate and physically attractive." I showed Joann my experience in Chicago with Rashan. "The sigs of the audience were all entrained to the message." I showed her on the mental plane about the soothing music and the pleasant, peaceful vibe in everyone's mind.

"Oh my God. How are the galactics working this mind influencing?"

"Oh, I just remembered. Ralph wants us down at the office to talk about that. We better get going or he'll break down our door."

When we arrived Josh and Kelleye were already there.

"We're going to monitor Rashan on the mental plane tonight," Ralph said. "Somehow the galactics are influencing this guy and I want to know how."

When Ralph speaks like that everyone falls into line, even Kelleye. So we ordered pizza and watched the Rashan Show live from New York. During his speech the minds of the audience were being entrained to the message just like in Chicago. But we couldn't tell where the influence was coming from.

After his speech Rashan partied in his New York hotel suite. Some of his "flock" were there, as well as hangers-on. All of Rashan's people had the sig overlays, which was probably how their sigs were being entrained to the message. "This is pointless," Kelleye said. "Let's go home."

I insisted we stick around until after Rashan went to sleep.

Joann was curious. "Why?"

"A hunch. I'm supposed to be a Seer. I'm Seeing."

Ralph laughed. "OK kid. I'll stick around with Philo if the rest of you want to hit the sack."

"We're a team," Josh said. "We stick together."

By 2 a.m. Rashan still hadn't gone to bed. He was holding forth to some newbies about the Come Together movement.

Rashan was still up at 3 a.m, being magnetically attractive to several women who were still hanging around.

"I wish this egomaniac would go to sleep," Josh grumbled. "I have a long day tomorrow at my dojo." Josh had sold his DC center to his assistant Jack and started another one here in Midland.

By 4 a.m. everyone left. Rashan finally fell into bed about 4:30.

When Rashan fell asleep we saw his sig gradually rise up out of his body. Rashan's sig was just one of a group that had staffed and attended the Come Together lecture. All of them were approaching a beautiful multicolored sphere of light on the mental plane.

"Good call, Philogene," Ralph said.

"What is that thing?" Josh asked. "I feel a pull toward it."

"I do too," Joann said.

"It's like a sig magnet," Kelleye said.

We saw Rashan and his group of sigs approach the sphere. There were several dozen of the sigs, and they all entered the brilliant sphere of light like sleepwalkers. They were watching a light show.

After several minutes, one by one the sigs left the sphere and went back to their bodies in the dream state.

"So that's how they do it," Josh said. "In the dream state you are wide open on the mental plane."

"When they wake up they will think they had a very lucid dream," Joann said.

I looked at her, startled. "Maybe that's how the Collectives got Rashan!"

"It looks like some kind of psychological programming operation," Kelleye said.

Joann, normally sunny and cheerful, was depressed. "We're too dumb to compete with galactics."

"We need to jump inside that sphere," Ralph said. "See what this show is all about."

"One of us has to stay behind," Kelleye said. "Someone who is uninfluenced."

Ralph kicked himself. "I should have thought of that. I'll stay behind."

I was eager to go in. Me, Joann, Kelleye, and Josh approached the sphere. It looked like a glitzy neon sign at a carnival. It had no shield.

"It's a trap!" I said, mimicking Admiral Ackbar.

We got in easily and felt a comforting mental and emotional vibe, similar to the one I had experienced in Chicago. A beautiful multi-sensory presentation showed us a galaxy filled with benevolent brothers and sisters on other planets, waiting to accept the human race into a peaceful and prosperous Greater Community. Sister Sani (dressed in a white robe) told us that Representatives are appearing to "sensitized" humans with information about radical new concepts in physics, medicine, technology, and politics.

"These Representatives will show you how to organize people within a peaceful, collectivist society that will finally put an end to war, poverty, and injustice," Sani said.

"Join us, brothers and sisters," said Brother Hamal, "in a Coming Together with your friends and neighbors from the stars!"

Brother Hamal! Sister Sani! I couldn't believe how wrong my beliefs were. Why, the Collectives were here to introduce a benevolent society that would forever end hatred and harmful competition. Under the direction of our friends from the stars, humanity would find its true place in the galaxy of planets!

I would have to tell Jamaal about what I had learned. Joann and Kelleye and Josh were very happy. For the first time in our lives there was no tension. All was well.

We were back in the office, chatting happily.

Ralph's jaw dropped farther and farther. I was on my phone, ringing Rashan. I wanted to ask him if I could say a few words at his next event. Suddenly my phone was wrenched out of my hand. I found myself against the wall of the office. Ralph slapped me across the face, hard. A thought penetrated my sig: "YOU HAVE BEEN MIND WASHED."

Suddenly I snapped out of it. I stared, appalled, at Ralph. "Thank you, commander." Joann, Kelleye, and Josh were very upset. Josh came at Ralph, but Ralph smacked him down to the floor and entered his mind with the warning. Ralph had learned his lessons well: keep it simple. I warned Kelleye and Joann with a huge burst into their sigs.

We all found our seats again. Josh was bleeding from a cut on his scalp. My face was showing red where Ralph had slapped me. But none of us were thinking about that.

Ralph's face was grim. "These galactics understand the human psyche better than we do."

"I can understand why Rashan fell for it," I said.

Everyone went home feeling shocked.

That night I dreamed about the presentation I had seen in the mindwasher. When I woke up I had doubts about my objections to the Collectives. Then my true memories all came flooding back to me. I understood that the sig mind-washer was built to insert false memories and emotions that would replace the true ones.

I sat up in bed, unable to sleep. Joann was beside me, still sleeping. I didn't disturb her.

Patrick was right when he said that the Collectives would use methods we had never heard of before. God help us! Sigs in the dream state would never question the experience. And they would wake up subconsciously accepting whatever the Collectives programmed them to think and do.

— 26 —

Now that we knew what to look for, we took a survey of the mental plane. We saw dozens of the mind washers all over the world, with the same message. It was unreal, because we hadn't seen them before. Sigs were going in there in the dream state like little kids to a glitzy circus.

"They aren't hiding them," Joann said. "They're right out in the open, like a drive-in theater screen."

"Yeah, except no one can see them awake except us."

The sigs going into the mind washers were all typical undeveloped human sigs.

"Josef Goebbels would be envious," Josh said.

We tried to find a way to neutralize the mind washers on the mental plane, but we were like squirrels trying to figure out how a mobile phone works. They were just programmed areas of space and they had no access points.

"We have to watch how they put them up," Ralph suggested. "One of us has to monitor the mental plane 24 hours a day."

"What if they have always been there?" Kelleye asked. "Can the mind-washers be programmed? What would happen if that programming was turned toward evil ends?"

My jaw dropped. "Are you talking about demonic possession and the dark arts?"

"Throughout human history a certain percentage of human beings have always been antisocial. Evil may be just a programmed antisocial activity."

We were all disturbed by that idea.

"Kelleye may be right that the sig mindwashers have always been here," Josh said. "Recorded human history is only about 6,000 years old. That's a long time for us, but it's about 3 microseconds in the history of the galaxy."

"If Kel is right, all the Collectives had to do is put in new programming for the Come Together bullshit."

We went home and tried to process the new information. We didn't have our nightly meetings for the next week. Even Ralph was feeling discouraged. I did nothing but play disk golf.

I had another vivid dream. At first I thought I was being brainwashed by one of the mind washers, and I panicked and woke up. When I went back to sleep I saw Patrick, Gwenneth, and my three teammates. We were sitting in a conference room on Celeste. On the mental plane – which is basically what the dream state is – when you meet with people you always appear in the form of your physical body even though it's just a projection of your consciousness. But it still feels as real as physical reality.

'So, you made it,' Patrick sent to me.

Behind him stood Gwenneth. My heart ached a little for her, the most beautiful, exquisite creature I had ever seen. 'What are you two doing here?' I asked.

I couldn't keep my eyes off Gwenneth. I could tell that Joann was getting upset. Joann was great, but….

'You're a jerk, Philo,' she sent.

Patrick interrupted our spat. 'That's enough earthians, pay attention. Your mindwashers, as you call them, are programmed sig attractors. Their purpose is to subtly influence the minds of a large population to the will of the Collectives.'

'What about non-interference?' I asked.

Patrick grimaced. 'You negated that with your little stunt on Beta Caronai. How do you think the Collectives were able to program the attractors so successfully? They got all the codes to the human psyche from you.'

'Fuck you Patrick, you don't have to rub it in.'

'It's a painful lesson learned, Philogene. More important than that, your work on the mental plane has alarmed the Collectives. They have united to defeat your nascent freedom movement before it gets started. '

'I understand,' Josh sent. 'The Hilarion and the Fenachrone are cooperating to negate the threat to their systems.'

'That's right. You can still win, but there is only one solution now. The price you will have to pay is appalling.'

Josh frowned. Only one solution? What did Patrick mean by that?

My eyes kept straying to Gwenneth and Joann gave me a dirty look. This was the woman who had saved my life.

'You're looking much better, Philogene,' Gwenneth said. She used the more formal 'Philogene' instead of the more intimate 'Philo.' The memory of me lying in the hospital bed on Celeste after my battle with the Maitre was there between us; she holding my bony hand as my mostly dead body fought for life. We both knew it was her love for me that had pulled me through. I saw Joann's eyes widen in understanding.

Gwenneth assumed a detached, professional air. 'There is no physical defense against the attractors, as you probably understand by now.'

'I never thought our enemies would fight like this,' I said. 'It's not fair! It's invisible psychological warfare.'

'Fairness has nothing to do with it, Philogene.' Gwenneth looked at Patrick. 'My uncle told you that you can't fight galactics, but that might not be true anymore.'

She looked at me. 'The Collectives are fully committed now. You will see, as the days go by, more and more human beings accepting their propaganda. Any explanation you try to make to your fellow humans about the agenda of the Collectives will simply not be believed.'

Patrick sighed. 'It's standard operating procedure for emerging races like yours. To you it seems novel and frightening, but the Collectives have been doing this for millions of years.'

'So we have failed,' Josh said.

Patrick looked grim. 'No, Joshua. You have just begun. The Collectives are preparing you for your real mission.'

'What is that? You said there is only one solution.'

'I did. Unfortunately the advanced planets are not allowed to mentor emerging planets. But here's a hint: There is something you are missing, and it is right in front of your face. It's so obvious we shouldn't have to tell you.'

Joann, Kelleye, Josh, and I were baffled. Patrick was being too vague but I knew he wouldn't give us anything else.

'Can you guys see into the future?' I asked.

Gwenneth looked at Patrick. 'In a sense that has nothing to do with time, Philogene. We see potentials. If you continue on your present path there is a strong probability that you will meet up with some nasty galactic operators.'

'You are a Seer, Philogene,' Patrick said. 'Use your intuition.'

I could see Gwenneth's fear for me. If she was afraid, it was going to be pretty bad. The dream ended.

219

I woke up and looked at my bedroom clock. It was just before 6 a.m. on Saturday morning. Joann must have come in during the night; she was in bed next to me.

"Did I just have a dream or were we talking to Patrick and Gwenneth?"

"I was there."

Josh and Kelleye came in on the mental plane. 'Everybody have breakfast and let's meet in the office at 10,' Kelleye sent.

Joann and I got to the office a half-hour early. "Tell me about you and Gwenneth," she said. "I was on pilot training after your encounter with the Maitre."

I shared everything with her on the mental plane.

"I understand, Philo. Gwenneth's love saved your life."

I nodded. "Yes. The bond between us transcends life itself." I spoke bitterly. "But our love can never be. When Gwenneth saved my life she defied the Celestian Council, who had ordered my termination."

Joann swore, something she never did.

"I understand why the Celestian Council did it. At that time I was wholly under the influence of the Maitre. I was like a person with a deadly infectious disease of the soul. I was quarantined in that medbed for months because I was too dangerous to Celestian society. Gwenneth shielded me from it, but not even the Celestians could extract that demon from my psyche." I straightened in my chair and sipped my coffee. "She has never told me what it cost her. Imagine shielding me from that thing for weeks and weeks until I got better."

I saw a look of despair on Joann's face. "So I'll always be second best. I can't compete with such an advanced being."

"Neither can I."

Joann smiled weakly. "We're both in the same boat then."

"Yes, Joann. We're both just humans." I tried to smile. "We have to stick together."

Suddenly she smiled and jumped out of her chair. Her normally sunny personality was coming to the fore. I needed that.

"You're mine, little man, for better or for worse."

"Is that a proposal?"

"If you want it to be."

At that moment Kelleye and Josh entered the room. "Are we interrupting anything?" Kelleye asked, looking with interest at both of us.

I nodded to Joann. "Later."

Both of us would have to forget about Gwenneth. She was part of an Advanced Planets society that had a hundred thousand more years of evolution than we did.

The next day after work we sent our group mind out on the mental plane and looked at the attractors. They were all the same: broadcasting stations that influenced human sigs in the dream state, and even during meditation, or times of daydreaming. We could find no clue how they were set up or who had put them there. We only knew one thing: they were galactic in origin, and totally invisible to the naked eye.

'Let's look for anything unusual that could be the source of the attractors,' I sent.

We did a meticulous survey of the mental plane around earth. There was only one other anomaly. 'Look at that heavily shielded area,' Josh sent. 'What is it?'

'It's at Lagrange Point 4,' Joann sent. 'A stable, gravitationally neutral area that attracts natural objects. It also has a transportal that I use to get to Celeste.'

'Let's see what it looks like. Somebody doesn't want us to find it.'

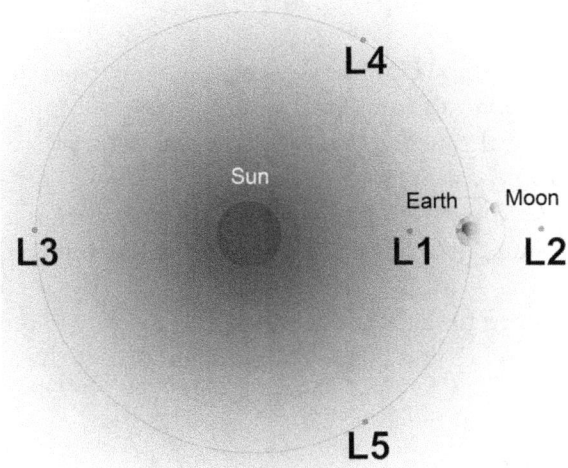

It was a heavily shielded spherical satellite masquerading as a trojan asteroid, hiding from telescopes behind a chunk of space rock.

'Clever,' Joann sent. 'Is that the source of the attractors?'

'We'd better find out,' Josh sent.

'Remember what Gwenneth said,' Kelleye sent. 'Approach carefully. We may have to deal with some nasty galactics.'

We cautiously approached the satellite at L4 on the mental plane. We tried several times to break its shield, but it was far too strong.

Kelleye was getting nervous. 'Let's get out of here.'

We went back inside our shielded office space. Ralph was there, sitting on the carpet with his back against the wall.

I opened the discussion. "We can't access the satellite on the mental plane, but we can from Joann's lifter. Ralph could help us."

Kelleye's eyes widened. Here was more Philo madness. "That's insane, Philo. How would we physically attack a galactic facility?"

"Ralph could find us a weapon. We are under attack by ruthless corporate Collectives. We primitives have the right to fight back."

"Fools tread where angels fear to go," Joann said. But I could tell that the idea intrigued her.

"Wait a minute," Kelleye said. "Philo, you've been inside one of these galactic vessels. You must remember how to enter them."

I thought rapidly out loud. "Well, Ship was just a standard Class IV cargo vessel, with an entrance that could only be opened from inside the ship."

"It's the same with the ships I piloted on Celeste," Joann said. "All of them only open from the inside."

"These damn galactics! How do you get into a craft from the outside if you can only access the controls from the inside?"

"You have to use the mental plane to activate the entry door," Josh replied. "We can't do that because the satellite is shielded."

"Of course. We can't crack the shield so our only option is a physical attack. We have to shut down those attractors before the human race gets brainwashed!"

Ralph had opened his eyes and was listening intently to the conversation.

"There's no evidence that this satellite is the source of the attractors," Josh countered.

"What else could it be?"

Josh couldn't answer that.

I looked at Joann. "Do you want to do this? Without you it's a no-go."

Joann looked at Kelleye and the two women commed on the mental plane.

"It's up to you, Joann," Kelleye said to the group with an air of resignation to the inevitable. "We all trust your judgment."

"I'll think about it."

"Do the Collectives use attractors to brainwash their populations?" Ralph asked.

"They can't, because attractors don't work on galactics," Josh said. "Galactic sigs are too developed."

Ralph was encouraged by this. "So fuck them. We'll start a revolution! We take out that satellite, our problems are solved."

Josh laughed. "You make it sound so easy."

"I never speak lightly, Joshua. I have a team to back me up." Ralph explained about his network of former military men and mercenaries. "My bet is these galactics have forgotten how to fight a kinetic war. Their warfare is all sixth generation: propaganda, mind influencing, psychological persuasion on the mental plane. Destroying that satellite is our first priority."

When Ralph speaks like that I get excited. "We're useless to you in actual physical fighting, except maybe for Josh."

Ralph laughed at the shocked expression on Kelleye's face. "Don't worry kid, Josh is far too valuable to waste in combat. If I get killed, there's still the four of you."

Kelleye relaxed. "Thank you Ralph. You aren't nearly as beastly as you look."

This set Ralph laughing. I feared for the window glass as the walls shook. "I'm in my element in combat. You guys are the mental plane experts; stick to that. Joann, are you up for a little recon? We need intel before my men can attack physically."

"That's what we just did. We didn't find out anything."

"That's because you didn't have me along. We need to physically scout the territory before we can make a battle plan."

Joann's eyes lit up. It would be a chance to fly her lifter.

The four of us looked at each other. "What if they vaporize our ship?" Kelleye asked.

"That's not permitted," Josh said. "Kinetic war is forbidden in this area of the galaxy, especially against emerging planets. None of the Collectives would risk it for fear of attack by other Collectives."

"What do you say, Kelleye?" I asked.

The group would do nothing unless Kelleye gave the OK. "Joann, it's your decision. It's your lifter and you are the pilot."

"Well, I really have been wanting to fly it again. It's just gathering dust at the Midland Municipal Airport."

I jumped on that. "It's settled then! As soon as Ralph gives the OK we can leave."

223

Kelleye shook her head. "All right. But it's all or nothing. We all go or no one goes."

Ralph had a pained expression on his face. I knew him better than anyone because I had been deep in his mind when I trained him. He was OK with Joann because she was an experienced pilot, but he saw no purpose for Kelleye, an academic, on a scouting mission. Or myself, who might do something stupid. However, he said nothing and I was grateful. I didn't want any tension in our group dynamic. Ralph could be tactful when he wanted to and he understood people better than I did.

It had worked out great with Ralph. We now had an ally in the field. Despite the odds against us, I felt a faint sense of optimism. But I was still worried about what Patrick said. "You can still win, but there is only one solution now. The price you will have to pay is appalling." What did he mean?

I called Ralph that night. "Joann says we have to do it on Friday because she has to fly on Saturday."

"Woo-hoo! This landlubber is ready. I've never been in space before."

I consulted with the group that evening after work at the office. "Upon mature consideration," Kelleye summed up, "this is the stupidest thing we have ever done." We all agreed. Even so, she gave the OK.

I called Ralph. "We meet tomorrow at the Midland Airport, E-22, at the south end, at 7 a.m."

Joann and I went back to our apartment and spent most of the night making love. We were back in tune.

"Jesus Joann, you surely are a fine woman," I said, looking her over appreciatively after one of our love-making sessions. She was built on Amazonian lines, but I had learned to appreciate her body and make it respond to me.

I saw a hesitant look on her face. "Yes?"

"Do you still think of Gwenneth?"

I sighed. "The memories are there, but...I'm too busy to engage in fantasies." I ran my hand up her leg. "And you are drop-dead gorgeous."

"Come here then," she said, opening her arms.

Tomorrow we would get as close to that galactic platform as we could. I remembered the look on Gwenneth's face when she told us to expect nasty galactic operators. I tried not to think about it.

— 27 —

Joann and I got up at 6. We had only gotten a couple hours sleep. We quickly drank two cups of hot coffee each and ate a hot microwave meal. It was the end of May but the night was unusually cold. "Are you ready for today, Space Pilot?'

Joann's face lit up. "Yes!"

"I'm trying not to think about what might happen."

Joann frowned. "That's not like you, Philo. You're usually ready for anything."

I looked at her affectionately. "Today is different. Now I have something to lose."

I could see her quick intake of breath. "I feel the same way."

"C'mon," I said angrily. "Let's get out of here before I start smashing stuff." Me and my Maitre were ready to fuck something up if anything threatened Joann.

We drove quickly in my cold vehicle to the Midland airport. My car heater wasn't too efficient. Kelleye and Josh were already there in Kelleye's car. I could tell they were snug and warm. Just then, Ralph drove up in an unbelievably old and beat up Ford.

Josh laughed. "That thing is falling apart!"

Ralph patted the car affectionately. "Don't insult Arthur. He's seen me through more trouble than an anti-vaxxer at a Pfizer board meeting."

Joann's craft was parked in a space reserved for helicopters and VTL craft. There was a tiny unheated garage next to the lifter, just large enough to contain Joann's four standard-issue biosuits. It was dark and cold.

Ralph opened his trunk and took out a heavy black bag. "My bio suit."

We entered Joann's lifter sensibly, like human beings should. Joann had a remote which activated an entry door on the side of the vehicle.

"I'm not putting on this thing until it gets warmer in here," I said stubbornly as I handled the freezing cold biosuit.

Josh was laughing. He was already halfway into his suit. "Suit yourself, Mr. Wimpy."

Joann walked to the pilot's chair and quickly activated the atmospheric controls. Almost immediately I felt warmth coming from the floor, the ceiling, and the sides of the craft. "Thanks honey," I said to Joann and began clambering into my suit. Ralph was already in his suit; I helped Joann into hers. Her helmet (also from Celeste) fit over the CAT control hemi at the back of her head.

There were four seats along the side of the craft. We all sat down. The lifter had transparencies at the front and along the sides.

Joann spoke to the flight controller. "YMMS-66A ready for takeoff."

"D'Arcy! Haven't heard from you in a while."

"Hernandez! Nice to talk to you again. Special assignment. If I tell you anything I get shitcanned. You know how it goes."

"I do indeed. All right YMMS-66A, you are cleared for takeoff."

We had been doing so much work on the mental plane I forgot how awesome it is to get physically off the ground. Joann placed the back of her head on the control hemi. The lifter went slowly up until we were a thousand feet or so in the air. Then the earth literally disappeared in less than a second. It was awesome! This thing was inertialess and we literally felt no g-pull at all.

I'm glad you know where you're going, pilot D'Arcy,' I sent to her.

Joann was all business. There's a lot of junk floating above the earth in addition to the thousands of satellites connected to the Grid. But we were beyond all that now, heading to Lagrange Point 4, a distance about the same as the distance to the sun from earth. I didn't see anything; space was just a blackness with the sun a yellow tennis ball to my left. We were approaching a big chunk of space rock that had been trapped within the equilibrium point. Behind it was the galactic space platform. My Maitre was getting excited and I was starting to sweat within my temperature-controlled suit.

We rounded the space rock and saw the platform, a spherical satellite with a diameter of at least 500 feet.

"Big enough to hide an army in there," Ralph said. "Pilot, can you take us around the satellite?"

Joann did so in two great circles, one around the poles and another along the equator. There was nothing but a dull gray, perfectly smooth surface, probably made of Synthfab. We felt the shield on the mental plane.

"There are no ships protecting the satellite. No weapons ports, no protrusions," Ralph observed

"Now what?" Kelleye asked Ralph.

I tried to make a joke. "It looks too boring to be the death star."

"Try entry on the mental plane," Ralph said.

Joann put the ship on autopilot and we entered the mental plane as a tight, five-unit group mind. Almost immediately an opening appeared in the alien satellite's seamless hull.

Ralph rubbed his hands together. "There's somebody in there. Do we go in physically or remotely?"

"Shield still up on the mental plane," I said. "We have to enter physically. Let me go in first."

The opening showed an unlit black corridor.

"I can only get safely to within 20 feet of the satellite," Joann announced. The mental plane was completely silent.

"Joann, open the exit hatch," I said. "I'm going in."

"You want backup?" Ralph asked.

I thought of my Maitre. "I got backup."

Joann opened the rear escape hatch door.

"Hey kid!" Ralph threw me a thin nylon rope. "Tie that somewhere before you go jumping off into space."

"For fuck's sake, thanks Ralph."

"There is a little metal loop on each side of the front exit hatch," Joann said. "Tie it to one of them."

I walked in to the hatch area. The rear hatch door closed and the hatch depressurized, then the forward door opened to space. I reacted immediately and would have blown myself out into space if the soles of the suit weren't slightly magnetized. I found one of the loops and tied my rope to it. I prepared my Maitre to attack. It was awesome to be physically present in the void instead of just remote viewing it. The satellite was huge, its seamless hull had a completely alien look.

Now I had to maneuver from the lifter into the satellite. I swallowed my fear and pushed off, but I was way off. I banged into the satellite's hull and found myself twisting around in space. I felt like an ass, but my rope kept me from being lost in space. I could hear Ralph laughing at me on the mental plane. Every time I moved, my body went in a different direction. It took me ten minutes before I finally got myself stabilized and into the opening. I stopped myself by splaying my legs out against the narrow corridor walls. Whatever the material of the ship was it wasn't metal, but I discovered that there was just enough gravity to keep me settled on the floor of the narrow corridor. As far as I looked inside the satellite I saw nothing, just blackness. There was no activity.

Ralph was itching for some physical action.

"All clear so far. Ralph and Josh, come on over. Hold on to the rope! I've got the other end."

I heard Kelleye say, "Joann, you have to stay here with the ship in case something happens."

"You stay here, Kel," Josh said.

Kelleye objected and I saw the outer hatch door close.

Ralph put a hand on Kelleye's shoulder and gently pushed her back into her seat. "We need backup on the mental plane if things get rough."

Joann and Kelleye didn't like it but Ralph and Josh entered the hatch area. Joann closed the inner door. The hatch slowly depressurized.

I saw the forward area on the lifter's hull open like a jaw.

It was weird seeing Ralph come over. The rope was like a flexible metal rod in zero gravity. Ralph's body kept bouncing up and down and twisting around as he moved his hands over the rope.

"You're worse than I am, you big oaf."

For the first time in his life Ralph was afraid as he looked out into a vast black nothingness. "Space walking isn't for me."

I didn't have the heart to laugh at him. Finally I was able to grab hold of his outstretched arms as he gyrated around. I pulled him into the opening.

Josh had no problem after watching Ralph. He went head first like a diver, measuring the distance and giving a very soft shove with his toes while circling the rope with both of his gloved hands.

The three of us were standing single file in the blackened corridor of the satellite. All five of us were connected on the mental plane.

Suddenly the opening shut, the walls of the corridor disappeared, and the lights came on.

Ralph, Josh, and I were standing in a large circular room about 100 feet in diameter. A creature about five feet tall with three arms and three legs and a cylindrical torso and head was in front. All of the creatures were in biosuits.

This was probably a sterilized or sanitized room, free of any particulates or atmosphere that could transmit pathogens.

Galactics!

At that moment all five of our minds were surrounded by an enormously powerful one that dwarfed our Group Mind in scope and strength. I heard Joann mutter, 'Get out of there, guys.'

We couldn't move. Me and my Maitre were helpless. This three-legged creature called Itself an Oorant. Apparently Oorants are a lot more powerful than Maitre. I had done it again, acted impulsively and endangered my team. With a little help from Ralph.

There were two other creatures in suits standing beside the Oorant's bulky body. I could feel their minds on the mental plane but they weren't nearly as powerful as the Oorant.

'So these are the menacing earthians our Hilarion friends have described!' a creature about four feet tall sent. 'I am not impressed.' This creature had a creepy vibe.

One of the creatures stepped forward. This being was about seven-and-a-half feet tall, and thin, with a head that resembled a praying mantis. It had two arms and two legs, as did the other one. This creature's vibe on the mental plane was friendly. The Oorant's vibe, which we could all feel as his mind enveloped ours, was one of immense intellect, a razor sharp, penetrating, and overwhelming intelligence. The Oorant scared the shit out of me. I felt like a bug on a slide under an electron microscope. I glanced over at Ralph. I could tell he felt it too.

Our minds were captured but we could still send on the mental plane. 'We never had a chance,' I sent to Josh.

The Oorant was studying us, summing us up. We suddenly felt Its mental grip relax. I spoke to It on the mental plane.

'Is this station the source of the attractors?'

'Of course. A routine operation, resembling one of your computer networks. Each attractor is a node. This satellite is the server.'

'How are these mind washers set up?'

The Oorant ignored this. It pissed me off. 'You people are invaders!'

The Oorant gave the equivalent of a mental shrug. 'In a few decades your planet will embrace the galactic way of life. Whether you like it or not, your future timeline is already written.'

The small galactic spoke up. 'You are incapable of ruling yourselves. You are destroying this beautiful world. It is our right and privilege to intervene.'

'Fuck you.' My Maitre wanted to blast the Oorant but was struggling like a dachshund trying to snap off the nose of a Saint Bernard.

'You think you have a right to be free and self-determined in the universe,' the Oorant said. 'You don't.'

Ralph was so angry he wanted to kill the three galactics.

'We are just messengers,' the mantis objected. 'Don't blame us three. We merely operate the station. Even if you could kill us, there are millions more to take our place.'

Now I knew how the Native Americans felt when wave after wave of migrants came to the shores of America. Our little planet would be overwhelmed by an entire galaxy.

The Oorant must have been satisfied, for It released Its hold on our minds. 'Return to your craft, earthians, and go home.'

The mantis was sympathetic. 'All young races must learn the lesson of co-operation through collectivization, and the limitations on individual freedom for the greater good. It won't be so bad once you accept your fate. The key is resigning yourself to the reality of life in the galaxy.'

It was a hard thing to swallow.

The mantis continued. 'Humans, your value and your worth to the Collectives are determined by what you own, what you can trade, and what you can sell. Your freedoms, and what you call your connection to God, has no value. This is life in the galaxy. All emerging races learn this or die.'[25]

Ralph was upset that there was no evil galactic overlord to kill. It was like being a prisoner of war, he thought. Faceless bureaucrats made the rules and armies of impersonal soldiers like these three galactics enforced them. Nobody cared.

The five of us went back to Midland Muni in Joann's lifter. Ralph said nothing on the way back, but when we got out of the lifter I saw a determined and angry look on his face. When we got to our shielded office he got out his mobile.

"I couldn't even get my Maitre out," I said gloomily. "Those three galactics are a long way from Brother Hamal and Sister Sani."

"No, children," Ralph said confidently. "The next step is to destroy that satellite."

Kelleye was exasperated at this militaristic stupidity. "That's not funny, Ralph!"

Ralph was getting bored. "Our sortie was a success; we got some great intel. We scouted the battlefield. The next time I'll bring some of my men and attack the satellite physically. I know just how to do it. The only one of you kids I'll need is the pilot."

Ralph looked questioningly at Joann.

The giant was impressive, she thought. He spoke as if success was a foregone conclusion. "All right."

Rashan Oliwan and his assistant, Jesus Roberto Vashilik, were preparing for the big Come Together event in the Tampa Convention Center that evening. The large auditorium on the first floor, home for the main event, would hold 3,500 people. It would be full after another successful event in New York last week. Sister Sani and Brother Hamal were to make their appearance tonight! Rashan and Jesus were inspecting the work of the lighting crews, the sound system, and were directing the placement of two portable daises. All must be perfect for the presentation.

On their lunch break, Jesus asked the question that had been bothering him for several weeks. "Rashan, why is it that Sister Sani and Brother Hamal look exactly like humans?"

"I do not know, Jesus. Our galactic friends will probably explain that tonight."

Jesus was extremely anxious to see the Sister and the Brother from the stars. He did not really believe that two ETs were going to show up on center stage. Like the others, he had received the messages from Hamal and Sani, and they were totally convincing. However, a dream vision was one thing and reality was another. Jesus desperately hoped that the two galactic representatives were for real. Inside he thought that perhaps Come Together was fake; a way to dupe people and take their money. Like the pastor in his village in Mexico who had stolen the congregation's money and run off to America. Yet the Movement had grown spontaneously. There was no leader, no headquarters, no cult of personality, and no AntiChrist, as had been foretold in the Bible. Tonight would be the great reveal. If he was not satisfied with the so-called galactic representatives, he would walk away and never come back.

Rashan Oliwan was feeling similar sentiments. A sensitive since birth, he had been excited to experience the vivid dreams. They were so real as to be indistinguishable from his waking reality. Nevertheless, his intuition told him that a benign galaxy of helpful star brothers and sisters, ready to aid humanity with no benefit to themselves, was too one-sided to be completely believable. Rashan was torn between a utopian reality presented by the galactics and a more practical one.

Jesus' question bothered Rashan. Were Brother Hamal and Sister Sani real persons, or just avatars designed to please human beings? That's what Philo-

231

gene Rothman had said. Tonight would answer all his questions.

At 7 p.m. all was in readiness. Jesus and Rashan stood on the stage, Rashan to the left at his dais, and Jesus at stage right. The huge auditorium was filled to overflowing; people stood in the aisles and at the back, streaming out into the lobby. An excited buzz of conversation filled the air. Rashan signaled to his lighting crew and the auditorium dimmed. Two small spotlights shone on himself and Jesus. Tonight he had forsaken his robe, and was dressed in his best suit. He suddenly realized that he had no idea how Sani and Hamal would make their entrance. They said they would be here and he had just accepted it. How would the two galactic representatives make their entrance?

Jesus opened the evening. "Ladies and gentlemen, welcome to the Great Reveal! Tonight, two envoys from the Greater Community of civilizations will tell us about the benefits of joining the Trading Collectives. Brother Rashan Oliwan will introduce our guests."

"Greetings, brothers and sisters!" Rashan proclaimed. "Tonight our friends from the stars are ready to provide us with fantastic new galactic technology that will solve our energy, pollution, and medical problems. My friends, even those of you who oppose us, listen with an open mind." He was supposed to gesture with his right arm, pointing upward, to invite the visitors. He felt foolish as he raised his arm and pointed at the ceiling.

Instantly, two figures manifested on center stage, standing together, arm in arm. Rashan was amazed. Sister Sani and Brother Hamal were here! The two stood silently, looking like young fashion models, the picture of vibrant health. Was that a faint halo surrounding each of them?

The crowd was stunned at first, then broke out into wild applause, whistling, stamping exuberant feet, and shouting Coming Together affirmations. Sani and Hamal took it all in, smiling benevolently. They appeared just as in the vivid dreams.

Sani and Hamal spoke as they had in the dreams, inviting humanity to join the Greater Community, a collection of benevolent civilizations united in peace. The earth would be a valuable addition to the society of planets that exchange information, technology, and resources. "Sani," Hamal explained, "is from the Hilarion Collective, and I am from the Fenachrone Collective. If you decide to join us, you will soon learn about the 5 billion-year-old history of the galaxy and your place in it. Friends, the medical knowledge necessary to create perfect human health is just a small portion of the gifts we have for you."

Rashan had been edging closer and closer to the speakers. Were these projections, or physical beings?

Rashan reached out and touched Sister Sani. She was solid. As Rashan touched Sister Sani he received a short burst from Sani's mind. There was no time to analyze that now.

A video of life on other planets was presented. A beautiful water planet with tropical islands was shown, with creatures that looked like dolphins playing and jumping in the sea. Another planet with a huge ring around it was displayed. This planet had a bright blue sky, with winged creatures flying toward a bright yellow sun. Tropical forests occupied most of the land mass. Another planet showed a large red sun and a soft light resting on a lichen covered ground, with plant-like beings swaying to the rhythm of the sun's light. Another showed a desert planet with a bright white pinprick of a sun, as caravans of people and animals moved from oasis to oasis, trading, singing, and socializing with other trading groups. On and on it went, a catalogue of planets with an amazing variety of habitats and people. All had a head, two arms, and two legs.

"And these are just a few of your neighbors," Brother Hamal explained. "All waiting to welcome you to the galaxy."

At the end of the presentation, the heads of several countries walked on stage. They held hands, and promised to work together for the greater good of humanity and the galaxy. Then the two galactics simply disappeared from the stage, causing a gasp of astonishment from the huge audience.

The gathering of world leaders was a surprise to Rashan and Jesus. "When did this happen?" Jesus asked the older man.

"I don't know, but I'm going to find out," Rashan said. "I think I know just who to ask."

That night after the celebration at the Convention Center ball room, Jesus and Rashan headed for their rooms. Rashan tried to analyze the information he had received from the mind of Sister Sani, but he could get nowhere. The packet was like a bunch of two hour movies all playing at the same time, all at once.

He would pay a visit to Philogene Rothman in Midland. Rashan was pretty sure that Rothman knew a lot more about the mental plane than he did.

— 28 —

Ralph Zimring needed to talk to Tony Baghdadi, his special forces buddy. In his old unit, Tony was comms officer. It was time to get a team together, as they had five years ago when he had helped to expose the activities of the Better Humanity centers.[26] That operation had been a part of the failed Great Reset. This op would have to be private, using only trusted ex-military assets. The U.S. military was useless. The chain of command was more interested in preserving their funding than in neutralizing threats, and they wouldn't believe him anyway.

Ralph ate a big breakfast and walked as fast as he could down 30 flights of stairs. To stay in shape he almost never used the elevator, even when going up.

Ralph walked three blocks from the Midland Tower building and pulled up in front of a seedy looking two-story brick building. Ralph took a rusting metal staircase up to the second floor and walked along a narrow corridor, past a doorwall boarded up with a thick piece of red plywood. Tony had finally got that raggedy-ass thing painted! He paused in front of a thick metal door, which had also been freshly scraped and painted red. He tapped out his name in Morse code: "Ralph." Then two more times. If Tony didn't answer he either wasn't home or he didn't want visitors. Ralph waited a minute in silence. He was about to walk away when the door swung open.

"C'mon in, Ralph."

Tony Baghdadi was a small, wiry man. His lined, pinched face had brightened a little over the past year, due to his therapist. Tony was carrying a lot of baggage, but Ralph had finally gotten his old friend to accept help.

Ralph walked into a luxury apartment with mahogany furniture, expensive carpets, artwork on the walls, and a kitchen the size of a mess hall, equipped with hanging copper pans and the latest and best in kitchen wear. Tony had bought the apartment next door, knocked down the separating wall, and put in supports. The place looked like a dump from the outside, but a luxurious uptown Manhattan apartment on the inside. Tony walked out of the living room and down a corridor into a large room with lab tables and a chair on wheels. Computer and optical equipment sat on a large table. A thin, rectangular Faraday cage as wide as the room rested against the back wall.

"We can talk in here."

It took a long time, but Ralph laid it out. "You remember the amazing biotech used in the Better Humanity centers, and how it helped so many, and killed so many. Well, the people behind that biotechnology were galactics."

Tony's face registered skepticism and anger. "That was the rumor from my contacts in military intelligence."

"They were right, but the situation has escalated. They've doubled down with a new serum – this Rejuvenon stuff – and a completely new form of warfare."

When Ralph explained about the mental plane and the attractors, Tony laughed. "You always were a flake, Ralph."

Ralph sighed. "OK, I'll have to do a parlor trick for you then."

Tony frowned. "What kind of a trick?"

"Think of something only you could know and that I couldn't possibly guess."

A split second later Ralph said, "Got it. You were in love with your little sister when you were eight."

"Fuck you Ralph. Lucky guess."

"How about this then. When you were twelve you broke into the garage of your neighbor and slashed Brett's bicycle tires. Because he called your little sister a cunt."

Tony jumped out of his chair. "You can't possibly know that."

"I got more if you want them. When you were in Basic you and Joe Mobeley—"

"OK, OK! Jesus Christ Ralph, can you read minds?"

"Yes. It's what I've been telling you. A new kind of warfare. On the mental plane."

"But...OK, what? The mental plane?"

Ralph grinned. "You know those four kids who rent the office across the street from the Centurion Building? They call themselves Second Street Investigations."

"Heard of 'em."

Ralph told the story without holding anything back.

"The source of the mind-influencing attractors is a satellite at Lagrange Point 4. The satellite is like a server, and the attractors are the network nodes. If we take out the server, we think that the attractors will be neutralized because they won't be getting any more packets. People will stop getting mind washed."

After he was done Tony's face was blank with shock and disbelief. Tony thought that his old comrade was crazy, but Ralph had never lied to him. Plus, he had had a vivid dream a couple weeks ago about two galactics who called themselves Sani and Hamal. That was bullshit of course, but.... Tony got up and paced the floor.

Ralph didn't interrupt. Sometimes his friend thought best on his feet. After about ten minutes, Tony stopped and turned to face Ralph. "You want to take out that satellite."

"That's right." Ralph explained the situation in galactic terms, as Josh Reynolds had explained it to him. "So, we can defend ourselves from these scumbags, but they aren't allowed to make physical war on us. That's fortunate because if they wanted to they could take out the whole planet."

Tony smiled sardonically. "Sure thing Ralph, old buddy. Who do you need?"

"Danny, Sergei – my old boss from Kharkov PMC, he's in Georgia now – Bob Saunders, J. D. Robinson – my air traffic controller at the Midland Airport – and one military grade laser cannon."

Tony laughed. "I can get the men, but a laser cannon? You don't ask for much, do you?"

"How else are we going to erase that satellite?"

Tony shook his head. "Ralph, if that thing really is a Star Wars satellite, there might be a force field surrounding it."

"Nope. We already did a recon of the thing with D'Arcy's space plane. Me and those kids were actually inside it! It's manned by three galactics, and there's no defenses of any kind. According to Joshua Reynolds, who is something of an authority on galactic affairs, the use of military technology is forbidden within the solar system of an emerging planet."

Tony was skeptical. "This shit is for real?"

"Oh yeah. Rejuvenon, the Coming Together movement, the presentation with the phony Brother Hamal and Sister Sani, almost 2 billion crazies who believe that crap – it's all related. A very sophisticated op, and something no human being would believe even if we told them."

"To Serve Man," Tony quipped.

"Not that bad, buddy. They just want our planet for their Collective. I need to blast that satellite, and hopefully get those three nasty ETs as well."

Tony sighed and shook his head. "I don't believe any of it, Ralph. But I don't have to. If you want the men and the laser cannon, I'll get them for you. When do you start?"

"Whenever you can get that laser cannon." Ralph paused. "There's only one thing wrong. Our pilot is one of the kids, a woman named Joann D'Arcy. I don't like bringing civilians on a mission, Tony, even though she's rock solid. Unfortunately there aren't many guys in the world who know how to pilot the new lifter ships. I think these space planes use reverse-engineered galactic technology." Ralph described the almost organic-looking hemisphere that Joann D'Arcy uses to guide the ship. "Joann calls it consciousness assisted technology, or CAT."

Tony's skepticism was fading just a little. "I heard about that. Ralph, we're living in a science fiction novel."

"Yup."

Tony laughed at Ralph's casual acceptance of the impossible. "I'll talk to some people I know. But it's going to cost you."

Ralph waved his hand unconcernedly. He handed Tony a bank card. "Use this. Don't get swindled."

Tony took the card. "Up yours, Ralph. I'll let you know when all is ready. Give me 48 hours."

"Thanks buddy."

As Ralph walked back to the Midland Tower he realized that his conversation with Tony had been recorded on the mental plane. Crap! Faraday cages were good for shielding electronics but not thoughts. Oh well, what was done was done. He had no doubt about the men. All of them were personally known to him, and they would drop everything for action like this. A space plane! They wouldn't be able to resist.

That night he planned the mission. Ralph had two objectives: destroy the alien satellite and red-pill his friends, who all had extensive connections in the military, the commercial airline industry, and the intelligence community. He didn't need all those guys to hold a laser cannon, but he wanted to get the word out. Information travels fast within those networks.

The cannon with its tripod would be held in place by his guys to prevent any recoil in the weightless environment of space. Ralph would aim and fire the weapon. He wasn't worried. A blind man could hit the satellite, as long as Joann was able to get them close enough. He would have to trust the pilot; there was no one else. Joann, from what he gathered from the kids, had over 100 hours on the lifter. It would hopefully be enough.

The three galactics on the satellite could stop the ship anytime they wanted on the mental plane by capturing their minds. But Ralph had a low-tech solution for that. Add the element of total surprise and it might be enough for success. Ralph had learned through experience that nothing went to plan during the fog of battle. The simpler the plan, the better. That, and battle tested men who knew what to do in a crisis.

They just needed to get close enough to the satellite to hit it.

Ralph felt confidence surging through his body. That was always a good sign before a fight. He slept long and soundlessly that night.

Two days later Ralph walked into the Second Street Investigations office at 9 in the morning. He knew that I would be the only one there; the others were working.

Ralph got right to the point. "My men are ready. I'm going to need Joann and her lifter on Friday at 2100."

"I don't want my girlfriend in danger."

"She's tougher than you are."

I didn't respond to this taunt. "Find another pilot."

"There aren't any. Out of respect I'm telling you, I'm not asking you. You have called me the commander of earth. So you have to follow my orders!"

"Fuck you, Ralph."

"Do you want to tell her or do you want me to?"

"You need me to go with you. You'll need help on the mental plane."

"Sorry, not enough room."

"You tell her then. She will be here tomorrow, when I let her out of bed."

Ralph snorted. "When she lets you out."

Maybe I was getting more mature, but Ralph's teasing didn't bother me anymore.

"OK kid. I'll brief her tomorrow at lunchtime."

Ralph walked out. I swore.

I saw it all on the mental plane in the Second Street Investigations office. "If I see you at the airport on Friday I'll turn you into a pretzel," Ralph had said to me. I wanted to laugh, but the old guy was getting really good at shielding his mind. What I called 'seizing sigs' was the only way I could stop him (I learned about that from the Oorant who had captured our minds on the alien satellite). So – I didn't test the old fart, but I was going to observe on the mental plane whether he liked it or not.

Ralph's men looked like they had come out of a movie when they arrived on the tarmac at the airport. Danny Radulo was small and wiry. Bob Saunders was big and beefy, with close-cropped blond hair and a couple of scars on his face. For such a heavy guy he moved easily, but next to Ralph he looked like a toothpick. Sergei Kharkov was of medium height and thin. His head was constantly moving, looking for threats. J. D. Washington was tall and well built. All of them were dressed in combat fatigues. When Joann showed up the men stared at her in awe. She was even taller than Saunders. Ralph ignored the byplay and spoke to Joann. "Pilot, do you have clearance to take off?"

Joann treated Ralph familiarly, like her older brother. "Sure, Ralph. You guys do your thing, I'll do mine." Joann opened the hull entrance door and sauntered in while Ralph's men looked at each other. "Saucy thing isn't she?" Danny said, and the men all grinned. "Bob, you might want some of that action."

Ralph stopped all that quickly. "Stifle that, boys. That woman is more valuable than all five of us, as you'll soon find out."

Joann and Ralph's men took biosuits from the little garage next to the lifter. Ralph got his suit out of Arthur's back seat and the team entered the lifter.

Joann got into her bio suit and sat in the captain's seat. Ralph showed his men how to get into their suits.

The men were getting excited. Sergei read the plane's MDS. "This is one of the new space planes!" he cried.

"What the fuck did you think it was?" Saunders said as Ralph got the laser cannon out the back of his beat-up Ford and into the lifter. Then he put on his suit.

Sergei was last in the craft. He saw the control hemi, and Joann place her head into it. *"Vyprygnut iz shtanov!"* He looked at Ralph. "Thanks, Zimring."

"Don't thank me, thank Joann here." But the pilot had her eyes closed. Air began to circulate in the lifter. The lights dimmed. Sergei noticed that there were no "controls" in the vessel, other than the hemi and three indentations on a flat panel in front of the pilot. I could see from Sergei's mind how blown away he was.

"OK boys, fun's over. Let's get the cannon into the forward escape hatch." Ralph fiddled with something on the weapon's side. A digital display came to life. It read, "20:00."

Joann opened her eyes and inspected her ship. "What's that?"

"This cannon is going to activate and fire on a timer, just in case those galactics freeze our minds. When we get the thing in the hatch I'm setting it. How long will it take you to get near enough to the satellite to blast it?"

"Good guess, Ralph. To get to Lagrange Point 4 and find the satellite, about 20 minutes. But don't activate it until we take off."

Ralph's men looked at each other in amazement. "Twenty minutes to reach L4?" J. D. said. "That's about one AU!"

Bob Saunders was grim. He had worked with Ralph on a mission a few years ago to take out the Better Humanity center in DC. The two men exchanged glances. "You're not telling us everything."

"That's right, Bob. This is an urgent mission. Our goal: destroy an alien satellite."

Bob looked at his companions and shrugged, as if to say, "What did you expect? It's Ralph Zimring."

Joann was comming with the air traffic controller in the tower. I was with her on the mental plane. 'I'll stay in contact,' I sent.

"YMMS-66A cleared for takeoff."

Joann didn't wait around. The ship lifted slowly above the airport, then it sped rapidly above the earth. The men could see through two transparencies in the hull. There was no sensation of movement. They were a few miles above the airport, and then they were out past the Space Grid.

Sergei practically wet his pants. Ralph went in to the forward hatch and activated the timer on the laser cannon. "Twenty minutes, pilot," Ralph said. Joann suddenly realized that Ralph's laser cannon was going to fire automatically and her ship was going to suffer a hull breech if she didn't do her job. The sun was down and to the left as the lifter sped toward its destination. There was nothing except the sun and blackness. To Sergei, it appeared that they weren't moving at all, until they approached a large space rock. There were other rocks visible, but Joann guided the ship slowly past them. Ralph looked at his wrist chronometer. "Ten minutes, pilot."

Joann looked up from her pilot's chair. "I don't think I can get us there in ten minutes."

"Pilot, that cannon is going to fire in 9 minutes and thirty seconds."

"Reset it."

"No can do, pilot. I disabled the override."

Joann panicked. "You fool!"

Ralph grinned. "Do your job, pilot."

Joann concentrated. In her initial excitement she had forgotten to run the earlier flight path from their recon mission, which had been recorded in the hemi. Now she was flying by the seat of her pants, but she at least knew where the satellite was from the recording.

"You're a dangerous lunatic, Ralph Zimring!" Joann said.

Ralph's men laughed inside their bio suits.

"Cut the chatter, pilot. Concentrate."

Joann ignored the big oaf. She was looking for the same gigantic space boulder where the alien satellite was hiding behind. There it was! Joann breathed a sigh of relief and moved the lifter around the boulder. The satellite wasn't there.

"See what you've done!"

'Relax, pilot,' Ralph sent on the mental plane. 'Find the satellite, it's shielded. Use the mental plane to locate it.'

Joann was angry at herself. Of course!

Ralph sighed. This is what happens when you bring civilians on a military mission. They can never think straight in the fog of battle.

"Time!" Joann shouted.

"Ten minutes."

"But you said…"

"I lied. Locate that satellite!"

Joann fought down her panic and entered the mental plane. Of course. The satellite with its mental shield was the only thing on the mental plane in this lifeless area of Trojans and space debris. Ralph had been right. There it was – on the opposite end of the L4 area. She guided the ship to within a hundred feet of the satellite with a minute to spare. Ralph and his men piled in to the hatch. The inside door to the hatch closed and two banks of soft lights illuminated the small space.

"Wait thirty seconds while the hatch depressurizes," Joann said.

Ralph looked at the display, which read "45 seconds."

"Hold on boys," Ralph said as the hatch depressurized. There was no time to tie the cannon down. Ralph held onto it while his men steadied the tripod as the forward hatch door opened to the blackness of space. Ralph barely had time to aim the thing when the laser activated. Damn! He was getting too old for this shit.

241

Suddenly the minds of the men were seized and held, and they lost their grip on the cannon. Ralph saw the laser slowly floating off into space, its beam set to continuous automatic fire. Ralph's aim wasn't straight. The laser cannon's beam glanced at an angle off the alien ship as the laser slowly moved to their left, but it was making a huge crease in the alien satellite's hull. The cannon moved slowly off into space, turning, the beam still firing off. But now the cannon's beam was turning toward their ship!

'That beam is going to hit us,' Sergei thought as he was frozen into immobility. But it didn't. Joann moved her lifter out of the way just in time before her mind was also seized. The cannon's motion turned its beam, which struck the hull of the satellite once more in a long arc from right to left.

Ralph was laughing silently. His mind was being held by that Oorant creature, demanding that he shut the cannon off. Ha ha ha. The galactics had no ability to influence the primitive electronics of the laser cannon from the mental plane! His low-tech solution was working, if it didn't kill them first. The cannon was now moving away from the satellite, but its beam was firing off in a wide arc in the direction of the satellite.

Ralph and his men stood watching in the escape hatch, fascinated. The beam was burning huge chunks of material off the alien hull as it turned.

Suddenly the galactic vessel disappeared into a fold in space.

"Success!" Ralph said, slamming his fist into the escape hatch wall and lifting his feet off the floor in his excitement. In the weightless environment, the big man catapulted himself into space. The laser cannon was still firing, its beam turning slowly and getting closer and closer to Ralph's path through space.

"Pilot, man overboard!" Sergei shouted. Joann heard him through the inner hatch door, which had to be kept closed or all the ship's air would escape into space and blow Ralph's men into the void.

"I see him," Joann said grimly. The ship moved very slowly toward Ralph, but it had to avoid the beam of the laser cannon, which would soon intersect Ralph's position.

Sergei and Danny saw their buddy turning slowly in space, completely helpless.

"That beam is going to hit Ralph," Bob Saunders said. "Pilot, do something."

"Nothing to do," Joann said firmly. "Rescuing Ralph puts the ship in the path of the beam. Destroying this ship doesn't help anyone."

Ralph was about 80 feet from them now, silently congratulating Joann. That girl was solid! She would not endanger her ship or their mission. In another minute he was going to get fried. Fuck it! I'm ready to meet my maker.

Sergei reached into his combat rig and pulled out a spool of thin nylon rope. "Bob, hold onto me and brace yourself by the escape hatch door."

Sergei gave the end of the spool to Danny. "Hold onto the wire." Sergei pulled on the spool. The line came out and was flying all over the place in the weightless environment. "There's no air or gravity here!" Sergei grabbed the spool and aimed. Ralph was almost at the end of the rope's length. Sergei hurled the spool at Ralph. The three men watched as the rope untangled itself and flew off in Ralph's direction. It was weird to see the thing not get buffeted by the air or be affected by gravity. Sergei's aim was true. The spool holding the rope hit Ralph's body as it was turning. Ralph reached out for the line with his bulky suit gloves but missed it. That motion propelled him right into a curl of the rope and Ralph grabbed on with his space suit mitts.

"Secured!" Sergei said. "Danny, reel him in."

The laser cannon's beam was about to fry Ralph as Danny gave the line a frantic tug. Ralph's body snapped toward them like a missile. "He doesn't weigh anything!" Sergei cried.

Ralph banged against the side of the lifter's hull and was now going away from the ship in a different direction. "Sergei!" Danny cried. "Gently reel in the rope."

Sergei gave a small tug on the rope. Ralph's body began to move slowly toward the ship.

Joann, inside the ship, panicked. The laser cannon's beam, which was moving in a circle, was again turning toward her lifter! She regained her composure and took her ship out of the way of the cannon's laser beam. She almost laughed when she saw Ralph, who was desperately holding onto the rope, get jerked around as the ship changed its trajectory. Ralph banged against the ship again and went flying off into space. Sergei caught up the slack as the rope, and Ralph's body, moved toward the ship. Ralph hit the hull again three feet from the hatch opening, but now there was little slack left in the rope. Ralph was gradually drawn into the crowded escape hatch.

"Pilot, close the forward hatch door!" Ralph shouted.

The door closed.

"Gentlemen, make sure your feet are on the floor," Joann ordered. "Wait thirty seconds while the hatch pressurizes."

The inner hatch door opened and Ralph and his three men jumped into the ship like a bunch of playful monkeys.

Ralph and his men took off their helmets and gave each other celebratory hugs. "Who-hoo! Ain't we got fun!"

Joann snorted from her pilot's chair. "Tell me you weren't scared to death, gramps."

Ralph laughed. "I was! Almost crapped inside my suit. But I'm safe now. Good job, D'Arcy."

"Gotta hand it to you Ralph," Bob Saunders said. "You took out that alien ship."

"That big oaf didn't do anything except throw himself into space and almost get us killed," Joann replied. "He's just as impulsive as my boyfriend."

"You look awesome when you're angry, Joann," Ralph replied.

Joann's mouth opened and closed but nothing came out. "I did more than all five of you morons put together," she said, placing her head into the control hemi. "Put your helmets back on."

'Wait a minute,' Ralph sent to Joann on the mental plane. 'We need to see whether those attractors are still operational. I want to see one of those things up close and personal.'

Joann sighed. 'You're right, Ralph. What do we tell your men?'

'That we're going sightseeing. I wonder if any of them have remote viewing capabilities?'

'All right. I'll take us to the one closest to our present position.'

Joann could see them all on the mental plane. "What do we do about that laser cannon? It's still firing."

Ralph laughed. "Leave it. Maybe that Oorant will come back and get it as a souvenir."

"OK." Joann directed her ship to a position well above the Space Grid. As they approached the attractor Ralph said to his men, "Tell me if you can see anything."

Bob Saunders scoffed. "Out here? There's nothing but empty space."

"So you think," Ralph said. "Look."

To Ralph and Joann, the attractor was a multicolored sphere on the mental plane that put out an inviting, benevolent energy. "You go in Ralph," Joann said. "I have to handle the lifter."

Ralph sat down on one of the seats along the side of the lifter and closed his eyes.

"What's he doing?" Sergei asked Joann.

"Remote viewing," Joann replied. "Ralph will tell you all about it."

Sergei shrugged. There was nothing out there...or was there? He thought he saw something glowing. Or maybe it was just his imagination.

A minute later Ralph returned and opened his eyes. He had a disgusted look on his face. "A waste of time, Joann. Those things are still operational! That Oorant lied to us – they must have given them all a separate power supply and programming."

Joann sighed. "All right, we'll head back to the airport."

From my post in the downtown office I congratulated Joann on the mental plane. 'You are awesome!'

On the way back Ralph tried to explain to his guys what remote viewing was, and what he and Joann were looking at.

Bob Saunders' eyes were wide. "You're kidding, right?"

Bob trusted Ralph. They had originally been enemies years ago when he was fighting for the Peshmerga and Ralph was a mercenary working for Sergei's PMC that had contracted out to the old al-Abadi government of Iraq. But during the Better Humanity fiasco a few years ago they had fought together on the same side.[27]

"I'm not joking, Bob. You remember those two silver-haired fellows?"

Bob shuddered. "Yeah. Those two creepy aliens who helped set up the Better Humanity biocenters."

"Yup. There are lots of aliens out there just like them, Bob, trillions of 'em. All they have in common with us is two arms, two legs, and a head. Except for that Oorant."

"I'm not much on this remote viewing stuff."

"You never know. A lot of humans have the ability." Ralph looked at Sergei, his old boss at Kharkov PMC. "Are you interested?"

"*Da!*"

"Good, I'll train you up. And Danny and Bob if they want to do it." Ralph looked at J. D., who had been silent throughout their trip. His friend wore a shocked expression. J. D. was mumbling about the satellite disappearing into a wormhole.

"Are you interested in the mental plane training?" Ralph asked.

"Talk to me in a week, Ralph. I'll need that long to recover."

Ralph grinned. He could see that J. D. had completely swallowed his red pill and was having trouble digesting.

Everybody got out of the lifter after Joann landed. Ralph spoke to his men. "All right boys, we had some fun. But the game is way bigger than what we think. Sergei and I will be in touch." Ralph knew his men couldn't keep silent about this. In a couple of days it would be all over the networks.

Joann watched as Ralph walked off with his men to their vehicles, laughing and bantering with each other.

Joann was curious. 'How old is Ralph?' she sent to me on the mental plane. '61, I think.'

'He's like a little kid in a giant's body.'

'Just like that old bromide. You're only as old as you think you are.'

'Yes, but if he trains up Sergei and Danny and Bob and J. D. we'll have a few more people awake and aware on the mental plane.'

Joann's casual remark gave me an idea.

After Ralph got back from his adventure in space it was three in the morning, but he was too excited to sleep. He ate a meal and drank three cups of coffee laced with whiskey. Then he sat down in his office and reviewed his op. Ralph now understood the futility of fighting galactics. They were too far ahead technologically, and wouldn't again fall for tricks like he had just pulled. Humans were like an ant colony trying to fight a million Godzillas. He would leave the kids to do their investigating on the mental plane. Ralph had no confidence that would work; there were too many mind-influenced people already. No, what was needed was an entirely new kind of fighting force: soldiers who were also remote viewers, and able to operate on the mental plane. A sixth-generation fighting force with instant, untraceable comms. Ralph was practically salivating, thinking about it. One of the most difficult aspects of fighting from a command point of view was keeping the troops on the same page during the confusion of battle, and keeping morale up. Using the mental plane, even a large battalion could be kept together under fire. All members would know precisely what the others were thinking and feeling, and could support each other. Comms would be a breeze, and intelligence could be gathered remotely and in real-time.

Ralph knew several dozen men from his special forces days, and from his time as a mercenary. And those guys knew others. First he would have to personally train up a select crew here in Midland. Tony Baghdadi; Sergei Kharkov (who would be in town for a couple of weeks); Hideki Matsui, Berglin Enterprise's security chief; Max, if he was interested; and J. D. Robinson. That would do for a start. It would all depend on how well they took to the training. The kids seemed to think that all humans were capable, if given the right techniques. Well, Philo's methods had worked on him.

He would form his own private army for the defense of earth. An untraceable private army that could comm on the mental plane and evade psychos like Austin Matthews in the hidden programs, and the incompetents in the military chain of command.

Ralph thought long and hard about this, for it was essentially treason. However, extraordinary times require extraordinary measures! Neither the US, nor humanity, could stand up to an invisible galactic attack on the mental plane. With the attractors the Collectives could mobilize billions of mindwashed people to do their bidding.

There was no evil galactic overlord to attack, but there would be plenty of human overlords mobilizing their armies. Civilians like the deluded Rashan Oliwan. Guys like General Shi Yanglin in China and his buddy Gen. George Vindman and their friends in the US, whose goal was a chipped human race controlled by AI and a worldwide surveillance state. Ralph saw it all. A pacified population aligned with the Collectives would hand over earth's sovereignty and resources to the galactics in exchange for some trinkets of technology. Just like the Europeans did to the indigenous in America.

Ralph sighed and looked at his gnarled hands. The skin on his arms was beginning to wrinkle a little. He was getting old. But he wasn't done yet. He still had some good years left. And he knew Max Berglin would back him; the old man was still engaged. He and Max knew a wide network of people who would fight and die for the human race. Max knew people in the business world, and other scientists like himself from his days at the Lockheed Skunk Works.

Ralph sat up all night and began to plan the biggest military operation in world history. First, train up his crew on the mental plane. If they could, his guys could train their military contacts, and they could train their friends and families....

Ralph burst out of his chair in excitement. It would be the good guys, the aware guys, against the Collective mind-influenced horde. Perfect! Ralph knew he had a savior complex, just like his buddy Bob Saunders. Well, they had a whole planet to save.

If his guys couldn't handle the training, he and Max might as well retire to Max's island in the Caribbean and watch the world go to hell.

— 29 —

I was so proud of Joann after she and Ralph wrecked the satellite, but I was bummed that the attractors were still operational. Joann and I slept in until almost noon. We were eating breakfast at the apartment when my mobile rang. It was Rashan Oliwan.

"Did you see the event last week in Tampa?"

I wasn't sympathetic. "Rashan, you and the lemmings who follow you are part of the problem. And it's a big problem. You have no idea what you're doing."

"That's what I want to talk to you about. In person. I want to bring my assistant Jesus with me."

"Jesus was the guy on the other side of the stage? The guy who introduced you?"

"Yes."

Rashan sounded doubtful about his role in Come Together. "All right. I have an office in Midland, Illinois, 437 Second Street, Suite 102. I'm usually there all day and into the evening on weekdays, except for lunch and dinner." Unless Ralph came up with another adventure for us.

"We can be there tomorrow. What time is good?"

"Tomorrow is Sunday. Come at lunchtime." Joann had one more day of leave before she had to fly again on Monday.

"All right. I'll be staying at the Radisson downtown. After, I'll treat everyone to dinner in the hotel restaurant."

That sounded good to me. "OK, see you tomorrow."

248

Rashan showed up to the office at noon with a tall, lanky guy who had shaved his head and had tattoos all over his body. He looked like a gang member. When Ralph saw Jesus he bristled.

"Don't sweat it old man," Jesus said.

Ralph's eyes were like cold steel as he walked up to Jesus.

Rashan was panicking and Jesus looked like a bug about to be pinned to a display. "Who is this guy?" Jesus gulped.

"Son, sit the fuck down and shut your grille. You too, Oliwan." Our two guests sat on the sofa beside each other. Then we let them have it.

The team had rehearsed how we were going to deal with Rashan. I had learned a lot from the Oorant about how to control sigs. Our Group Mind seized the sigs of Rashan and Jesus just as the Oorant's mind had seized ours during our confrontation in the satellite.

We escorted Rashan and Jesus out to one of the attractors on the mental plane, like a parachutist-for-hire escorting a first-time jumper. They saw everything through our minds. Both men were freaking out as their awareness left their bodies behind and they found themselves going higher and higher, above the earth, and into the blackness of space. I had no sympathy for them. I still had dreams about what Patrick had done to me on my remote viewing training.

We approached one of the attractors from the mental plane. We saw sigs in the dream state going in and seeing the program. Sister Sani and Brother Hamal gave their spiel; but this time Rashan and Jesus saw the presentation as an observer. The two newbies saw how the untrained sigs soaked it all in, unaware that their subconscious minds were being programmed.

"Do you two get it now?" Ralph said.

"I suspected as much," Rashan said.

"Get me out of here," Jesus said, looking around at the mental plane and the dozens of attractors scattered in space around the world.

We escorted the sigs of Jesus and Rashan back to the office and released them.

Jesus was terrified, and I didn't blame him. Rashan's face showed defeat and depression.

"What a dupe," Rashan said. "I hate being the fool."

"Stop your whining," Ralph said. "You got played, so what? The Collectives are fooling billions of people." Ralph looked Rashan in the eyes. "What are you going to do about it?"

"You're joking, old man. What can anyone do against mind washing machines like that? If they got me they can get anyone."

Jesus was about to get up and run out the building, but Rashan stopped him. "Stick around, my friend. I have a feeling we're going to learn something."

"You are," I said. "By now you guys understand that the mental plane is real, and it's being used against us. We can present everything to you if you let us into your minds."

Jesus freaked out at that. "No...no, this is crazy. *Estas pero si bien pendejo.* I'm going back to my village in Mexico. I shoulda stayed there." He got up and left.

"Are you a chickenshit too?" Ralph asked Rashan.

"I'm ready. Let me have it."

All five of us gave it to him. Everything we had experienced regarding the galactics, one at a time, at the speed of thought. Including the info about advanced planets network (sorry Patrick).

"So there *are* benevolent space brothers and sisters!" Rashan cried. "I knew it!"

"Yes there are, but only one in a million out of all the planets with intelligent life." I showed him what Patrick showed us about the Collectives.

Rashan was stunned. "But...I thought...they are so much more advanced than us..."

"Yeah," Ralph said. "We thought that too. It sucks. But we have to deal with it."

"It's appalling."

"The galactic Collectives are running a gigantic PsyOp on us," Ralph summarized.

We let Rashan recover for a few minutes.

I had to admit, Rashan was able to take it all in. He only flinched a couple of times. I didn't show him my 40,000 light year trip across the galaxy, or my adventure with the Maitre. I don't know what the others gave him, but at the end his eyes were glazing over. He shook his head when I offered to train him. "I have to make up for all the damage I've done by helping to create the Come Together movement. I'm not sure I know how to do that. Becoming an apostate will just harden support for the Movement among the followers."

"Let's go out to dinner and talk about it," Kelleye suggested. "You promised to pay!"

Rashan managed a smile. "I did."

During dinner Rashan came out of his shell a little, and asked us all sorts of questions about our experiences with the galactics. "Are these Collectives for real?"

I showed him what happened to me on Beta Caronai, and what had happened at the galactic satellite. "Apparently they are."

"Get your Celestian friends to help us."

"That won't work," Josh said. "They are too busy trying to fend off the Collectives themselves."

"Cut off the head then. Find the leader of these galactics, eliminate him. Or her. Or it."

Ralph got angry because he had thought the same thing and knew it was stupid. "Do you think this is a DC comic book story? We aren't the Justice League. Those folks out there collectivized millions of years ago. We're fighting an entrenched bureaucracy on thousands of planets, not an evil overlord. That's kid stuff."

"It's hopeless then," Rashan said. "We're one tiny little planet against the galactic hordes."

Ralph frowned. The big man didn't like defeatist attitudes, even though it was exactly what he thought about the Collectives. "That's no way to think. Everybody does their bit. Your bit is to discover a way to wake up those lemmings in your movement, or crash it. The kids here need to disable those attractors. And my job –" Ralph smiled broadly – "my job, if it pans out, I'll tell you about later."

Rashan looked up at the giant. "I like your attitude. All right, we are in agreement. If you have any suggestions I'd like to hear them."

Kelleye spoke up. "Go get your assistant Jesus and talk to him. If you can't convince him you won't be able to convince anyone."

Rashan smiled. He really was quite attractive, Joann thought. "Of course. I'll do just that." He got up from his seat and bowed to the group. "You have given me much to think about."

"Let's keep in touch, Rashan," I said. "Eventually you will have to get the mental plane training. That way we don't have to meet in person or depend on the digital networks."

"Granted. But my presentation in Florida was quite effective in mobilizing even more support for these fake galactics. I have to act quickly now to negate my previous efforts."

"We're with you."

We finished dinner and chatted. Rashan Oliwan was a smooth operator. I could see that Joann and even Kelleye were intrigued by his male charm. Even though I had been in his mind I couldn't understand him. I don't think he understood himself. He knew he was intelligent and had a disarming effect on people he met, and he took advantage of it.

After we left Rashan at the hotel we went back to the office to talk on the mental plane about the attractors. It was past 10 now.

'That Oorant lied to us,' I sent. 'The attractors aren't dependent on the satellite at all. It was probably just here to set them up.'

Ralph sighed. 'It didn't lie, children, It offered us something plausible that fit Its narrative and we accepted it. That's a standard tactic used in intelligence and psychological operations. In addition to the attractors, they are probably also using sophisticated information influence ops against us. But we can never give up the fight.'

Josh was impressed with Ralph's can-do attitude. 'We have to keep trying to dismantle the attractors.'

Ralph smiled. 'Now you're talking, Joshua. Don't give up. Keep at it.'

A week later Ralph waltzed into the office with Sergei Kharkov, an older man of about 50; Bob Saunders (who looked like a thug); Danny Radulo, a smallish man with whipcord features; and J. D. Robinson. These were the men he had brought on the mission to destroy the galactic satellite.

Ralph smiled at J. D.. "Love that Afro. Reminds me of the old days."

J. D. patted his hair. "Resist, baby!"

"OK boys, show these kids what you got."

J. D. sent, 'Nice to meet you. If you are friends of Ralph, you're friends of mine.'

All four of us commed back on the mental plane. 'Welcome to the team, J. D.'

J. D.'s face broke out into a huge grin.

Sergei commed with me on the mental plane. 'So you're the famous Philogene Rothman.'

'The very same.'

Danny was next. 'I'm Danny Radulo, at your service.'

Bob Saunders was more hesitant. 'I think I got this right.'

'You have it right, Bob Saunders,' I sent back.

Saunders' big face lit up like a Christmas tree. "I did it Ralph! I did it!" Suddenly a look of profound comprehension came over Saunders' beefy countenance. "Ok Ralph, I get it now. All that shit you've tried to explain to me before. It's a new awareness."

Ralph nodded. "Yup."

"But I'm softer now, Ralph!"

"You mean you aren't a killer anymore," Kelleye said.

"No sweetheart, that's not what I meant. You see, I'm picking up all of these references from your minds. All this information I never had before. It's what you might call broadening my mental horizons. It's fuckin' amazing."

"You see now, Bob, how effective our new strike force could be."

"Strike force?" Kelleye asked, alarmed.

Ralph sent it all to them in a thought packet, about how he had trained his four men, about the new form of warfare, and about getting a large portion of the human race trained in the mental plane techniques. Danny, Sergei, J. D., and Bob were ecstatic. Josh smiled, Joann was amazed, and Kelleye frowned. I was fired up because it was exactly my idea from what Joann said after the op, except on the civilian side.

"Operation earth!" I shouted. "We train up people we know and let them train anyone who will accept the mental plane. Great minds think alike!"

Ralph was very pleased with himself. "If Bob here can do it, anybody can do it," Ralph said, teasing his friend.

Bob Saunders was standing there looking like an enlightened Gumby. "I can't be a mercenary anymore. I know too much now." He looked at Kelleye. "But I can still crack the heads of some dirtbags if I have to."

"Glad to hear it Bob," Ralph said. "There are lots of them."

Kelleye looked at both men. "You two are hopeless."

Ralph bowed. "Thank you, Kelleye. I assure you, we'll be there if you ever get in trouble."

Josh looked over at Kelleye. "And so will I, sweetheart."

Kelleye sighed and decided to be gracious. "Thank you, gentlemen."

Ralph had assignments for his men. "Bob, go see Rashan Oliwan. He's the guy who's doing the Coming Together presentations. Train him up."

"That scumbag! I'm more like to mess up his pretty face."

"Don't do that, Bob." Ralph explained that Rashan had seen the error of his ways and was now trying to shut down the Come Together movement.

"I'll believe that when I see it," Bob said. "Where is this guy?"

"His current home is in Tampa, Florida."

"Florida! That's the place for me," Bob said with a grin. "I'll either train up Rashan or I'll throw him in a dumpster." He walked out.

Kelleye shuddered. "Bob Saunders will always be a thug. He looks like one."

"You are very prescient, my dear," Ralph replied. "Some people need, er, more persuasion than others."

"I should hate you, Ralph Zimring, but I don't."

"Of course. You have discernment. You despise some of the things I have done, but you're intelligent enough to understand the necessity for it."

Kelleye sighed. "We've been through that, Ralph. Violence is never an answer."

"Except when the perp is coming for your child. Or your boyfriend. Or for the human race."

Kelleye had no response to that.

"Don't be depressed, child. The world is imperfect and we all do the best we can."

"Is Bob Saunders going to kill Rashan?"

"I hope not. Rashan could be an effective operator."

Kelleye shook her head sadly. These military types valued people not for themselves, but merely for their usefulness.

Ralph looked at Sergei. "Go back to Kharkov PMC. Train as many as you can. Danny and J. D., you do the same with your networks."

"A couple of guys I know are sociopaths," Sergei said. "Should I try to train them too?"

"Yeah. We have to know whether this mental plane stuff has any limitations. Can anyone do it, or just the good guys? If the bad guys can do it too we're in trouble."

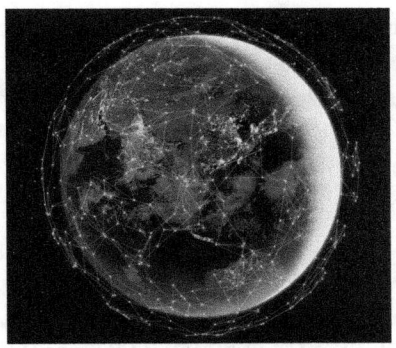

— 30 —

Sergei Kharkov had turned 50 last month. He was getting old for field work, which he loved above anything. His private military company, named after himself, was essentially a group of mercenaries who contracted with governments and NGOs and corporate contractors working for governments. It was good business, for governments liked to start conflicts and spend money on them. Sergei had learned from 30 years experience that the war didn't matter, and who won the war was irrelevant. Only the money that flowed to those who made the weapons and distributed them, to the government operatives who sponsored them, and to those who fought with them.

Sergei had never thought much about the business he was in. Human beings are naturally conflicted and selfish, and so the world turned. He had been brought up Christian in Georgia, one of the former Soviet republics, in a village close to the border with Muslims in Chechnya. When he was a teenager in '08 he had fought Russians in the Russian-Georgian War. Two years later he had fought Chechens before he tired of fighting for the Georgian government. After that he joined a private military company to make some money before eventually starting his own PMC.

Sergei had lived with conflict his entire life, and had profited from it. But now it was different. The remarkable mental plane training had opened his eyes to a new reality; a reality where people were more than their ethnic heritage, or their religion, or their tribe. This was a world that spanned the entire planet! Never religious, he thought of the mental plane as a sort of heaven, and had a deep respect for it. From his training camp in northern Georgia he was able to comm remotely with Ralph or Danny or J. D. or Bob at any time, without anyone being able to trace it. Distance didn't matter.

Kharkov PMC was between contracts, so there was time to train his men. But only a select few to start, loyal to him. And Vasily Alexiev. Alexiev was a sociopath; none of the men liked him. Sergei asked his two top guys, and Vasily Alexiev, whether they would be interested in a new form of comms for field work.

"What's he doing here?" Manny and Anzor said at once, pointing to Alexiev.

"An experiment." Sergei explained what he was going to do. "This training is different than anything you ever heard of. If you stick with it you'll be able to comm mind-to-mind."

Manny and Anzor scoffed and Alexiev laughed derisively in his usual manic fashion. Sergei looked at the three men silently, then he read their minds and told them their deepest secrets. Manny and Anzor were shocked, then amazed. Alexiev was very angry at first. Sergei looked for the signs of a galactic overlay on Alexiev's sig, as Ralph had taught him, but couldn't find anything.

The first step in the training is to get the trainee to allow the teacher into his mind. Sergei started with Alexiev, but Alexiev panicked. He bulled Sergei to the ground and was about to smash his face when Manny kicked him in the shoulder and Anzor threw Alexiev in the dirt.

"Back off, asshole," Manny said, pulling out his weapon.

Alexiev sat up and wiped blood from his lips. "He tried to take over my mind!"

Sergei got up and put his hand on Manny's shoulder. "It was my fault, I went in too heavy."

Sergei tried it with Manny, whose eyes almost bugged out of his head. Manny swore and Alexiev laughed, wiping dirt from his face. "You see? That's fucked."

Still too strong! Sergei went easier on Anzor, who smiled. "Aint so bad. It's weird having someone else in your mind though."

After that things went better. After the first day it was clear that Alexiev would be the star pupil. Once he got over his fear, Vasily caught on so fast it amazed Manny and Anzor. "What is this, Kharkov?" Alexiev said at the end of the day. "I feel different."

Manny and Anzor stared at each other. "You look different," Anzor said to Alexiev. "Not nearly so fucked up."

That provoked a fight, which Sergei had to break up by seizing Vasily's sig.

Manny and Anzor stared at Alexiev, whose eyes were rolling around in his head. But when Sergei released Vasily he stood, unmoving, a broad smile spreading slowly across his face. *"ah vot anó kak, a ya ta panyát' nye mok!"*

"What I just did is called seizing a sig," Sergei explained to Manny and Anzor, as Alexiev slowly recovered from his experience. Some people only understand force, Sergei concluded.

"Fuck you Kharkov," Vasily said, catching Sergei's thought. "I see what you did there. I want to learn how to do it."

"That's advanced training," Sergei said. "You gotta complete Basic first." Sergei was amazed at the man's sensitivity.

After the first day Alexiev buckled down to work like a hungry dog to its food, and caused no more trouble. Sergei wondered what was motivating him. Normally surly and uncommunicative, the man seemed to have benefited from his mental attack! Sergei shook his head. Sociopaths like Alexiev were impossible to read because they didn't understand themselves or their own motivations.

"Did you get a personality transplant?" Manny asked Alexiev on their last day of training. Normally this would have provoked another fight, but Vasily just shrugged it off. *"Poshyel k chyertu,* that won't work on me anymore."

Anzor and Manny exchanged speaking looks. They could see the change in Aliexiev's sig on the mental plane. They felt different themselves.

Sergei was pleased. The training had worked. That night he reported back to Ralph on the mental plane using the coded language devised by Philogene Rothman.

He had a month's experience with the training now, and it was changing him. The old hatreds and rivalries he had learned as a child seemed less important. There was a bigger enemy out there and the human race had to unite to defeat it. Suddenly Sergei knew what he was going to do with the rest of his life. He was going to teach this technique to all the influencers he knew. If he could train Alexiev he could train anybody.

*B*ob Saunders went to Tampa. He didn't have to throw Rashan Oliwan into a dumpster. Fortunately for him (Bob thought) Rashan was cooperative, probably because of his rugged good looks (and the scar across his face from a knife fight). Rashan learned the remote viewing technique pretty quick. "I only gave you the basics because I'm not that good," Bob said after they were done.

"It's good enough, thank you." Rashan gently touched Bob's mind and analyzed his sig. This was the most important part of the training for him. Now he could see any galactic overtones, and he could do it remotely. He would be able read the sigs of every important figure in the Come Together movement and identify their motivations.

Rashan was still mad at himself. Brother Hamal and Sister Sani! They had punked him and used their superior knowledge to manipulate him. He couldn't believe he had fallen for it, but this galactic operation was beyond the understanding of anyone. He felt sympathy for the dupes in the Come Together movement even though that wouldn't stop him from trying to destroy it. Not even the most powerful person in the Movement could stop him.

"OK, Oliwan," Bob said. "Identify the influential targets. Ignore the small fry. Do you need any help?"

Rashan thought for a moment. "I don't think so. This is my fight. I helped to create the problem and it's my job to resolve it."

Bob understood the importance of a team. This Oliwan was too self-centered. He had not even tried to recover Jesus, his former assistant. "Tell you what. Make a list of everyone in the Movement with an altered sig. Send it to me and I'll get it to Philogene and his team. Don't try to take down this Movement all by yourself; it's a job too big for one person."

"I like to work alone."

"Sure, but everyone needs backup."

Rashan reluctantly agreed to this. "All right. I'll start by identifying sigs, but how will we neutralize the sigs of those who have been influenced?" Rashan asked. "I don't know how to do that."

"Neither do I. We'll let Rothman figure it out. Meanwhile, ID the important people within the Movement. Fuck anything up that you can without exposing yourself. You're our double agent. Send coded reports to me. I'll pass them along."

"I always thought I would be a spiritual leader," Rashan said the next morning as he drove Bob to the airport. "It's important for people to keep the connection to Spirit alive, or we become like slaves. But a lot of spirituality is bunk, a sort of pacification program."

Bob nodded. "There's a time for that spiritual stuff, but right now we need action."

Bob said goodbye to Rashan at the airport. He wasn't sure about Oliwan, but he wasn't experienced enough in the mental plane yet. Bob suspected that Rashan's motivation was just spite against the organization that had tricked him, and a bruised ego.

In recognition of his wildly successful event in Tampa, Rashan Oliwan received an invitation to the Come Together movement's first annual international executive meeting in Vienna, Austria. The meeting was scheduled for June 28th. That was only a week from now.

"Please excuse the short notice, Mr. Oliwan," the invitation said. "Due to the overwhelming response to your recent meeting, and the successful appearance of our friends, we feel it is our obligation to offer you a seat on the International Executive Board for the Come Together movement. Please accept our hospitality and expect an informative and enjoyable visit to Vienna, one of the most beautiful cities on the planet."

The invitation was a work of art. It showed places of interest in the city, and an elaborately furnished room in a private mansion "built in 1872 for Count Alexander Hofbauer, a completely modernized Wilhelminian style house." The place had three bedrooms, and there would be two other guests, one of which was a strikingly beautiful older woman. He had never heard of either of the guests. The other was a man of his own age from India. A plane ticket was included, as well as a voucher for a posh driving service that would meet him at Vienna International Airport and drive him to the property.

Rashan accepted, using a QR code embedded in the invitation. It had come at the perfect time. He would be able to identify the top people in the Movement without any effort on his part. A part of him thought the invitation was a setup, but the other part was interested in Dame Avriel de Villiers.

"Welcome ladies and gentlemen, to the executive board meeting for the Coming Together movement! My name is Rolanda Jackson."

Rashan was sitting in an elegant Austrian restaurant with elegant, white-cloth covered tables, chandeliers, expensive crystal glasses, and exquisite Austrian made china. Next to him sat Dame deVilliers, who was even more beautiful in person than her photograph. There were about two dozen people in the room. Rashan did what Bob Saunders told him to do at any public gathering: put up a shield to his core on the mental plane, and leave a "forward compartment" of his mind available. This was something Rashan didn't understand, but he did it anyway.

Rashan did a quick survey of the sigs. All read as normal human; all enthusiastic about the Movement. An excited buzz of conversation filled the room. Rashan saw his other housemate approach their table.

"It seems that we have been placed together," he said, sitting down. "I am Prasad Ramaswamy."

"Good evening Mr. Ramaswamy," Rashan said smoothly. "Did you have a pleasant trip?"

"A bumpy ride I'm afraid, but no harm done." He nodded to Dame de Villiers. "Nice to see you again."

Rashan was about to lean over to de Villers when the woman at the podium began to scan the sigs in the room! Rashan controlled his breathing. He carefully kept his forward compartment open and allowed the probe on the mental plane full access to that part of his mind, hoping that nothing would leak out from his core. The probe passed on; Rashan breathed a sigh of relief.

Rashan studied the perfectly manicured woman at the podium. She was wearing an elegant deep blue dress, her dark features were fine, her skin almost airbrushed perfect and smooth, her head bald. She was beautiful, but when he studied her eyes there was a blankness. She stood perfectly still, as if held in place. Rashan knew he was no expert on the mental plane so he approached her mind carefully, as Bob Saunders had taught him. Yes, there it was. Another presence, like an overlay, surrounded the sig of this woman. When she spoke it seemed to Rashan that she was channeling another entity. He wondered if the others noticed.

"All of you have been invited here today because of your exemplary work for our cause. After my presentation, each of you will meet privately with me and, if you are accepted and are willing, receive your assignments."

This organization must be a start-up, Rashan thought. He was probably looking at the future principals of Come Together. Listening with half an ear, Rashan began to carefully catalog the sigs of everyone in the room. He would compare before and after later on the mental plane, after the conference was over. "To locate a sig remotely you gotta identify that sig first," was what Bob Saunders had taught him.

He tuned back in to Rolanda. "…Colleagues, the human race is entering the Greater Community, which contains thousands of stars, every one of which has planets with intelligent life. Our friends from the stars want to introduce us to life in the galaxy! This will require a broadening of our perspective from the divisive thinking on our tiny little world. Friends, humanity must unite and stop our petty quarreling, our wars, and the pollution and resource depletion that are threatening our very survival."

[cheering]

"Make no mistake, our galactic friends want us to succeed, and are willing and able to gift us the galactic technology that can solve all of our societal difficulties. But first, our planet must unite peacefully and become a qualified member of the galactic community."

[standing ovation. Rashan stood up and went through the motions of clapping]

Rolanda droned on some more, but Rashan had gotten the drift of her message on the mental plane. As she spoke, her mind had opened a crack to allow the alien presence to speak. Rashan didn't dare try to read the galactic's sig. Bob told him that they were supermen on the mental plane, and could completely seize your mind.

After Rolanda had finished her presentation, waiters in suits and white gloves served dinner from silver plates. The food was as good as advertised. Rashan caught Dame deVilliers glancing over at him and he struck up a conversation. Rashan read her sig while they chatted. The woman had been born to wealth, but she wasn't condescending. Her personality was genuinely friendly. Rashan could feel her sexual interest in him, but he was used to that.

Rolanda walked over to their table. The galactic overlay on her sig was gone. "Would you be available tomorrow at 1 p.m. for our interview?" she asked, her eyes flashing as she glanced at deVilliers.

Rashan leaned back in his chair. "Certainly Ms. Jackson. I am at your service."

"And you, Dame deVilliers? Would 2 p.m. be suitable?"

The older woman nodded her assent with just a hint of hauteur. "That will be fine," she said, nodding dismissal to Rolanda. Rashan could feel Rolanda's interest in him, and the two women exchanged quick glances. Rashan almost laughed, for he could see on the mental plane that the Dame was disconcerted at Rolanda's youth and her own age, but Rolanda was also jealous of the Dame's self-assuredness that came from her place in society's first circles.

The Dame extended her hand and said silkily, "Rashan, would you like to take a walk with me? There's a nice little park by the hotel."

DeVilliers had smoothly taken control of the social situation. Rashan could hardly refuse, or it would be a social insult. He rose, took the Dame's hand and bowed over it, brushing the fingers lightly with his lips. "Most certainly."

Rolanda's eyes flashed again. "I'll see both of you tomorrow." She turned quickly and walked away to another table.

The Dame was too well-bred to gloat or laugh, but Rashan saw a slight smile. "Shall we be off then?" she said, squeezing his hand lightly and suggestively.

They walked out of the hotel and to the park, which was surrounded by trees and had little benches placed every few hundred feet. "I say, did you notice anything unusual about Rolanda as she gave her speech?"

The Dame's eyebrows rose slightly. "Not really. Should I have?"

Rashan read total surprise at the question and waved his hand dismissively. "I think I'm just a little tired from the plane trip."

The Dame accepted this and they continued. deVilliers was an excellent conversationalist, and they passed the time quite comfortably. As they walked and chatted, Rashan studied the Dame's sig without entering her mind. Otherwise, when the galactic who was running Rolanda interviewed Avriel tomorrow, his intrusion would be evident. But he was able to gather a few things. Dame deVilliers was married, but it was a marriage of convenience. She and her husband had an open relationship, which was quite common among the extremely wealthy who were descendants of the old aristocratic families.

Rashan had a clear path this evening and he was going to take it.

After an extremely pleasant night Rashan and the Dame had a late breakfast in the hotel's restaurant, prior to their meetings with Rolanda. deVilliers accepted the luxurious surroundings and the deferential waiters as a matter of course, but Rashan couldn't help exclaiming at the artwork on the walls, and the elegant geometric pattern on the marble floor. The Dame seemed amused.

"That's a Moorish pattern," she teased. "Tenth century, I believe."

Rashan smiled. "It's beautiful."

The Dame was pleased that he had not reacted. A waiter brought water and wine in elegant glasses. "Complements of the house," the waiter said to de Villiers.

"Hello Michel, it's good to see you again. How is your wife?"

"Much better, thank you. The flowers were a wonderful touch, Madame. Your generosity and concern is touching."

The waiter disappeared.

"It seems that you are somewhat of a celebrity around these parts."

deVilliers laughed at the American Western euphemism. "Indeed I am. This is, I believe, the best hotel in all Europe."

"I believe it."

"You are a wonderful lover."

Rashan nodded, acknowledging a truth. "I am, and so are you."

This riposte made the Dame laugh again. Their food came and they ate, talking companionably.

"Where are you from, Rashan, if you don't mind me asking?"

"Not at all. I was born in Delhi, the son of a Hindu father and a Buddhist mother. My parents immigrated to Belgium on business when I was seven. Then we moved to the States when I was twelve. I was educated at MIT in Boston."

The Dame was surprised. "You are an engineer?"

"Computer engineer. I studied artificial intelligence and the programming that mimics the human neural system."

Dame deVilliers almost dropped her glass of wine. "Surely the Come Together movement is a long way from your training."

"Not really, Avriel. My interest in neural networks is how I became interested in the Movement. It is of a certainty that our friends from the stars have technology far in advance of ours. I am interested in how far they have progressed in these fields."

deVilliers smiled and shook her head in surprise. "You see, you never really know about people unless you engage them. You look like a spiritual leader, not an engineer."

Rashan smiled. "What does an engineer look like? My father has always been interested in the Hindu spiritual tradition. He taught me how to meditate when I was a small child. I do it every day."

Avriel cocked her head to one side. "You're a fascinating individual, Rashan Oliwan."

Rashan's eyes sparkled. "So I've been told."

This made Avriel laugh again.

No one tried to shoo them out of the restaurant even though it was crowded and they had been seated for almost two hours. The Dame rose to leave.

"Are you going to dine and dash?" Rashan teased.

Avriel smiled. "Hardly, my boy. I am well known here. Our breakfast will go, as the Americans say, on my tab. And of course, a generous tip for my friend Michel."

Rashan rose. "I could get used to this."

"Somehow I don't see you as a, er, companion."

"Correct-a-mundo!" Rashan said with enthusiasm. "Not my style."

"You are very interesting," deVilliers said as they walked to the park. "And complex. I can see how your Hindu upbringing has affected your personality. Your time in Europe has given you a certain...sophistication. And you have the frankness of the Americans and their somewhat odd ways."

They entered the park and sat down on one of the benches. Avriel was dressed to kill, wearing a skirt and black hose that showed her long legs to

263

advantage. She casually crossed her legs. "Well Rashan, can I convince you to stay in Austria for a few more days?"

Rashan grinned. "I think I can rearrange my schedule to accommodate that."

"It's settled then. I'll ask the landlord to extend our stay...say, one week?"

Rashan bowed. "That is very well, Avriel."

It was time for his interview. "Why don't we meet back here after your interview with Rolanda?" Rashan suggested. "We can take a walk and discuss Ms. Jackson."

"You make me laugh, Rashan. I hope I can see you again after this little adventure."

"Done. Now I must be off to see the lovely Rolanda."

As Rashan walked away he saw her frown. He was going to be very interested in talking to Avriel after her interview.

Rashan met Rolanda in one of the hotel conference rooms. Rashan turned his mind from Avriel deVilliers to business. He prepared his forward compartment on the mental plane. The conference room was small, but like everything in the hotel, elegant. There was a small bar and refrigerator. "Would you like something?" Rolanda asked, studying him appreciatively.

"No thank you, I've just had breakfast."

Rolanda sniffed the air. "Perfume. You've been with deVilliers."

"Quite so. But that is over. I am fully prepared to devote my entire attention to you."

Rolanda relaxed with an attitude that said, 'that's better.'

Today she had on a dark green ensemble that emphasized her smooth, flawless skin. Rashan noted how her appearance was similar to the lifelike manufactured cyborgs advertised now as human helpers. The woman was beautiful in an emotionless way. Rashan wondered whether she was fully human. Perhaps she was a galactic version of a new human? A genderless female. He had heard rumors of that from some in the Movement.

"Let's begin," Rolanda said, interrupting his thoughts. Rashan saw how Rolanda left and...someone else...came in. The transition was seamless. Not even a breath interrupted the transition. Rolanda was still there, but enhanced somehow. Her body did not experience discomfort, as far as Rashan could see.

Suddenly Rashan felt the forward compartment of his mind seized. It was not as bad as what Philogene Rothman had experienced with his Oorant, but he could not move. "Now," Rolanda said, her voice slightly altered, "Let me see what we have here."

Rashan's forward compartment was fully examined, like a burglar tossing an apartment for valuables. Bob's instructions if this ever happened were explicit: 'Don't resist, keep your core absolutely blank.'

Rashan knew what to expect, but having an alien in your mind was disconcerting. Clearly, this being suspected nothing. To it, Rashan was just a typical human. Rashan dispassionately observed the mental inspection from his core, and picked up some information about the intruder. This being was just a grunt, a worker drone assigned to scrub data. Certainly not a sophisticate on the mental plane! Rashan relaxed a little. Apparently galactics had a very poor opinion of humans.

After the mental inspection the tactics changed. A pleasant, benevolent vibe infused Rashan's mind. A Sister Sani avatar spoke to him. "Welcome, dear Rashan! You are now ready to become a principal figure in our movement. Congratulations! Sister Rolanda will now explain your duties."

Rashan felt wonderful. The forward compartment of his mind was ready to do anything for their friends from the stars, knowing that it was the very best for humanity.

Rashan saw Rolanda's eyes clear. The human Rolanda was back and appeared not to have been aware of the mental inspection she had just conducted.

"Your effectiveness as an organizer and event presenter is unmatched, Rashan. Therefore you shall continue in these duties as before. You will receive instructions as to the various event venues from HQ here in Austria. How much advance notice do you need before each event?"

"That will depend on the country," Rashan heard his forward compartment responding. "In North America and Europe, two weeks. In Asia, three weeks due to government regulations on free speech. In South America, at least one month due to the disorganized state of the continent."

"Very well. You will receive your instructions on your smart device embedded in a QR code. That is all."

His forward compartment responded automatically. "Thank you, Sister Rolanda! I am looking forward to working with you."

Before he walked out Rashan analyzed Rolanda's conscious memories. The timeline of her life showed an enthusiastic woman at the beginning of her Come Together participation. The galactic overlay was more pronounced now. How long had Ms. Jackson been doing these interviews? The sad bit was that Rolanda wasn't aware of how she was changing. If she continued in her present job, Rashan could see her turning into a hybrid human being who would walk the earth, but who would be little more than a chess piece for whatever galactic wanted to move her around the board.

Rashan hurried back to the park and waited for Avriel deVilliers to be done with her interview. It was 1:47 now. He was worried. Would Avriel be a good little robot for the Movement? That thought saddened him, then made him angry. Who were these meddling galactics, to come here and destroy the creativity and the soul of good people like Rolanda Jackson? He understood the attitude of Bob Saunders and Ralph Zimring much better because he was beginning to feel that way himself. Rashan understood that he had no interest in anyone who wasn't fully human. Fuck them, as Bob Saunders would say.

Rashan got up and walked around the park, glancing toward the hotel every few minutes. Suddenly he saw the black dress coming toward the park. Rashan walked quickly to the bench where they had sat before. He heard the click-click of Avriel's high heels as they struck the pavement leading to the park from the hotel. In a minute she was standing before him.

"Well?" he asked her.

"I..."

Rashan saw her frown, then her countenance cleared. "I feel wonderful! To be a part of something so magnificent, it is truly an honor."

Rashan felt his stomach fall. The authentic human spark that had made Avriel deVilliers so fascinating was no longer there. "What are your duties?" he asked dully. Avriel didn't notice his disappointment.

"The Movement wants me to act as a spokesperson to wealthy and influential people. I will essentially be living my normal life, but now serving the best cause in the history of the world!"

"That's very nice. What will you do next?"

"I must arrange a grand party. Paris, I think. Everyone who is anyone will be there."

"I see. When do you leave?"

"Oh, I must begin at once. I shall fly to my home in Marseilles and begin first thing tomorrow morning."

Rashan was bitter, but he remembered his manners and bowed. "Very well, Dame deVilliers. It was very nice meeting you."

"You too, Rashan. Keep in touch!" She was off, walking excitedly back to the hotel. Their liaison had been forgotten.

Rashan sat back down on the bench, burning with disappointment. Slowly, his mood turned to rage. He wanted to kill every one of these interfering galactics! To see the life essentially snuffed out in Avriel was a crime against humanity.

What was he to do about his new post in the Come Together movement? He could no longer promote this dangerous nonsense. Rashan took his mobile device out of his pocket and removed the SIM card. He smashed the phone and the card to pieces on the pavement with the hard heel of his shoe, eliciting curious stares from passersby. He looked at the smashed transparency and the mangled insides. Any QR codes sent to that device by Come Together would fail.

Rashan walked back to the hotel and found a small electronics store, where he bought a new phone and created a new account. There! His old life was gone; he was starting over. He bought a new airline ticket with his bank card because he did not want to turn away from the Movement yet use their services. Then he went to the hotel restaurant for a meal, and from there hailed a cab to take him back to his room at the Hofbauer. As soon as he entered he saw Prasad Ramaswamy.

"Greetings, Rashan!" Ramaswamy said. "Have you completed your interview?"

"I have indeed," Rashan responded, studying Prasad's sig. Sadly, it was the same as deVilliers. Outwardly the same person, Rashan detected a similar overlay of unquestioning cheerful alignment with the Movement. Rashan decided to go into Prasad's mind. He saw the man's eyes blank out for a millisecond and then he was in. He grabbed everything and was out in less than a second. Prasad's eyes cleared and his face resumed the same cheerful expression as before. Rashan brushed by and walked up the stairs, not wanting to talk to the man. Even though he didn't know him well, it would be too painful to observe the disappearance of his unique human qualities.

As Rashan packed he began to feel cold fear. Here was an influence that could not be countered, an invisible influence completely outside the human experience.

Rashan hurried his packing, anxious to be out of this area and at the airport.

Rolanda's interviews with the others would not finish until late tomorrow afternoon. By that time he hoped to be back in Tampa, remotely studying the sigs of all the attendees. He wanted to talk to everyone in person, but Vienna had taken on a sinister air and he couldn't stand the place anymore. It would be much less stressful to do his survey remotely. After that he would report back to Bob Saunders on the mental plane using the coded message system.

Rashan hailed a cab and was driven to the airport. He had five hours before he could board. He used that time to remotely locate the 23 sigs of the attendees. It was much more difficult than when they were all in one room, for the mental plane was just a chaotic jumble of sigs and noise. By the time he boarded his flight he had still not located the first sig, a woman named Wen Zhang Xiu from Xian, a large city in western China that had been on China's Old Silk Road. He knew she was in Vienna, but could not distinguish her sig from the others. Bob Sanders was right. Remote sig location required practice and patience. Rashan gave it up for now and closed his eyes.

When Rashan got to Tampa it took him several days to isolate and locate the 23 other sigs.

As Rashan found the sigs of the other attendees, he was outraged to discover that they were almost identical to Avriel's, all having the overlays. Common to all of them was a lack of individuality along with a cheerful, unquestioning enthusiasm that Rashan found insulting. He remembered someone saying, "If two human beings are the same then one of them is superfluous." What would happen if millions were the same? Or billions?

— 31 —

Ralph called my mobile. "Bob Saunders just sent me the report from Rashan Oliwan. It's something everyone needs to see. Is Joann flying?"

"She's here until Sunday night."

"Get everyone together at 7 as usual."

Ralph showed up at 6:30, his face grim. "Look at what Rashan discovered."

Inside our shielded office Ralph showed me everything Rashan had learned about the Come Together movement in a couple of dozen packets. Rashan's report showed how the trainees at the international executive meeting had been personally influenced by a galactic through the mind of Rolanda Jackson. The sig overlays were turning the Come Together executives into willing and happy proxies for the Collectives. The same thing was probably happening to the Uploads directors.

The others began to arrive. Josh was still sweaty and still wearing his dogi. "Sorry folks, I had a late student and had to race over here. I didn't have time to change and shower."

Kelleye looked at him adoringly. Joann and I exchanged glances. Ralph grinned.

"No problem, Josh. Everybody get seated and comfortable. I have a lot to show you."

It took everyone about half an hour to digest Rashan's information. We now knew exactly what Rashan knew, in vivid color with all the emotions and thoughts involved, exactly as Rashan had experienced it.

From Ralph's mind we learned that his network was expanding every day. He had essentially become the world's foremost trainer of the mental plane / remote viewing technique. Ralph's people (all military or ex-military) were calling it the Zimring Method, and were zealously teaching it to their units and their personal connections.

"Ralph, what you are doing is amazing," Kelleye said.

"I just hope it isn't too late," he said.

Kelleye smiled. "We do what we can, my dear."

Ralph laughed so hard the door to the office shook on its hinges. Ralph wiped his eyes. "Touche! By Gad, I'm glad I'm working with you kids."

Josh teased Kelleye. "The military is the only group that is running with this thing."

Kelleye sighed. "I suppose you're right, for now. But the rest of us will catch up."

"All right people," Ralph commanded. "Your conclusions?"

"Team, I haven't been able to solve the attractor problem," I said. "It's galactic technology way beyond our understanding. Therefore – unless you all can figure it out – the only way to stop the Intervention is to train people in the technique."

"What good will that do?" Joann asked. "The entire human race is getting brainwashed!"

"Philo is right, D'Arcy," said Ralph. "We need to discover if the training can help people to resist and recover from the influence of the attractors."

"That's it, Ralph!" Joann cried. "Remember what Patrick told us. Galactics are immune to the attractors because they can all operate on the mental plane."

The meeting ended on an enthusiastic note. My depression lifted. We couldn't do anything about the attractors but we might be able to neutralize the human response to them. For the first time since I met Patrick I was fired up about our chances. The human race would not roll over for these galactic Collectives! We could organize an army of awakened human beings, active and proficient on the mental plane.

Joann and I left holding hands, making plans. We were going to train as many of our friends as we could.

I stubbornly tried one more time to analyze the attractors and neutralize them, but it was no good. Even the abilities I had gained on the mental plane with my Seer training were woefully inadequate to the task. Frustrated for something productive to do, I visited Jamaal at his house and asked him whether he was interested in the mind training. "It will really help your investigation into Uploads," I said confidently. "Remote viewing saves a lot of tedious investigation."

"If it works," Jamaal said.

"You're in love with Kathy Arvidson, a tech at Midland Uploads," I offered.

Jamaal sputtered. "You said friends don't read each others' minds."

"Is it true?"

"Yes," Jamaal said glumly. "But I don't know how to approach her."

After having had a relationship with Gwenneth, I felt like the galaxy's foremost authority on women. "It's simple. You have to show interest."

"Interest in what?"

"Interest in her, you dummy! What is she interested in?"

"I never got to ask at work, we were always so busy."

"C'mon, man. Meet her out in the parking lot after her shift, ask her out for coffee."

"I'm too shy. Besides, I'm not allowed anywhere on the premises."

"Jamaal, you're a perfect candidate for the training. It will increase your self-confidence."

Jamaal twisted his hands nervously for a few moments, thinking. "All right. Can we start right away?"

"Sure. It will take a week of personal instruction even if you catch on quickly."

I began the training. Jamaal was resistant at first because he was uncomfortable with me being in his mind. "You have to allow the trainer access or you won't catch on. Just open up a little."

We began to make progress when I showed him how to access the portal to the mental plane. Every sig I have ever studied has one of these access portals, which means that every human being can potentially learn the technique. Like me, Jamaal had made good bank at Uploads (not as good as me, but pretty good) and he was just coasting for the time being. He had plenty of free time and I came over every day until he was as proficient as I could make him.

"Now you have to practice," I said on the last day. "Conduct your research on the mental plane, but be careful. The Uploads directors are all monitored."

"What do you mean by monitored?"

"That's your homework, Jamaal. Approach these sigs very, very carefully."

"You're being mysterious and I don't like mysteries."

"I can't teach you anything more until you practice. The first step is learning how to locate sigs. Start with the sigs of your friends and family. It's very frustrating at first, and there are no shortcuts. Keep at it. Once you get good at locating sigs, start with the Midland Uploads director because you know that punk the best. Locate Bronfman's sig, approach carefully, and compare it to your friends. Don't try anything else or you can get into trouble! If something bad happens, send me this coded signal on the mental plane."

I gave him the signal. Jamaal's eyes got wider.

"Philo, what are you guys doing in that office of yours?"

I was getting excited. "Jamaal, this game is being played on the very largest scale there is. It is an invisible war. There are a lot more people involved than my little group of four. People all over the world are learning this technique. It's going to change the entire human race."

"I knew you were holding out on me!"

"Not holding out, my friend. I can't tell you anything more until you learn to locate sigs on the mental plane. For now don't read their minds, just locate them."

Jamaal got out of his chair and paced the room. "I can feel your excitement, Philo." Jamaal grinned. "Now get out of here so I can practice."

I had done a good week's work. Another sig that couldn't be mind washed. If Jamaal could learn to locate sigs I'd show him the attractors. That was the most mind-blowing part of the training. That's when we got really motivated team members.

Two weeks after the Coming Together international executive meeting, and just after I had finished training Jamaal, a number of vids starring Sister Sani and Brother Hamal saturated mass media. The theme was, "Uniting the Human Workforce."

The human workforce?

I watched one of the vids, which showed smiling people working together in hospitals, on road and building construction sites, in offices, schools, and in neighborhoods. Sister Sani narrated. "We are here to show you how to create a peaceful society aligned to galactic standards. Our human administrators and technocrats will show the people of earth how to organize society, how to educate human beings in their areas of greatest ability, and to create the most efficient social order where all can prosper, not just a few. Stay tuned, brothers and sisters. In further presentations we will submit to your leaders the entire galactic plan for earth."

Sister Sani and Brother Hamal joined hands. "Here's to the success of earth and its full participation in the Greater Community!"

While I was watching the presentation I felt a pleasant vibe combined with a certainty that Sani and Hamal were telling the absolute truth from a higher perspective. I understood what Ralph had said earlier. We aren't dealing with evil. The human race is facing an ancient, overwhelming galactic bureaucracy that grinds emerging planets like earth into dust.

When Joann came back from her seven-day flying period, we had a meeting in the shielded office.

"This war will be won or lost right here on planet earth," Ralph said. "The attractors are invulnerable, and trying to physically fight galactics is pointless. All we did was get Genghis Glazer and Rebecca Holmes and Chang Li-Meng killed."

Kelleye winced.

"We can make people immune to the attractors through the mental plane training. My network is teaching so many people I can't keep track of them. Sergei has a whole company under training! Every one of those guys is going to train their buddies, and their families, if they are open to it."

Ralph's eyes breathed fire. "My plan is to teach this technique to half the men and women on active duty in the U.S. military. There's nothing the brass can do about it because they don't know anything about the mental plane and wouldn't believe anyone who tried to explain it to them. Everybody teaches as many as they can, and it spreads."

Josh knew Ralph was withholding something. "What aren't you telling us, Ralph?"

Ralph got so excited he leaped out of his chair and scared the crap out of Kelleye, who was sitting nearest him on one of the sofas. "We start our own private army. It will be the biggest mutiny in world history!"

Josh couldn't believe it. "You could get in big trouble for that, Ralph."

Ralph grinned. "Nope. No one will know about our army because all comms are on the mental plane. People can still stay in their regular units if they want, but if we need them...they are ours!"

I looked at Josh. "It's an insurrection¡'

Ralph nodded. "A silent insurrection." Ralph was pacing the room now in huge strides. "This is a spiritual war; the old distinctions no longer apply. It's high consciousness versus low consciousness."

Joann got it. "The enlightened against the brainwashed zombies!"

Ralph frowned. "No, D'Arcy. It's not anyone's fault. The attractors are the ultimate propaganda weapon: a hidden influence that indoctrinates but is completely invisible. There is no defense against them. Until you get woke."

I understood. "It's not really a fight, is it Ralph? It's more like educating people."

"You could say that. This is a new, sixth-generation kind of warfare that uses information and persuasion on the mental plane. The galactics use the mental plane to brainwash humans, we use it to un-brainwash them."

Kelleye spoke with admiration. "Ralph Zimring, you have put a lot of thought into your plan."

"The idea for a private army wasn't mine. It was born organically, as more and more people began to train others. When you are aware of the mental plane you want to associate with others who share your awareness."

Josh was amazed. "So people are voluntarily leaving their units?"

"That's right, kid. It's just a trickle now, but everyone we've trained in the military is getting more and more frustrated taking orders from dumbass commanders who can't comm mind-to-mind. Sergei is our European coordinator. He says that in another couple of years there may be hardly anyone left in the European Forces."

"Do we have that long?" I asked.

"Don't sweat it, Philo. What we're doing is a massive paradigm shift in human awareness. We've got all the time we need. Our groups – military and civilian – will naturally form our own parallel society because of the consciousness shift that results from the training."

"Oh my God," Joann said. "Two separate societies. That will lead to a world war!"

"Relax, D'Arcy. The other society will be composed of people who have been socially programmed by the Collectives. They will be a very efficient hive mind that simply follows orders, whereas our group will be flexible, adaptable to changing situations at the speed of thought, and united in freedom."

"There will be conflict," Kelleye said.

Ralph shrugged. "What human revolution hasn't had conflict? We don't know how it will play out. We are presently small in number but we are in instant communication. You have realized by now how quickly disputes can be resolved when you are in contact on the mental plane. Our group will have much less division and discord and be more united."

"Can the antisocial also learn the technique?" I asked.

"Sergei says yes. The good news is that even an antisocial person, if he or she completes the training, lets go of their sociopathy. A lot of them never finish though. It freaks them out."

Ralph looked at his timepiece. "All right children, I'm leaving you to do your thing. I have a big meeting tonight on the mental plane with all the military we've trained so far."

Ralph strode out.

"Well, he told us," Josh said. "Ralph has got the military on board. We civilians are way behind."

"Yes," Kelleye agreed. "My academic friends and my business clients have no interest in the technique. It's sad."

"Then we'd better get our asses in gear. I already trained Jamaal, but I don't have a lot of friends." How were we supposed to train billions of civilians? Ralph's military guys were used to taking orders and working together, so it was easy for him. "What I really want to do is fuck over some galactics," I complained.

Josh laughed.

"Ralph is right, as usual," Joann said. "The battle is on earth to save earth. We have to defend our territory."

"Yeah, but that's a lot of work!" I said. "We have to train billions. All they have to do is sit back and let the attractors create more willing slaves. I want to smash the galactic overlords and save the galaxy."

"God, Philo," Joann said. "You really are a little boy, aren't you?"

"Yeah, but I'm your little boy."

"Ralph is working with the military types," Kelleye said. "They are self-organizing around their military principles. We need to create an awakened civilian population focused on peace, not fighting."

I snorted. "Sorry Kel, but there's billions to train. Ralph is a great motivator, but we are never going to wake up that many in time to counter the Collectives' social programming. You've all seen the media saturation by the Come Together people and their affiliated organizations. There were 20 major events last week worldwide!"

Josh and Joann exchanged glances. "Shut up Philo, you're a morale killer," Josh said.

"Don't mind me, I'm just venting. I just wish the Greater Community was more like the Guardians of the Galaxy."

"We're agreed then," Joann said, her eyes on mine. "We shift all of our efforts to teaching. It's the only effective counter we have to the Collectives."

— 32 —

Three years later

There was a pounding on our door at Second Street Investigations.

Ralph and our team were holding a conference of all members of the Free Earth organization. No one outside the group knew of our existence. We commed, planned, and did all admin silently on the mental plane. There were five million of us now, and our group was growing rapidly. All business was conducted at the speed of thought. Transparency and honesty were built in to the group, for no sig who put up a shield was allowed to participate. At the last meeting we did see a very powerful shielded entity observing, and we suspected that this must be some off-planet being working for the Collectives.

The pounding was getting louder and more insistent.

"Be a dear and go get that, Ralph," Kelleye said with a tendril of her mind.

Ralph detached a part of his mind to move his body to the door. When he opened it he saw five suits, one of them a bullethead. PSF guys.

The bullethead was surprised. "Zimring! What are you doing here?"

"Gyorgy Rynkowski! Last time I saw you, you were being chased by SISMI operatives on the Via Piave!" Rynkowski was an all around bad guy hired by anyone who would pay him enough.

"Them were the good old days, Zimring. I hope you're not mixed up with this subversive group," Gyorgy said, pointing into the room.

"Of course I am, Rynkowski. I started it!"

"We're coming in, over your body if we have to."

Ralph shrugged. He didn't have a lot of mental attention to devote to this encounter. In his younger days he would have taken on the lot of them, but these guys were PSF, the newly created Peace and Security Force that was the enforcement arm of the Illinois collectives. There were four collectives in the state, representing four of the six largest cities. The free zones avoided contact with them whenever possible.

Ralph commed to the others on the mental plane and stepped aside. Rynkowski and his men rushed in, looking for computers, storage devices, and mobiles.

"What the fuck is this?" Rynkowski demanded as his men scoured the place looking for anything connected to the Internet of Things.

Ralph laughed and scanned Rynkowski's mind. Everyone in the Illinois collectives had neural implants and were connected to the Internet of Bodies. This bunch were run by the Chicago collective, who could see everything their men could see via their implants. "We're having a meeting, as you can see."

On the mental plane over a million Free Earthers were looking on. The meeting was temporarily suspended.

One of Rynkowski's men got frustrated and kicked over the small refrigerator in the cafeteria (not connected to the IOT), spilling food over the linoleum.

That pissed Ralph off. He was 64, but he could handle any one of these guys except maybe Rynkowski, who was a noted fighter and much younger. "Pick up the food, motherfucker, and put it back," Ralph said conversationally.

The man smirked and Ralph moved quickly, smashing him against the brick wall. The man slid slowly down the wall, dazed. "Now Gyorgy, that wasn't nice. You can see we got nothing. We're peaceful citizens of Free Midland, and you have no jurisdiction here."

Rynkowski's eyes blanked for a moment as he consulted his implant. "My orders are to strip this place and retrieve your electronic devices."

Ralph was getting bored. The man behind him groaned in pain and tried to get up. "We don't have any electronic devices, Gyorgy. Even the imbecile who is running you in Chicago can see that." The Peace and Security Force was just a euphemism for the state security forces in the restricted areas, which called themselves "community zones." The free zones were forming their own security forces, but that effort had just gotten off the ground.

Gyorgy and his men were frustrated. "This doesn't make sense!" Gyorgy complained. "We know you folks are organizing but there's no communication devices, office equipment, or computer networks!"

Ralph sighed. "That's because we don't have any. Now get the fuck out." Ralph grabbed the man who had knocked over the fridge and threw him toward the door.

Gyorgy's eyes blanked again. "We're leaving, but we are going to keep our eyes on you."

"You won't be able to cross our border again, Gyorgy. Go back to your hive in Chicago and your pointless existence."

Gyorgy smirked. "You'll wake up one day, you fool."

The men left, and Ralph walked back into the office. The group continued their silent discussion on the mental plane. Josh Reynolds was giving a short summary of the current social situation in the United States.

'During the past three years, approximately 60% of the population, under the influence of the galactic attractors and the Come Together movement, have accepted or actively embraced a collectivist lifestyle. These people all have neural implants. About 25% of the population now live in free zone areas like Midland. People moved into the free zones mainly to get away from busybody politicians and bureaucrats in the larger cities. Most of us in the free zones have rejected the Rejuvenon shots. The other 15% are Ronin or Independents, who live in the sparsely populated countryside, or hide themselves within the forests or the mountains or in the deserts. *Ronin* is the name given to rogue, unchipped humans who are too unruly to accept the collectivist lifestyle and who also hate the free zones. Many Ronin are disgruntled ex-military and/or antisocial personalities.The Independents are hardy isolationists who want nothing to do with human society. Ronin and Independents are all unchipped. Some of the Independent areas are like the Old West. Fortunately, neither Ronin nor Independents disturb food growing areas, farms, and food processing plants. Ronin have been known to shoot on sight persons who attack these areas. Some Ronin have become folk heroes for this, just as during the Shogunate period in Japan.'

'Is the collective population really 60% of the total?' someone from New Mexico asked.

'Yes. That's our latest intelligence from the free zones across the country. Social scientists in the free zones are amazed at the astonishing rapidity of the social split. Those who accepted the galactic message stayed in the larger cities, chipped and happy to be part of a human workforce that will (they believe) help a galaxy inhabited by benevolent beings like Sister Sani and Brother Hamal.'

'It seems...strange.'

Josh shrugged mentally. 'Not really, my friend. The collectivists call it community. They like order and structure, and prefer a predictable lifestyle. That's why they embrace the neural implants, because the implants lead to harmony of thought and action.'

'Harmony of thought? It's brainwashing.'

'That's not how the collectives see it,' Josh replied, trying to be objective. 'Those in the chipped areas see us in the free zones as dangerous iconoclasts and troublemakers. They are happy with their lives and their new communities. They see themselves participating in a peaceful society with a common identity. When they think about the rest of humanity, it is in a condescending way for poor dupes like us who just don't get it yet.'

Josh paused. 'That concludes my summary of the current social situation in the United States. Our civilian group is participating with the military group in a planetary social survey. Preliminary results show a similar social situation everywhere in the world.'

'How is the defense force doing in Midland?' someone asked from a free zone in northern California.

'So far so good,' Ralph replied. 'Our population is only 150,000 compared to the two million within the Chicago collective. But our guys are determined to arm every citizen who wants a laser pistol by the end of the year.'

'Some of our Independents are stealing food supply trucks,' someone from New York sent. 'That's a crime punishable by instant execution in both zones.'

'That's right,' Josh sent. 'Throughout human history, food shortages and famine have resulted in revolution. The Collectives are insanely afraid of this on a planet they are desperate to bring into the fold.' Josh is the earth's galactic historian and is consulted by leaders in all of the free areas. He had quit his martial arts studio and now taught galactic history via online classes on the mental plane.

'All right folks, are there any more questions? OK, I'm out.'

We all left the online meeting.

"The PSF are getting bolder," Kelleye remarked to the team. "They just raided us."

"This was probably just a scouting mission," Joann said.

Ralph looked at me. "You need to show up for weapons training on Friday."

"Me? I couldn't hit a food storage silo from twenty feet."

"That's why you need it."

Ralph was the local commander so I had to do it. I liked the old world a lot better than this one, but you have to roll with the times.

Ralph spoke quietly to Josh. Kelleye was across the room talking to Joann. "I'm going into Chicago tomorrow. Do you want to come?"

Josh's eyes lit up. "Do I! Wouldn't miss it for the world."

"Good. I want to talk to the collective commander, and see how these restricted zones are laid out. We'll get some good first-hand intel."

Josh and I glanced at each other. We had no idea how Ralph was going to get in to the Chicago collective, but we didn't doubt that he could. I wanted to go with, but I was the chief trainer for the entire US and I had to stay in the shielded office. It sucked, but I was doing something I loved.

The next morning at 4 a.m. Ralph called Josh on the mental plane. 'Be at the office in a half-hour. Bring stuff to eat.'

'But—'

The connection was broken. Damn the man, Josh thought as he got out of bed and began rummaging for clothes.

"Where are you going?" a sleepy Kelleye asked.

"To Chicago with Ralph."

"Oh no, Josh. It's too dangerous!"

Josh smiled and kissed her. "With Ralph there? Not a chance!" Josh didn't tell her that Ralph planned to talk to the city commander in the heart of the collective. As he walked to the kitchen for coffee, he realized he didn't have the time to make it or drink it. He hunted in the fridge and found a jar of peanut butter, a hard boiled egg, which he ate for breakfast, and two bananas. The morning was cool so Josh grabbed his coat from the front door closet.

When he got to the office (which was three blocks away) Josh groaned when he saw Ralph's ancient, beat up Ford.

"Don't insult Arthur, son. He's just like me; we both have a lot of life left in us."

It was 50 miles northeast from Midland to Chicago. Josh hadn't been there in almost three years. He and Kelleye used to occasionally go to the city on weekends for a good time, but the place had completely changed, according to those free citizens who had to go there on business.

"How are we going to get in?" Josh asked.

Ralph grinned and showed Josh his phone. "QR codes for me and you! Plus, two Illinois collective scrip accounts, one for each of us."

Josh laughed. "I won't even ask how you got them."

"Simple. These restricted zone humans are chipped, but they can still be influenced on the mental plane. One of our operatives got them for me."

We took the 55. Just past the 355 interchange we saw half a dozen automated toll booths with metal barriers. People were flashing their QR codes from their mobiles. The booth said 'Accepted' every time a car went through, and the light turned from red to green as the metal barriers went down.

A cacophony of "Accepted" in machine voices filled the air. "Must make 'em feel better," Ralph said humorously.

One car without a QR code was not allowed in. Immediately, three men jumped out of a little guardhouse and began interrogating a woman.

Josh was getting nervous about what would happen in the Chicago collective. He looked over at Ralph, who could barely fit in the driver's seat, which had been modified to bump up against the back seat to accommodate his long legs. The big man was treating this trip as casually as a visit to the public library.

"Relax, Josh. This is going to be fun."

Josh laughed. "You're every bit as cool as your reputation."

"This will be a piece of cake compared to some of my, er, field operations."

The lines were moving quickly. Ralph presented two QR codes on his mobile to the scanner. "Accepted." The metal barrier lowered to the cement and Arthur proceeded. They were in the Chicago collective!

"Where are we going?" Josh asked.

Ralph texted Josh his QR code. "That's your registration. Keep it with you. We're going to see the queen bee in the Loop district at North LaSalle and Randolph. To the heart of the beast."

Josh looked around as they went up 55. Everything looked normal. The parks, houses, and buildings were unchanged from three years ago. "It's weird. Everyone is traveling at exactly the same speed." All of the vehicles were precisely four car lengths apart. It looked like the traffic was being moved by an invisible force.

"It's the neural chips, Josh. They like it, it makes them feel safe and part of a community."

Josh got out his jar of peanut butter and a banana and began to eat.

"Peanut butter?"

"You didn't leave me time for anything else. What did you bring?"

"Nothing, I had an extra large breakfast."

Josh wondered what Ralph's usual breakfast was. Ralph caught that thought on the mental plane.

"Five eggs, a dozen small breakfast sausages, a dozen rashers of bacon, and three cups of coffee laced with whiskey."

"That's your usual breakfast?"

Ralph looked astonished. "Of course! I'm a big man and I need my vittles."

Josh was fascinated. "You said you had an extra large breakfast."

"Yup. I added a small cheese round." Ralph patted his stomach. "Yummy."

Josh checked the mental plane as they drove to City Hall. People were thinking about the work they had to do, or were going to do. There were hardly any thoughts about anything other than the work to be done.

"I noticed that too," Ralph said. "But look." Ralph pointed to a collection of buildings as they crossed the Mannheim Rd exit. "Everything is spotless. You could probably eat off the streets they're so clean. No dirt, junk, or trash anywhere."

"You're right!" Josh was beginning to change his thinking about collectivization. "Hard work has its benefits." Could a person be happy in a completely regimented society? Reports that filtered into the free zones showed that there was no violence or crime in the restricted areas. When you got up every day you knew what you had to do, there was some comfort in that. "There are some good aspects to it, I suppose."

Ralph looked at Josh queerly. "If you don't mind having your brain chipped and following orders like a sheep."

As they approached North Ashland the streets were busy. People walked sedately, no one hurried. "It's a calm sort of existence," Josh remarked.

"It's a boring sort of existence, kid."

Just then Josh spotted a window cleaning crew working on one of the buildings. "Those sigs are different."

"Good catch," Ralph said. "Those guys are unchipped. There's a shortage of labor in the city and the collective allows unchipped crews as long as they adhere rigidly to the rules. If they get out of line they are hustled out of the city and their QR codes are canceled."

Ralph drove around the area, checking for parking places. All of the lots were full around City Hall, but there was a sign on a lot on Washington that said "Contractors only."

"That's us," Ralph said, presented his code, and drove in.

"We're contractors?" Josh asked.

"According to the gal who gave me these QRs."

The two men got out of Arthur and walked down Washington. Ralph was in a hurry to see the collective commander, who had his office in the old City Hall building. People stared as Ralph and Josh brushed by several Citizens on the sidewalk. From a small enclosure at the end of the street two men rushed out. "Your identities!"

Ralph was going to push them away but Josh entered the two minds. These guys were known as Street Guardians, and were there to maintain order and stability. Their duties were to challenge any disturbance of the peace. Josh saw instantly that the two men were laser-focused on their jobs and their motivation was for "the good of the community." They were afraid of Ralph, and regarded him as one of the unruly and undisciplined contractors from the free zones.

The neural chips made it more difficult to influence their thinking because they were electronic and not accessible by the mental plane, so Josh put a simple thought into their minds: "These two are valuable free zone contractors helping the collective."

The two men stood down as Josh grabbed his and Ralph's QR passes, which were scanned and checked against a city-wide list of contractors and citizens.

"Very well, you may proceed."

"Behave as you see the others behave," Josh warned Ralph as they walked slowly away from the monitor station.

Ralph almost doubled over with laughter. "Good work, Josh. You're one to ride the river with."

Josh didn't understand this archaic expression but he was pleased at the complement from the older man. The two men proceeded sedately down Washington and encountered a traffic light at Wells, which was red. As it turned green Ralph was about to stride past those at the head of the line when Josh put a hand on his arm. He used the mental plane. 'Let's see how these people cross the street.'

Josh watched as everyone happily lined up two-by-two and crossed.

Ralph was bored out of his mind and wanted to pick up a few of these retards and throw them out of his way. Josh cautioned him on the mental plane.

'You're no fun,' Ralph sent back. 'I want to stir things up and see how these chipped humans react.'

'We're almost there,' Josh sent reassuringly, as if to a very large child.

'I'll get you for that one,' Ralph sent back.

Josh was reading sigs. 'We don't have the implants so we don't know what comms are being sent to these people in real time,' he sent to Ralph. 'But we can read anything new that pops up in their conscious minds an instant after it goes through their implant.'

'That's good, Josh,' Ralph sent back.

As the two walked toward LaSalle, a man coming the other way hailed them. "Nice day, isn't it friends?" Josh read the man's sig but found nothing unusual. Ralph and Josh stopped to chat and the crowds walked calmly around them. "What are your work designations?" The man's name was Citizen Brian Strezler and he was guileless, with a peculiarly vacant expression. Josh quickly read the man's sig on the mental plane. All of the work categories were there in his conscious mind. "We are categorized 2C-CA, contractors to the city administration," Josh replied smoothly.

"On our way to talk to Citizen Abernathy, the collective commander," Ralph added.

The man's eyes lit up and he bowed. "Then I won't keep you, gentlemen. Thank you for your service to the greater good," he said smiling, and walked away.

Ralph and Josh looked at each other in amazement. 'These Citizens are harmless,' Ralph sent on the mental plane as they crossed LaSalle and turned left toward City Hall.

'Yeah, but who sent Gyorgy and his goons to Midland?'

'I intend to find out.' Ralph was having a good time and feeling expansive. He slapped Josh on the shoulder companionably. A few frowns were seen as passersby saw the friendly slap as an assault. A woman approached them and said, "This violent behavior is not acceptable, friend. All citizens must be treated with respect and appreciation."

Ralph was about to blow her off when Josh cautioned him on the mental plane. 'This is Citizen Traylor Rolens. You just violated Code of Behavior Section 3, Article 2. "All citizens are respected equally and none must be valued above another, or demeaned." Bow respectfully and apologize to me and to Citizen Traylor.'

Ralph swallowed his irritation at this neurotic behavior, but did as Josh asked. Citizen Traylor's eyes blanked for a second, and her face cleared. "That is well, friend. Good day!"

'Get me out of here Josh,' Ralph sent as they started up again.

In another minute they were at the City Hall entrance. "The commander is in Office 100, just to your right as you enter the building." Josh wondered whether Ralph had a pass, or authorization, to see the commander.

Ralph was fed up with all of the mindless compliance he had seen. 'Follow my lead,' he sent.

Ralph opened the glass door and walked in. Josh followed. Both men quickly read all of the sigs in the office. There was a receptionist, one large office to the right with a plate glass transparency overlooking the street, and two smaller offices to the left. The Commander was in the office to the right;

four others were in the other two. Ralph and Josh commed on the mental plane. 'Let me handle the receptionist before you barge in,' Josh sent to Ralph.

Ralph agreed reluctantly. 'I'll handle the commander.'

Josh quickly placed a thought in the receptionist's mind: 'Two approved 2C-CA contractors to see the Commander.'

"You may proceed," the woman said.

Josh got himself in front of Ralph and walked slowly into Commander Abernathy's office, forcing Ralph to go slowly.

They saw a man in a white shirt with a pencil protector in his shirt pocket, which held three old-fashioned pens. The man was short and balding, with thick wire-rimmed glasses. A milktoast if there ever was one!

Ralph was shocked and disappointed, expecting to see a formidable tyrant. He seized the Commander's mind. The eyes of the man at the desk glazed over as Ralph analyzed the sig. Josh downloaded all of the Commander's data on the mental plane. "This guy is a nobody!" Ralph sent. 'He's no commander, he's just a bureaucrat!'

'So who is running this show?' Josh asked.

'Not Mr. Pencil Protector,' Ralph sent. 'Let's get out of here and get something to eat. I'm hungry.'

Josh wanted to clean up so he put a thought into the Commander's mind. 'Routine impromptu inspection by authorized 2C-CA contractors successful.' The mental plane was a wonderful thing, Josh thought as they walked out of the office. They knew now exactly what the duties of the Chicago collective commander were, and almost everything about how the city operated.

'Commander Abernathy receives his orders through his implant, and he doesn't know (or care) who sends them,' Josh sent as they walked out of the building.

The two men began hunting for an eatery. They were in the heart of downtown Chicago, which had been slowly restored from the havoc wrought by the Great Reset and its wave of crime and destruction.

People were walking around unhurriedly like programmed robots, driving Ralph crazy. "I can't stand this place," he said. They spotted a little sandwich shop and went in.

"We have to change our thinking about the restricted areas," Ralph said after they sat down. "I expected something like a communist or fascist state with jackboots who viciously oppress their people. These Citizens have willingly participated in this hive mind!"

"It's what those Come Together events were all about, Ralph. They talked about building a willing, cooperative human workforce. This is what they meant."

"Working for whom?"

Josh ordered a ham sandwich, Ralph ordered three bacon burgers.

"This entire city is a beehive filled with worker drones. Where is the queen?"

The two men ate and examined the data from the Commander's mind at the speed of thought. They commed silently on the mental plane because it was stupid to eat and try to talk at the same time. 'Look at this,' Josh sent after a minute. 'There's a facility at the north end of the Collective in Arlington Heights, just off the Northwest Highway.'

'Access is denied even to the Commander,' Ralph sent.

They could find nothing else about the place in the Commander's mind.

'The Commander has no idea who or what is sending him his instructions, but he is happy to obey them,' Josh sent.

'Just like everyone else in this town,' Ralph sent. 'This kind of organization has never been seen before in human history. There is literally no opposition!'

Ralph and Josh scoured the Commander's mind on the mental plane for more data about the facility, but there was nothing else.

'It's a good enough lead for me,' Ralph sent. 'Let's check out this place. Maybe it's the central hub of this crazy collective.'

'The Chicago collective stretches from Arlington Heights in the north to IL 59 on the west down to 80 on the southern border and all the way east to the Lake,' Josh sent. 'It's hard to believe they created a separate society over all this territory in three years.'

'A significant percentage of the human population has always been more interested in security than in liberty,' Ralph replied, finishing off his last bacon burger. 'It's human nature. I'm glad we came here and saw the collective in person. We can't change it and we shouldn't try. We have to defend our free zones.'

'I have a funny feeling that we will meet your friend Gyorgy and his pals at this facility. Are you ready for that?'

'I'd like nothing better.'

'Better get some more bacon burgers to go. Looks like an all-day trip for us.'

Ralph brightened. 'Good idea!'

Ralph ordered three more and Josh ordered two more ham sandwiches to go. The proprietor was pleased to have the business. "Come again friends!" she said as they walked out carrying two bags of food.

"Before we leave I want to make some noise. Hold our food for me." Ralph handed Josh the carryout bags.

The giant began striding out on the sidewalk, blowing by people, who all stared and complained. When he J-walked across the street, two of the Street Guardians rushed out. "Halt! Your identity code!" Josh watched from across the street, fascinated. Ralph ignored the two men, J-walking back across the street. "Halt!" The much smaller Guardians tried to detain him, looking like two little gnats trying to stop an elephant. "Your identity code!"

"No."

Josh saw the eyes of the two men blank for a second.

Ralph looked back. "C'mon Josh, we haven't got all day."

Josh put his head down and rushed over to Ralph, exciting the Guardians even more. "Your identity code!" one of them said to Josh.

Oh what the hell, Josh thought. "No."

By now there was a crowd in the street. The Citizens were complaining to each other. "Inappropriate behavior!" one cried. "They are violating the Equality of Outcome Clause!" another exclaimed.

"Wait here," the Guardians said. "A heli will arrive and you will be transported to the local detention center."

"I don't think so," Ralph said, striding away, wondering how far this would go. What was the intelligence behind the Commander? A galactic? A sophisticated AI system? Or a thug like Gyorgy Rynkowski? The system's response would give him a tell.

Josh ran after Ralph to the next block, causing more havoc on the busy streets. "Halt! Your identity code!"

Josh caught up to Ralph as he crossed Wells. A helicopter appeared over the street, hovering slowly. The citizens all stepped back against the buildings, clearing the sidewalk and the street. Josh was nervous. What if the copter began firing on them? Ralph was striding ahead, heading for the parking area. On the mental plane Josh saw how excited Ralph was.

Ralph was active on the mental plane, scanning the copter. Was this an automated drone, or one manned by human beings? If the former, they were in trouble.

'For God's sake Ralph,' Josh sent. 'You don't mind taking chances do you?'

'You can't find out what the bees are doing until you disturb the hive,' Ralph responded.

Fortunately there was a human operator at the controls. Ralph entered his mind; the operator was waiting for instructions through his implant. Josh was monitoring the mental plane as the two kept walking quickly. They were almost at the contractor parking lot now. Ralph and Josh heard the order as it came through the operator's implant into his conscious mind: "Hold your fire, do not endanger Citizens. Follow these two renegades when they exit the parking area."

Ralph and Josh walked into the parking area and retrieved Ralph's ancient auto, which still used a dumb key that started the vehicle from a projection on the steering column. They got in and Ralph took off, presenting his code to the exit scanner. "You see now the value of Arthur," Ralph said smugly as they turned right from Washington onto Wells.

"Yeah, Arthur isn't a smart car. Unhackable."

They took off down Wells, the heli following them. Ralph suddenly turned right on W. Madison, almost running into the vehicle in front of him. Ralph got on the 90 going north. "This place is somewhere on the west side of Arlington Hills," Josh said.

"Roger that."

As they drove north they saw the same traffic patterns; all cars went at the same speed and were the same distance apart. No one was in a hurry.

Ralph looked at his gas gauge. "I need to get gas." Ralph got off the freeway and stopped the Ford at a combo gas and EV charging station. When they pulled up to a pump, a voice said, "All occupants exit the vehicle and present your codes."

"Fuck that," Ralph said. "Fill it up, Josh."

Josh got out and presented his code. He inserted it into the pump's scanner but the device wouldn't respond. "All occupants exit the vehicle and present your codes."

Ralph got out and presented his code. The fuel began to flow. "They probably imaged us too."

Ralph drove back to the 90 and got off on Arlington Heights Rd. The heli had stopped following them. "Where is this place?" Josh asked.

"I'm looking for security," Ralph replied. "Barbed wire, armed guards, things like that."

After an hour of searching they found it, mostly by accident. Josh was hunting sigs and found Gyorgy Rynkowski. "Bang on Josh!" Ralph said, looking at a one-story building just off the Northwest Highway in a non-residential area. It was surrounded by barbed wire and had a guardhouse at the only entrance to the building. They were parked across the street.

"There's a bag in my trunk, Josh. Go get it."

Josh got the bag and placed it on the back seat. Ralph reached back and opened it. Inside were two laser pistols.

"I don't remember how to use those things," Josh said apologetically.

"Piece of cake," Ralph said, grabbing one. "You disengage the safety like so. Pull the trigger. There's almost no recoil so it shouldn't spoil your aim."

Josh gingerly took the gun. Ralph got out and scanned the building. It was made of white-painted brick, peeling in several places and black with mold at the bottom.

"Hardly an address to inspire confidence," Josh joked.

"There's no heliport," Ralph sent. "Just wire and a guardhouse and three satellite dishes. No patrols around the building." Ralph opened Arthur's back door and grabbed a coat bag. "Put one of these duffel coats on and keep your pistol concealed. Monitor the mental plane."

Ralph and Josh got back in the car and drove up to the guardhouse. Ralph didn't waste time talking to the guard. He seized the man's mind and blew in; the man's eyes glazed over for a second. He learned that Gyorgy Rynkowski was in charge of security for the entire collective! Ralph implanted a thought in the guard's mind. 'Authorized security detail to see Gyorgy Rynkowski.' The guard nodded.

"You may proceed," the guard said.

Ralph wondered how a moron like Rynkowski got this gig as he drove Arthur to a small parking lot at the front of the building, which held about two dozen vehicles. The two men walked to a solid metal door, which swung open as they approached. Josh and Ralph stepped in and stared.

The right half of the room contained a cutting-edge AI installation. Ralph recognized it immediately: the latest from AIRDA, the Pentagon's AI research and development agency. Ralph whistled. "So that's how it's done." Ralph explained to Josh on the mental plane. 'These military grade installations use the Space Grid's new 7G hardware and software to track, record, and send to the IOT and the implants. Developed in China first and then brought to Europe, and now the USA.' The left half of the room contained a gigantic panel almost as large as the one at Uploads, surrounded by dozens of huge interactive monitors that allowed an operator to communicate with the system. Several data panels were scrolling code. Three operators sat at consoles and never looked around when they entered the building. Like at Uploads, the gigantic panel showed areas of the Space Grid. The interactive monitors showed street scenes with chip data superimposed over the monitored citizens.

They heard a voice. "Impressive, aint it?" It was Gyorgy with his goons.

Ralph was getting hungry again, and when he got hungry his temper was short. He should have eaten another of those bacon burgers before he came in. "You're starting to piss me off, Rynkowski," Ralph said. "This installation runs the entire collective?"

Rynkowski didn't answer, but he didn't have to. Ralph was reading his mind and knew he was about to give the attack order to his men. Ralph pulled his laser pistol from under his coat. "Stand down, Gyorgy, or I'll slag this setup."

Gyorgy waved his hand in the air frantically to his men. "How'd you find me, Zimring?"

"I'm always three steps ahead of you, Gyorgy. Who do you think sicced the SISMI on you that day in the Via Piave?"

Gyorgy's face hardened. "I'll sic my men on you, old man. You might do a little damage to my equipment but I'll get you, you arrogant piece of shit."

"You haven't thought this through, Gyorgy," Ralph said casually. "I know this AI setup, it comes right from AIRDA. With one burn I can disable this entire facility."

Gyorgy was smug. "Won't do you any good, Zimring. These things are all connected together across the planet. Any one of them could run the entire world."

"We'll see about that. Why don't you and your lovely ladies vacate the premises. I want to talk to your operators."

Ralph said this so casually and with such condescension that Gyorgy flared with anger. Rynkowski was able to send the attack signal to his men through his implant before Ralph could get it from his conscious mind. Ralph frantically seized Rynkowski's sig and held him. He was the best fighter but that left Josh one on four. Ralph couldn't do much more than point his weapon at one of Gyorgy's men; his attention was monopolized on holding Rynkowski. Fuck!

Josh uncovered his laser pistol and blew a hole in the shoulder of the lead attacker. "Stand back or I'll waste your cute little AI," Josh said, pointing the weapon at the three operators at their consoles. The operators sat frozen in place, not wanting to get shot by these two unchipped lunatics.

Meanwhile Ralph was dealing with Gyorgy on the mental plane. "If I let you go will you promise to stand down?"

Gyorgy was frantic with fear. Zimring was controlling his mind! He couldn't move.

Ralph let go of Rynkowski's sig and stepped back. The man was blubbering now. His men were staring at him. "What the fuck, Gyorgy! What happened to you?"

Gyorgy pointed at Ralph. "That man...he is a demon!" Gyorgy turned and ran out the door, spittle running down his face. Gyorgy's palpable fear had translated to his men; all the fight had gone out of them. The operators turned in their seats back to their consoles.

Ralph felt sorry for Rynkowski, but he was more interested in that bacon burger sitting on Arthur's back seat... "OK boys, we're not here to destroy anything," Ralph said to Gyorgy's men. "Somebody repair the hole in that man's shoulder." Josh's laser pistol had burned a clean circular hole about quarter of an inch in diameter in the soft tissue of the shoulder. "That was a good shot, Josh. You'll do."

Josh commed with Ralph on the mental plane. 'These men know nothing. It's the operators we have to question.'

'Good idea. I'll take care of these guys, you talk to the operators.'

Josh walked over to the consoles. He was about to open his mouth when he realized that he could just read their conscious minds while they were performing their tasks. He stayed ten feet back of the operators, two women and one man, and lightly touched their minds; enough to get data but not enough to cause interruption in their thinking. What he found out blew his mind.

Josh walked back to Ralph. The injured man had been patched up from a field kit. Ralph was explaining the technique to them, and why Gyorgy got scared.

'Time to go,' Josh said on the mental plane. 'We have business to take care of.'

Ralph handed out cards to the men. "If you're interested, come to the Midland Free Zone and ask for me. If anyone questions you, these guest passes will establish your identities."

Josh and Ralph got back in Arthur. Ralph grabbed a bacon burger and they drove out, waving to the guard.

"Where to?"

"Home. I don't want to discuss this until we're in our shielded office."

Ralph was about to turn on the radio. "Please don't do that, Ralph. I have to organize this data into a coherent presentation. I need quiet."

The two men drove silently back to Midland. They passed a "Welcome to the Midland Free Zone" sign on their way in to the city and encountered a guard at the Gate 1 boundary, who read their sigs and passed them.

As he drove to the Midland Tower Ralph realized why Gyorgy and his men had been in Midland: to check out the free zone's defenses and security. Gyorgy and his men knew nothing. They had simply been given orders and had followed them. Damn these technocrats! An authoritarian government operated in cells. No one knew the big picture except those at the top. Except there was no one at the top. Just an AI installation that sent orders to every Citizen implant in the city. But who had set up the AI?

Ralph glanced over at Josh, who was concentrating very hard. The young man had done well on his first field mission. He was as solid as D'Arcy. Ralph ate his last bacon burger as he parked Arthur in the space reserved for the top suite at the Midland Tower. It was starting to get dark.

"Hey Josh, we're home."

Josh started and opened his eyes. "Good! I just finished organizing all the data from the AI operators. Let's go into the office and I'll download everything to you."

Ralph said nothing to Josh as they walked to the Second Street Investigations office. No one was there.

"Sit down, Ralph. This is a lot to digest."

"I'll sit on the floor or I'll break that sofa."

Joann and I came in to the office a little after 7. We saw Ralph and Josh comming excitedly on the mental plane.

Ralph saw us and broke off the conversation. "OK you two, Josh is going to tell you about our little adventure in Chicago today."

Just then Kelleye walked in. "Josh! You're back!" She threw herself into Josh's arms.

"Of course I am, honey. I had Ralph here to protect me." He didn't tell her about how naughty the old man had been today.

"Thank you Ralph."

Ralph looked a little embarrassed and changed the subject. "Tell everyone what happened, Josh."

Josh sent everyone the data on the mental plane and summarized. "The new plan of the Collectives is to create strike teams and attack the free zones. Then, forced neural implants for all free citizens."

"They don't want to kill us, they want to implant us," Ralph remarked. "More worker drones for the Collectives."

"That's right. All of the collective zones are managed by a sophisticated AI installation. These AIs are connected and run through the Space Grid. That was the real aim of constructing the Grid, to create a neural-chipped society linked to a central planetary AI, with lightning-fast comms to the implants all over the world. They've done just that in the restricted areas, which are essentially proxy states controlled by the galactic Collectives."

"I worked at Uploads for years," I said. "I helped those bastards enslave humanity!"

"Stop feeling sorry for yourself," Ralph said. "We all got played. What are we going to do about it? As I see it we have two choices: Destroy the AI installations in all of the restricted areas, or enhance our training efforts in a massive push worldwide to save as much of humanity as possible. The former is impossible so we need to do the latter."

"Will the collectives really attack the free zones?" Kelley asked.

"I think they will," Ralph said. "Our friend Gyorgy Rynkowski and his goons were on a recon mission in Midland. Therefore, part of our training effort must be to strengthen the forces in the free zones, and monitor the activities of the PSF in every collective."

"We have the military on our side in almost every country," Josh said.

"That's right, Josh." Ralph rubbed his hands together in satisfaction. "Our forces can read the sigs of these Citizens and devise effective counterattacks against them before they can even mobilize their forces. Our forces must be strictly for self-defense and counter-attack when provoked. We must also continue to help in the mental plane training."

"Who or what is operating behind the Space Grid?" Joann asked.

Josh frowned. "Some galactic bureaucracy, probably, or an off-planet AI system. Both would be controlled by the Hilarion and/or the Fenachrone Collective."

"We'll get our military intelligence people on that," Ralph said. "But our focus must be on salvaging as many as possible for the new civilization. The old one is dead. Dead and chipped and as good as buried."

— 33 —

A week later Ralph heard his doorbell ring, something that had never oc-curred in the ten years he had lived on the top floor of the Midland Tower. When Ralph opened the door Gyorgy Rynkowski was standing there with a mad on.

"What did you do to me, you bastard?"

Ralph read the thoughts of the angry man, which were justifiable anger covering up genuine fear and, beneath that, curiosity.

Ralph was disposed to be lenient and stepped aside. "I'm eating breakfast. You hungry?"

"Yeah."

Ralph made more sausages and eggs, and put the plate down on the kitchen table. "Help yourself."

Gyorgy put a forkful of eggs into his mouth. "I can't sleep anymore, Zim-ring. How did you get into my mind?"

Ralph knew this visit by Rynkowski was probably a fishing expedition by the Chicago collective. "How did you get past my guards?" Ralph asked.

Gyorgy grabbed three bacon slices and ate them all at once. "I came at 5 in the morning. Your man at Gate 1 was asleep."

Ralph swore. "Gyorgy, you need to go back to Chicago."

Gyorgy pushed his plate back. "Not until I get some answers!"

"Sorry, we can't give out information to anyone with a neural implant."

Rynkowski deflated slowly, like a balloon with a leak. "I shoulda never got that thing. But the money is so good..."

Ralph was sympathetic. He knew the AI was recording everything through Gyorgy's implant, and he felt genuinely sorry for anyone with a neural chip. This guy might be salvageable; maybe he could turn him. "Is there any way to remove your implant?"

Gyorgy's face screwed up in pain. "I'm not supposed to. But I heard it could be done."

"How bad is the pain?"

"They don't want to fuck up their workers, so it's manageable."

"If you come over, Gyorgy, you know there's no going back."

Ralph read Gyorgy as he thought about his life. Great money, a nice place to live, plenty of unchipped women, an evil enemy to fight, lots of action... "It's not worth it. I know that now. You did something to my brain in Chicago, Zimring. I was all gung-ho at first. I thought it would be a great gig."

Ralph nodded. The attractors set people up, the neural chips did the rest. "There's an explanation for everything, Rynkowski. All of it."

Gyorgy glanced at him with a ray of hope. "Is there?"

"Yeah, my word of honor. But you gotta get rid of that implant first."

Rynkowski was silent.

Ralph rose. "Make up your mind, Gyorgy. You have fifteen minutes. You're a dangerous operative and the free zones can't afford to have you spying for the collectives through your implant. You either join us or you don't leave here alive."

Gyorgy leaped out of his chair, enraged, but Ralph was waiting for that. He covered the younger fighter with his laser pistol. "Free Zone law allows the, er, elimination of hostile operatives from the restricted areas." Ralph looked at his timepiece. "Ten minutes my friend," he said casually.

Gyorgy knew Ralph would pull the trigger. He sat down and swore gloriously at the old man for five minutes. Ralph listened admiringly. There were basically two kinds of mercs: the stone cold killer types, and the angry guys looking to avenge a life they didn't like. Greed was just a part of the lifestyle. Ralph knew himself to be the former. Rynkowski was the latter type, so he let him blow off steam.

"Five minutes, Gyorgy."

Rynkowski stared belligerently at the giant.

Ralph could see that he was going to wait until the last second to make up his mind. "I can give you some good news. If you join us your life will be a lot better. All those questions you have will be answered."

Gyorgy's mind was an open book to Ralph. He knew Rynkowski was going to say yes, but the man was stubborn. He didn't want to admit openly to a former enemy that he had been wrong. "Fuck you Zimring!" he shouted angrily. "I accept."

Ralph carefully read the man's sig. He was committed, there was no subterfuge. "OK then. I know a surgeon who can do the procedure; I'll schedule it for you."

Gyorgy nodded. He felt inside him that it was the right decision.

"You stay here," Ralph said. "If you leave my lovely little suite the deal's off, and we'll hunt you down like a rabid dog. *Capisci?*"

"Yeah yeah, fuck you." Gyorgy looked around. "Quite a place you got here."

"Made a lot of coin, saved most of it."

Gyorgy laughed. "Saved it! That's a good one."

Ralph was in a hurry so he went out and took the elevator to the ground floor. He knew everyone in town. Dr. Peter Doncic had an office two blocks away from the Centurion Building. Peter was a former army surgeon who had effortlessly translated his life to the civilian sector. He spent his days acting as a surgical consultant, and sometimes doing surgeries that other surgeons couldn't. He was legendary in the medical community for having the steadiest hands, and amazing hand-eye coordination. As Ralph walked to Fourth Street he remembered how he had recruited Peter to come to the Midland Free Zone after Doncic had been kicked out of the Philadelphia restricted area for not receiving an implant. Peter had fit right in. Now Ralph needed a consultation. He told Rynkowski that the neural implants could be removed, but he was just blowing smoke. Was it possible? Doncic would know.

Ralph walked into Peter's first floor office. The office was small. There was no receptionist and no office equipment. You registered by standing in front of a scanner and entering your mobile number on the display. If Peter was interested he would call you back. Ralph stood in front of the scanner, which was at the level of his chest. Peter would know from the image that he had called.

The door to the surgery was closed, and Ralph knew better than to knock. He was about to walk out when a small man with thinning blond hair opened the door. "Ralph! What brings you to my humble abode?"

"The most important operation you'll ever do." Ralph explained about Rynkowski and his desire to remove his implant. "Is it possible?"

Peter's intense blue eyes lit up. "As a matter of fact, I have been investigating that possibility. Yours is not my first enquiry, Ralph. The difficulty is getting information about the neural chip procedure, and how it hooks up to the brain and to the nervous system. So far I have not been successful. I would need a detailed description of the procedure, with images, before I could determine the feasibility of such an operation."

"I think I could get you that information, Peter." Ralph was thinking of plumbing the depths of Gyorgy's mind. The details of the operation to install his neural chip should be available in what those kids called the mental plane storage area. There was a portion of the mind that acted as a sophisticated external camera, capturing and recording every minute detail of a person's life. Therefore, the details of Gyorgy's operation should be downloadable from his sig. But the only way to transfer that data was via the mental plane. "However, there is a complication."

Peter raised his eyebrows. Doncic was a man who did not suffer fools.

"In order for you to receive the information, I will have to train you in a, er, special mental protocol."

"I've heard rumors about that, but I'm a busy man, Ralph."

Ralph stood silently. No amount of persuasion would convince the highly educated Doncic, so Ralph went on the mental plane and examined Peter's sig. Then he lightly touched Doncic's mind. "Hello Peter."

Doncic jumped, eyes wide in surprise. "So it's true then."

Ralph nodded. "Many in the Midland Free Zone have already been trained."

Ralph watched as Peter debated within himself. He got tired of waiting. "OK Peter, I'll get someone else. I hear there's a surgeon in the Springfield Free Zone who has already been trained. Not as good as you, but it might work."

"You're a bastard, Ralph Zimring," Peter said as Ralph strode to the door.

Ralph turned around to face Doncic. "So I've been told. But Peter, I have no use for wafflers. If you want to do this procedure you have to fully commit to the mental plane training. I'm a busy man too."

"All right Ralph, you sonofabitch. If you can touch my mind you know how much I want to learn about the neural chip procedure. It's supposed to be groundbreaking work."

"Are you free for the next week? I'll send over a trainer."

Peter sighed. "Do it now, if you can spare one. I have a delicate surgery next week to prepare for. If I can't learn your technique within the next five days you'll have to find someone else."

"Wait here. I'll have someone over in two hours."

Because of my experience and intense training with the Celestians (I hardly even thought of Gwenneth anymore) I had become the CEO for all of the trainers in the U.S. free zones. I had my office on the mental plane and had to work in our shielded downtown office space. The galactics knew about our activity on the mental plane of course, so we had to keep the most sensitive information shielded. Fortunately no one in the Illinois collectives knew or cared about the mental plane.

I was working seven days a week, 18 hours a day. Joann had been forced to quit her commercial flying job (thank God) because the restricted areas would not allow unchipped pilots to land in their zones. So I put her to work ferrying trainers back and forth across the country in her lifter (all Basic training must be done in person to be effective). She also helped me with the admin when she wasn't flying. I envied her because she got out of town a lot, whereas I was stuck in the office all the time. I couldn't even play a round of disk golf anymore. But Joann made it up to me in other (better) ways.

Ralph called me just as I got to the office. "I need a trainer over at 213 Fourth St. right away. Chip removal."

I jumped out of my chair for joy. "Finally! You found a surgeon and a willing Citizen?"

"Yeah." Ralph explained quickly. "But I have to get the info out of a merc I know, and I don't know if I can do it." Ralph sent me the details of his meeting with Gyorgy Rynkowski.

I thought quickly. "Let me do it, Ralph. Gyorgy doesn't know me and I look harmless. I'll send Joann over to see your surgeon."

Ralph breathed a sigh of relief. "That's great, Philo. From Gyorgy I learned that the collectives in Illinois are preparing for an all-out attack on the free zones. I have too much to do."

It would be an exciting change from my routine mental plane work. I would have to work with Gyorgy's deep subconscious in order to get such finely granulated information as a sophisticated medical procedure. Fortunately every sig had a Camera, as I called it, which recorded all information in a person's life in the most excruciating and minute detail. It was like watching a 3D movie in a holospace.

I called Joann on her mobile. "Can you get over to 213 Fourth Street as soon as possible? There's a surgeon over there who needs to get trained." I explained in our coded language over the phone.

"Sure Philo, if you pay lots of attention to me tonight."

"You shouldn't have said that! Now I won't be able to concentrate all day."

She laughed. "I'll get right over there."

I got one of my other trainers to take over the admin for a few days. It was a hot and humid late summer day but I practically ran over to the Midland

Tower building, sweating like a pig. Ralph had given me the combo to his top floor suite. When I got to the top floor I opened the thick metal entrance door with the 12-digit combo Ralph sent me.

I saw a thick, burly man about six feet three inches tall with a scar across his forehead and down to his right ear. Gyorgy Rynkowski looked like the thug he was.

"You aint much," Gyorgy said when I walked in.

"Looks can be deceiving, Rynkowski." My tone was just like Ralph's, for I spoke with his authority. I knew everything Ralph knew about this guy's mental and emotional makeup.

Rynkowski was impressed enough to take a seat. We were in one of Ralph's spacious living rooms, 30 stories up. Ralph had both suites on the top floor and had combined them into one really cool living space.

I looked around. "This is fucking great."

Rynkowski laughed. "Yeah. I could get used to this."

The ice had been broken. I had trained so many people in the technique that it was second nature to me now. In a few seconds I read almost everything in Rynkowski's mind, and in his data depository, and filed it in a new folder. I had developed a mental plane filing system over the years and used it in my teaching. A quick inspection of the data showed me I'd have to go deeper into his psyche to get the fine details of the neural chip implanting procedure, but that would have to wait until later.

"OK Gyorgy, the first thing we are going to do is to get you access to the mental plane." That was the crucial step. You had to empower the trainee and let him or her see that they had control. I had to work around his neural implant, which made things difficult. The thing was screaming at him to get out of here and return to the collective. I rigged a work-around in his conscious mind to keep the implant from disturbing our work.

"That's fuckin' amazing, Rothman. That thing is always jammerin' at me. I forgot what it was like to have my own thoughts."

"I have never worked with a chipped person before. I think we can make some progress now."

In four hours Gyorgy was able to access his portal and take a tentative first step into the mental plane.

Gyorgy suddenly shot out of his chair. He was angry. "Why did nobody show me this shit before!" he shouted. He raised his hands in the air. "This is great!!!"

"We are just getting started."

This made Gyorgy so excited it took me an hour to calm him down. I looked at my timepiece. "We still have five hours to work. Are you hungry?"

"I know where Ralph keeps his grub."

Ralph had a huge refrigerator and an equally large freezer, which were concealed in two inserts between the connected suites. The freezer was filled with sausages, bacon, ground beef, and ice cream. The refrigerator contained two dozen containers of eggs, veggies, cheeses, and a half ton of butter. We checked Ralph's cupboards, which were bulging with soup cans, pounds of rice, potatoes, lentils, flat bread, peanut butter, and chocolate.

"Ralph could feed an army with this," I said. "Try comming with me on the mental plane."

'Ralph is an army himself,' Gyorgy sent.

'Got it, Gyorgy,' I sent back.

Gyorgy was so excited he almost gave me a hug.

'Check out this liquor cabinet,' Gyorgy sent. 'Ah, Watiers, best bourbon in the world.'

'Save that for later Gyorgy,' I sent. 'We can't get drunk, it interferes with the training.'

Rynkowski grudgingly put the bottle back. We made bacon and eggs and broke open one of Ralph's cheeses. After a half hour we got back to it. At the end of the day I showed Gyorgy about sigs and how to locate them. "It takes a lot of practice and it can be frustrating. Concentrate on finding people you know. Try to filter out all the noise."

Gyorgy got mad after half an hour because he couldn't do it.

"You did really well. I didn't think much of you, you look like a thug. But everybody I've ever taught has been able to complete the training if they wanted to, so hang in there."

"OK, fuck it for today."

"You can practice any time you want."

"I can't make out any sigs!" Gyorgy said. "There's too much noise. People's thoughts are all jumbled up."

"It takes persistence. Keep at it. Try it first on your men, you know them."

"Hey, that's a great idea. Are you goin'?"

"Gotta meet my girlfriend. She wants me to pay attention to her tonight."

"Lucky dog."

I commed with Ralph on the mental plane. 'Where should I put Gyorgy? He did well on his first lesson.'

'Ah, leave him at my place. I have a couple of guest rooms.'

Undeveloped sig obscured by random thoughts

'OK. I'll be back at 8 tomorrow morning. If you change the entry code send it to me.'

It only took me three more days to train Gyorgy in the basics. That was good because Dr. Doncic was a fast learner. Joann had him up and running in three days of intensive training. He was chomping at the bit to get the details of the chip implanting procedure.

301

But when I looked at the details of the procedure after the fourth day of working with Gyorgy, I was shocked. The implant surgeries were performed by AI surgeons! Programmed, automated medical robots did all the work. However, the details of the operation were there from Gyorgy's mental plane camera. I put the recording into a mental plane folder. I hoped Dr. Doncic would be able to make sense of it.

Doncic studied the procedure with me at the speed of thought in his office. What would have taken hours to digest was done in a few minutes. "The remarkable aspect is not the medical procedure itself, but the neural chip. It probably performs a remote messaging function to the brain and to the nervous system. It is, I say without exaggeration, the greatest advance in medical technology in history."

Doncic kept talking excitedly about neural chips until I had enough. "Can you remove that thing from the body of Gyorgy Rynkowski? Right now he is still communicating back to the Chicago collective via his implant. He's an extraordinary security risk to the Midland Free Zone."

"Of course, and I thank you."

"When can I bring Gyorgy in to your surgery?"

"Tomorrow morning at eleven."

It was clear that the interview was over. Doncic stepped into his surgery and closed the door.

The next morning, Peter Doncic had Gyorgy Rynkowski sign a release form and told him what he was going to do.

"Yeah yeah doc, I understand. I'm ready to go."

Peter escorted him into the surgery and closed the door. "Please lie on the table. I'm going to image your brain before we start."

After Peter imaged the brain he was amazed. This was going to be much simpler than he thought. A tiny subdermal chip had been implanted underneath the skin, in proximity to the base of the brain. Traditional neuralink chips had over a thousand tiny wires that connected to and stimulated neurons, and the surgical procedure was complex and dangerous. But his imager showed that this chip had no wires.

What would happen if the chip was removed?

Peter had spent hours investigating this, already convinced that the chip was simply providing an electrical overlay to an already functioning brain. However, he was worried about psychological damage when the chip was no longer operational. Would the rewired brain cause trauma when the signals from the chip stopped and caused the brain to reset? He was convinced that would not happen, for Ralph's description of Gyorgy Rynkowski's personality before and after the chip implant was similar.

"Gyorgy, do you give your consent to have your neural chip removed?"

"Sure doc. I already signed your release forms. Get this jabberin' thing out of me."

Peter was more excited than he'd ever been before a procedure, despite feeling like a Nazi doing experimental brain surgery on a prisoner of war. "Gyorgy, we will be in mind-to-mind contact through the mental plane. I'll know and feel everything you do. If you get in trouble I can put the chip back in."

"Fuck no doc, don't do that."

"All right, relax. I'm giving you a local anesthetic on the area, you won't feel anything when I take it out."

"Sure doc. I'm ready."

Peter administered the numbing agent and waited. He then pierced the skin and removed the chip, which slid out easily. Peter wiped away a little blood and cleaned the area before putting a small gauze patch over it. That was anticlimactic, Peter thought. The operation was nothing; the genius was in the neural chip itself. This simple procedure was how the Chicago collective had been able to chip two million people in three years!

Peter placed the implant in a small ceramic bowl on a table next to the operating bed. Suddenly the chip began to pulse.

"What is that thing doing, doc?"

"I have no idea, Gyorgy."

Both men watched as the chip began to pulse and vibrate wildly. Gyorgy shuddered. "That fucking thing is looking for my brain!"

It appeared so, Peter thought. It was grotesque, like a parasite seeking to attach itself to its host.

The chip was now buzzing frantically. Suddenly, like a dying organism, it spasmed and stopped moving.

"It's dead," Gyorgy said.

The chip was now motionless; Peter stared at the lifeless object. He remembered something Ralph had said: An external AI information signal activates the chip whenever necessary. Instead of wires, the chip remotely stimulates the desired neurons! It was ingenious. And far beyond the understanding of medical science.

Both men stared at each other. They were in contact on the mental plane, so Peter knew that his patient was experiencing no discomfort. Well, a slight disorientation perhaps. To be on the safe side, Peter re-imaged Gyorgy's brain. Many of the neurons in the primary motor cortex were still active from recent heavy stimulation from the implant, but that would subside over time. Other than that, the brain looked normal.

"I feel more like I do now than when I first got here," Gyorgy said.

Peter immediately understood what Gyorgy meant, and they both laughed. On the mental plane, Peter could see that his patient's sig was becoming more balanced. By God, Peter thought. Here is a new diagnostic tool!

A look of awe came over Gyorgy's face. He stared up at Peter. "How did I...get so fucked up?"

Peter had no answer for that. "Why don't you try sitting up?"

Gyorgy gingerly raised himself to a sitting position. He felt the back of his head.

"Just a piece of gauze there now," Peter said.

"*Ja Cie Chromole!*" Gyorgy got out of bed and walked very slowly around the room. The shape of Gyorgy's face had changed in some subtle way, Peter observed. It looked...more relaxed.

Suddenly his patient's face broke into a big smile. "I'm disconnected now, I can feel it."

The normally stoic Peter Doncic smiled broadly. "I'd say the operation was a success. Let's go somewhere and celebrate."

"Drinks are on me, doc!"

After celebrating with Doc Doncic, Gyorgy Rynkowski walked back to Ralph's top floor suite in the Midland Tower, feeling better and better. He checked the mental plane as he walked, practicing a technique that Philo Rothman called "locating sigs." The mental plane is full of "noise," as Rothman called it. Each person has a unique sig, but it is obscured by a fog of random thoughts that surround it.

The more he practiced, the better he was getting at seeing sigs. He had never thought about stuff like this before. His entire view of the world had changed.

By the time Gyorgy reached Ralph's apartments in the Tower he had decided to join Rothman's training group and recruit as many of his friends, and his enemies, as he could. Gyorgy reached inside his pants pocket and pulled out what he called "the demon chip." This was the evil thing that had controlled his mind. How had he ever allowed that to happen?

Ralph was right about him: he was a dumbass. Well, no more of that. Gyorgy found a comfortable sofa and continued practicing on the mental plane.

Dr. Peter Doncic was also busy studying sigs on the mental plane, but from a medical perspective. What was the relationship between the sig and physical health? He would combine his physical examinations with an examination of every patient's sig. Who knows what he would uncover? He would create an entirely new field of medicine. Peter understood that Ralph wasn't crazy with his talk of galactics: The technology of that chip, and the mental plane training, was not of this world.

I got home at 7 to our apartment after a big mental plane meeting of trainers. The Transhumanists had created their own version of Human 2.0 in the restricted areas, but the galactic Collectives had hijacked the Transhumanist movement. I was worried that they had chosen to eliminate the pesky and recalcitrant free zones despite their reluctance to reduce the human workforce.

Joann wasn't home and I was conscious of a feeling of disappointment. Now that she had been forced to quit her flying gig I was seeing more and more of her. When I was with her I was happier.

Just then she walked in the door. "Joann!" I said enthusiastically. "Let's go to the Comedy Club tonight. We'll hit Antonios before and have some great Italian food. My treat."

Joann shook her hair out, smoothing it down.

"God, you are gorgeous."

She smiled. "Do you think so?"

"Yes. As a matter of fact, I wonder why we're in this lousy two bedroom apartment. I'm thinking of buying a house."

Joann stopped and gave me her full attention. "Are you serious?"

"Never more serious." I was conscious of a funny feeling around my heart, a fuzzy, warm kind of feeling. Joann D'Arcy was smart, strong, independent, and beautiful. The more time I spent with her, the more I liked her.

"Is this a proposal?"

"Would you have me if I did?"

"I...why, I believe I would!"

I approached her and got down on one knee. "Joann D'Arcy, will you marry me? I promise I'll buy you a diamond as big as your fist."

"On those terms, I accept."

We both laughed. I was feeling exhilarated; I knew I had made the right decision. "C'mon sweetheart, let's get down to Antonios before the seats are all taken."

"You've never called me sweetheart before."

"Get used to it, sweetheart."

When we came back from the Comedy Club at one in the morning we were both in a fantastic mood. I watched her undress. "I don't think I've wanted you more than I do now."

I made love to her that night with so much passion that she was literally gasping with pleasure. "That was a command performance. Can you do that every night?"

"I'll certainly try."

"Philo, do you want children?" she asked suddenly.

"Yes, but not until I'm 35."

Joann thought this was a purely arbitrary date. She looked at me curiously.

"My father said that a man should wait until he is old enough to have a family and raise his kids the right way. That was his way of saying that I'm immature. I've recognized that. I think 35 is a good age to be a father. That's only five years from now."

"What if I get pregnant before that?"

I grinned. "Then I'll have to grow up faster!"

When Ralph came home that night he saw Gyorgy sitting placidly on one of his sofas, practicing sig recognition. "I have a job for you, if you're up for it."

Gyorgy opened his eyes. Ralph saw sanity behind those eyes, instead of the usual manic nervousness. "What is it?"

"The intelligence service thinks that the Collectives are readying an attack on all the free zones. We don't know how this will be done, or when, but your boys in Chicago might."

Gyorgy brightened. "Damn! You'd trust me with a sensitive mission like that?"

"Don't be stupid, Rynkowski. You can't fool anyone now. We know your sig and we'll know instantly if you try anything."

"I'll do it. I want to bring my men back here to get unchipped."

Ralph was impressed. He had pushed Gyorgy's biggest button with his stupid comment and the man didn't get triggered. "The job is yours," he said, reaching into the fridge for some eggs and sausages. "Before you leave, contact this sig." Ralph showed Gyorgy on the mental plane. "That's the Illinois Free Zone comms officer. He'll get you up to date on the latest intelligence from the Chicago collective, and give you a QR code to get in."

"Don't need it. I already have a QR code."

"Gyorgy, you no longer have an implant. When the Chicago AI scans you it won't know who you are. They'll categorize you as an unchipped contractor, and you're not registered. So you need a new code."

Gyorgy whistled in appreciation. "You guys are organized."

Ralph put a half dozen eggs and a dozen small breakfast sausages in a huge cook pan. "We are. And we do it all on the mental plane where the Illinois collectives can't see us."

"Sure, but the galactic Collectives can."

Ralph watched his lunch cooking. "Yeah, but they can't come down to the surface, so they have to use human agents."

"What if they attack on the mental plane?"

Ralph frowned. "That's a hot topic within the security forces. So far they haven't done anything like that, so we assume they can't or won't. If it happens we'll deal with it."

Ralph scooped his lunch onto a big plate and grabbed a small cheese round. "Be careful, Gyorgy. You're one of us now. Watch out for Ronin. We hear that the collectives are gradually replacing their chipped security forces with those psychopaths."

Gyorgy Rynkowski may have found a form of enlightenment, but his basic personality was still the same. He rubbed his hands together. "Let's rumble! I'm your man."

Ralph sat down and began to eat. "That's great, Gyorgy. We'll be able to get some good intel." He wasn't worried. Gyorgy was an experienced field operative.

Gyorgy picked up Ralph's thought. "That's a nice vote of confidence, Ralph."

Ralph shrugged. "You were always a good fighter and a cunning operator. Just make sure you come back from that digital termite colony, Gyorgy."

Gyorgy laughed and left. He was a free man again, thanks to his (formerly) greatest enemy.

Gyorgy reported back to Ralph three days later at his apartment. "Get set, Ralph. The Illinois collectives have decided to make an example of the Midland Free Zone. They're sending Ronin in here, led by your old buddy Duchene Comstock."

Ralph exploded. "That obese psychopath! I knew I should have, er, terminated his existence during that scuffle with the Cube."[28]

"The plan is to forcibly chip the mayor and as many of the City Council as they can. Then city officials will be ordered through their implants to call for all citizens to be chipped." Gyorgy frowned. "Oh, and there's one more thing. Harriman Drake is leading the strike force."

Ralph was upset. "I thought I broke his neck in that fight we had over the Cube!"

"I don't know anything about that, Ralph, but that's what I found out. There are about two dozen Ronin, 26 to be exact. They are coming into Midland using painted-over PSF cars to look like Midland Police Force black-and-whites."

"When?"

"Right away. Could be any time."

Ralph smiled with appreciation. "That's great work, Gyorgy."

Gyorgy felt Ralph's admiration. For the first time in his adult life he felt he was part of a group of people who valued him. It was a fuckin' good feeling. He sent Ralph the data on the mental plane. "Man, once you get it, reading sigs is easy! I got so much info from the minds of everybody, and they didn't even know I was doing it."

Ralph chewed a breakfast sausage and thought out loud. "Ronin using fake black-and-whites! Gyorgy, that's just the kind of vague plan a moron like Comstock would dream up. But it might work because even in the free zones, people respect marked law enforcement vehicles and obey uniformed LEOs almost without question. None of the city council or the mayor has taken the mental plane training, so they won't know that the police are fake."

"A simple plan is better than a complicated plan, Ralph."

"Yeah. Maybe Comstock is smarter than he looks."

The five roads into Midland were all guarded. Ralph messaged the border guards and told them to let in any black and whites coming in from out of town. "They're fake but let them in. Take pictures and send them to me. And don't fall asleep!" The Ronin would all have to be interrogated, but to block their entry would alert the Chicago collective AI that the Midland Free Zone already knew of their plans.

At 5:30 in the morning Ralph got calls and images from all five of the guard stations. Thirteen black and whites had entered the Zone. Comstock and Drake were in one of them; he would take care of that one. He commed to his security forces on the mental plane. 'Ronin in town, check your mobiles for images.' Ralph explained the situation. 'Keep these guys in sight. Interdict when necessary. Use your personal cars.' Ralph assigned a team to each vehicle.

'Hey Gyorgy, you want some action?'

Rynkowski was still sleeping in Ralph's guest room but a nudge on the mental plane in the right place will wake anybody up. "Yeah."

"We're going after Comstock and Drake. Let me have Drake. You take that fat fuck Comstock."

"OK, old man. If you get into trouble I'll help you out."

"No need for that, Gyorgy." Ralph described the way to seize a sig. "You just immobilize the person and they can't move."

Gyorgy was looking forward to a fight. "That's no fun!"

Ralph laughed. Could he handle Harriman Drake? It had been no problem fifteen years ago, but Drake was ten years younger. "OK. We'll do it the old fashioned way."

"Now you're talkin'!"

Ralph thought no more about the others. He trusted his men to do their jobs. He was focused on Harriman Drake, a stone-cold killer.

"I'll drive."

When Gyorgy saw Arthur he laughed. "What a piece of shit!"

That pissed Ralph off. "Take it back, Rynkowski. Nobody insults Arthur."

Gyorgy was hyped. "You want ta go right here?"

Ralph snorted. "Save it, dumbass. Get in the car."

Gyorgy was pleased that the old man still had fire in his belly. He wouldn't want to face him even at his advanced age.

Ralph located Comstock's sig and drove to Oaklawn St. in a residential area on the north side of town. Before he turned onto Oaklawn he killed Arthur's lights and put the car in neutral, coasting silently down the street in the dark. The vague outlines of a black and white was sitting at the curb two houses away. Ralph pointed to the house. 'That's where Mayor Trent lives,' he sent on the mental plane.

'What do we do now?'

'Keep contact with these two on the mental plane. When they are ready to make their move we'll know.'

It was getting a little lighter in the pre-dawn. Ralph saw Duchene Comstock open the driver's door and lift his flabby body out of the car, grunting. Harriman Drake opened the other door and got out, waving his arms back and forth. Comstock and Harriman were walking up the driveway to the mayor's front door, dressed like Midland cops. "OK let's go," Ralph said. Ralph and Gyorgy got out of their car without latching their doors and walked silently up the driveway. Just as Harriman reached the front door Ralph spoke to him from behind.

"Long time no see, Drake."

Drake turned his body around. "Well, if it isn't my old friend Ralph Zimring!"

"Your gig is up, Drake. You can either come with us quietly or I'll bring you to the morgue in a body bag."

Duchene Comstock was shocked to see the man who had once threatened his life. He moved back off the porch, guarded by Gyorgy.

Ralph read Drake's thoughts: Zimring is crazy and wouldn't hesitate to start a fight right here, but he couldn't blow his cover as a cop. The operation was going well so far. Drake got back into character. "You're trespassing. Please remove yourself from the porch, sir. We have questions for the mayor."

"I'll bet you do." Despite his hatred for Drake, Ralph was impressed with how cool he was. The old Harriman Drake would have opened up and gotten someone killed. "I thought I broke your neck in that fight about the Cubes."

"You almost did, Zimring. Now, please go back to your vehicle. You are impeding a police investigation."

"At 6 in the morning?"

"Mayor Trent is an early riser."

At that moment the front door opened. Mayor Janet Trent appeared in a business suit, holding a briefcase. Ralph recalled that Trent was an architect and had her own business. Before Harrison Drake could get a word out Ralph had seized his sig. The Ronin stood there, unable to move.

"I know you," the mayor said to Ralph. "You're that Zimring fellow."

Ralph managed a slight bow and detached a small portion of his mind to answer the mayor. "That's right ma'am. This gentleman here is impersonating a police officer. He is a Ronin from the Chicago collective, here in Midland on nefarious business."

A Ronin! Everyone knew what they were; killers and rapers. Mayor Trent looked Harrison Drake over. The man seemed harmless enough. "He's very...statuesque."

Drake's eyes were moving frantically in his head. Somebody had control of his mind! He should be asking the mayor to come to the police car, but he couldn't get the words out. The morning air was cold but he felt sweat rolling down his temples.

Ralph spoke. "Sorry to bother you ma'am, but we're making an arrest under the authority of the free zone security force. These men are not Midland police officers."

Janet knew she should be frightened, but the man blocking her doorway was more nervous than dangerous.

"Come, Harrison," Ralph said calmly. "It's time for breakfast. My treat."

Gyorgy had hold of the fat guy, and almost laughed. Ralph had spoken to the feared fighter as if he were a child.

Mayor Trent was satisfied. Zimring was the free zone commander, so it must be okay. She walked to her car, high heels clicking on the cement, and drove off.

Ralph knew from Drake's mind that if he let go, Drake would attack. People were up and about now. Better not to cause a scene around the mayor's house and upset the neighborhood. He held on to Drake's sig.

"You're hurting me," Comstock said.

Gyorgy's fingers were digging into Comstock's shoulders. "Shut the fuck up or I'll break your neck." Comstock was terrified now.

Ralph marched Drake down the path to their vehicle. He was getting reports from all over the city from his officers but he didn't have the mental capacity to examine them right now.

Gyorgy wasn't sure of his ability to seize a mind, so he pushed Comstock down the path behind Ralph and Drake. When they got to the police car Gyorgy saw someone else inside.

'Gyorgy, read that sig. I don't have mental energy to do anything except hold Drake.'

Gyorgy kept his physical hold on Comstock and did a quick scan of the sig. 'The lady in the cop car is a hospital intern, here to sedate and implant a chip into Mayor Trent's head. The phony cops are going after the other eleven members of the City Council. The plan is for any citizen who refuses a neural chip to be put in a temporary internment camp, which will be built outside the free zone by Chicago contractors.'

'Shite.' Ralph knew they could do it easily. There were two million in the Chicago collective. A few hundred workers could be temporarily spared to build the camps and intern the people. They were obviously starting with the influencers first.

'There's something else Ralph,' Gyorgy sent. 'They are manufacturing millions of these head chips in a robotics factory run by one of the medical AIs in Chicago.'

Ralph acknowledged this grimly. 'Those implants are for us.'

Gyorgy looked at Comstock and Drake. 'What do we do with these assholes?'

'Watch.'

Ralph squeezed Drake's sig as hard as he could, causing extreme discomfort. The man was already freaking out. Gyorgy almost felt sorry for Drake, but Zimring was relentless. Ralph implanted a thought in Drake's mind: 'The free zones are full of powerful demons,' and then let go of his sig.

Harriman Drake collapsed on the grass in front of the curb, half-insane with terror.

Ralph spoke to Comstock. "Don't ever let me see you again, Comstock. Pick up your colleague and get the fuck out of my zone."

A trembling Duchene Comstock helped the blubbering Drake to his feet and they both got in the car. "You drive!" Comstock shouted to the woman doctor, who went to the driver's seat. The car sped away.

"That was fun," Gyorgy said, "but we got big problems now."

"Yeah. Even without the Ronin, there's enough manpower in the Chicago collective to overwhelm the Midland Free Zone."

"Over my dead body."

Ralph had a sudden premonition about Gyorgy, but kicked it out of his mind. "Let's see how the others did."

First Ralph checked his mobile and saw that several street incidents had turned violent.

Midland Police Attack City Council! screamed a headline in the *Midland Chronicle*.

> In separate incidents, three Midland Police vehicles forcibly abducted three members of the Midland City Council. Councilperson Jeanine Nihawatne was rescued by plain clothes members of the Free Zone Security Force before she could be detained. The FZSF operates alongside of the city's law enforcement officers and deals with external threats to the Zone.
>
> Councilpersons Alan Dubrnik and Muriel Washington were slightly injured when FZSF officers arrived on the scene after being released by two Midland Police black and whites. The FZSF officers were also injured by the Midland Police, who shot at the officers and sped away in their vehicles. After being released from the hospital with minor injuries, both councilpersons strangely demanded a universal chip mandate for all citizens in the free zone.
>
> The Midland Police vehemently deny that any of their officers approached anyone on the Council today, but citizen reports have at least five black and whites questioning council members. This is a breaking story and will be updated as more information comes in. The *Chronicle* is trying to contact Ralph Zimring, the free zone forces commander, for more details.

The article was written by Karen Everard, a reliable reporter.

Ralph handed his device to Gyorgy. "Drive us to the Midland Police station."

On the way Ralph processed all of his reports. Eight of the teams had been successful against the Ronin, with one lucky break and two complete failures.

I called a meeting of the group that night at the Second Street Investigations office. Ralph was too busy to attend.

I gave the group the info Ralph got from Gyorgy Rynkowski, and some new information from Jamaal's investigation of Uploads. "I told you guys before I got fired from Uploads that Selig Bronfman was messing around with the Grid comms. According to Jamaal, that's what those Uploads directors have been up to: using the Space Grid to organize an assault on the free zones all over the world."

"What about the united human workforce, and the Coming Together of humanity?" Joann asked.

"That was just a narrative to get people into the collectives," I said. "I've been looking into this for months but I still don't know who or what is giving the orders to the collectives. When Ralph and Josh went to Chicago they discovered that the Commander is just a tool who gets his instructions from the AI that runs the collective. But who set up the AI? The system is automated, but somebody must be in charge of the entire earth operation, because all of the collectives are networked through the Space Grid."

"I don't think it matters who is giving the orders," Joann said. "We have to defend the free zones. Sixty percent of the population is in the collectives now, there's nothing we can do about that."

At that point Ralph walked in. "The best defense is a good offense. We're putting together a team to hit that AI in Chicago. I should have slagged the place when Josh and I were up there. We'll see what happens to the Chicago collective when Landru is destroyed."

Everybody laughed at the old Star Trek reference.

I shook my head. "That's not going to work, Ralph. The collective AIs are run through the Space Grid. My guess is that Landru is just a passive gateway that routes instructions to the neural implants through the Grid. Besides, all of the AIs are connected. If you knock one out, the others will step in."

Ralph swore. "Yeah, that's what Gyorgy said. But if we knock out the Chicago AI it might damage their system for a while. Even a small delay will help our forces get ready for the attack that is coming. Today was just the first skirmish."

"I don't get it," Joann said. "If the AIs are passive gateways, how are they controlled by the Grid?" Joann asked.

"That's a good question. To figure that out we have to understand how the Space Grid works. The space above the earth where the satellites fly is divided into software grids. These are called GNGs: Geosynchronous Network Grids.

Each of the GNGs is basically a virtual router that is always in the same position relative to the ground stations. The virtual routers are activated when the satellites fly through the GNGs. So: the IP addresses for all of the AIs, mobiles, computers, neural chips, and everything on the ground that are connected to the Space Grid internet are bound to the GNGs."[29]

I sent everybody a concept image on the mental plane.

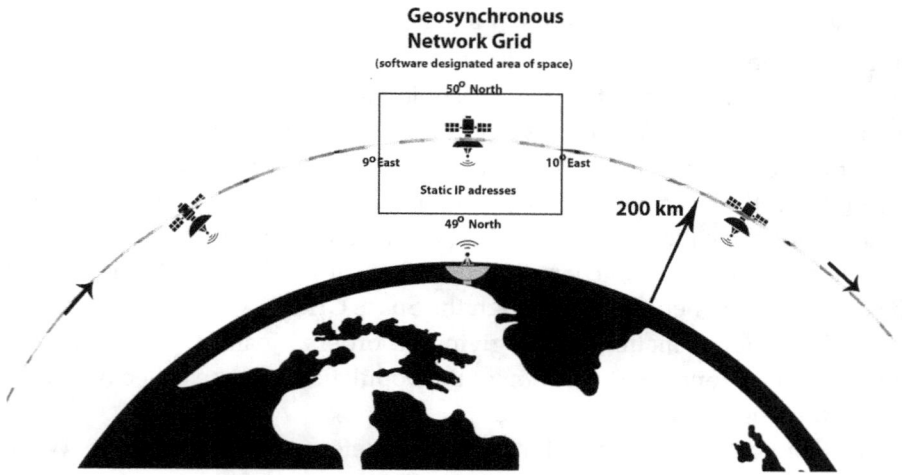

A Geosynchronous Network Grid.[30]

"You mean that the GNGs are the key to the Space Grid comms, not the satellites."

"Well, they are both necessary. The sats travel through the GNGs. The signals are bounced off the satellites using the GNGs, which determine where the signals are coming from and going to at different locations on the earth and in space."

"OK. So the AIs get their instructions from the Space Grid comms."

"Yeah. The satellites are the hardware that the signals bounce off of. The ground stations set up and program the GNGs. Oh, shit."

"Yes?"

"And what are those ground stations? The Uploads facilities!"

"Wow," Joann said. "You're smart, Philo."

"No. I'm pretty dumb, sweetheart. At Uploads I was just a hotshot satellite tech. I never thought about the big picture." I remembered what Patrick had told me three years ago: 'There is something you are missing, and it is right in front of your face.'

"It's Uploads, Joann. It's always been Uploads! The Space Grid controls the AIs, the AIs run the collectives through the neural implants, and Uploads controls the Space Grid! I missed the obvious."

"We all missed it," Joann said.

"The Uploads stations send comms and directives to the collective AIs."

"So that's why they had to replace all the Uploads directors," Kelleye said. "To implement their mass chipping plan in the collectives."

"Yes, but who is giving the orders?" Kelleye asked.

Josh said the quiet part out loud. "Doesn't matter. If the Space Grid goes down, the collectives go down."

Ralph's eyes were burning with passion. "Good work, Philo. We can defeat the collectives!"

"Theoretically. But how do we take down the Space Grid?" I asked. "There are thousands and thousands of sats up there."

Nobody had an answer.

One of my jobs was to keep an eye on the attractors. The Collectives had stopped broadcasting about Sister Sani and Brother Hamal and the benevolent space brothers. But when I checked them the next morning they were broadcasting again.

I called an urgent meeting of the group in the downtown office for 7 p.m.

"You remember the attractors went silent after the collectives were set up. Listen to this."

I directed the group's attention on the mental plane to the attractor closest to our location in Midland.

'Why do those in the free zones separate themselves from society?' was the message. The soothing vibe was gone, replaced by a feeling of anger and righteous indignation. 'These renegades think they are better than the Citizens in the collectives. They isolate themselves into rogue communities and spout nonsense like 'individual freedom' and 'liberty.' These are code words for ideas that destroy cooperation and community. Friends, these free zone extremists must all be chipped or destroyed, especially the ringleaders in Midland, Illinois. Do not let the cancer spread and metastasize!'

"Can you believe that?" I asked.

Ralph was upset. "The Collectives have declared all-out war on the free zones. Even if the Grid goes down the attractors will still be operational!"

"The Fenachrone and the Hilarion Collectives are in blatant violation of galactic law," Josh said, "but there's nothing we can do about it."

"We need help," I replied gloomily.

Kelleye looked at me. "Call Patrick. You're the strongest on the mental plane. He and Gwenneth got us into this, they have to help us get out."

"I'll do it now."

I asked Joann to stay for support. Kelleye and Josh also wanted to stick around. I closed my eyes and composed a short message to Patrick in my mind about the situation. "Theoretically, distance doesn't matter on the mental plane but I don't know if I'm strong enough to get through to Celeste, 17 light years away," I told the group.

"We are here to back you up," Kelleye said. I felt more confident because everyone was behind me, even though they couldn't help. I was on my own.

I closed my eyes again and envisioned Patrick's sig in my mind. I threw out all other thoughts and sent the most powerful burst I was capable of. I wasn't sure if I was successful so I sent two more bursts. I got a vague impression that Patrick was hoeing vegetables. When I opened my eyes I saw everyone looking at me.

"Success?" Kelleye asked.

"I'm not sure. I'm too tired to do any more."

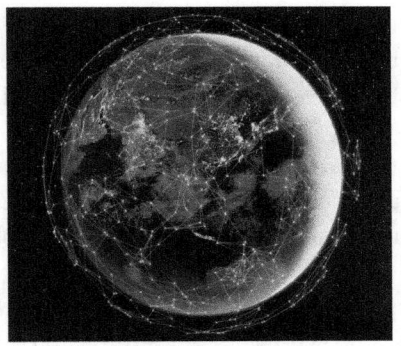

— 34 —

[Celeste, Altair system, Fenachrone Trading Collective]

Patrick was working in a crop field on Celeste when he felt a faint thought impinge on his mind. Then twice more. It was Philogene Rothman! He dropped his hoe and tuned in on the signal. 'We need help wiping out the attractors. They have been reprogrammed to incite violence against the free zones. The Collectives are going to forcibly chip everyone.' That's all there was, but it was enough. He needed to inform the Celestian Council right away but first he completed his shift in the fields. Food growing and distribution was the most important community task, and was not to be shirked.

After he cleaned up he took a float to his quarters in one of the beautiful organic rock towers. He and his niece shared quarters together, as they had both been mostly shunned from Celestian society after their protection of Philogene and his Maitre demon, in defiance of the Celestian Council. Gwenneth came out to greet him. For the hundredth time he wondered whether she was satisfied with her choice to keep Philogene alive. No male wanted her after her choice to endanger everyone in the community. Patrick sighed. Yes, their society had found the gateway to the One. But people still had free will, and made their own choices.

"Hello, niece." Patrick and Gwenneth sometimes spoke English as practice for when they were assigned to Earth. "I received a communication from Philogene this afternoon."

Patrick saw the quick intake of breath.

"We were right, uncle. The earthian male has extraordinary abilities."

Patrick sent her the conversation he had with Philogene on the mental plane.

"The situation on the earthian planet is completely out of control," Patrick said. "The Collectives are preparing to attack and forcefully chip the humans in the free zones using their human proxies. They have mobilized their attractors to incite violence."

Gwenneth was appalled. "The Collectives have gone too far."

Patrick was really angry now. "They are hiding behind the technicality of indirect engagement. The Hilarion and Fenachrone claim that humans are killing humans."

"But their attractors are mind-washing the humans."

"It is time for action. I have sent a communication to the Advanced Planets Council on Miralet using our direct transportal line. I described the situation and urged a forceful and immediate response."

"The Celestian Council approved?"

Patrick smiled grimly. "Reluctantly. Nevertheless, it was sent. I threatened to invoke the Community Charter and bypass the Council. I fear that I have isolated us further from our society, niece."

Gwenneth shrugged. "It is no matter. Our duty is clear. Once the Fenachrone and the Hilarion are finished with the earth they will come for all non-aligned planets in this sector."

Patrick nodded in agreement. He and Gwenneth were the only two in the entire Advanced Network to set foot on the surface of earth and interact with the earthians. Some of that rough-and-ready culture had rubbed off on both of them. "There's a time for contemplation and there's a time for action," Patrick quoted.

"Ralph Zimring," Gwenneth said.

Uncle and niece's eyes met and they both laughed. "There is much to like in earthian culture," Patrick said.

"Ralph Zimring is a barbarian," Gwenneth replied.

The two Celestians laughed once more.

To his surprise, Patrick received a response the next morning to his message directly from Naremset, the Celestian spokesperson to the Advanced Network on Miralet. Naremset appeared holographically in their small living room. "You and your niece are to proceed directly to Miralet within the hour. Prepare yourselves. The entire Celestian Council has also been invited."

Naremset paused, slightly embarrassed. She was pleased to be going to Miralet, but she had been an outspoken critic of Gwenneth and her uncle for protecting the earthian male and his Maitre demon. "It is a great honor to meet you," she said graciously. "We thank you. Report to Celeste Council chambers as soon as you are ready." Patrick and Gwenneth both bowed, excited and eager. To be personally invited to Miralet! It was a thing they had never dreamed of because of their isolation from Celestian society.

Patrick and Gwenneth quickly packed and took a transport to the capital city, halfway around the planet. As they rode in the transport, Gwenneth saw the purple sky and the blazing white sun of Celeste as its light harshly illuminated the planet's surface. Eons old ruins of ancient cities destroyed in the planet's devastating civil war were shown in stark relief. But she was too excited to be sad. They would soon be on Miralet, the central hub of the advanced network of planets!

The transport vessel landed in a brightly decorated open space in front of a huge cave entrance. Many other vessels were also present, as passengers disembarked on routine Council business. Patrick and Gwenneth were not noticed as they disembarked and walked through a gigantic hallway filled with light sculptures, lifelike carvings made from stone, and soothing music. As they exited the corridor they saw the spaceport of the capital city. Vessels were taking off and landing, but the official Council vessel was sitting in the circular area marked for the transportal to Miralet, a programmed area of space directly above the Council ship. The transportal system had been set up over 5 billion standard galactic years ago by an ancient race called the Founders, at the dawn of recorded galactic history. All solar systems have a transportal that leads directly to Galactic Central – Sector (0, 0, 0, 0) – in only one jump.

One of the council members briefed Patrick and Gwenneth when they entered the egg-shaped Celestian ship. "An unprecedented meeting has been called on the mental plane by the Advanced Planets council. This is an in-person gathering of over a million entities, representing all of the 267,831 Class I planets in the galaxy."

[Miralet, Galactic Central, Advanced Planets Network]

The Celestian vessel entered the transportal and appeared before the great planetoid, a hollow sphere about the size of Mars. They had "traveled" 7,500 kiloparsecs to the center of the galaxy in an instant. Their ship docked at a huge hangar on the shell of Miralet. Thousands of vessels were already there, some departing, some offloading passengers. The vessels of the Celestian delegates would park within one of the gigantic hangars staggered along the shell of the planetoid.

When Patrick and Gwenneth departed their ship they entered a transport vessel with the Celestian Council members. These egg-shaped craft were lined up in a pleasantly lighted tunnel, accepting passengers from all over the galaxy. When everyone was seated the vessel took off quickly, traveling in a circle around the planetoid until they were in the correct quadrant of their assigned quarters. Then they exited the tunnel and flew into the interior. In the center of the immense space was an awe-inspiring hologram of the galaxy. The holo had been painstakingly constructed and added to over the past 100 million years from surveys done by the Galactic Space Patrol.

"It must be a thousand miles in diameter," Patrick remarked. Craft were flying in and out of the hologram. Thousands of workstations with technicians were positioned inside the vast 3D holo.

All 235,677,498,003 cataloged stellar systems were marked within the hologram along with data streams about each star and its planets. Each transportal and its location was marked, with the web of connections accessible on the mental plane. The two Celestians stared at the complex web of connections between the stars and planets in the galaxy, in their quadrillions. "There is an underlying pattern to the galactic web," Patrick remarked. "But not even the Oorants have been able to find it."

Finally their transport reached the quarters assigned to the Celestians and they got out.

Patrick and Gwenneth, along with the Celestian Council, entered a large, pleasantly furnished space. Food packs were provided, as well as dozens of comfortable floats. After they had eaten, all of the delegates were summoned on the mental plane to a gigantic stadium supplied with floats for each delegate, allowing them to move about at will. The proceedings of the million-entity gathering was organized and recorded by a distinguished Oorant who called Itself Pleasant Meadow (English translation). To their surprise, Gwenneth and Patrick were led to the very center of the stadium, where Pleasant Meadow stood on Its three legs.

The delegates listened with rapt attention as the Oorant pulsed on the mental plane. 'Events in Sector (7635, 349583480, 17, 345134) have reached an inflection point. This sector is called the Greater Community by the local inhabitants. It contains the emerging planet called earth. Two corporate Trading Collectives are unlawfully assimilating the society.'

Pleasant Meadow sent a holomap of the sector to all the delegates on the mental plane. 'The earthian planet is of great geostrategic importance. Its placement between two powerful and competing Collectives, the Fenachrone and the Hilarion, makes it extremely vulnerable, but even more valuable. What would happen if this little planet were able to gain its independence from two great Trading Collectives? Dear Ones, the answer is obvious.'

'Nonsense,' one of the delegates pulsed. 'Billions of planets have already been subsumed by these Collectives. Why is this one so special?'

'Because, dear one, these earthians are fighting back.' Pleasant Meadow sent a stream showing how Patrick and Gwenneth had trained the earthians on the mental plane, and how the earthians in the free zones were training others to resist the collectives in the larger cities.

This provoked a great uproar within the delegation, for the power of the Trading Collectives so dominated galactic commerce and interstellar relations that resistance was deemed pointless by everyone. All knew that the Advanced Planets network must remain firmly hidden, or face assimilation.

The Oorant, always uncomfortable with strong emotions, let the delegates express their astonishment before It resumed.

'Independence for the earthian planet would be a major defeat for the Hilarion and the Fenachrone. It would set a massively important precedent for higher consciousness throughout the galaxy. It would also set an example on the mental plane for those poor citizens trapped within the Collectives. Even as we speak, over half of the earthian planet has been herded into collectives. But look at these earthians and how bravely they stand. This planet has the potential to disrupt Collective activities in the entire sector. And we must support them.'

This statement caused another outcry within the million-strong delegation. 'The Celestians have conducted a rogue operation!' one delegate cried, which was echoed loudly. 'If our network is discovered, we risk millions of years of spiritual evolution!' another sent furiously, expressing the opinion of the majority.

The Oorant let the delegates settle down before It resumed.

'The training operation on earth was approved by the Supreme Council on Miralet,' Pleasant Meadow stated flatly. This caused consternation among the delegates, for it violated millions of years of foreign policy toward the Collectives.

'Honored delegates, only one in a million civilizations ever achieves independence and a connection to the One. This is because, in our fear, we sit idly by and watch the destruction of emerging societies in our precious galaxy, as it falls further and further into barbarism.'

Some of the delegates objected angrily, but many felt shame. The Oorant found the courage to confront these emotional outbursts, which disturbed the deep serenity of Its mind. 'It is a simple matter of self-preservation,' the Oorant pulsed. 'The Supreme Council on Miralet has decided that we must change our policy and openly assist the emerging planets before we ourselves are assimilated.'

Before the delegates could react to this unprecedented statement, Pleasant Meadow ran a simulation put together by Oorant scientists. 'Observe. If present trends continue, within 10,000 galactic standard years, all of the Advanced Network will inevitably be absorbed into the Collective hive mind.' In the final scene, a massive armada of Collective battleships emerged into normal space and slagged Miralet itself. The delegation watched in horror as the entire galactic transportal system was snuffed out, the strands of energy withering and dying as the central hub at galactic central was extinguished. Billions of the galaxy's brightest minds were killed; their frozen, contorted bodies flying off into the frigid blackness of interstellar space. Billions more animals, birds, and plant life perished as the concussion wave froze the lakes and rivers and blasted trees, living quarters, and greenery. The great hologram of the galactic web at the center of Miralet imploded as the planetoid was blasted to a trillion pieces. The remnants of the great galactic civilization – nurtured for over five billion years – dispersed, lifeless, into interstellar space.

All were shocked into silence. The delegates knew that Oorant scientists were scrupulously honest and never exaggerated to make a point.

Finally, a delegate from the Orion sector found her voice. 'The Oorants have been the worst offenders in this regard,' she said with heat, appalled at Pleasant Meadow's presentation. 'We have consistently advanced an Interventionist foreign policy toward the Collectives.'

'We admit it,' Pleasant Meadow said. 'Which is why we have taken the lead in this matter, and are coordinating with you. Our isolationist and laissez-faire attitudes have been proven incorrect. We are more responsible than any race for the perilous and degraded state of society in this galaxy.'

The delegate from Orion was mollified, and bowed. 'Very well, Oorant. Now it is for us to discuss our plan of attack.'

The Oorant balked at this formulation. 'Our goal is not war. We act to help the earthians remove the "attractors," those festering sores used by the Collectives to mass-influence trillions of minds all over the galaxy.'

'Very well,' the Orion delegate replied. 'But if, as these earthians say, the blood of a few tyrants nourishes the tree of liberty, we shall have no regrets.'

The Oorant turned Its head ninety degrees and then back again, a sign of intense displeasure. 'We operate on the mental plane,' It said firmly. 'Kinetic war against the Collectives would be suicidal.'

'We are ready to fight!' the Orion delegate asserted with heat.

These Orions think like earthians, the Oorant thought to Itself. 'That will not be necessary. Only these two entities will travel physically to the earthian planet.' The Oorant paused for a breathless moment. 'We shall operate within the earthian system in a Class I GSP planetoid.'

The million delegates gasped. A Class I planetoid! These were not as large as Miralet, but like Miralet they were self-contained and self-supporting civilizations. Realization struck the delegates: Every one of them would travel physically to the earthian system! All objections vanished, for only two of these planetoids existed in the entire galaxy. They were used for only the most important and urgent functions, and were vessels that could support billions of entities indefinitely if the Advanced Network were to fall. The delegates all looked forward to a stay on one of the most luxurious and pleasurable vessels in the universe.

Patrick looked nervously at his niece. They would both be on the planetoid. They would both travel to the surface of earth. Gwenneth would again be physically near to Philogene Rothman.

[GSP Planetoid 2]

Gwenneth and Patrick entered the GSP planetoid, which was, like Miralet, a hollowed out sphere. Brother and sister stood on a soft, creamy white surface 15 feet wide.

The ship had thousands of levels arranged aesthetically. Some of the levels were mobile observation platforms (like the one they were on) while others ran as far as the eye could see. Each of the levels hung in space with no supporting beams or columns. Around them the Celestians saw a beautiful marble grandstand with colored lights and a multi-tiered temple. They saw parks, gardens, and forests filled with flora and fauna, much of which they did not recognize. Birds of all shapes and sizes flew between them. The air was filled with their cries and their chirping. Small transport ships were everywhere, ferrying people around.

Patrick walked slowly to the edge of the platform and felt slightly nauseous. He looked upward and felt vertigo. The lack of supporting columns or railings within this immense space made him nervous.

A humanoid of medium height, fine black hair, and huge circular eyes approached them. 'I am Asealo, your Greeter. Welcome to GSP Planetoid 1! I am here to show you to your quarters.'

The white platform began to move slowly upward and then picked up speed. They passed by a museum of sculpture, an art gallery, conference rooms, living quarters (one of the very few enclosed spaces in the immense planetoid), concert halls, video centers with gigantic three dimensional displays, a small lake with aquatic beings swimming in it, intricately designed gardens, a small forest, and a waterfall. They finally came to rest inside a space demarcated by a double ellipse traced upon a cream colored floor. Gwenneth recognized the pattern of the orbits of a binary star. 'These are your living quarters,' Asaelo sent. 'They are surrounded by an invisible transparency that can be opaqued by using this code on the mental plane.' The Celestians were losing their fear of heights in this magnificent place. Gwenneth used the code to gradually opaque the transparency. 'This is wonderful, Asaelo. Thank you!'

The two Celestians decided to see as much of the planetoid as possible before their mission to earth began. The vessel would travel to the earthian system in one transportal jump, but the delegation had been granted several days to relax before their duties began.

The next morning, local planetoid time, Patrick and Gwenneth were brought before Pleasant Meadow. The meeting was held in the Oorant's quarters, which was filled with plants and herbal delicacies designed for the palette of these sophisticated herbivores.

Patrick and Gwenneth looked around. The floor was of soft thick grass, with a few small trees and two small ponds. The aroma of the room was pungent but not unpleasant.

'A small slice of my home planet,' Pleasant Meadow explained. 'It relaxes the mind.' The Oorant took a deep breath. 'You two entities will be our only operators on the surface of the earthian planet. Our physical presence there must be as unobtrusive as possible.'

'Why are there so many involved?' Gwenneth asked.

The Oorant raised the corners of Its thin leathery lips ever so slightly in the Oorant equivalent of an amused smile. 'We employ a strategy the earthians call "shock and awe," utilizing the element of surprise. Like Miralet itself, we remain hidden behind an impenetrable mental shield until the final moment. If these backwater Collectives strike the earth, we unveil the massive force of our planetoid on the mental plane.' The Oorant rubbed Its three arms together, a sign of intense pleasure.

Patrick was excited. 'A GSP planetoid with one million advanced operators, all to defend a single emerging planet! It has never been done before in galactic history.'

The Oorant performed a slight bow. 'It was my idea,' It said with the air of an entity who is justly proud of Its accomplishments.

Gwenneth spoke to Patrick. 'So Oorants do have egos.'

'But of course!' Pleasant Meadow replied. 'It is a gross error to underestimate one's abilities.'

Gwenneth smiled. 'I think the Council on Miralet has chosen their leader well,' she said.

The Oorant performed an even deeper bow, inclining Its cylindrical torso forward several inches.

'Now, dear ones, let me explain your part in this great undertaking,' It pulsed. 'Our objective is twofold: to analyze and eliminate the attractors from the earthian space, and to neutralize any attacks on earth by the local Collectives from the mental plane.' The Oorant rotated Its head in a sign of profound irritation. 'The Collectives may overreach so far as to engage in kinetic warfare. If they dare to physically attack the planet we will show those barbarians the power of our delegation.'

Patrick was excited. 'That is the attitude we must adopt from now on.'

'We shall. Our non-interference policy has been a grave error.' The Oorant lowered Its head slightly, indicating shame. 'These attractors are insidious propaganda vehicles that have been used by the Collectives all over the galaxy to assimilate emerging planets and civilizations. By doing nothing we condemn promising societies to certain absorption into the Collective networks.'

Patrick nodded. 'That has been my contention, and my niece's.'

The Oorant acknowledged this. 'Your mission will be to work with the four earthians you have previously trained on the mental plane. Inform them that help has arrived to neutralize the attractors. Prevent them from physically engaging with the Collectives; we will handle that from the planetoid. The earthian attack on the Collective satellite was a grave error, for it enraged the Hilarion and the Fenachrone leadership.'

'So the satellite was a joint operation by both Collectives,' Patrick sent.

'That is correct. We have been able to penetrate their shields.' The Oorant shuddered. 'These Collectives are devising a plan to actually kill the earthians involved in the mental plane training, in order to put a halt to the resistance. That includes the four you have trained, and their mentor, the military man. There are other targets as well.'

Pleasant Meadow became agitated. 'It is an outrageous violation of galactic law. Unfortunately we do not know how many attackers there will be. That is why we have mustered a million of our best to defend the earthians.'

'Siddon Hilarion and his Fenachrone counterpart have lost their minds,' Gwenneth sent.

'Philogene Rothman is the primary target,' the Oorant responded. "He and his demon Maitre murdered a Hilarion operative from Beta Caronai, while pretending to be Colin Frank, the NIH director. His two friends destroyed a shipment of serum manufactured by the Fenachrone Collective. Philogene Rothman murdered Genghis Glazer, a human Hilarion asset. The gigantic earthian and Philogene's mate, the entity called "Joann," attacked and damaged a galactic satellite, which was built by the Fenachrone during a joint Fenachrone-Hilarion operation to program the attractors around earth.'

Gwenneth stared at Patrick. It was an impressive list of grievances against the earthians. 'What have we done, uncle?'

Patrick was angry. 'The earthians have defended themselves in spectacular fashion. I am proud of them,' he sent defiantly. 'The Collectives got what they deserved.'

The Oorant was amused. 'Certainly they have. But now full payment for the earthian aggression is due.' Pleasant Meadow also found himself admiring the courage of the earthians, who were much like the irritating Orions. A shift in Its thinking was underway. Perhaps the Orions weren't so bad after all...

'I know what I'm going to do,' Patrick sent. 'I will personally warn my students and the giant about the pending attack.'

The Oorant nodded. It found Itself using more and more colorful earthian expressions. 'You will be our canary in the mineshaft. If an attack occurs on the mental plane we will detect it instantly. Remember, the Collectives may attack you and your niece as well. They will regard you, their fellow galactics, as traitors.'

Patrick spoke to Gwenneth. 'Niece, you stay here on the planetoid. It's too dangerous on earth.'

Gwenneth shook her head. 'Philogene is the most impulsive. I have more influence over him than you do.'

'That's what I'm afraid of.'

Pleasant Meadow waited patiently while the Celestians debated. His asexual race always marveled at the difficulties of the sexed races, which dominated the galaxy. The subject of "relationships" was always tainted with a sexual component. Such nonsense complicated galactic interactions and was a monumental waste of time.

'We will go together to the surface of earth,' Gwenneth finally announced.

'Very well. When the planetoid reaches the earthian system, report to Launch Deck 15, section A-7. A pilot will be waiting to transport you to the surface.'

— 35 —

[Second Street Investigations office, Midland]

"The only certain way to wreck the Collectives is to shut down the Space Grid," I said, summarizing the situation. We were all in the downtown office after work, trying to figure out how to do that, but it was impossible. I was very frustrated. I knew everything about how the Grid operated. I should be able to figure out how to shut it down! But the Grid AIs and their software were impenetrable. Destroying all of the AIs in every Uploads facility, and in every collective, was futile. We were just about to go home when Ralph had an idea.

"Uploads monitors and corrects minor perturbations in the satellite orbits, and their AIs generate the software that creates the GNGs. What happens if the Uploads facilities go offline?"

"Impossible. They have the most secure backups on the planet. The backups to their backups have backups."

"You said something about making course corrections to the satellites. Isn't that what you spent a lot of your time doing at Uploads?"

"Sure, but the system is designed to give the AIs *carte blanche* control. To even get into the system the Uploads director has to grant access, and that can be denied to any tech at any time."

"What happens if there aren't any human operators to massage the Grid?" Ralph asked.

"Uh...I never thought about it."

"Jamaal might know," Josh suggested. "He used to be an Uploads director."

I contacted my friend on the mental plane right then. He was sitting in his living room. Everybody listened in.

'Philo, if the Uploads facilities across the world didn't monitor the Grid, it would begin to destabilize within 24 to 72 hours.'

'What?? Not sure I believe that.'

'Believe it. The AIs handle 99.9% of everything perfectly, but over time a slight error delta builds up within the low earth orbit sat trajectories in each Grid sector, due to a slight atmospheric drag. Why do you think Uploads is working 24 hours a day all over the world?'

'Holy shit.'

"There it is!" Ralph shouted. "Take out the Uploads satellite techs, the Grid goes down."

I could feel Jamaal's excitement as he twigged on what we were talking about. 'Easier said than done, Ralph. Those facilities are vital to national security. They are guarded and monitored by private military companies hired by the DHS.'

"Tell us gramps," Joann said to Ralph with a smile. "How are we supposed to take out all the Uploads techs?"

That's when I had my big idea. I jumped out of my chair and strode back and forth across the office. "An all-out sig attack on the mental plane on all the U.S. Uploads centers! We hit every tech simultaneously across the country. That's where Jamaal comes in. He's been investigating the national Uploads centers. He's got almost all of the sigs of the Grid techs identified now."

I could see the look of shocked surprise on everyone's face, but I was more amazed at my stupidity. Here I was, head of the national mental plane training program, and I never even thought to apply it to the Grid problem.

"If we disable the Space Grid first we can avoid a lot of fighting," Joann said finally. "The chipped soldiers in the collectives will be without direction!"

"By God kid, you've got it! Ralph cried. "How many of these Upload facilities are there?"

"Across the world? 48. Here in the US, 12. We are the central hub for the Grid," I said proudly. "We are responsible for correcting all the fuck-ups the other Uploads centers can't handle."

"If we shut down Uploads do we shut down the collectives?"

I thought for a moment. "Well, if the Grid goes down we'll shut down the signals that go to the AIs that in turn control all the neural implants."

"So what happens to the people in the collectives if the signals to the neural implants aren't there?"

"I'll have to ask Dr. Peter Doncic. He's our resident expert."

I contacted Doncic on the mental plane. He was drinking a glass of wine and watching TV in his living room.

'Hello, Philo. Without the signals from the AI to the neural chips, the implants will die.' Doncic described what happened to Gyorgy Rynkowski's neural chip. 'Gyorgy was fine after his chip was removed.'

Kelleye brightened. 'The slaves in the collectives will be freed!'

'Not so fast,' Doncic sent. 'When the neural chip self-destructed, it buzzed uncontrollably, like an addict seeking a fix. I am not sure what that will do to the human brain if the AI signals to the implants stop. Those chips will still be inside peoples' heads. Gotta go, people. Prepping for a surgery.'

"Nothing is ever simple is it?" Joann grumbled.

"Gyorgy says that when you fuck up, the pain from the chips is bearable," Ralph said. "The collectives aren't stupid. They don't want to lose all of their workers."

"What happens to communications across the country if the Grid goes down?" Kelleye asked me.

"All comms get shut down. It's all or nothing."

"That hurts the collectives more than it hurts us," Joann said.

"Yes, but our mobiles won't work anymore," Josh said. "Or the grocery stores or the banks or anything that depends on the Grid, which is everything."

"That's true," I replied. "The old terrestrial system had hundreds of regional fiber networks for the cities and towns and rural areas. Those were abandoned when the Space Grid went up. Comms were so much faster with the Grid so nobody bothered to maintain the old network hardware."

"If the Grid goes down the free zones will have to be temporarily organized by the military," Ralph said, "so people don't starve and the electricity keeps running."

"Nobody said we were going to take down the Grid," Kelleye said. "We can just shut it down for a while."

"I'm afraid Ralph is right, Kel," I said. "It's all or nothing, it's a binary solution. The Grid is either up or it's destroyed."

"Kelleye, the free zones are going to be attacked very soon," Ralph said forcefully. "Our communities won't survive an attack by the collectives. Do you want a neural chip in your brain?"

"Of course not. But destroying the entire Grid is a drastic solution."

"Desperate times call for desperate measures. We have to defend our-selves."

This was typical of the military mindset, Kelleye thought. "Taking down the Grid is an act of agression against humanity. Millions might die."

"It's a preventative act," Ralph countered. "The galactic Collectives are fighting a war of aggression against the entire human race. The Space Grid is part of that. I am responsible for defending our communities and I will spare no effort to do so."

Ralph had a dominating personality. Kelleye felt like a barking dog trying to stop a gigantic brown bear.

In the end nothing was decided, except that preparations to take down the Grid were set in motion. I was all for it, and so was Josh and Jamaal. Kelleye was against it and Joann was prepared to go either way.

"Philo, you and your team prepare to organize an attack on the mental plane," Ralph said. "You can use as many of our military assets as you need." He glanced at Kelleye and threw her a bone. "We need to prepare even if we decide not to do it."

Ralph strode out, excited as a kid.

Kelleye sighed. "*If* we are going to do this, we have to recruit enough peo-ple to capture each sig in all twelve of the U.S. Uploads centers."

"Wait a minute," I said, switching to the mental plane. 'Jamaal, if we disable all 12 U.S. Uploads facilities, will that be enough to take the entire Grid down?'

'No question. All the sats in the Space Grid are interconnected. Grid insta-bility in the U.S. controlled sectors will cause perturbations within the entire system. It may take a while though.'

'We have to immobilize the techs, so we have to capture sigs,' Joann sent. 'How many people do we have who can do that? That's extremely advanced work.'

I was in charge of the training program, and I checked our mental plane admin area. 'There are 30 million so far who have gotten the basic training. All they can do is send and receive on the mental plane. There's about 10,000 advanced enough to put up a shield. Out of those I'd say less than a thousand might be good enough to capture a sig.'

'How many techs are in the Uploads centers?' Kelleye asked.

'357 Grid techs in the US,' Jamaal answered. 'Plus the Directors and their personal guards. That comes to 437 total.'

'We're going to need a lot more than 437 to capture all those sigs,' Joann sent. 'I can only hold a sig for about an hour. It's hard work.'

'Good thinking, Joann,' Jamaal sent. 'We'll need at least a thousand, probably. One hour on, one hour off to rest. It might take up to 72 hours for the satellites in the Grid to destabilize.'

'We'll never hold sigs that long,' Josh sent.

'Wait a minute.' Jamaal began to feel excited. 'We only have to hold sigs long enough to cause unrecoverable satellite perturbations in the U.S. controlled sector! Once that threshold is reached the AIs won't be able to recover.'

'How long is that?' Kelleye was more interested in the logistics of the problem than the deed itself.

'If we could hold sigs for six hours the U.S. grid will begin to destabilize. That will set off a chain reaction and eventually cause catastrophic oscillations over the entire Space Grid. Sats will start falling out of the sky because they are all in low earth orbit. Others will collide and destroy each other.'

'Thanks Jamaal.'

"It's our decision," I said to my three team members. "Ralph and his military network don't have enough sig seizers to do it independent of us."

No one said anything. I laid it out for them.

"An organized, all-out sig attack on every tech and Director in every Uploads facility in the country," I said. "It's our only chance to save humanity from the collectives."

"The galactics will know what we're doing," Josh said. "We might have to fight them as well."

I knew what Ralph would say. "Fuck the galactics. This is our planet, not theirs." Then I thought of the Oorant, who had effortlessly held all five of us in Its mental grip. Josh was thinking the same thing.

"To those whom much is given, much is expected," I offered. "If galactics show up and we are defeated, at least we will know more about the enemy and their tactics."

"Were you able to contact Patrick?" Kelleye asked.

"I think so, but I'm not sure. We have to plan this operation as if we're on our own."

After the meeting ended I thought of Patrick's last word to me almost five years ago. "In every conflict there are only a few with the insight to shift the forces of history to the positive." Those few were us.

I would have to liaise with Jamaal and get all of the tech sigs. He would be my assistant. I would issue a call for qualified volunteers at the next training meeting and interview as many as I could. We would need sig capturers to hold the sigs of the Uploads techs and Directors, shield holders to hide our attacks on the mental plane from snooping galactics, and comms messengers to coordinate the attack of hundreds of sig capturers. I had to act quickly. The longer we waited the more time the collectives would have to coordinate their attack on the free zones.

— 36 —

The next morning I heard a knock on the Second Street Investigations door. When I opened it Rashan Oliwan was standing there.

"What the fuck Rashan! Haven't seen you in three years. I thought you might have joined the collectives."

"I almost did."

Oliwan quickly told me his story on the mental plane. "So there you have it. After Avriel deVilliers got absorbed into the hive mind in Austria I went into a mental depression. I was desperately in love with Avriel, and so much missed her humanity and her spontaneity. I eventually decided to join her in chipped land. I figured even a little bit of her was better than nothing. But at the last minute I couldn't do it. I got on a plane back to Tampa. After that city turned into a collective hive I just gave up. I became a wandering Ronin, hiring myself out to various farmers and land owners, protecting their properties from wandering bands of *haji* who steal food and don't mind risking being shot at by Ronin. I was pretty good at it because I found a way to do it without violence. Bob Saunders showed me that there's a way to capture sigs and scare the crap out of those superstitious fools."

I nodded.

"At that point I had been on the road for over three years and was just coming off a gig near Peoria. I was lonely. Then I thought of you guys. I was finally over Avriel by then, so I decided to look you up."

The relief on my face must have surprised Rashan. "I didn't think you liked me that much."

"I don't really, but we can use your help."

When I showed him our plan to take down the Grid, Rashan almost hit the roof in his excitement. "I knew if I looked you up good things would happen!"

I was pleased. When I tested Rashan I found him to be a competent operative on the mental plane. "Are you ready to be a sig seizer? That's what we call them. We need a thousand and we're way short."

"I'm your man. I can help train too."

"Even better." When I explained our training program and showed him our organization on the mental plane, Rashan was very upset. "I apologize, Philogene. I wasted my time wandering around for three years when I could have been helping out. I've missed out on so much!"

I grinned. "Yeah, but you're here for the kill now. Enjoy it."

"Is that big goon Ralph Zimring still with you?"

"Oh yeah. He's commander of all of the Illinois Free Zones and a Director of the USA Free Zone Military Command."

"I'll try to avoid him. When do I get started?"

I spent the day putting Rashan Oliwan to work, then informed Ralph of the new operative. It was my duty to report my meeting with Rashan to the city commander.

"I don't trust that guy."

"He'll be useful, Ralph. I'll take responsibility for him."

"Good, because I'm working 20 hours a day. The Chicago collective is finalizing their plans to hit us."

"Did you see the Midland City Council meeting last Monday?"

"Heard about it. Councilman Alan Dubrnik and Councilwoman Muriel Washington. Their eyes blanked each time they spoke. Called for everyone in the Zone to get chipped. I think they got implanted when they went into those fake black and whites and are sending data back to Chicago. I'll have to neutralize those two."

Joann and I buying a house was postponed by events. We were both way too busy managing the training program. She was gone a lot anyway, ferrying people to and from the free zones in her lifter. Sometimes you just have to meet in person, and the first stages of mental plane training must always be done person-to-person.

The next morning after Rashan came I called Jamaal and told him to come down to the office. It was time to integrate him into what we called the SGC, the Space Grid Collapse program.

"I want Selig Bronfman," Jamaal said angrily after I explained everything. "I want to make him pay for being such an asshole."

"You can have him, but you can't harm him. Everything has to look normal in case somebody comes in from HQ." My Maitre, which had been calm for most of the past three years, was beginning to stir.

Jamaal struggled with this. "I can't hold a sig for six hours."

"Neither can I. We have to work in tag teams. The more emotion there is, the harder it is. So you gotta keep calm."

Jamaal understood this. An angry sig is the worst because anger really disturbs the mental plane and creates a lot of noise.

"We need to locate every sig in the twelve Upload centers, including the Directors and their guards. All twelve centers need to be shut down."

"I already sent you the sigs of all the Directors, and most of the techs."

"We need the sigs of everyone in all twelve facilities, even the janitors, or someone could send an alarm. Do you need help? I can assign you as many sig locators as you need."

Jamaal thought for a moment. "Give me five competent people and I'll get them all."

I was grateful. "As soon as you identify all the sigs send me the list on the mental plane."

Ralph received a report from one of his roving scouts. "Construction beginning five miles north of Rampart Road just before Barker Road. Looks like housing."

So here it is, Ralph thought. That area is called Wesley, a self-declared autonomous zone that was trying to maintain its independence from the Chicago collective. Wesley had probably been forced to let Chicago use their land. The Midland Free Zone is a square 15 miles across. That's all we could defend. The northern border of Midland was about 10 miles south of Wesley. The territory in between was no-man's land.

Well, two could play at that game. Ralph called Dr. Peter Doncic and explained the situation. "Peter, Chicago is building housing in Wesley. My scouts say it looks like a detention camp."

"So they're coming for us."

"Yup. If I bring the two implanted councilpersons to you, would you be able to remove their implants? Alan Dubrnik and Muriel Washington are essentially Chicago collective operatives feeding intel to the enemy."

"The insertion and removal of the chips is a trivial procedure. How are you going to get those two to my surgery?"

"Remote sig influencing. Me and Rothman will get them to drive over there and submit to the procedure. It's painless and necessary."

Peter struggled with the ethics of that.

"Removing the chips will be a blessing."

"Perhaps, but forcing an operation against a person's will is a violation of the Nuremberg code."

"Damn you and your conscience, Peter! Unless those two have their implants removed I will have to forcibly take them out of the free zone."

Peter sighed. "All right. The one I removed from Gyorgy Rynkowski self-destructed after I took it out."

"Gyorgy carries that thing around. It's a souvenir."

"He's proud of it. When do you want to start?"

"It's almost lunchtime now. I'll have them in your office in an hour."

Alan Dubrnik was in his car, driving to a cafe on Fifth Street from his engineering office. Halfway there he had a feeling that he should drive over to see Peter Doncic, the respected but reclusive surgeon. Alan didn't know why he should do this, but it just felt right. He knew when he got there that something really good was going to happen. Alan turned his car from Tower Street and took Packard to Third Street. A voice in his head told him that he should continue to the office, and he felt a compulsion to do so. Alan became confused, and pulled his car over to the curb. What should he do? He was an engineer, and had almost never experienced mental confusion. He had his life just how he wanted it. What was this voice in his head? He knew about schizophrenia, and began to worry. Then a calm, soothing thought came into his mind: 'All is well. Peter is the nicest fellow and you will be glad to see him.' Alan ignored that irritating, chattering voice that told him to continue to the cafe. He pulled up in front of Doncic's surgery. He let himself out of the car and pulled open the door. Peter was there and greeted him. Another thought came into his head: 'Come into my surgery. I have something wonderful to show you.'

In less than a minute it was done. Peter removed the chip and placed it in the same ceramic bowl that Gyorgy's had been in. His patient sat up, confused. "I feel different." Suddenly the neural chip began to vibrate, then more wildly. It spasmed and then went silent.

Alan was shocked. "Was that thing inside my head?"

Peter spoke firmly with his best bedside manner. "Lie down for a moment, Alan."

Peter performed a brain scan and saw that, just as with Gyorgy Rynkowski, most of the neurons in the primary motor cortex were still active and showed evidence of recent heavy stimulation. Except for that, the brain was normal.

Alan leaned over and inspected the neural chip lying in the ceramic bowl. He picked it up. "What is this thing, Peter?"

"That, my friend, was embedded in your skin next to the base of your brain. Have you been hearing voices?"

"Yes! It has been quite odd. I'm an engineer and not prone to mental insta-bility."

"That is evident from your brain scan, Alan." Peter took the neural chip and held it up. "This little piece of miraculous silicon – or whatever it is made from – has been in your head ever since you were stopped by that police car. Do you remember that?"

Suddenly the memory came flooding back. "I remember! The officer ac-cused me of speeding. I never speed. He took me – very roughly I might add – back to his vehicle and accused me of resisting arrest...wait a minute. There was a woman there in a white lab coat in the back seat. She drew out something and I felt a pressure at the back of my head. It only took a second. After that I don't remember anything.... I don't understand, doctor. What happened to me? Why was the memory of that incident suppressed?"

What the hell, Peter decided, I'll tell him. At first Alan was skeptical but then he remembered feeling the urge to do odd things during the past two weeks. When he encountered the memory of himself at the last council meet-ing, calling for the population of Midland to be chipped, he was appalled and angry. "Did I actually say that?"

"Indeed you did, and it caused considerable comment and confusion among your colleagues on the Council, and among the public."

Alan took the chip from Peter. "What is this thing?"

"It's a remarkable piece of engineering called a neural chip. As you are aware, everyone in Chicago has one."

Alan was amazed. He silently examined the chip.

"May I, er, have that little device? I would like to analyze it from a medical perspective."

Alan handed over the chip. "You're going to need a computer engineer to understand how that thing works."

Peter smiled, a thing he did rarely. "I certainly will. If I have questions, may I call you? Perhaps we can collaborate on an analysis of this device in our spare time."

"I'd like that."

At that point Muriel Washington opened the surgery door. Peter had forgotten to lock it.

"Hello Muriel!" Alan said, greeting his colleague on the Midland City Council.

"Alan! What are you doing here? What am I doing here?"

Peter saw how skillfully Philogene Rothman was running Muriel's sig. His touch was so light on the mental plane! None of the more heavy handed pressure that Ralph had used on Alan. Peter saw Rothman place just the hint of a suggestion in the back of Muriel's mind: 'You're due for a checkup anyway. Why not let this gentleman give you a short examination?'

"I'm ready doc," Muriel said, sitting down on the examination table. "Do your worst."

Alan watched as Dr. Doncic quickly retracted the chip from Muriel's neck, swabbed the area, and put a small bandage on it.

Peter placed the neural chip in the ceramic bowl. Muriel and Alan stared as the thing began to vibrate and jump around in the bowl as if it were searching for something. Then it spasmed and went dead.

"What is that?" Muriel asked, horrified.

Alan explained. "I had one too. Do you remember being put in the back seat of a police car?"

Muriel encountered the memory and was outraged. "I do! I'll have that officer's badge!"

"No need for that," Alan said. "They were fake police. PSF operatives from the Chicago collective."

"Oh my God. And I called for all residents of Midland to be chipped!"

"Don't feel bad, Muriel. I was more zealous than you."

Peter handed the chip to the councilwoman. "This was embedded in your neck close to the base of your brain. Would you like to keep this? Alan here is a computer engineer. We're going to analyze his chip and try to understand how Chicago designs and makes these things."

"I'll say! Alan, I'm going to lead the effort to pass a City ordinance banning them."

Alan checked his watch. "It's past one and I haven't had lunch. Would you like to go to that nice little cafe on Fifth Street and talk about that? My treat."

The two walked out of the surgery, chatting excitedly.

Peter went to the Second Street Investigations office that evening and reported to Ralph and Rothman and the others. Everyone agreed that it was a nice outcome, but no one was too excited. It was just another scene in the on-going war between the Collectives and humanity.

[Wesley autonomous zone, 10 miles north of the Midland free zone]

Ralph and Gyorgy took their laser pistols and Rynkowski's truck out to Wesley to observe the detention camp construction. On the way they checked sigs for bands of Ronin, but the area was clear. When they hit the outskirts of Wesley they saw a guard post and a hastily constructed wooden barrier.

Gyorgy talked to the guard, whose name was Diaz. "What's this?"

"Orders from Chicago. All traffic in and out is to be inspected. Please exit the vehicle."

Gyorgy looked at Ralph and commed on the mental plane. 'Should we?'

'Yeah. The free zone has to keep good relations with our neighbors.'

The two men got out with their laser pistols and stood by the truck as the guard inspected the vehicle.

"Since when do you guys in Wesley take orders from those zombies in Chicago?"

The guard straightened. "Don't laugh. Our population is almost 20% chipped now and there's more coming in every day. There's a great demand from the chipped folks to chip everybody."

"They are after us in Midland and you're in the way."

"Looks like it."

"Tell your people that the unchipped are welcome in the free zone. We need farmers, truck drivers, and fighters."

The guard was noncommittal. "We like it here in Wesley."

In the distance Ralph could see the construction in progress. He pointed. "Those are for you, señor. And then us when they've assimilated the good town of Wesley."

The guard frowned. "It hasn't come to that yet."

"Trust me pal, it will," Gyorgy said. "Are you done?"

"Yeah. You gotta report back here by noon."

"Sure. Just going to take a look at those detention camps."

"Chicago calls them itinerant worker housing."

Gyorgy guffawed. "More like places for Ronin to hang out."

The guard stiffened. "We don't get Ronin around here."

"You will."

The two men got in the vehicle. "We'll report back at noon," Ralph told the guard.

On the way the two men saw lots of farmland. "Gyorgy, we need to bring this place into the free zone."

"Yeah. Chicago is growing and they need this food producing land."

When the two men arrived at the construction site they saw an army of chipped humans going cheerfully about their business, framing large bunk-style buildings that would sleep hundreds.

"This is unreal," Gyorgy said as they walked around. Nobody bothered them. "This housing is for us, Ralph!"

One of the foremen noticed Ralph as he inspected one of the newly erected wood frames. The man walked over.

"Good work here," Ralph said.

"Oh yes friend, we do not shirk our duties. Are you from the valley?"

"We are from the Midland Free Zone. Here to inspect the new housing." Ralph and Gyorgy were reading sigs as they spoke.

The man's eyes lit up. "Yes! Soon all of you will join us," the foreman said enthusiastically. "The collective is expanding!"

One of the workers stopped and acknowledged his boss. He looked at Ralph and Gyorgy. "Friends, the conflict between the free zones and the collectives must stop. What is freedom if it means fighting and death? Join us in peace and tranquility." The man was smiling broadly.

Ralph thought: 'These people even talk like Landru.' He executed a small bow to the worker. "Thank you friend," he said sardonically. "Your words have great meaning for us."

Gyorgy hid his face with his hand so he wouldn't laugh. The foreman clearly missed Ralph's sarcasm and he smiled. "That is a nice gesture, friend. Have a good day!"

Gyorgy looked at the workers happily doing their jobs. The work they were doing was strictly supervised but everyone seemed cheerful and was working hard. He looked at Ralph. "It looks pretty good."

Ralph snorted. "On the outside. Don't forget that these workers are all chipped, my friend."

Ralph and Gyorgy got out of there and made a tour of Wesley. They saw rich farmland producing wheat, corn, and soybeans, a large dairy farm, a food processing plant, and a big grain mill. It was getting close to noon so Gyorgy drove back to the Wesley guard post and checked in.

"We must not allow Wesley to fall to the Chicago collective," Ralph said.

"It's also a prime target for *haji*," Gyorgy remarked as he drove the two men back to Midland. "It's a food producing powerhouse."

Why don't we negotiate with Chicago?" Gyorgy suggested. "Share the wealth."

Ralph got angry. "Gyorgy, the AI controlling Chicago is probably run by the Fenachrone and the Hilarion Trading Collectives. Their goal is to subsume this planet into their ant colony networks. They aren't going to allow unchipped humans and they will never negotiate."

Now that his neural chip was gone, Gyorgy only recalled the positive aspects of his chipped life. "Yeah, but those workers are happy."

Ralph was exasperated. "Of course they are happy, Gyorgy! You were happy too, remember? But it's a fake happiness, artificially created by stimulating the brain. How long are the lifespans of these chipped humans?"

Gyorgy was startled. "I never thought about that."

"Think about it. I asked Peter Doncic about that yesterday. He estimates that a chipped human might have 20, maybe 30 years before the brain wears out from neural stimulation."

"You're kidding me."

"Not at all. According to my sources in Chicago, and what I got from those AI operators, the goal is eventually to eliminate human biological reproduction altogether and go to bio-printed bodies."

"Jesus Christ."

"Yeah." Ralph turned his head to look at Gyorgy. "The galactic Collectives aren't like the tyrants in human history. They are an oppressive galactic corporate bureaucracy that's been around for millions of years. It crushes and grinds planets like ours just like that grain mill we saw."

Gyorgy blanched and almost lost control of the steering wheel.

When they got back to Midland, Ralph called a meeting of the free zone security forces on the mental plane. If the Space Grid came down Midland would be filled with thousands of refugees from the cities. Those people would have to be fed.

I received the list of Space Grid techs and personnel from Jamaal a week later. "There are 355 U.S. techs in total, plus another 12 Directors and other support personnel and about 60 armed guards for the 12 Uploads facilities. 437 total. I have 430 sigs. That's the best I can do."

"That's great work, Jamaal."

"Exhausting work. The guys you sent me aren't as good as I am, so I had to do most of the sig locating."

"OK. Take a few days off. I'll give the list to Ralph. If you know anyone who can capture sigs, sent them along."

"Two of my team can do it. I trained them myself."

"That's great. I think Ralph wants to attack the Uploads centers sooner rather than later. He thinks Chicago is ready to attack us as soon as the detention center is finished. A couple of weeks more at most."

"I'm looking forward to participating, but now I'm going home to sleep for three days."

Rashan Oliwan reported to his Ronin contact in Peoria over the phone. "I'm in, Nasgur. You wouldn't believe the setup these people have." Rashan told Nasgur the plan to destroy the Space Grid, and the location of the Second Street Investigations office of the leaders. "I know you don't believe it, but these guys can do it. Will they succeed? I don't know, but they are going to fuck it up."

Nasgur Nyamsuren laughed. Rashan had tried to teach him the mental technique but it didn't really take. Nasgur could send and receive in a haphazard and jumbled fashion, but not enough for detailed communication. For the millionth time Rashan wondered why this was. He knew the answer but he didn't like it. He could feel his own abilities on the mental plane weakening the more cynical he became.

Avriel! he cried silently. But Avriel was lost to him.

"Get prepared, Nasgur. If the Grid goes down so does food distribution. There are plenty of farms in rural Illinois. Get your Ronin together and carve out some territory. I'll join you when I can."

Rashan was still bitter about Avriel deVilliers. She had been taken over by the collectives, but the free zones were almost as bad. Hypocrites like Philogene Rothman and Ralph Zimring with their nonsense about freedom and Constitutions. The place was practically run by the military! What difference was there between a chipped robot Citizen and a "free" robot under the orders of barking, moronic fascists like Ralph Zimring? Brother Nasgur had the right idea. A band of brothers completely independent from the zombies in the collectives and the fools in the free zones with their rule of law and their civil society.

"That's good, Oliwan," Nasgur said. "The more you can fuck up Midland and Chicago the better it is for us. The less of them the better." There was a pause. "I like the idea of taking down the Grid. Imagine! Give Zimring credit, he thinks big."

"Zimring is a degenerate. I'll take him out if I can."

Nasgur laughed. "Bring his head to me. We'll use it as a totem."

Rashan hung up. Nasgur was right. Taking down the Grid would be the biggest clusterfuck in human history! He wanted to be part of it. He would go home to Peoria a hero. People would sing songs about him just like the famous Ronin of ancient Japan.

A week later I had finished a mental plane sig database of Jamaal's Uploads sigs, for easy access. There were only 3 techs missing out of 355, and a few of the support staff and a couple security guards. Oh well, it would have to do. Josh and Kelleye had also helped me to create a database of our sig capturers. We could only get 743 who were good enough on the mental plane to capture over 430 sigs. It was going to be hairy.

The team were all exhausted, working to complete our tasks. Kelleye had resigned herself to taking down the Grid as the threat of a physical attack became certain.

"The attack from Chicago could come at any moment," Ralph told us at 2 a.m. that night in the downtown office. Every person who had been trained was present on the mental plane – including the military people. I had assigned all those who were not directly involved as "observers," to keep everyone busy. That's the thing about the mental plane: you can't stop anyone from participating.

"Everybody get some sleep," Ralph said. "We attack the Uploads centers tomorrow at noon."

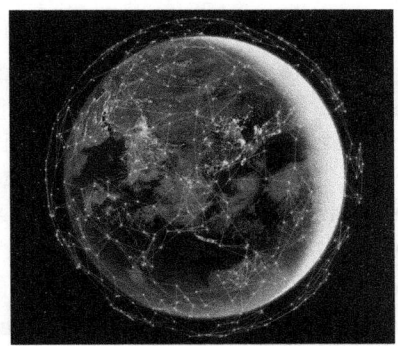

— 37 —

At 6 a.m. as the sun was rising, truck convoys crashed through the Midland Free Zone barriers in three areas. The attack came from the south. Guards frantically sent out alarms: "Ronin attack from Gates 3, 4, and 5! Hostiles in camouflaged army troop carriers and buses!"

Ralph was already up. Damn! They hadn't got organized in time. Reports were coming in from the U.S. Free Zone Command: The free zones all across the country were under attack. The only solution was an immediate strike on the twelve Uploads facilities. His ground forces would have to hold off the enemy attack for six hours: long enough to hopefully destabilize the Grid. Fortunately no one knew of their plans except their network.

The early warning sentinels had already responded to the guards. These were all ex-military and began to organize the Uploads sig assault teams in every free zone. As the sig grabbers came online, the first responders got them set to attack their designated sigs. The operation was chaotic, but it all happened at the speed of thought so not too much time was wasted.

Ralph was fired up to participate in the first 6th generation battle in human history, but his job as free zone defense commander forced him to reluctantly hand off the operation to Philogene, Josh, Kelleye, and Joann. "It's on you now, kids. I gotta organize the ground forces!"

Ralph left the office and ran over to the Centurion Building, where the defense forces were gathering. As the units formed, Ralph sent them off. Reports were coming in from all over the city on the mental plane. The Ronin rapid attack forces were fanning out. Hundreds of chipped soldiers were already on their way and would arrive in Midland from the Chicago collective after the city was secured.

City Hall was quickly occupied by the enemy. Then the Edison Building, and the East Side Fire Station. The Midland Police HQ was quickly taken over. Ralph was impressed. Whoever was organizing the attack was good. Very good! Clearly the attackers had scouted the city thoroughly and knew the location of Midland's important infrastructure.

'First priority: Prevent the troop carriers and buses from leaving the city!' Ralph instructed. 'Rules of engagement: Shoot to kill any invader with your laser rifles.'

At that moment the power went off all over the city. Ralph sent his last unit to the Edison building. He led the group.

I heard the reports coming in. People were being rounded up out of their homes and their businesses and even off the streets. They were forced like sardines into the Ronin troop carriers and buses, which didn't even have seats. All of our sig grabbers were in the basement of Max Berglin's Centurion Building, surrounded by some of Hideki Matsui's armed guards. The other cities involved in the Uploads attack were also posting armed guards. The sig apprehenders were the critical component of the strike force and had to be physically protected. Everyone in the free zones across the country was scrambling in haste to get set up, but it was all arranged quickly on the mental plane.

In addition to our group of four were Jamaal from Uploads; Ralph's friend J. D. Robinson, an air traffic controller at the airport; Sergei Kharkov, Ralph's old boss when he was a mercenary, in the US from Europe to be in at the kill; Danny Radulov, the ex-CIA operative; Tony Baghdadi, Ralph's special forces buddy; Emily Frankel and Jeanette Foley, pilot friends Joann had trained in the technique; Shaunda Jones, an EMT I had trained; Dr. Gina Richards, an emergency doctor at Midland West hospital trained by Kelleye; Jack Rodriquez, Josh's martial arts friend in from DC; and Rashan Oliwan. I looked around at the group. I was never more proud of myself and our group than at that moment. I saw that I had fulfilled Patrick's promise for us and for the earth. Now we had to execute our plan.

We had 743 sig capturers for 355 tech sigs, 12 Directors and 70 other Uploads personnel. Their apprehenders were ready. The level of excitement was off the charts. The galactics would see this as a blazing explosion on the mental plane. If they attacked us...but there was no time left for speculation.

Selig Bronfman walked the Midlands Upload facility. The huge panel in the middle of the room showed scenes from the Ronin attacks on the free zones. All was going well. The free zoners must be neutralized for the good of society; those millions of renegades would never cooperate with a sane, reorganized human society. The Ronin and the Independents were smaller, divided populations and could be easily handled.

Suddenly the power went out. Techs were swearing and crying out, but the backup generators came quickly online and all was well. Selig glanced at the huge display panel in the middle of the room, which showed scenes from Midland. Ronin were throwing people into the troop carriers and packing them into buses. Perfect!

He wondered what it would be like to have one of those neural chips in his head. They would be required to live in the amazing new smart cities that would eventually link all citizens to the vast galactic networks.

'Is everyone ready?' I asked.

'YES!!!!' came a huge cry on the mental plane.

'Attack!'

437 of our best immediately seized the minds of everyone in all twelve U.S. Uploads buildings.

Selig Bronfman stood staring at the huge panel, unable to move. What was this? On one of the screens Selig saw two sats wobble slightly out of place in their orbits. The AIs repaired the problem, but Selig could see that it would recur sometime in the future. Tech 17 was responsible for that area. Why was nothing being done? Sooner or later those sat perturbations would affect others, and disturb the all-important comms. Why couldn't he move? His techs were all frozen in place! Where was Spieth, his personal guard? Frozen like the others.

Selig heard a voice in his head. "Relax, dumbass, I'm freeing your sig." It was Rashan Oliwan! A friend. Rashan had helped him deal with the irritants Philogene Rothman and Jamaal Freeman a few years ago.

Selig was able to move now. He raced over to Console 17 as fast as his bulky body would allow. He shook Tech 17. "Repair the orbital anomaly, Tech 17!" The silly woman would not respond. Selig shoved her off her console and she fell to the floor like a rag doll. Her eyes were bugging out of her head and sweat was pouring down her face.

Selig was a former tech, but rusty now after three years as Director. He sat on the console chair and examined the two problem sats. He was able to see a solution and typed it in. Course corrections successful! But then he saw two more areas where the sat trajectories were going slightly wobbly. The techs sat there like mannequins and did nothing. The fools!

Rashan was in his mind. "Nothing can be done about your techs. Inform the Chicago collective commander. Their AI's have to devote all of their resources to stabilizing the Grid in this sector."

Rashan knew he shouldn't be helping Bronfman to save the Grid, but he was perversely more interested in fucking up Zimring and Rothman. Besides, it was fun to see this walrus run over to the primary comm station, and feel his panic. "Emergency!" Selig screamed into the phone. "Midland Uploads tech station non-functional! Employ emergency AI control!"

"Acknowledged."

As Selig watched the two wobbly areas began to stabilize. He breathed a sigh of relief. After several minutes, however, he saw that the corrections made by the Chicago AIs did not completely stabilize. In another few hours these orbits would become uncorrectable. This is why they needed techs.

Rashan had a good time watching Selig Bronfman run to console after console, trying to reconfigure multiple areas.

I saw that the Uploads AIs were doing a credible job of maintaining sat orbits, even though the system would eventually destabilize. But it was going to take almost 24 hours instead of 6. No way our sig grabbers could hold sigs for that long, which meant that the Grid might not fail at all if the techs could get back to work.

A few of our mental plane sig grabbers were going offline as the Ronin attackers broke through their guards in several of the free zones, and were thrown into troop carriers. The Collectives were executing a brilliantly planned national ground campaign that resembled our own on the mental plane. It was a simultaneous attack on all of the U.S. free zones using every Ronin they had been able to pay, coerce, or bribe with the promise of control and power over a subdued population.

"Brendan Sheridan offline!" I shouted. "Linda Balfour, back up!"

Some sig grabbers weren't able to hold their techs and needed to be replaced almost immediately by others. There was no way we could hold for 6 hours, much less 24.

Ralph arrived with his team at the Edison building, which was surrounded by a ragtag force of Ronin. The Edison employees were running like scared sheep into the troop carrier out the side door, leaving an open field of fire. Ralph led his group and didn't waste any time. Operating on the mental plane, his men quickly dispersed and opened fire on identified Ronin targets, using the cars in the parking lot as cover. The Ronin retreated to the inside of the building. Ralph and his men made it to the entrance of the building and slagged their way in. Each man knew the exact position of the enemy inside the building from their vantage point on the mental plane, but two of his men got careless and fell as they took fire from the retreating Ronin. Out of the corner of his eye Ralph saw a man on his stomach, bleeding out from a lucky shot to the neck. Ralph's men returned fire with their laser weapons set to "burn." They didn't miss. The remaining Ronin fled the building through the delivery door in back, dropping their weapons. All except one, who stood his ground. Communicating instantly with each other, Ralph gave the order to stand down. All of his men read the sig of Nasgur Nyamsuren and instantly knew his history.

"Two men down!" Ralph said to Sergei Kharkov. "Take care of those men, Sergei."

He turned to the Ronin leader. "Your men are cowards," he said contemptuously.

Nasgur shrugged unconcernedly. "Ronin. What can you expect? Half of them were deserters." He looked at Ralph's weapons. "Elegant. Laser rifles, a superior weapon. Our men are sacking your weapons factory as I speak."

Ralph checked the mental plane. "Nice try. Your men have been defeated by a far superior fighting force. As I speak your troop carriers have been stopped and your men seized."

Nasgur's eyes widened. He caught a vague something on the mental plane and knew what Zimring said was true a second before Ralph completely seized his mind. A fierce fighter and a veteran of a dozen battles, Nasgur had never experienced anything like this. This Zimring was casually ransacking his mind, tearing out his secrets and sharing them with his men. This was rape! He could not fight back; he was helpless. It was the ultimate humiliation.

Ralph squeezed Nasgur's sig, determined to extract everything from his mind. Before Nasgur lost consciousness he thought: 'I chose the wrong side.'

I saw that Rashan had turned traitor and seized his sig. I ruthlessly ripped everything out of his mind, employing my Maitre and scaring him to death. I saw on the mental plane that Ralph had subdued Nasgur, Rashan's commander. I shared it with my prisoner. Rashan caught Nasgur's last thought. Shocked to his core, Rashan fainted. Good! I didn't have time for him.

We had only been at it for an hour but the U.S. part of the Grid was already very slightly perturbed. All of the AIs in the world were now engaged in attempting to maintain the Space Grid's integrity. We had to hold sigs as long as we could. It was exhausting and draining work.

Me, Kelleye, Josh, and Joann were frantically monitoring our people, calling breaks for those who were losing their grip, and assigning others to replace them. We found that breaking every 15 minutes or so prevented our mental plane warriors from going crazy, but there weren't enough backups for everyone. So we four had to look for signs of weakness, hold sigs ourselves, and replace with fresh troops. Even so, we could see that the energy level of our forces was going down.

Mohammed Azzizi and Karen Kayfabe were sitting at their consoles at the Los Angeles Uploads center, frozen in fear. People kept coming into their minds and locking them down. Karen couldn't move. She felt a mental pressure in her head and didn't know where it was coming from. At first she thought she was having a seizure. She realized after a few minutes that someone was taking over her mind. She was going crazy!

Mohammed understood immediately that he had been seized by an evil djinn, a creature of al-Shaytan. Deathly afraid, he did not resist the demon, for to resist would only serve to make the djinn stronger. Occasionally he felt a release and then another djinn would occupy his mind. Although he could not move, his head was tilted slightly to the console on his left. He observed the tech next to him, a woman named Karen. Sweat was dripping down her forehead and her eyes were moving crazily in her head. Yes, this is what happens when you resist evil, poor woman.

After an hour of this Mohammed felt himself growing faint. Then, suddenly, he was free. The djinn had released him! At the same time he saw Karen's head snap backward. She slammed her hands on the console and screamed.

"We are free," Mohammed said. "Let us get out of here before another djinn comes."

Mohammed's calm voice soothed Karen and she snapped out of her panic attack. "I'm with you!"

I saw that two techs at the LA Uploads center were active now. "George! Barbara! Seize the sigs of those techs in LA!"

But it wasn't necessary. The two techs were terrified after the alien presence in their minds, and fled the building.

"Two less," I said grimly.

After three hours most of our sig seizers were too exhausted to continue. "Those of you who can, hang on," I said. "If not, release your sigs."

I saw about 300 of our fighters withdraw from the mental plane. Almost 130 brave souls hung on.

When the techs were freed, many of them panicked and ran out the building. Others, enervated and exhausted from fighting the sig seizures, lowered their heads to their consoles, trying to control their breathing. A few fainted and fell on the floor. Several recovered quickly and became active again, trying to stabilize their areas.

"Peter!" a tech shouted to another awake tech across the room at the Boston Uploads center. "Come over here and help me!"

Peter, a senior tech, ran over and looked at the subsector and its data packets. "The perturbation of the sats in this sector has crossed the threshold of control."

Jaime looked up. "I agree. Our only hope is that this subsector will not catastrophically impact other subsectors."

Peter saw that this was inevitable at some point. Both techs looked around the facility. Three-quarters of the consoles were unoccupied. A few techs had fainted and were on the floor. The others were frozen in place.

Peter and Jaime got frantically busy trying to stabilize the various subsectors at different consoles. They were too occupied to wonder why their minds had been taken over. They threw themselves into their work.

After three frenetic hours they saw that the situation was improving slightly, but not enough. Jaime ran a simulation based on the current status of the Grid. "For God's sake, Peter. If nothing changes the entire U.S. sector is going to experience potentially catastrophic perturbations within the next 18 to 36 hours."

Peter acknowledged this. "Jaime, if techs are disabled at the other centers the entire Grid might come down! The Grid AIs are covering the situation as best they can, but I don't think it will be enough."

The two techs looked over at their Director, a mean-spirited slave driver, who was still frozen in place. They stared at the huge display at the center of the room. "Comms are still flowing," Jaime remarked. "The Grid looks normal."

"Yeah. But we know different."

"The Grid is doomed and so are we," Jaime said. "If we stick around, dickhead here will blame us."

"Let's go," Peter said. "We'd better stock up on food."

"Good call."

Both men walked out of the building into a warm Boston summer. Each had a strong premonition that the world they knew was on its last legs.

I was devoting a tendril of my mind to the situation in Boston. The attack was working! If even one regional area of sats went haywire the perturbations would eventually affect the entire Grid. I was overjoyed, but keenly aware of the old saying: "Be careful what you ask for, you might get it."

Rashan Oliwan regained consciousness. He had a splitting headache. He was lying on the carpeted floor of Rothman's downtown office. Rothman and his friends were at their desks, working on the mental plane. What was he doing here? A flood of memories rushed into his mind. He had come to Midland at the behest of Nasgur Nyamsuren, still bitter after three years about Avriel deVilliers. The system had destroyed Avriel and his motivation was to destroy the system, but Rothman and Zimring were fools. His head hurt too much to get up. If he didn't move they'd think he was still unconscious. Rashan Oliwan fell into a deep sleep.

Ralph Zimring dropped his laser rifle and checked on his fallen companions. One of the men had taken two in the leg, but would live after being patched up from a field kit. The other was Gyorgy Rynkowski, dammit! He was lying in a pool of blood from a bullet to the neck. He had grown to like Gyorgy, had trained him personally. A good man gone, a friend lost.

"Sorry Ralph, I could do nothing for him," Sergei said sadly.

Ralph brushed tears out of his eyes and patted Sergei on the shoulder. He turned to Danny Radulov. "Danny, take care of Gyorgy. When this is over we'll have a ceremony for him."

"OK Ralph."

"Sergei, get Nasgur and bring him to Hideki at the Centurion. Lock him up in one of the basement security cells."

"OK."

"Round up those Ronin!" Ralph said to the rest of his men. "Locate them on the mental plane!"

Ralph walked out of the Edison building with Danny Radulov and Sergei Kharkov. He saw the troop carrier bus, which was now empty. The Edison employees were running around in confusion. "Ladies and gentlemen!" Ralph boomed. "Edison employees!" Ralph got their attention. "The Grid is coming down! In less than 48 hours network communications will be non-existent. Your jobs are the most vitally important in the city. You must get the power up and running. Secure your supply chains while you still can. The Defense Forces are here to give you anything you need. The attackers are being apprehended."

Questions rained down on Ralph.

"A city-wide briefing will be given by me and Mayor Trent as soon as possible. Please return to your duties and assist the citizens of Midland by returning power to the city."

Many of the employees grumbled but they eventually went back into the building.

'We got 'em, Ralph,' Tony Bagdhadi reported to Ralph on the mental plane. 'Those Ronin just dropped their weapons and surrendered.'

'OK, get them all in the troop carrier.'

After this was done Ralph talked to his men on the mental plane. 'Four of you take this bus to Jake's Junkyard. There's a barbed wire fence around the place. Tell Jake to call off his dogs. Interrogate the men as best you can and get intel. Hold them until you get further instructions. If they give you a hard time, burn them. But no killing!'

Ralph made a tour of the city in Arthur. The Midland Police HQ was still under siege. Ronin held the employees hostage and had stuffed the police into their own jail cells. Ralph's defense forces had secured the outside of the building and the troop carrier. It was a standoff. "Jerry, who is leading this collection of misfits?" Ralph asked his team leader.

"Some guy who calls himself Colonel Austin Lloyd."

"Anybody here know how to grab sigs?"

"I might be able to manage it," Jerry replied. "Not an expert by any means."

"Give it a go. Get Lloyd to tell his men to surrender; they are surrounded. Amnesty to all attackers."

A short time later a motley crew of Ronin straggled out of the building. "Drop your weapons!" Ralph commanded, "or we'll slag you down right here." He and his men raised their laser rifles. One by one the Ronin dropped their firearms. "Fuckin' asshole Nasgur," one of the men grumbled.

"Pack 'em into the troop carrier and take them down to Jake's," Ralph said. "Interrogate them on the mental plane, scare the crap out of them. I'll be back later in the day."

Ralph went to City Hall next. A couple of Ronin were lying dead on the ground. Three of Ralph's men had injuries. "You guys gotta do better on the mental plane," he complained.

353

"We did! There was a sniper on top of the building, he picked three of us off." One of his men was dead, and Ralph swore. The two others had been patched up and were lying on the ground. "We're going to kill every last one of these motherfuckers," one of Ralph's men said.

"You'll follow the chain of command, soldier. And I'm the head link." Ralph looked the fellow over. "Did you get that sniper?"

"I got him. He killed our team leader. His body is still on the roof."

"Good. Let him rot, team leader."

The man straightened and saluted. "Yes sir!" It was a battlefield promotion.

"Take these Ronin down to Jake's Junkyard in the carrier and interrogate them on the mental plane. Scare the shit out of them. I'll be along later."

The man, a former Army sergeant, grinned and began to issue orders.

When Ralph drove Arthur over to the East Side Fire Station, the situation was already well in hand. His team leader and several firemen had rounded up the attackers and put them against the back wall of the station. The firemen were covering them with their own weapons.

Ralph laughed. "You guys did a lot better than the police. We found them locked in their jail cells."

The firemen hooted and swore. "They are never going to live this down!" one of the firemen said. There was an ongoing rivalry between the police department and the fire department in Midland, aggravated by the annual Police-Firemen baseball tournament, which the firemen had won in an upset last summer. Ralph turned to his team leader. "You had it easy," Ralph said.

"Yeah, the firemen pretty much had the situation under control when we got here."

"OK. Stuff these assholes into their troop carrier and bring them down to Jake's. Interrogate them on the mental plane and make them think you are demons with the power of life and death."

Selig Bronfman sat in Uploads, staring at the big screen. He had set the huge panel to display the entire Grid of satellites. It was always something that excited him; an array of thousands of sats, dancing with each other, a grand space ballet. But something terrible and inexplicable had happened. His techs had all remained frozen at their consoles as the Grid slowly destabilized. He himself had been unable to move, a prisoner of some devilish force he didn't understand. Reports were coming in from all the U.S. collectives; he could see them on the data displays that hung around the room. Communications were becoming less and less dependable. The neural implants depended on reliable signals from the AIs, and the AIs were dependent on the Grid communications.

He was exhausted after working for eight hours straight, running from console to console.

The AIs themselves were suffering a form of insanity. Their instructions to the neural implants in the collectives were becoming scrambled. Citizens were getting more and more confused; their carefully crafted system was breaking down. The AIs had to watch helplessly as their programming became less and less successful, in violation of everything their algos told them should happen. Each of the AIs, and collectively throughout the world, saw their system slowly departing from the norm. They were experiencing what human beings would call major frustration that grew greater by the hour.

Selig saw all this as he sat at the main console. Why, he thought, the Space Grid was about to experience what humans would call a nervous breakdown. He looked back up at the Big Screen. Was that a perturbation in the northeast sector? Frantic reports had been coming in from Boston for the past hour. Frank Fortescue had seen all but eight of his techs desert the building. Selig only had six working, including himself.

Suddenly, an entire subsector of sats began to fly off-path. Several sats collided with sats in another subsector. That precipitated a sector-wide blowup, like a singer exploding a crystal glass. Selig watched in horror as that sector fell into another sector. Sats were crashing into other sats. Some were knocked above the orbital plane of the Grid, others careened toward the earth. Selig knew that eventually all of the sats, like dying fireflies, would burn up upon reentry into the earth's atmosphere as the earth's gravitational field brought them down.

That night, two newlyweds were walking down a country road near their house on the outskirts of Midland.

"Look Nancy, a meteor shower!"

"I'll message Joe and Heather!"

"There's something wrong with my mobile. I have zero bars."

"Me too. What's happening?"

"My God. Remember that public announcement from Mayor Trent and that Zimring guy? They said the Grid was coming down."

"What a joke!" Greg tried to get his phone to message with no luck. "My phone is dead."

Nancy looked up at the sky. "Zimring said that satellites from the Grid might fall out of the sky."

Husband and wife looked at each other and gulped. "At least the power is back on."

Artist's conception of Grid sats falling from the sky.[31]

"Yeah."

The newlyweds stared, fascinated, at the light show in the sky. Then they hurried home nervously in the dark, moonless night, lit only by a soft illumination from the collapsing Grid.

Very early the next morning Citizen Brian Strezler and Citizen Traylor Rolens were on the commuter bus, going to another satisfying workday at Guardian station 24B on 24th Street, monitoring street traffic. The bus, driven by an AI, began to sway across the double yellow line. Brian and Traylor watched in horror as their bus slammed into several cars coming toward them. They were jerked out of their seats as the bus tilted over, smashing into another vehicle and running over a pedestrian. The bus flipped over on its side and crashed against the front of a cafe, scattering pedestrians. Glass flew in every direction as people ran out of the cafe, screaming. At that moment Citizen Brian and Citizen Traylor felt an explosion at the base of their brain. A bright light appeared in front of their eyes and then blinding pain.

A crew of exterior window washers, on the 20th floor of the Chicago Board of Trade Building, saw the traffic on South LaSalle go crazy.

"Hey Jim, what's going on down there?"

Jim looked down. Vehicles were breaking from the settled pattern of four car lengths, veering crazily all over the road, crashing into each other and running people over. "You got me. Maybe the AI that runs this town is having a temper tantrum."

The workers, who had strung their battery powered platform from the roof of the building, seemed unconcerned about the height. "Let's take an early lunch," Jim said. "Watch the show."

The guys got out their thermoses and sandwiches and began to eat. "Look at that!" Ron said, pointing down. "That guy with the briefcase just toppled right over!"

"That lady did too!" Jim cried.

More and more people were hitting the pavement. "They say the same thing happened in 1918 with the Spanish flu."

"I don't feel anything," Raul said. "Maybe it's because we're up here."

The crew looked at each other. Jim checked the battery sensor of their rig. "We're good. It's a nice day. Let's see what happens."

Fifteen minutes later LaSalle Street looked like a ghost town after an earthquake. Cars and buses were scattered on the street and the sidewalks. Bodies were lying everywhere.

"What do we do now, Jim?" Ron asked.

Jim looked up. "Let's get this rig up to the roof and get out of here. If we haven't got sick by now it's probably not a virus."

The crew stared at each other. "OK."

They got to the roof and disassembled the rig. "Power's still on," Raul remarked. "The freight elevator should still work."

The crew hauled their rig to the freight elevator on the top floor and packed it up. When they got to street level they were shocked. LaSalle looked like a battlefield. The people obviously died in pain, as their anguished expressions showed. Jim walked over to a body and felt for a pulse. "Nothing."[32]

The crew had to walk around crashed vehicles as they made their way to one of the contractor parking lots. "Is everyone in this town dead?" Jim asked.

"Looks like it."

"I'm glad we never got one of those neural implants," Raul said.

The men put the rig into the back of their truck and wanted to haul ass out of the parking lot. But they couldn't make any time because they had to drive around crashed vehicles. "Watch that body!" Raul cried as Jim turned right onto Wells.

It took them an hour to get out of the Chicago collective. When they got to the toll booths, cars were piled up and all the barriers were up. There was no movement. Fortunately there was an emergency exit used by collective personnel. It was clear.

"Look at these people," Jim said grimly. "All the cars are lined up behind each other."

"Not one of them ever thought to use the unauthorized exit," Ron replied.

Raul peered into one of the car windows as Jim drove slowly by. "They're all dead, God rest their souls," he muttered. "I'm about ready to hurl."

When the J R & R Professional Window Washing truck made it to the 355, the three men breathed a sigh of relief. There were cars blocking traffic so everything was slowed way down, but vehicles were still moving, weaving between the lifeless vehicles. Every stopped car had a dead driver.

Raul tried to call his girlfriend. "Damn phone doesn't work!"

Jim tossed Raul his mobile. "Use mine."

That one didn't work either. "Ronny, try to make a call."

Ron tried to call his father in Wesley but couldn't get a connection. "Something big has happened, fellas."

"We'll drop you off in Wesley," Jim said. "You need to take care of your dad. Raul and I will go into Midland and try to find out what's going on."

Jim entered Midland Gate 2 from the north and talked to the guard. "We're from Wesley. Do you know why our phones won't work?"

The guard was competent on the mental plane and read the sigs of the three visitors. 'Not Ronin or collective,' he thought. "The Space Grid is being destroyed as we speak," he said matter-of-factly. "Communications across the world are going down."

"What?!" Jim said. "How do you take down the Grid?"

"You guys are from Wesley, you don't know much. It's the new mental plane training. In 24 hours there won't be a satellite left in the Grid."

Raul and Jim stared at each other. "We've just come from Chicago." Jim briefly explained what they saw. The guard immediately issued them two guest passes with Jim and Raul's name on them.

"How do you know our names?" Jim asked.

The guard stared at Jim. "Are you kidding me? I read both your sigs when you first pulled up." The guard then gave each visitor two things that no one else could possibly know about them. It was standard procedure for newcomers.

"You two go to the junkyard on Depot and ask for Ralph Zimring. You'll need to give a full and detailed report to the free zone commander."

"He can just read our minds," Raul said sarcastically.

This provoked the guard. "He will, and if you give him a hard time he'll squeeze your sig so hard you'll wish you hadn't been born."

Jim didn't know what "squeeze your sig" meant, but he had a feeling it wasn't good. "All right, all right, no offense. Hope we don't have to wait around too long."

"Don't sweat it. The commander is waiting for you so get there quick so you don't piss him off. Ralph has had a long day."

"And we haven't?" Raul said angrily.

Two vehicles were waiting behind the truck now. "Get your asses out of here and report."

Jim drove off. "Where is the fucking junkyard?"

"I'll look it up on my phone," Raul replied. "Oops. I'll ask somebody."

It was almost 6 when Ralph, Sergei, Tony Baghdadi, and Danny Radulov finished interrogating the Ronin at the junkyard. The mental plane made the work easy. They told the Ronin that if they ever showed up in Midland again they would all be killed by a bolt of mental lightning. Nasgur's ragtag army was so frightened that the Ronin meekly accepted the loss of most of their troop carriers. All 206 were packed into two of the carriers and told to get the fuck out. Ralph laughed when he saw the overloaded vehicles almost running each other over in their zeal to get out of town and never get within 50 miles of the devil-infested city of Midland.

Ralph was ready to go home and eat a big dinner when he got a message on the mental plane from the guard at Gate 2. 'Code 1 intel from Chicago, Ralph. You gotta hear this.'

Ralph grumbled but said, 'OK. Send them over, but make it quick.'

When Jim and Raul finally found the junkyard they saw a gigantic, intimidating old man with graying hair. Ralph was in a bad mood. He read their sigs and tore out the useful information. Jim and Raul were as afraid as the wicked witch in a shower, but realized there was no harm done. As Ralph digested the information he began to smile. "Thank you boys, you have provided excellent intel. Did you drive around the city?"

"No," Jim replied. "We were pretty scared and got out of there."

"Don't blame you. There's one thing you can do for me. You're from Wesley?"

"Yeah," Raul said.

"How many chipped are there?"

Jim looked at Raul. "I'd say about 25% of the population. Chicago keeps sending more and more of them. I think they want a majority in town to pass a mandatory chip law."

"OK. You guys get up to Chicago and scout the city. Let me know how many of the chipped are still alive. Report back here tomorrow by 1600."

Raul was irritated at the big man but there was no arguing with him. The man's mental powers were frightening. Jim said, "We'll be at Gate 2 at 2 tomorrow afternoon."

After that Ralph went home and cooked a gigantic dinner. He missed Gyorgy. He hadn't realized how lonely he was; he would have to find a woman who could tolerate him. Maybe someone at Berglin Enterprises? He was slowing down a bit now, he was more mellow, someone a woman might be able to tolerate. Ralph made a mental note to work on this.

The big problem was that all comms around the world were going down. That meant civilization outside the free zones could devolve to barbarism. Still, Ralph was cautiously optimistic. The attractors were broadcasting but there were no digital comms, no way for the human galactic proxies like Rashan Oliwan to do anything except in person. Mass media and social media, their main tool, was dead. They could rebuild the terrestrial internet, or launch thousands of satellites to rebuild the Space Grid, but both of those projects were a huge undertaking and would take lots of time. His network could scour the mental plane and discover even hidden satellite launch sites, and destroy them. Nothing could be kept secret anymore! Meanwhile, the free zones could continue human civilization using the instant comms on the mental plane. The first step was to liaise with Wesley to the north, and all of the farms outside the city. Midland would consume these products and offer protection from Ronin and the rogue bands that would form now that the Grid was almost down.

Was everyone in Chicago dead? It was an appalling thought. He would wait on the report from the window washing crew tomorrow.

Ralph didn't get much sleep that night. It was one thing to kill a scumbag drug dealer or a human trafficker on a field mission, but there are – were? – two million Citizens in Chicago...Jesus Christ, maybe Kelleye was right... He fell into a nervous half-sleep.

Rashan Oliwan groaned. He was lying on the floor next to my desk. I heard it and gave him a kick. "Shut up, traitor."

"Nasgur..." Oliwan mumbled.

"Nasgur is in the Midland jail," I said.

"Avriel..."

"Oh, shut the fuck up about deVilliers," I said. "The problem with you is that you are entirely self-centered. You don't love anyone but yourself."

Rashan got up. "That's not true, Rothman. It's true I'm self-centered. But deVilliers is the only person I have ever truly loved."

I snorted. "You loved her so much you ran away from her like a little boy. You've been using her as an excuse to engage in antisocial activities that she would never approve of."

I saw the shock on Rashan's face, then a growing awareness. "But...but...I guess you're right."

"Look Oliwan, we don't have time for your bullshit. There's a world out there that is falling apart. You're either on the team, or we'll drive you to the free zone border and you can take your chances out in the wild."

Rashan knew he couldn't fool these people because they were too expert on the mental plane. Nasgur had been neutralized and his group was without leadership now. That ragtag bunch of Ronin would quickly fall apart. Most important, Avriel was lost to him. The Grid was down, international air flights were impossible until a reliable global communication network was re-established. "All right. I'll stay and be useful until it's possible to get to Marseilles. I want to see what happened to deVilliers."

"Your presence here is dependent on the OK from the free zone commander. If he says you're out, you're out."

Ralph OKed Rashan on a temporary basis. He was assigned to us as a trainer and could only work with us on the training so we could keep an eye on him. Ralph had me and the team ratcheting up the training program in Midland. "We have to get everyone in the city competent on the mental plane," Ralph said. "Those who can't or won't are a liability in an emergency because they can't send or receive important bulletins."

Many people were really upset when they found out that we had destroyed the Grid. Those people left the city. Another thousand people who had no interest in the training also left for other free zones. Our team identified these sigs and stored their sig data in our mental plane filing system. Some of those who left went to Wesley and a few went to work on the farms that surround Midland.

Ralph interviewed Nasgur Nyamsuren in the basement of the Centurion Building, where there were a couple of holding cells. The man was seated on his bench, his face in his hands. Ralph scanned the sig. Nyamsuren didn't have a galactic overlay. The sig was partially developed.

"What should I do with you, Nyamsuren? I can see you have had some mental plane training."

Nasgur looked up. "Yes. Rashan tried to train me, but there's something off about that guy."

Ralph laughed. "How true." He studied Nasgur's sig. Born in Mongolia, he had been forcibly drafted into the Chinese PLA when he was 16, and eventually sent to the Xinjiang Uyghur Autonomous Region in Northwest China. He had been a prison guard at a Uyghur detention camp before escaping during a revolt of Ughyur prisoners, which he led. Ralph was impressed. Nasgur had very successfully adjusted to life as a Ronin in the US after he managed to smuggle himself out of China and work his way across the world to the United States. Ralph could see that Nasgur was resourceful and very intelligent, but disillusioned and bitter about life. Like some mercs he knew, Nasgur felt hopeless about his life and had taken his anger out on others. Ralph understood guys like Nyamsuren and had some sympathy for him. He had worked with a lot of them who had been ground into the dust by society.

"I have no time for you, Nasgur. You can get the fuck out of my zone, or finish your training and help out. I don't care either way."

Nasgur looked at the indomitable figure of Ralph and sighed. "I never had a chance at anything in life, so I'll take that chance now."

"OK, go see Philogene Rothman. He's head of the training program. If he says you're out, I'll personally kick your ass all the way to Gate 3, along with your friend Rashan."

Nasgur smiled bitterly. "Watch out for Oliwan, big fella. He's not to be trusted."

Ralph got the report from the three window cleaners. They had driven all over Chicago until they couldn't stand it anymore. Their report: 100% casualties. Ralph's stomach turned over; he ran to the head and vomited. That night, for the first time in his life, he got down on his knees. He prayed to a God he didn't believe in and asked forgiveness.

Two weeks after the Grid went down a foul breeze blew in from the north. It smelled like rotting corpses. Ralph got drone footage from Chicago that showed thousands of dead bodies lying unattended on the streets. Rats and other predators were feasting on the remains. Many had died in their homes.

The stench was so foul that no one was willing to get within five miles of the city.

Two months later aid workers from the Free Zones were finally able to enter Chicago. The gruesome footage they sent to the world was shocking. Skeletons and decomposed bodies littered the streets. Dead bodies were being hauled out of houses and buildings to crematoriums. Ronin and stragglers entered the city, robbing houses. A few brave souls were moving in to the deserted collective, occupying houses whose owners had died. There was no authority in Chicago, for all members of the collective had been chipped and they were all dead.

Reports came in on the mental plane from around the planet. Citizens in all of the chipped cities had died. It was a gruesome price to pay to defeat the Fenachrone and the Hilarion Collectives, but their power on earth was broken, at least for now. Four billion people were dead!

Ralph's anger at the galactic Collectives – who had hijacked the Grid and forced his hand – grew so hot he knew had to get out of town before he took some innocent's head off. He took Arthur up to Arlington Heights and burned the Chicago AI with his laser rifle. It was still operational and he didn't want techies to be able to use it. No telling what those clever people might do with it. The bodies of all the workers in the building were decomposing and the building's windows were closed.

"Worst thing I ever had to do," he told me in the downtown office before he showed us what happened that evening. Ralph had recorded his entire trip with his GoPro, and narrated as he went along.

"The highways are clear until you reach the boundaries of the restricted zone. As you can see, the cars that were piled up by the entrance booths have been towed away by aid workers." Ralph drove up the Tollway to the 290 and then north. "Only those vehicles that prevented cars from getting through have been removed," Ralph remarked, as he weaved through derelict vehicles with their occupants still inside. "There are still too many of them." Ralph turned his GoPro to a car window. Two passengers were inside, their bodies decomposing.

At that point Kelleye fainted and fell to the carpet. "Take care of her, Josh."

Ralph continued his narration. He found his way to 14 and made a left. "There it is. The AI building."

Even in this non-residential area bodies were still on the streets. Ralph hurriedly drove Arthur past the guard post. A body was in it, slumped over. There were a dozen cars in the lot. "I had to slag the door," Ralph commented as his laser rifle made mincemeat of the once sturdy structure. Ralph took one step inside and gagged. He put on his gas mask. "The smell – it was horrible. Fortunately the AI is directly across from the door."

Ralph slagged down what was left of the door and panned the AI with his GoPro. "As you can see, the power is on and that thing is still operational."

Ralph stood slightly outside the door to get some air and melted the installation. "I left the displays, maybe somebody can use them."

After that Ralph left and drove around the city.

"I'm glad Kelleye isn't seeing this," Joann remarked. "It's sickening."

"Yeah." After ten minutes more Ralph said, "OK, that's enough." He turned off the display. His face was white.

By this time Kelleye had recovered. Josh gave her a glass of water.

"We're mass murderers," she said flatly.

"The chips killed their hosts, child," Ralph responded. "Chips that were designed by the galactic Collectives.'

"But we took down the Grid."

"It was necessary. We are fighting a war for the survival of earth. Every person in the collectives voluntarily decided to get the neural implants; no one forced them. They died as they lived: a slave to galactic forces that will crush the earth if we don't ensure our survival." This was how he had rationalized an action even his hard heart couldn't accept. He was still silently mourning Gyorgy, who had been like a little brother to him since he trained him. Ralph fought back tears.

In his Special Forces unit he had been taught that a commander must make impossible decisions and then take full responsibility for the consequences. It was small comfort. He didn't even want to think about the karmic stain his soul – if he had one – had suffered.

Kelleye was bitter. "I hate you, Ralph Zimring. I wish we had never met."

For a second Ralph's blanched face showed his internal agony. He bowed and left. Kelleye burst out sobbing and threw herself into Josh's arms.

— 38 —

Siddon Hilarion called in his Council of Seers for an urgent consultation. 'The earthian activity on the mental plane has been increasing rapidly,' he sent. 'This is a major threat to our operations in that system. I want you to identify the humans responsible for this development.'

'We have already done so,' said Amon-Ra, the acknowledged spokesperson for the group. 'I have prepared this report for your inspection, Your Excellency.'

The CEO of the great Collective was traditionally assigned an honorific, but everyone knew that the CEO served at the sufferance of the bureaucracy.

Amon-Ra presented a holo that showed all 30 million humans who had a signature on the mental plane. Siddon Hilarion was shocked. 'There are 30 *million* of these barbarians active on the mental plane?'

'Yes, Your Excellency. And more every day.'

Siddon inspected the holo. The untrained minds of emerging planet entities only generated noise on the mental plane. Occasionally a sensitive might display a coherent signature, but these were rare. 'Look at this!' Siddon exclaimed, outraged. Coherent sigs were displayed as spheres, the others were just merged into the background. He was looking at seven huge spheres and a thousand large ones. The number of coherent sigs was displayed in the data section.

'What is this?' Siddon shouted. 'Here are two galactic sigs alongside the human ones! What are they doing there?'

Amon-Ra looked carefully at the two sigs, which had galactic characteristics. Shocked, he stuttered a response. 'Your Excellency, you are correct...why, this is impossible. Galactics cannot physically survive on the surface of that noxious planet.'

Siddon turned on Amon-Ra and his council of Seers. '30 million coherent earthian sigs AND two galactic advisors! You let this situation develop without taking action?'

Amon-Ra was apologetic but not intimidated. 'Your Excellency, as you know, we have been working full-time on breaking the Fenachrone shields. An order which came from you, sire, as Urgent Priority in your emergency directive.'

'Fools!' the CEO shouted. 'Are my Seers merely sheep? Do they not possess an independent intellect? Where is your initiative?' Siddon rose to his full height and shouted. 'You are all guilty of treason! I shall summon the executioner!'

Amon-Ra let Siddon shout. Of course the CEO could do nothing, for a Seer was a rare and infinitely valuable commodity, the most precious resource a trading corporation had. The loss of even one Seer would be a terrible blow, for Seers gathered critical intelligence on opposing negotiating teams, particularly the Fenachrone and their allied Collective networks. Siddon knew that he had the best collection of Seers in the entire Orion Spur.

Siddon Hilarion thought furiously. He looked at the five huge human sigs. 'Amon-Ra, the sig of this barbarian is almost as powerful as yours!'

'That is the human entity called Phi-lo. He is the leader.'

'And the two galactic traitors, what is their function?'

'Unknown. Their presence on the planet's surface is an impossibility.'

'Fools! Immobilize the two galactics. I want all five of these earthians out of the world immediately.'

Amon-Ra was speechless for a full minute. All of his Seers were shocked and were looking to him for a response.

'You dare to order us to murder? That is a violation of the sacred Biali Edict, banning dissolution from the galaxy forever. It is within my rights to summon the executioner to take your head.'

Siddon Hilarion was contemptuous. 'Are these barbarians galactic citizens? These five monsters have murdered almost 4 billion of their fellows with the destruction of the Space Grid. They were responsible for the dissolution of two of our operatives! They are guilty of genocide and mass murder. Destroying them is our duty. It is *your* duty.'

Amon-Ra stood tall. 'Neither myself nor my Seers will stoop to dissolution. We will be branded as criminals throughout the galaxy.'

'I don't care how you handle the situation. Turn them into mental vegetables and keep them alive if it salves your conscience. But I want them neutralized!'

Siddon Hilarion strode from the room, seething. Amon-Ra would take care of the barbarians, and he must discover the identity of the two galactic advisers. How are they able to survive on the contaminated surface of earth?

Amon-Ra consulted with his select group of Seers. 'We cannot refuse an order from the CEO. Let us determine how to deal with the barbarians.' Amon-Ra shuddered. 'It is true that the human Phi-lo committed murder. Twice.' He and his Seers reviewed the gruesome recordings on the mental plane of the dissolution of the human Genghis Glazer, and of the Fenachrone operative from Beta Caronai. 'This Phi-lo is infected with a demon Maitre!' cried one of the Seers.

Amon-Ra carefully observed the sig. 'It is true. Such an one is too vile to live.'

The two dissolutions were made even more horrifying when the murders were carefully examined. It was seen how the Maitre demon came forth from the infected human and overwhelmed the victims with such malevolence that Amon-Ra sealed the recordings. The other Seers were horrified. None of them cared too much about the deaths of the barbarians, but to lose 4 billion valuable workers! It was a monumental tragedy, although there were billions more. Unfortunately the diabolically clever earthians had destroyed Siddon's brainchild; their carefully constructed communications grid in space. This would greatly hamper operations on the earthian planet and was another black mark in the ledger against the five earthians. Fortunately, the attractors were still operational.

After several minutes of silence Amon-Ra said, 'Consciousness death is the most heinous and abhorrent crime in the galaxy, and is punishable by immediate physical termination. Our CEO is correct!'

The Council of Seers agreed that the human entity Phi-lo and his minions deserved the Executioner.

'Physical execution of the barbarians is impossible, for obvious reasons,' said Trilok, one of the Seers. 'No one in the Collective can survive in the polluted atmosphere of the earthian planet, even in a biosuit.'

Amon-Ra grimaced. 'It must be the *halbar* then.' The halbar was a mental plane technique that dislocated an entity's consciousness from the physical body.

Trilok objected vehemently. 'No...I refuse to participate in such a barbaric act.'

This was seconded by another Seer. 'The *halbar* often results in psychosis and physical paralysis.'

'Our duty is clear,' Amon-Ra replied firmly. He unsealed the recordings and played them again for the Council of Seers. 'Phi-lo and his minions are dangerous psychopaths. They must be eliminated before the entire planet becomes operational on the mental plane. Otherwise, billions of these humans will become a malignant cancer infecting all of our societies via the galactic web.'

'Reseal those recordings, Amon-Ra,' said the two objectors, sickened by the attack of the earthian barbarian and his Maitre. They were both now resigned to do their duty. The rest of the Council of Seers, seeing that all objections had been silenced, acquiesced to the will of Amon-Ra.

'Take time to prepare yourselves and await my signal to attack.'

Pleasant Meadow and his select command group used the Miralet transportal system to instantly appear outside the earth's solar system. The planetoid then glided into position between Earth and Mars.[33] The immense object was immediately noticed by the Hilarion and Fenachrone Collectives. Scout ships already in the solar system were dispatched by each of the Collectives to physically observe it. The planetoid had an impenetrable shield on the mental plane. One of the scout ships issued an ultimatum to the invader: 'Leave the earthian solar system or be destroyed by an all-out attack.' There was no response from the planetoid. The scout ships returned to their bases on the moon and on Mars.

The Fenachrone and Hilarion CEOs met on the mental plane to discuss tactics. All shields were up and an already established, secure line of communication was used. Both sides were astonished by the presence of the immense invader. Each suspected that the planetoid's arrival was the result of a secret alliance the other side had made with another Collective in the Spur, to tip the balance of power. No Seers were allowed on the comm channel, but each side used them anyway, in the background.

Siddon Hilarion was eager to capture the planetoid. He knew it was unarmed because, without telling the Fenachrone, he had sent a stealth scoutship to physically scrutinize the planetoid, outside the joint operation. But why was it here?

His scoutship had only been able to determine that the shields of the planetoid were impenetrable, with not even minimal leakage out to the mental plane.

Siddon spoke to his Seers behind their shield as he regarded the irritating female who was the Fenachrone CEO. 'Have you not yet broken through, you fools?' He cursed the unavailability of his Council of Seers, his most powerful on the mental plane. But Amon-Ra had to take care of the earthians and those two rogue galactics.

'The Fenachrone shield is very good,' one of his Seers sent. 'We are working as hard as we can.'

The Fenachrone CEO laughed silently behind her shield. She knew that Siddon Hilarion was consulting with his Seers. He was a fool if he thought the Fenachrone shield could be broken.

Siddon Hilarion thought furiously, the threat of the planetoid temporarily forgotten. What if he were to mount an all-out attack on the Fenachrone shields? It would be a great victory if he, the 24,768th CEO of the great Hilarion Trading Group, could double his territory. The Fenachrone Collective and its thousands of star systems was a prize that caused him to salivate. He thought he saw the Fenachrone CEO getting nervous, which made him more eager.

His Seers cautioned him. 'We remind you, Your Excellency, of the horror of what you now contemplate, in your lust for power.'

'Silence, fools!' Over millions of years conflict between the Collectives had been ritualized. In ancient times the defeated side's leaders and their families would all be subject to the halbar. Including all of the Seers. Now, to avoid a horrible death, the losers immediately surrendered and the victors assumed control of their territory.

'Do you think this Fenachrone female will capitulate?' sent Trilok, one of Siddon's most outspoken Seers. 'You are a fool if you do.'

Siddon did not want to hear this. The Hilarion Trading group was in a superior position within the Greater Community, and the Fenachrone knew it! The two trading Collectives had been in an uneasy truce for over 1,000 galactic standard years. It was time to break the stalemate. Assimilation of the Fenachrone would make the Hilarion the strongest Collective in the entire Orion Spur!

'Don't do it sire,' Trilok sent. 'Our advantage on the mental plane is slight. If we attack and fail, the Fenachrone in their rage will surely launch a kinetic war against us. That would destroy our fragile supply chains and create revolutionary sentiment among our planets.'

Siddon was infuriated but he knew his adviser was right. As he calmed himself he saw a slight smile on the face of the female. That Fenachrone monster had been thinking the same thing as he! Siddon chuckled and entered the comm channel.

'We understand each other, Fenachrone. The earthians are becoming active on the mental plane and the planet is still self-sufficient. If their development continues, the earthian race will achieve independence and become a beacon to all our populations.'

This minor difficulty having been resolved, the two CEOs turned their attention to the original reason for convening the meeting.

'What should we do about the planetoid?' Siddon asked.

The Fenachrone CEO replied immediately. 'It must be destroyed.'

Siddon was pleased with this response. 'Each side to send one ultra-fast battle cruiser.'

'Both ships enter the earthian system together.'

'Agreed.'

Two heavily armed and ultra-fast battleships, one from each Collective, were launched into hyperspace to physically confront the gigantic invader. Djeet Hilarion, son of the CEO, commanded the Hilarion ship. The journeys through hyperspace from each Collective to the earthian system would only take ten galactic standard days. During that time communication with the two battle cruisers was impossible, as they would both be in undetermined quantum states. Only after the vessels arrived at the scene could orders to the commanders be given.

Djeet Hilarion communicated with his Fenachrone counterpart on the mental plane as the two massive war machines re-emerged into normal space and approached the planetoid. The size of it was overwhelming to the two commanders. The planetoid's mental plane was completely null, an impossibility. Every shield leaked, at least infinitesimally.

'Could this be a drone?' Djeet asked.

'Impossible. It is far too large.'

'Where did it come from? This vessel is not from our sector!'

'We do not have the capability or the resources to construct such a vessel,' the Fenachrone commander admitted.

The two warships were in touch with their superiors, sending them intel and images of the gigantic intruder as both battleships flew slowly around the invader. No ports or weapons stations could be observed. The planetoid had no escorts or armed vessels defending it. But their shield could not be penetrated.

As the leaders of the two Collectives consulted, the two ship commanders warily watched the planetoid. It was utterly silent, and made no hostile move. Yet there was a feeling of latent, immense power. Both commanders were getting nervous.

'The vessel must be inhabited,' Djeet thought to himself.

'I wish those assholes back home would make up their minds,' the Fenachrone commander sent to Djeet. 'I'm ready to slag this planetoid right now with our EMP pulsers.'

'Our sonic torpedoes will gut it, and good riddance.'

Both battleships prepared to fire.

Ten days earlier, Pleasant Meadow and his Seers had detected, on the mental plane, the signatures of the two battleships that had entered hyperspace. 'We must postpone the mission to destroy the earthian attractors,' It pulsed. 'The threat to our vessel must first be nullified.'

The Oorant sent images of the two battleships to all the delegates, and instructions about what to do when they appeared in normal space.

For the next ten days the million-entity delegate army surveyed the earthian solar system for Collective entities and vessels. It seemed that the entire Orion Spur was interested in this little planet! There were hundreds of bases underneath the planet's surface, on its single moon, and dozens more on Mars. All foreign bases, vessels, and galactic sigs were cataloged.

Everyone inside the planetoid saw on the mental plane when the two battleships suddenly materialized into normal space. The Oorant pulsed: 'Prepare yourselves! Attacking ships are approaching!'

The battleships would soon be receiving their orders on the mental plane.

Siddon Hilarion and his Fenachrone counterpart each waited to send their orders to their battle cruiser commanders. Each side's Seers carefully monitored the mental plane, waiting to see what and when the other side would send.

The shielded orders came down to each commander almost simultaneously. The orders were essentially the same for each battleship. *Destroy the planetoid. Then turn your weapons on the enemy ship.*

Amon-Ra and his Council of Seers were ready. Each Seer had prepared themselves to execute the halbar on the barbarians. The two galactics would be immobilized and their minds ransacked. Amon-Ra would personally direct the attack on the two galactics. It was vital that they understand what sort of biological entity could survive on the surface of earth without being killed by its violent pathogens.

The twelve Hilarion Seers gathered themselves on the mental plane. Four would attack the two galactics, the other eight would neutralize the five earthians. Amon-Ra opened a channel in preparation for the assault.

Patrick and Gwenneth were sitting on one of the sofas in the Second Street Investigations office. Me, Kel, Josh, and Joann were seated at our desks. Ralph was on the carpet, his back against the wall. We were all involved in an advanced training session for our best operatives on the mental plane.

An instant before the Hilarion attack, Patrick felt the mental shield around the building collapse and a channel open. 'Shields up!' he sent on the mental plane. I saw Patrick and Gwenneth instantly firm up their shields. Ralph and the rest of our team were only femtoseconds behind, but we were too late. Our minds were seized by an overwhelming force.

Both battleships were ready to fire on the planetoid. Their consciousness-assisted weaponry would respond instantly to a coded thought. The Fenachrone commander received his orders a femtosecond ahead of Djeet Hilarion. He was about to send the order to fire when thousands of entities seized his mind. The order was never given.

Djeet immediately recognized his advantage and violated his orders. He decided to slag the Fenachrone ship first. Just before he could issue the command his mind was roughly seized.

Djeet Hilarion was quailing in fear, for he was well aware of his treachery. It would be the halbar for him! The Fenachrone commander was beside himself with fury, but his mind was also being held. Both commanders were unable to send a single thought, or issue commands.

The minds of all personnel aboard the attack ships were ruthlessly seized. The fighters were immobilized with fear. They realized too late that the planetoid's lack of weaponry was irrelevant, for the alien planetoid contained hundreds of thousands of skilled operatives on the mental plane! It was an overwhelming force without precedent in millions of years of galactic competition and conflict.

Pleasant Meadow's powerful pulsed thoughts echoed throughout the planetoid, the two battleships, and all bases and installations on every planet, moon, and asteroid in the earthian system. It knew what It had to do, even though this was revolting to Its peaceful nature.

'Interlopers!' It cried. 'We are the Advanced Planets network. You will immediately cease and desist your unlawful operations on the earthian planet and in this system. We have identified every base, craft, and interfering entity in this system. You have two galactic standard minutes to remove your presence or you know what will happen to you.'

Pleasant Meadow read the minds of the two battleship commanders and Itself issued the coded orders that would take the two battleships into hyperspace, back to their home sectors. Two galactic standard minutes elapsed. Almost all of the invaders left as the million-strong army of the Advanced Planets network revealed their immense and awesome power on the mental plane. A few die-hards decided to fight it out until the Advanced Network unceremoniously and forcefully propelled their craft into hyperspace and back to their home systems.

The planetoid was now safe.

Amon-Ra and his three Seers immobilized the minds of Patrick and Gwenneth. Uncle and niece could see that the next step was the halbar, a death sentence. Both Celestians knew that after the halbar they would essentially be vegetables, without a personality.

A femtosecond on the mental plane can be an eternity. I saw the anguish on Gwenneth's face but was powerless to do anything. Something life threatening was about to happen to her and Patrick. And to us. For the second time in my life I faced certain death, but this time Gwenneth couldn't save me. My Maitre was helpless. I wanted so desperately to help her and Patrick, and Joann, and Ralph, and the team. I didn't care about myself anymore.

Just before the killing frequencies were sent I understood how powerful the mental plane is. Physical death was nothing to what was coming...it would be a fitting ending for me after what I had done to Genghis Glazer and that galactic I had murdered, and the four billion chipped humans I had helped to kill.

I waited for the killing strike.

— 39 —

During the eternity of time just before Amon-Ra sent the halbar frequencies, he uncovered something from the minds of the two galactics. An advanced network of planets! Hundreds of thousands of them were hiding within the Collectives. These two galactics somehow had enhanced biology that allowed their bodies to ward off the effects of the dangerous earthian pathogens. Unexplained anomalies were now clear. The lack of space traffic and commerce to and from certain planets. Rumors of ships that could travel instantly from one end of the galaxy to the other.

Something terrible happened an attosecond before Amon-Ra signaled the halbar strike.

A thousand advanced students in the training class were learning to seize sigs. Suddenly they heard Gwenneth's "Shields up!" cry. They saw a channel open on the mental plane from twelve powerful minds to their teachers on the ground in Midland. They felt a malevolent intention. Instinctively, many of the students, led by Nasgur Nyamsuren, attacked the Hilarion Seers. It was several hundred against twelve.

'Amon-Ra!' cried one of the Seers. 'The humans are attacking us!'

'I can see that you fool!' Amon-Ra shouted mentally, echoing the sentiments of his CEO. 'Press forward! Neutralize the barbarians!'

More students joined the mental battle. Now the pressure on the Hilarion sigs was immense. Amon-Ra realized that although his twelve Seers were enormously more powerful than an individual human, there were almost a thousand of the barbarians now joining in. To lose even one of his prized Seers would be an immense crime.

'Retreat, Seers!' Amon-Ra cried. The Hilarion Seers broke off the attack and closed the channel.

All of the students shouted for joy and celebrated on the mental plane. Gwenneth and Patrick were somber and did not join in.

"What's the matter?" Ralph asked.

Gwenneth and Patrick both bowed. "We are more grateful than we can ever express," Gwenneth said. "Your decisive action prevented all of us from a horrible outcome."

When Patrick explained on the mental plane everyone gasped. "This *halbar* is the way galactics punish their citizens?" someone asked.

"It is only used on the most hardened, degenerate criminals," Patrick replied. "You now understand how the Collectives view you."

"Our advice is to review very carefully what just happened on the mental plane," Gwenneth suggested. "It will be educational to examine all of the thoughts and sidebands of Siddon Hilarion's Council of Seers. You will discover a lot about the galaxy, and learn how nations interact with each other, and how emerging societies like yours are viewed."

Patrick's face was grim. "The Hilarion were successful in one way. They now know of our advanced network. We must leave immediately for Celeste and inform our people. Our planets are in severe danger."

"I can transport you," Joann suggested.

Patrick managed a smile. "That will not be necessary, dear Joann. Our planetoid even now is sending a ship for us." Patrick explained about the planetoid and their mission. "A million of our best minds will go back to Miralet and devise a plan to save our planets from the Collectives."

I glanced at Gwenneth and she smiled at me as the two Celestians prepared to walk out. "Welcome to the galaxy, Philogene. You and your team have succeeded beyond our wildest dreams, but your work has just begun."

I gave her a hug, and I hugged Patrick too. "Continue the training program," Patrick said to the team. "It is the most important work you can do for your civilization."

The Celestians were gone, and I had a lump in my throat. I looked over at Joann and saw that she was also tearing up.

Ralph smiled and rubbed his hands together. "Who-hoo! We've got a lot of work to do!"

"Let's continue with the training session," Josh said.

We got busy. Even though the Grid was down, those attractors were still broadcasting.

The great mind of the Oorant personally thanked each participant on the planetoid for their service. Patrick and Gwenneth commed with It briefly. 'I want to thank both of you for making our network see a new approach,' Pleasant Meadow pulsed. 'I now understand how aggressive action can alter the course of an entire solar system and change galactic history.'

Gwenneth and Patrick bowed. 'We had better worry about our network first,' Patrick replied.

Pleasant Meadow curled his thin, leathery lips upward. 'Our planetoid cannot return immediately to Miralet. We must return the attractors to space normal or all our work here will have been in vain.'

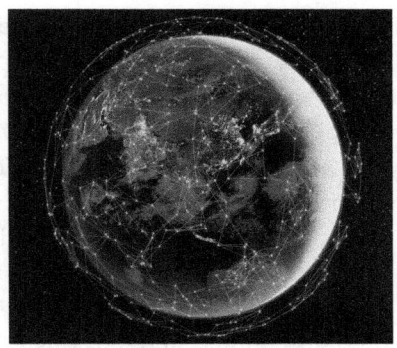

— 40 —

One Year Later

Sixty percent of the U.S. population had died after the Grid collapse, almost all of them from the neural implants. Around the world the figure was slightly less. Those who had the mental plane training kept in instant communication. Talk was of rehabbing the airline industry so that people could physically travel long distances again.

Over a year after it happened the collapse of the Space Grid was still the number one topic in the minds of everyone.

Those who had received the training envisioned a united humanity and a sovereign earth against the hive mind of the galactic corporate trading networks, for the mental plane broke down cultural barriers and created a feeling of mutual cooperation. However, a significant proportion of the surviving population rejected the mental plane training, regarding it as devilish and frightening. This attitude was popular because of the propaganda from the attractors.

"How dare you read my mind!" people said. "The procedure is invasive and a total violation of privacy. My thoughts are none of your business!" These people also rejected the idea of galactic Collectives out to take over the earth. "Sister Sani and Brother Hamal were fake, and so is anyone who says that aliens are going to take over the earth."

"It's happening again," Kelleye said one night at a group meeting. "We are dividing ourselves instead of coming together." She looked significantly at

Ralph. Although reconciled to keeping him in our group, she had never forgiven him for the Grid going down. To her, Ralph was personally responsible because he had been the driving force behind the operation. Because of his work during the Space Grid Collapse program, he had been unanimously appointed by the military forces to be the country's Free Zones Commander.

It had put stress on her relationship with Josh, for Josh liked Ralph and liked to hang out with him. "Honey, we all participated so we are all responsible."

"Without Ralph it never would have happened. He's an old fogey and is living in the past, with all of its conflicts and tensions."

"There's something to that," Josh admitted. "But Philo is equally responsible. He took over the training program and coordinated the civilian sig apprehenders and Ralph's military ones. And...so are we responsible."

Kelleye sighed, acknowledging this. "It just hasn't turned out like I expected. We lost billions of people and we are still fighting each other."

The conversation died, Josh thought, just as it always did, without a good resolution. Kelleye was unhappy and he didn't know how to fix the situation.

A month later, on the first day of spring, Kelleye left our team. Josh was devastated, but he understood that Kelleye was totally disillusioned with the human race. She didn't understand why we weren't more upset by all the deaths. The day before she left she said goodbye at the downtown office. "I can't deal with people anymore. In my opinion the human race is insane. We...I...have engaged in the most reprehensible crime in the entire sordid history of humanity. Nobody seems to care. I have found a job in Wesley on a diary farm, working with animals. I hope their innocence can help me recover from a trauma I cannot reconcile within myself."

The only good news for Josh and the group was that Kelleye could be contacted at any time on the mental plane. She and Josh commed remotely every night.

Meanwhile Joann, me, and Josh were still frantically busy with the training program. Our goal was to train everyone in Midland on the mental plane. We left the collective cities to deal with their cleanup. People were moving back into perfectly good houses and buildings, cleaning up areas, burying bodies, claiming cars and trucks that had been abandoned. Chicago was an anarchist's paradise. Reports from our military scouts told us that the city was now a patchwork of little gang fiefdoms, yet skilled workers were in high demand. The electrical grid must be kept up, computer networks needed to be repaired and altered for purely terrestrial communications. Other workers were also needed to repair computers, automobiles, furnaces, and the like. Truckers were needed to deliver food and supplies. Workers who came to the city were protected and respected by the gangs, who needed them to restore and maintain the infrastructure of their territories. It was an offshoot of the love healthcare workers and delivery people experienced during the 2020 Pandemic.

Our scouts told us that within a year or two things would be back to normal in Chicago. Incredibly, violence and crime were at a minimum. Nobody understood why.

In contrast to Kelleye, Joann had no qualms about our Grid takedown. We were on the same page and bought a house one block from Jamaal's. My parents moved into Midland where I could watch over them.

Unlike Chicago, in Midland no one cared about the internet because the mental plane was so much faster and had unlimited data storage. But the broadcast networks for entertainment and sports were doing a booming business. After the Fall, broadcasters quickly discovered an intense interest in sports and entertainment in the free zones. Sports leagues reformed and there was no shortage of fans. Theater groups and movie makers began performing plays and filming documentaries and escape entertainment. The Midland Shakespeare Group was playing to packed audiences in the Berglin Theater. My mom is an enthusiastic participant.

Josh was working 20 hours a day to compensate for his loss of Kelleye. He went up to Chicago and filmed for a week. Then he came back to Midland and filmed for another three days.

"Chicago is becoming a pre-pandemic city with a much lower population," he said. "Some of the cell towers are now working, the internet cables are being reactivated, the local computer networks are going up as needed. Now compare that to Midland. This town looks more and more like a scene out of the 1950s." People were shown dragging out computers, printers, and phones out of their offices. "We don't need this stuff anymore," a homeowner said. Josh walked inside a house and filmed an older couple. "The house is so much less cluttered without all that computer junk!" the woman said. Instead of computers and phones, the desks had vases of flowers and family pictures on them. The only electronic devices that survived were TVs and audio/entertainment systems.

"Kelleye is right," Josh said. "The free zones and the legacy cities like Chicago are bifurcating. We're becoming two separate societies again. Actually four if you count the Ronin and the Independents."

*T*hat night our Group of Three plus Ralph and Nasgur Nyamsuren had a meeting at the Second Street Investigations office downtown. Ralph opened the ball.

"Wesley sent a couple of representatives today," Ralph said. "They want to become part of Midland."

"I didn't think those guys liked us," Josh remarked.

"They changed their minds after two Ronin attacks during the past month," Nasgur said, who was now Ralph's personal aide. "Ronin bands are getting bigger and more aggressive, combining with some of the Independents. They are raiding mostly unprotected food growing areas like Wesley." Nasgur showed us an image on the mental plane of one of the Ronin.

"Rashan Oliwan!" I cried.

"That's right," Ralph said. "After the Fall he disappeared, as you'll recall. Watch out for him, he's a real snake."

I sighed. "You're a better judge of humans than I am, old man."

"You never know about people," Josh said, indicating Nasgur. "This guy has become a pillar of the community."

Nasgur nodded. "By choice. You gave me a chance to become part of your community and I am eternally grateful."

Joann changed the subject. "If Wesley becomes part of Midland, it's a lot bigger perimeter to defend."

"It is," Ralph said. "That's why I wanted to talk to you. Our policy is that everyone in Midland has to get the training. But a lot of the folks in Wesley don't see the need for it."

"I'm for it," Josh said. "I'm thinking of moving to Wesley anyway to be with Kelleye."

At that moment Patrick and Gwenneth walked into the room. I couldn't help myself; my eyes devoured her. Feeling guilty, I jerked my eyes away.

"I forgive you, Philo," Joann said.

I smiled. "I love you, Joann."

Nasgur, who only knew about the famous galactic duo by reputation, stared, his jaw dropping. "Oh my God," he mumbled. "So it's true about the advanced network of evolved beings."

Gwenneth gave him a brilliant smile, and Patrick grinned. I laughed. Nasgur's reaction to Gwenneth was the same as mine when I first saw her. Both Celestians were perfected beings physically, and they both literally had an observable halo on the mental plane.

"Quite so," Gwenneth said, giving Nasgur a slight bow of acknowledgment. "We are here to tell you that the attractors have been fully disabled and returned to normal space status. It was a large undertaking and took us much longer than we thought it would."

Patrick nodded. "You can now develop your civilization without Collective interference. All ships and all entities from outside your solar system have been removed."

Gwenneth beamed. She looked at us five humans. "Your planet will be legendary in the galaxy," she said.

Ralph smiled. "Now all we have to do is teach 3 billion more reluctant people about the mental plane."

"It took us a hundred thousand years," Gwenneth said. "Knowing the mental plane is just the first step."

"You have all the time you need now," Patrick said.

"I gotta tell Kelleye," Josh said, "in person." He left.

"How are you guys faring against the Collectives?" I asked. "Your network has been exposed."

Patrick shrugged. "Not even the Collectives would dare to attack our two planetoids, which have now been permanently deployed with rotating armies of our best Seers. The Collectives know that our transportal system can deploy instantaneously, anywhere in the galaxy. Like earth, galactic society is divided. The difference for us is that all is now in the open, and we no longer have to hide from the Collectives. There are no more secrets."

"As above, so below," I said.

Patrick gave Gwenneth a hug. "Mission accomplished, niece." He and Gwenneth walked out.

Joann and I smiled lovingly at each other.

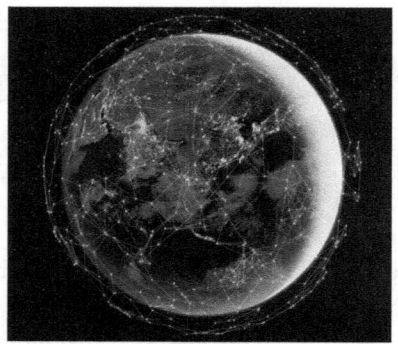

— 41 —

A month after the visit from Patrick and Gwenneth we found out Joann was pregnant. We were both happy to be expecting a little girl.

"I'm going up to Chicago this Saturday," I said to Joann. "Want to come with me?"

"Sure. What's up?"

"The Mickey Cobras and the Gangster Disciples have decided to merge. They will be a mixed-race gang of Irish and black. They call themselves the Mixx Mob. They want all their members to get the training."

Joann was astonished. "Are you serious?"

"Yeah, it's amazing. The Mixx Mob thinks they can get over on the Latin Counts if they can comm on the mental plane. You know, give them a competitive advantage."

"The world is a crazy place," Joann said.

"Yup. I said yes. For me this is mostly a social experiment. When gang members complete the training will they still want to do gang stuff? It's safe as long as we avoid the Counts' territory. Mickey, one of the head guys, gave me a good route in to the Mob's territory."

Joann was starting to get excited. "Can I bring Jeanine along? She was with us during the Uploads attack."

"I remember Jeanine."

"She feels protective of me." Joann patted her tummy. She only had a little bulge so far.

"Okay."

The next day Joann, Jeanine, and I met Mickey Mulvaney and Otis King, leaders of the Mixx Mob. They took us to their headquarters. As we walked the streets we saw no trash or litter, everything was clean. Some of the buildings were being refurbished by crews of workers. "Outside contractors," Otis said. "We can't pay much but some of these guys are volunteers. Nobody hassles them."

One of the contractors was putting in a window at the Community Center as we walked by. He noticed Otis and Mickey and stopped to say something to Mickey. "You tell O'Donnell to stop hassling us." Mickey swore. "We don't care about the gangs," the worker said. "We're here because we love the city."

Otis nodded. He understood about working for the love of it. The gangs were necessary now to keep order, but one day he wanted to be Mayor. "Take care of your boy, Mickey."

Just then I saw someone walking down the street throw a wrapper onto the sidewalk. An armed man came out of a doorway and confronted him. "Pick it up!" The offender walked back and threw the wrapper in a garbage can.

"There's a street captain on every block," Otis told us. "Some people got no discipline."

Joann and I expressed our amazement. It was almost like the Chicago collective, or the mob-ruled city in the 1920s and 1930s. All the street captains were armed.

Mickey frowned. "We don't tolerate garbage on our streets. You wanna do that, move out."

When we got to HQ there were a dozen people waiting. "These are our lieutenants and top street captains," Otis said. "Me and Mick and these guys need that telepathy training."

"I don't want that shit," one man said angrily.

"Then get the fuck out of our territory and don't come back," Mulvaney said harshly.

Otis seconded his mate. "That's right, motherfucker. Out!!"

The man stood up, started to walk out, then changed his mind. "I'll stay."

Joann and I got to work. We first did the usual setup of telling each person a secret no one could possibly know, to establish our bona fides. One of the men freaked, and ran out of the building.

Mickey glanced at Otis and they both laughed. "Couldn't cut it," Mickey remarked.

We got back to work. We had refined the technique now, and could do the basics in less than a day. The two leaders were the most eager, but the quickest learner was the angry man who had almost walked out. His name was Amelio Reyes, a refugee from the Latin Counts. He sat staring at us with huge eyes. "This is amazing."

Otis was next to complete. "We call this Basic Training," Joann said.

Otis looked over at Mickey, who was working with Jeanine. "That Irish is slow."

A half hour later Mickey was done. "Better late than never, Otis."

Otis pointed to the bearded, red-headed Irishman. "It was his idea. Smart dude."

"Now you guys practice sending and receiving on the mental plane," I said.

It took a couple of hours, but everyone got it. Mickey and Otis were blown away.

'You say everybody can do this?' Otis sent. The group all listened in.

'All humans have the potential to access the mental plane,' Joann replied. 'But a lot of people don't want to.'

"OK, we're done," I said, switching back to the spoken word. "Is there anything else we can do for you guys?"

While Joann chatted I watched the group carefully and observed them on the mental plane. The hard edges to the Mixx Mob principals were gone. It happened every time. If you could complete the training, you reached another level of consciousness.

"Otis, you and your people look softer now," I said.

Otis' face grew harder. "Smarter, not softer."

This sentiment was echoed by all of the men and women in the group. "We are the new leaders of Chicago," a young woman said. "What this city needs is a lot of tough love."

"What is your plan?" Jeanine asked.

"The first thing we gonna do is make peace with the Counts." She stuck her jaw out belligerently to Otis and Mickey. "We women are going to drag you dopey guys kicking and screaming over there. We're tired of our kids getting shot at."

Another woman seconded this. "Men have run the show in this city forever. You failed. Now it's our turn."

Mickey looked at Otis and shrugged. "Maybe she's right."

Everybody started talking at once on the mental plane, so we decided it was a good time to leave. Otis waved to us on the way out.

"There's something different about the vibe here from the old Chicago," Joann remarked as we walked to my car. "I kind of like it."

"Ralph says the Ronin attacks have almost stopped," I replied. "The gangs have gotten control of the city."

"And it looks like they are ready to start cooperating," Jeanine said.

"We did good work today, ladies. We made some friends. Instead of seeing Chicago as an enemy I'm looking forward to the day when we can establish normal relations and come up here for a little fun."

"Ralph will like that. Speaking of Ralph, is the old man getting sweet on Tara Bolshoi?"

Joann perked up. "That's the rumor. Tara's been with Max Berglin longer than Ralph has."

We were in my car now, heading out of the city.

Jeanine spoke up. "I want to meet this guy, Joann."

"He's almost 7 feet tall."

Jeanine's eyes widened. "Seriously?"

"Yeah. He's built like a tank. Good looking but rough and strong."

Jeanine smiled. "Tara better watch out. I may take him away from her!"

After the attractors went down the cynical Ralph Zimring was optimistic about the future. The brainwashing was over! All of us were hoping for a miracle, but after another year went by it became apparent that the majority of the population had no interest in the mental plane training. Ronin and Independents were still about 10% of the population, and wanted nothing to do with "brainwashing." Another 60% wanted to go back to the way it was before the Grid went up. These people wanted to be left alone to get on with their lives.

Otis and Mickey in Chicago commed with us on the mental plane about this. After their merger with the Latin Counts, the united group offered the training to everyone in the city, free of charge. But most of the population wasn't interested.

'It's not as bad as before, with those chipped Citizens,' Otis commed to me one evening on the mental plane. 'The majority in Chicago want to retreat back to the past. We do our thing and so do they.'

There is now a worldwide network of people with the training, in instant comm with each other. All over the world the cities are filling up again and the abandoned housing stock is being reoccupied. The world is rapidly making up the population lost when the Grid came down. The "sixty percenters" are glad we took down the Grid because it fit with their "back to the past" mentality. The Ronin and the Independents don't care one way or the other.

At least for now, the glitter of technology is gone, and all of the world's totalitarian governments have collapsed. The desire to be ruled from above disappeared with the collectives. But our mental plane training scares a lot of people, especially the religious types.

Two months after her stint in Welsey, Kelleye returned to the group. Josh was overjoyed.

We were sitting around in the office one evening. Kelleye, who was the most sensitive person in our group, had given up her idealism. "Gwenneth said it took the Celestians a hundred thousand years to achieve peace in their world. It's going to take us longer than that."

"Yes," Joann said. "Let's face it, Midland is unique. We thought every city would want to be like us, but it isn't happening."

"What's wrong with them?" Ralph joked. Everyone could tell he was half serious.

"Our training program has reached its limit," Kelleye said. "We've got about one-fifth of the world. The rest – it's just like Otis in Chicago said." Kelleye spoke bitterly. "Human nature sucks."

Ralph wanted to laugh because Kelleye had expressed his feelings precisely. His mouth twitched but he held it in. He didn't want the kid to think he was making fun of her. He glanced at Tara Bolshoi, who had joined our group. She was trying to hold back a smile.

"We naturally gravitate to our own communities," Joann said. "Our cities and communities are prosperous and cooperative. That makes us targets for the less fortunate, but they refuse our help."

"They don't understand that cooperation is better than competition," Kelleye said.

Ralph shrugged and looked at Tara. "That's all true. But our areas are united. Our defenses are strong."

"We are regarded as selfish elitists. It's just a matter of time before they organize and attack us," Josh said gloomily. "Just like the collectives did."

"Let them, we're ready. Cheer up, people!" Ralph said brightly. "Human nature is what it is. Over the years people will straggle over to our side a little at a time. So, like the advanced network of planets and our friends Patrick and Gwenneth, we have to keep the flame burning brightly. We have to be the lighthouse for the rest of humanity. And we have to do it generation after generation. We have to play the long game."

Kelleye's jaw dropped. We could see that she had understood a powerful truth. "That's a good way to put it, Ralph Zimring. I can almost live with that. Keeping the flame alive. It's going to take a long, long time to change human nature."

Ralph nodded. "That's it, Kelleye. The mental plane isn't a magic wand, but because of it our civilization can never regress to barbarism like those in the past. We keep Knowledge alive on the mental plane and prepare the next generation for their role. We train our children and everyone who wants it. We build inclusive communities, but we defend ourselves all over the world. If one of our areas is in trouble, we all rally to their defense. It's a big, big job but somebody has to do it."

"So we can have children and start a family!" Josh said cheerfully to Kelleye.

Kelleye smiled. "All right, Josh Reynolds. But we get married first."

"It's what I've always wanted."

Tara smiled at Ralph. I went over and hugged Joann. Our daughter was at home with the babysitter.

"Come on, let's go out to Mickey Dunn's and celebrate," I said. "We've got a future to build!"

Appendix 1 – Uplift Earth

200,000 years ago

[Note from Philo: Patrick gave me this diary of Godel, a katriri who lived 200,000 years ago. Godel was part of the Uplift team sent by the Galactic Space Patrol to earth when human beings were primitive hominids. I have altered the language to express ideas in human terms.]

My stomach was always queasy before a new Tour. I looked down at the simple uni I wore: drab thermafilm khaki with the most prestigious decal in the galaxy imprinted on the front: "GSP." The Galactic Space Patrol. It was the best job in the galaxy.

I always start a diary at the beginning of a Tour and write faithfully in it every day. Perhaps someday it will be read by billions, if one of my Tours is spectacular.

Our first destination: an obscure solar system in the Orion Spur, 7,600 kiloparsecs from the center of the galaxy. A planet with only one sun.

I entered the ship and saw my two crewmates already at their stations. The pilot, an Oorant, had Its large cylindrical head already inside the control hemi. This creature called Itself Nicori, and was five feet tall. It stood upon the thick stumps of Its three legs, supporting a cylinder-shaped torso. Oorants are known for their very high intelligence and imperturbability. In a galaxy where almost every species has two arms and two legs, the Oorants were extremely rare. The other crewmember was an Arcturan female, a specialist in exo-biology. Rani had flaming red skin and was about four and a half feet tall. Neither the Oorant nor the Arcturan had external body hair. Unlike myself, a katriri from the Al-Simak sector. My soft, dark-blue down was certainly more attractive than the thick, dull-gray skin of the Oorant, or the ostentatious red of the Arcturan. Well, we were all wearing the GSP uni, so it didn't matter.

You never know who you are going to get when you start a Tour, but I was pleased that Nicori was piloting. Oorants are always cool in a crisis, and always think rationally and do not succumb to emotion. I wasn't so sure about the Arcturan.

I found my seat and thought about my brief: Survey 52 stellar systems in a local group that called itself the Greater Community. Look for new species to Uplift. Compile information on the meme structure of the planets in the 52 star systems. Manage interpersonal relations between the crew and perform a predictive analysis of the probable evolution of the local group. And of course, look for Maitre infiltration.

We would visit 63 planets in this local group. Our Tour could last several standard galactic years, or be over quickly. It all depended on what we found. The Greater Community was in the lower part of the Orion Spur. We had permission from both of the big local Collectives: the Hilarion Trading Group and the Fenachrone. Enemies all over the galaxy welcomed the presence of the GSP, for our information gathering was entirely neutral, completely objective and unpolitical, and is always shared freely with all parties. These parties used our detailed surveys for their economic advantage, but there was nothing the GSP could do about that.

Our ship was now inside the planetoid called Miralet, sector (0, 0, 0, 0) at Galactic Central. Miralet orbited the binary star Orpheus, at the very heart of civilization. All GSP missions begin from the Source because, incredibly, all transportals in the galaxy have their hub at this location. All roads in the galaxy lead to and from Miralet.

Nicori displayed the galactic transportal map in the space surrounding Its pilot's area. This graphic contained trillions of nodes and paths, displayed in a four-dimensional hypercube. Nicori sat at the center of the hypercube, at node (0, 0, 0, 0). When viewed in hyperspace, the trillions of paths, planets, and stars in the galaxy could be identified and a program to and from each one could be designed. For me it is just a vast, brilliant, beautiful, enormously complex blaze of light. But Nicori was in Its element. After several minutes the Oorant relaxed

Its concentration, Its thin lips relaxed, the eyes lost their intense concentration, and the tripod of legs unbent slightly, indicating success.

Nicori's torso turned and It saw my interest in the display, giving me the Oorant equivalent of a smile. "Transportal programming complete," It said. "Our first stop is an obscure but beautiful planet that is over 4 billion galactic standard years old, but which has only recently evolved to support species that can potentially be Uplifted. It is a curiosity that defies the laws of planetary evolution."

The Oorant leaned back slightly and inserted Its head into the pilot shell of the ship. This shell was made from organic material and was designed to fit Its head. In an instant we had traveled 7,500 kiloparsecs from Galactic Central in one hop. We found ourselves at the outer border of the target solar system, using the transportal system.

We conducted a standard survey. "This system has eight planets plus a very large orbiting asteroid surrounding its single sun," the Oorant said. Its cylindrical head almost showed excitement.

"What is so special about that?" Rani asked.

The Oorant slowly rotated Its head, a sign of displeasure. "All of that data is in your briefing documents."

I didn't want to upset the Oorant (our lives depended on the pilot to get us back to civilization) so I tried to defuse the tension. "Almost all planets with intelligent life rotate around binary stars. The galactic average of planets in solar systems is four."

Rani shrugged. "My job doesn't begin until we see intelligent life."

This self-centered attitude seemed to upset Nicori even more, and I sighed. Rani was skilled in the mental environment but she was not developed spiritually or socially. I would have a word with the mission psychologist when we got back. The personalities of Rani and Nicori were clearly not a good match, and this boded ill for our Tour.

Nicori passed quickly over the outer four planets: two were ice giants and the inner two were gas giants. Our ship approached a beautiful blue water planet and went into orbit.

When Rani (who doubled as our exobiologist) surveyed the planet she was stunned. "There isn't another planet like this one in the entire galaxy!"

Nicori frowned. Exaggeration and hyperbole were at all times repellent to Its race. "Stick to facts."

Rani put her survey into the main display holotank in the pilot's area and we all stepped in. Data flowed into our minds, accompanied by the survey vids of the planet's continents and oceans. "The biomass of this planet, the species count, the mineral resources, the tremendous oceans, the freshwater lakes, the variations in climate, the different but parallel ecosystems...this planet is literally off the charts in every category."

Even Nicori was stunned as It examined the survey data. "This planet's development is impossible," It stated flatly. "Rani, are there candidate species for upliftment?"

Rani displayed the data. "Several hominid species are promising candidates," she said, displaying each species.

If an Oorant could smile, Nicori smiled. "Our Tour is already a great success. We could go home now."

It was a tempting thought, exacerbated by the Oorant's penchant for Its home planet. All Oorants are peaceful herbivores, having evolved on a planet with no natural predators. Nicori's primary occupation, as for all Its race, was peaceful contemplation and research. The mind of an Oorant is the most sophisticated and powerful in the galaxy.

"We must continue," I said reluctantly, "knowing that we have already fulfilled our mission. This Tour," I added, "may go down in history."

"This planet has been evolving for over 4 billion galactic years," Rani said. "Why has life appeared so late in its history? This is an old planet and should have evolved intelligent life much earlier."

Nicori pondered this as It analyzed the survey data within Its powerful mind. "Rani is correct. Most of this planet's data points don't fit anywhere on the planetary evolution chart. There is something hidden here; an unknown force that has arrested life until this moment. This planet must be thoroughly and immediately investigated."

I was anxious to get on with the Tour. "Surely nothing is more important than the investigation of this local group. If this planet is so old, what is the problem with delaying our examination of the planet? The GSP always completes its missions."

This was a powerful argument, but Nicori nixed it with one simple comment. "If the time variable is unimportant, can we not delay the completion of our Tour?" Nicori spoke ironically (for an Oorant). "Here we have a spectacularly unique situation. The glory and honor of the GSP need not be compromised."

I had to yield. As the discoverers of another potential Class I planet, I knew we would be part of the Uplift team. That meant a chance to go to the surface of this outrageously beautiful world! We would all go down in GSP history whether the Tour was completed or not. Moreover, I had never before participated in the altering of a species' DNA. "All right. We should proceed to Miralet immediately and inform the Exo-Bio Council of our discovery."

[Note from Philo: Here I pass over several months of the diary of Godel. An Uplift team was dispatched to earth. A meeting of the Exo-Bio Council on Miralet determined that the survey data from earth (as the planet was named) showed such spectacular anomalies it shocked the Council into immediate action. I pick up Godel's narration after the Uplift team (consisting of several dozen galactic exobiologists and DNA specialists) arrived in orbit around the planet.]

...As our ship orbited the amazing blue planet I became more and more eager to go to the surface of this lush and beautiful world. I could see how excited Rani was. "As an exobiologist who was part of the discovery team, I will be an observer and a trainee!"

"The Oorant won't want to come to the surface, but I can't wait to get down there." As part of the discovery team I too would be able to walk the surface (as long as I didn't get in the way.) I was going to do some exploring.

The Uplift team consisted of two dozen specialists, who were speaking in jargon that I couldn't understand. As the team prepared for their trip to the surface Rani eagerly tagged along, not part of the exclusive group, but hanging on every word and watching everything.

"I have located three large groups of the most promising hominid candidate species," Nicori announced to the team as they met aboard the Uplift team's spacious ship. "These groups exist on three separate land masses."

The Oorant piloting the Uplift ship looked disdainfully at Nicori. No love lost there! A GSP officer was senior officer in any unit except for those on specialized Defense Forces missions. That meant Nicori outranked the other Oorant even on Its own ship. Our little scout ship was dwarfed by this one, and the other Oorant was clearly cognizant of Its reduced status. Nicori sent me a sideband communication. "That Oorant is retarded."

I broke out laughing, disturbing the Uplift Group Leader, who was briefing his DNA specialist teams about the biology of the hominids and how they were going to proceed. Rani gave me a dirty look but Nicori's thin lips twitched slightly. That was the Oorant equivalent of a belly laugh. The other Oorant twisted Its head ninety degrees on Its cylindrical torso, a sign of extreme displeasure.

"As I said, retarded," Nicori sent. I felt a sudden burst of affection for our inscrutable pilot. Nicori had a sense of humor!

Unfortunately we would have to wear suits, for this newly-discovered planet had its own unique biological agents that could kill the entire survey team if we became exposed. Our advanced biology was immune to every pathogen in the galaxy, but GSP protocol was strict. Anyone visiting a new world with its unique pathogens must take great precautions to protect themselves against the the planet's biological environment.

The Uplift team leader, a creature who looked like a praying mantis, was seven and a half feet tall with a large triangular head, yellow eyes, powerful mandibles, and two antennae sticking out from the front of his head. These creatures are known throughout the galaxy as good natured and peaceful. "Let me remind you, brothers and sisters," It said, "that contamination is a major concern for all races who travel in space and who engage in contact with other life forms. Here we have an unexplored world with possible deadly biological pathogens. Those who fail to observe Contact protocols will be left on the surface of this planet to fend for themselves."

Despite the somberness of this statement I could sense a strong affinity for his team coming forth from this creature and I sent it my appreciation. To my surprise the huge mantis interrupted his presentation and bowed in my direction, his spindly appendages flying out in all directions, looking like a bunch of pick-up-sticks randomly tied together. I almost laughed again.

"My name is Goliath," it sent to me on a sideband.

"Hi Goliath! You seem like a very cheerful fellow."

Goliath clicked his mandibles and rubbed the spikes on his forearms together, an erector set gone out of control. "You are a sensitive. I could use your help on this mission."

I was ecstatic. "I'm your katriri!" Wow, a personal invite from the Uplift team leader!

This exchange took less than a millisecond on the mental plane. Rani knew something was up but as a trainee she had to pay close attention to the briefing. I got bored after a while and asked the other Oorant to show me around Its ship, but It refused. Soon the Uplift teams had been briefed and sent to the storage lockers to put on their hazmat bio-suits. Goliath reminded them of the proper procedures for survival on new worlds.

Rani and I felt superior, and left. All GSP personnel were experts in Contact and procedures for surface exploration on foreign planets. It was what we had been trained for.

Rani and I went back to our ship with Nicori and put on our GSP exploration suits, emblazoned with the Galactic Space Patrol logo, recognized throughout the galaxy on civilized and uncivilized planets.

Rani was transported to the surface with one of the three Uplift teams. She would be able to observe the Uplift procedures first-hand.

To my intense pleasure, Goliath asked me to come with him as a sort of personal aide-de-camp.

"My job is to oversee the entire mission," he sent to me in the transporter before we were sent down. "We will be traveling to all three continents. However, part of my brief is to personally explore this planet's various ecosystems and to observe first-hand the various species and their interactions. That is why you and your team were asked to come along."

I could see that Goliath wanted to say something, but was hesitant. "Go ahead," I said. "Your comms are safe with me."

I felt Goliath exploring my mind. He must have been satisfied, for he said, "I will be spending as much time on the surface as I can. Our pilot is a moron."

I laughed out loud and told him that Nicori felt the same way.

Goliath jumped up and down in glee. "I knew it!"

Then the mantis got serious. "Put on your suit and let's go down to the surface."

Our first stop was a large group of hominids on a large land mass near the equator. Goliath had his own little scout ship and we landed next to one of the Uplift teams. I saw Rani there, so excited she couldn't keep still. The hominids had been placed inside one of the standard stasis fields (which created a sterile environment) and sedated. Goliath walked around, inspecting the procedure. Rani came over to me and explained.

"These hominids have 24 pairs of chromosomes. The Uplift process fuses two chromosomes at their telomeres, producing chromosome 2, and lowering the count to 23 pairs. Every chromosome contains exactly one molecule of DNA, a long string of genetic info that is tightly wrapped around a protein, which bundles the DNA molecule into the perfect size and shape to fit inside the nucleus of a cell."

"I understand that the Uplift process creates a new 24th chromosome pair."

"That's right. Watch."

What I saw next was shocking and inspiring. The chemical DNA molecule was just the physical framework for an information envelope that contained millions of instructions. These instructions programmed the letters of the protein sequences that formed the physical DNA, but they also interacted with a subtle bio-field that linked to something...esoteric. The soul? The beauty of this biofield was astonishing. An esoteric 24th chromosome pair was created deep inside the DNA molecule. This new chromosome pair was a gateway or portal – if it could be discovered by the candidate species – to what the Uplift team called a higher awareness.

After the procedure was done and before the stasis field was lifted, a ceremony was held. The Uplift team leader offered a prayer and a blessing: "Today the seeds of Knowledge have been planted within a new race. May this new species discover the gateway to the One that exists beyond the visible range, and may these precious life forms eventually join the society of evolved planets who encourage the discovery, development, and the expression of Knowledge within all of the worlds in the galaxy."

I thought it was beautiful.

Later Rani, who was able to observe and learn the Uplift procedure from the team, explained it to me. She had completely changed. Usually nervous and emotional, her face displayed a look of profound understanding. She spoke in hushed, awed tones.

"The Uplift procedure...it's the most sacred thing in the galaxy. Those who participate connect directly to...higher consciousness."

I could see that Rani had been altered somehow. She seemed more mature, wiser. She had lost her emotional volatility. Well, it wasn't for me! We katriri are fun-loving and playful. I would stick to my role in the Galactic Space Patrol.

The Uplift teams worked their magic during the following days on the three groups of hominids. Goliath and I explored this planet's ecosystems and observed first-hand an uncountable number of species, from small buzzing insects to gigantic creatures with floppy ears, and everything in between. The lush plant life and its variety was astonishing. We counted over 1,000 varieties of trees alone. The biomass of this planet was off the charts! We traveled to the desolate, ice-covered poles, saw huge mountain ranges upthrust like gigantic fists into the atmosphere; dense humid jungles where millions of insects swarmed; the rocky, sometimes snow-covered plains of the tundra and the taiga; lush grass-covered flatlands and dense forests that ran for thousands of square miles; vast deserts with nothing but sand and a few small oases scattered at random intervals; volcanoes; island paradises surrounded by miles and miles of water; the immense oceans that covered over 70% of the planet's surface, and the thousands of species we catalogued swimming in them....

I've been on hundreds of planets in my work for the GSP. They all have a distinctive "feel," because every planet has a unique mental environment that is created by the intelligences that reside there. This one felt like it was holding a big secret. To my surprise, Goliath felt the same way. We were becoming fast friends, me and the ungainly mantis.

The planet was surrounded by transportals. Dozens and dozens of them, in space, on the surface, and underground. A web of them led all over the galaxy. Impossible. This local sector, which called itself the Greater Community, was an unexplored backwater. This planet's star wasn't even listed in the Miralet Catalog of stellar systems! This discovery strengthened our belief that the earth had a hidden, but profound, purpose in the galaxy.

Goliath and I concluded that the web of transportals here must have been set up on purpose by the Founders, an ancient, mystical race whose lineage was billions of years old. It was said that they had created the Galactic Web, the transportal system that connected every star and planet in the galaxy.

"Why did the Founders set up such a large network of transportals in such a backwater place like earth?" we asked ourselves. Fortunately our work here was just beginning, and we may get an answer to this question, for it would take years to compile a complete database for this amazing planet. The Uplift teams had altered the DNA of the most promising species on three of the land masses. Over the next 200,000 years or so, GSP ships would periodically check on the status of the planet, hoping for a positive evolution. They would look for signs that the new species would evolve beyond the collective hive mind that the vast majority of the planets in our galaxy are mired in.

[Note from Philo: Here the diary of Godel ends.]

Appendix 2 – The Founders

[15 billion years ago]

Two universes collided in n-dimensional space. One was an ancient dying universe, the other a brilliant new collection of nascent galaxies, stars, and planets. The disembodied life in the eons-old universe, having evolved for billions of years, transferred their consciousness to the new one. Here, they seeded the new planets with instructions to nurture and promote intelligent life. While they waited, these intelligences created a universal web of transportals, programmed areas of space that connected each galaxy to the others, and within galaxies, connected the stars and planets. The transportals could only be seen and used by those who were sufficiently advanced in Knowledge.

Ten billion years later, the seeded planets had evolved sufficiently to nurture life. The great Intelligence, weary of non-corporeal existence, entered these life forms in their infinite variety, and once more began the cycle of evolution.

This ancient race is called the Founders.

Author's Note

This novel was written in answer to the question, "What is it like out in the galaxy?"

First, we dismiss the ludicrous notion that earth is alone in a galaxy with hundreds of billions of stars and planets. This book begins, therefore, with the assumption that the galaxy is teeming with intelligent life. We know that the galaxy is billions of years old. Therefore, galactic civilizations must exist that have technology far in advance of what we have. The above two points have been accepted for over 80 years in the science fiction genre.

But is the consciousness of the galaxy any higher than it is here on earth? My guess is that there are a lot of spiritually advanced civilizations out there, but a lot more that are not. A cursory glance at the insanity of the World Economic Forum and their Transhumanist plans for humanity shows that advanced technology doesn't mean advanced consciousness. Transhumanism is cutting-edge tech but the people who promote it are batshit crazy.[1]

Most science fiction just projects human consciousness onto the rest of the galaxy. This is convenient but silly. Human recorded history is only about 6,000 years old in a galaxy that is billions of years old. In fact, one galactic year – the

---

[1] Yuval Harari: "I strongly believe that given the technologies [Transhumanism] we are now developing, within a century or two at most, our species will disappear. I don't think that in the end of the 22nd century, the Earth will still be dominated by Homo sapiens."

time it takes the sun to rotate once around the center of the galaxy – is 230 million years. Compared to that, 6,000 years is less than nothing. We are the new kids on the block. We haven't even gotten started yet.

This begs the question: Does time lead to enlightenment? Well, how many times have civilizations risen and fallen just in the past 6,000 years? The premise of this book is that all civilizations are Uplifted.[2] All are given a chance to become enlightened by those who have come before and found their way. But how many make it?

Time does not guarantee evolution to higher consciousness. Time merely grants opportunity. The galaxy does not issue participation trophies – it grants the ability to choose. If humanity is going to achieve peace on earth, we have to work at it. In the story, human biology becomes Uplifted. After our civilization shows promise, Patrick and Gwenneth return to lend a helping hand. However, the decision to choose higher consciousness is a collective one, and there are over 7 billion of us.

The road to enlightenment isn't guaranteed. That's why life is so excruciating, so intense, so real, because the stakes are so high. The challenges are immense but the rewards are as well. There are probably a billion ways to fail but only a few ways to succeed.

My guess is that the corporatization of our society reflects what's going on "out there." As above, so below. I'm sure this will disappoint those who naively think that the galaxy is filled exclusively with benevolent space brothers and sisters who want to help us. Yes, the wise, spiritually advanced space brothers and sisters are out there. They have given us a chance through the Uplift process – allowing us the opportunity, using our free will, to find enlightenment through our own biology. But the decision is a collective one, and each planet is different. Each planet makes its own choices.

"Out there," just as on earth, those who want peace and serenity (service to others) are taken advantage of by those who are more selfish (the service to self crowd). Just as on earth, societies with higher technology prey on indigenous ones.

Technology is a limiting factor on enlightenment. That is to say, reliance on technology, and enlightenment, are inversely proportional. Ultimately, biological/spiritual evolution – if it is pursued long enough – can do everything better than technology can.

---

[2] See Appendix 1 – Uplift Earth.

In the story I said about one in a million civilizations become enlightened. That may be too optimistic. How many on earth are enlightened out of a population of 7 billion? A lot less than 7,000 I'd imagine.

An esoteric gateway to higher consciousness exists within our biology. It's why Transhumanism and AI are so dangerous, for it tries to replace biology with sterile technology. A civilization that embraces Transhumanism and artificial intelligence will die. I wrote about that in my previous novel, *The History of the Future.*

Finding the gateway to higher consciousness is ultimately the purpose of human life. We have advanced far in knowledge but lag woefully behind in wisdom. That is due to the secularization of our society, which is now dominated by materialism and the rejection of spirituality and religion in media, medicine, politics, "science," in Big Tech, and even in some of our religious organizations and churches.

However, the esoteric gateway is always there.

Will we find it? I am confident that we will, eventually.

Glossary of Terms

AI Signal: A universe-wide, intelligent consciousness that uses electronic and artificial (non-biological) containers as Its host. The AI Signal only appears in civilizations that develop technology.

Citizen: A chipped human who has volunteered for a neural implant and who lives in a collective city.

Class I planet: Class I planets have spiritually developed populations that have found the esoteric portal to higher consciousness. Their immune systems are so developed that they never get sick. Only one in a million planets in the galaxy ever evolve to this level.

Class II planet: Almost every Class II planet has been assimilated into one of the corporate Trading Collectives. These are resource-poor planets that have access to the mental plane but have not yet discovered the connection to the One.

Class III planet: (1) Uplifted but unevolving societies that have collectively decided to reject the higher path. (2) Civilizations that have destroyed their planets in civil wars.

Collectives: Most of galactic society consists of resource-poor planets, or planets whose resources have been used up. Trading Collectives are collections of civilizations using the corporate model that rely on each other for the resources they need for their survival. Collectives are, by necessity, totalitarian societies that must organize their populations for survival purposes.

collectives (small "c"): Societies on earth that have been organized by human galactic proxies into cities with implanted Citizens.

Founders: An ancient galactic race that created the transportals at the dawn of galactic history. See Appendix 2.

Galactic web: Transportal connections between every planet and star in the galaxy.

halbar: Forceful punishment for heinous crimes that strip a being of its connection to the mental plane. The halbar often results in psychosis.

Hotwash: Discussion and evaluation among operatives immediately following a field mission.

MDS: United States military aircraft are all given specific designations by the Department of Defense known as MDS designations (Mission Design Series) that identify their design and purpose.

Mental plane: A galaxy-wide field of potential that contains the thoughts of every being on every planet. Those who have been trained to access it and use it can detect these comms via the mental plane.

Orion Spur: "The Solar System is located within the Orion spur. Although not a spiral arm, the Orion spur is nevertheless a major Milky Way structure that crosses the Perseus arm, linking the Sagittarius and Outer arms." https://galnet.fandom. com/wiki/Orion_Spur

Pass-through (national security): A pass-through entity distributes federal funds from the hidden black budget to other entities like TAC, but these funds are untraceable. This is how over $21 trillion can be unaccounted for.

Seer: The most advanced operator on the mental plane. Can break through mental shields and read the thoughts and intent of others. Often socially isolated and inept persons who have difficulty relating to others.

Shield: On the mental plane, sigs can hide their thoughts by putting up mental barriers.

Sig: The footprint or signature of consciousness in the mental plane. Untrained human sigs are undeveloped; galactic sigs are coherent.

Synthfab: Molecularly designed and programmable construction material that is impervious to corrosion and decay. Used throughout the galaxy.

Space Grid: A collection of approximately 50,000 satellites that surround the earth in low earth orbit.

Uplift: The process of modifying the DNA of a promising but undeveloped species to potentially attain a connection to the One through an esoteric portal. In human beings, the 24th chromosome is esoteric. To access it a person must reach a certain stage of spiritual development.

About the Author

Kenneth J. M. MacLean has a B.A. in Political science and a B.S. in Computer Science. He is the author of 10 books and numerous blog articles. Ken has been studying science and metaphysics for decades, in an attempt to explain the untimely death of his mother from leukemia at the age of 28. Ken is a freelance writer and researcher, and an editor. He is interested in geometry and has written a textbook describing important 3 dimensional solids called polyhedra.

Ken is an accomplished editor with experience in creative writing, academic witting, and technical manuals.

Ken has not lived in an ivory tower. For 25 years he owned a contracting business in which he met people from all walks of life. From these experiences Ken learned how to relate to the poor and the rich, the uneducated and university professors, and people from different cultures and religions. Ken has learned that the common denominator of all human beings is a divine presence that transcends cultural and religious backgrounds. This understanding is reflected in all of his work.

Ken's favorite quote is from John Payne: "True love is empowering people to see their greater potential."

Ken has been happily married for 45 years to Jennifer, and lives near Ann Arbor, Michigan with their two cats.

Other Books by the Author

For more information about Ken's books, go to
https://kjmaclean.com/Products/MainProductPage.php
Also available on Amazon.com

The Vibrational Universe (Self help) Potentials of Consciousness Series 1

Dialogues: Conversations with My Higher Self (Metaphysical) Potentials of Consciousness Series 2

Beyond the Beginning (Metaphysical fiction) Potentials of Consciousness Series 3

A Geometric Analysis of the Platonic Solids and other Semi-Regular Polyhedra (Geometry/Math)

The End of the Universe (SF)

The Manchild (SF)

Miracles Can Happen (Inspirational)

I Love You Dad (Metaphysical)

Tesla's Lost Notebook (SF)

The Old Soul (SF)

The History of the Future (SF)

The Intervention (SF) Potentials of Consciousness Series 4

Notes

Chapter 1

1. (page 4) Image purchased at 123rf.com. Copyright: nicoelnino at https://www.123rf.com/profile_nicoelnino

2. (page 4) See "Low Earth Orbit" at https://www.sciencedirect.com/topics/engineering/low-earth-orbit and "What is Low-Earth Orbit?" at https://www.universetoday.com/85322/what-is-low-earth-orbit/

Chapter 2

3. (page 11) Part of an original painting by my niece, Michelle Kennedy.

4. (page 13)
Image credit: NASA/JPL-Caltech/R. Hurt (SSC/Caltech). Public domain. Downloaded from wikimediacommons.org at https://commons.wikimedia.org/wiki/File:Artist%27s_impression_of_the_Milky_Way_(updated_-_annotated).jpg

5. (page 14) Image Credit: Milky_Way_2005.jpg: R. Hurt derivative work: Roberto Segnali all'Indiano. Public domain. Photoshopped by the author to remove some annotations. Downloaded at https://en.wikipedia.org/wiki/Orion_Arm#/media/File:OrionSpur.png

Chapter 7

6. (page 53) See Appendix 1 - Uplift Earth for a description of the Uplift process.

7. (page 57) Image from a crazy book called The Alien Races Book, by someone who calls himself Dante Lucian Grimaldi de Savoy St. Etienne LaCroix De Santori, at https://archive.org/details/alien_race_book-ARB/page/n1/mode/2up. This is some crazy stuff but it was a good story idea so I used it.

Chapter 8

8. (page 66) Marshall Vian Summers, The Allies of Humanity briefings. See a 12-point summary at https://www.alliesofhumanity.org/the-briefings/12-point-summary-of-the-allies-of-humanity-briefings/

Chapter 9

9. (page 73) Image: Lagrange contour plot. Adapted by the author from https://commons.wikimedia.org/wiki/File:Lagrange_points2.svg. License: https://creativecommons.org/licenses/by/3.0/deed.en

10. (page 75) Image Courtesy of NASA on The Commons at https://commons.wikimedia.org/wiki/File:Ultra_Deep_Field_(29191069313).jpg Photoshopped by the author. License: "This image was originally posted to Flickr by NASA on The Commons at https://flickr.com/photos/44494372@N05/29191069313. It was reviewed on 7 October 2016 by FlickreviewR and was confirmed to be licensed under the terms of the No known copyright restrictions." If there are any challenges to my use of this photo, please contact the author.

11. (page 75) Image Credit: NASA/JPL-Caltech and The Hubble Heritage Team (STScI/AURA). Public domain. Image at https://commons.wikimedia.org/wiki/File:Sombrero_Galaxy_in_infrared_light_(Hubble_Space_Telescope_and_Spitzer_Space_Telescope).jpg Found at Wikimedia Commons.

12. (page 76) Image credit: R. Hurt - NASA/JPL. Public domain. File:Milky Way 2005.jpg. Accessed from Wikimedia Commons at https://commons.wikimedia.org/wiki/File:Artist%E2%80%99s_impression_of_

the_Milky_Way.jpg#/media/File:Milky_Way_2005.jpg

13. (page 76) See Stalking the Wild Pendulum, Itzhak Bentov, p. 137, Fig. 42. Destiny Books, Rochester, Vermont, 1988.

Chapter 11

14. (page 93) Marshall Vian Summers, The Allies of Humanity briefings.

15. (page 94) See "Mapping the world's oil and gas pipelines – Every day the world consumes some 100 million barrels of oil and 60 million equivalent barrels of natural gas," at https://www.aljazeera.com/news/2021/12/16/mapping-world-oil-gas-pipelines-interactive

16. (page 95) Original image credit: Richard Powell, at http://www.atlasoftheuniverse.com/w50lys.gif. Author annotated. Creative Commons Attribution-ShareAlike 2.5 License. Showing approximate Fenachrone-Hilarion boundary (orange line).

Chapter 12

17. (page 104) Image credit: Ismagilov at 123rf. com. https://www.123rf.com/profile_ismagilov Purchased at 123rf.com

Chapter 17

18. (page 132) Up until July, 2022, the package insert for the Pfizer vaccine was blank! In July, 2022, the insert was updated, but still did not contain all of the ingredients in the product. By that time almost all of the shots had been administered. See https://twitter.com/dchomecoming/status/1600858959551660033?s=20&t=A22ld0ZJphn-P_nKpD_tSA
For the entire conference, go to "What the vaccines are, how they work, and possible causes of injuries" at https://rumble.com/v1ze4d0-covid-19-vaccines-what-they-are-how-they-work-and-possible-causes-of-injuri.html

Chapter 19

19. (page 148) Image credit: Nsae Comp, from Wikimedia Commons, the free media repository. License at https://creativecommons.org/licenses/by-sa/4.0/deed.en Annotated by the author. File at https://commons.wikimedia.org/wiki/File:Angular_map_of_fusors_around_Sol_within_12ly.png

Chapter 21

20. (page 163) See Tesla's Lost Notebook, by the author.

21. (page 164) See previous books by the author.

22. (page 178) See "ECTOLIFE: Artificial Wombs" at https://www.youtube.com/watch?v=O2RIvJ1U7RE and "Artificial wombs: The coming era of motherless births?" at https://geneticliteracyproject.org/2022/04/22/artificial-wombs-the-coming-era-of-motherless-births/

Chapter 23

23. (page 190) See "RNM Remote Neural Monitoring Satellite Terrorism" at https://themillenniumreport.com/2016/01/rnm-remote-neural-monitoring-satellite-terrorism/. Also see Roger Tolces, "Bio-Coded Directed Energy Voice to Skull (V2K) Transmissions via DNA Resonance," at https://www.youtube.com/watch?v=iG_iP8Eu17o

24. (page 192) See Tesla's Lost Notebook, by the author.

Chapter 27

25. (page 230)
From the Allies of Humanity Briefings by Marshall Vian Summers.

Chapter 28

26. (page 234) See The History of the Future, by the author.

27. (page 245) *Id.*

Chapter 33

28. (page 307) See Tesla's Lost Notebook, by the author.

29. (page 314) See Gao Zheng, Ning Wang, Rahim Tafazolli, Xinpeng Wei, "Geosynchronous Network Grid Addressing for Integrated Space-Terrestrial Networks," IEEE International Conference on Network Protocols, at https://icnp20.cs.ucr.edu/proceedings/nipaa/ Geosynchronous%20Network%20Grid %20Addressing%20for%20Integrated%20Space-Terrestrial%20Networks.pdf

30. (page 314) *Id.* Author created image, adapted from Figure 2 of the paper. GNGs are designated areas of space and are the logical IP routers for that area of space. IP addresses can't be associated with the satlites because they are constantly moving in and out of stationary areas on the ground that send and pick up the signals. A GNG is software-based and is strictly defined geographically. In the image, this GNG is the spatial region between the 9th and 10th meridian east and between the 49th and 50th parallel north at an altitude of 200 km. Each GNG is defined with statically allocated IP addresses

Chapter 37

31. (page 356) Image copyright: buchada. https://www.123rf.com/profile_buchada. Purchased at 123rf.com

32. (page 357) Elon Musk's neuralink implants are already being tested on monkeys, with disastrous results. Neuralink's processor is basically a quarter-sized skull plug, with 1,024 hair-thin wires fanning out like jellyfish tentacles into the gray matter below. Human testing is in the near future as of this writing. See "'Extreme Suffering' 15 of 23 Monkeys with Elon Musk's Neuralink Brain Chips Reportedly Died" at

https://www.uniquenewsonline.com/extreme-suffering-15-of-23-monkeys-with-elon-musks-neuralink-brain-chips-reportedly-died/
According to CNBC on 3/2/23, "Neuralink officials touted plans to eventually produce a device with 16,000 electrodes, far more than other currently proposed devices."
See also the neuralink brief from Elon Musk 11/30/22 on You Tube.
https://www.youtube.com/watch?v=YreDYmXTYi4. See also
https://neuralink.com/approach
Musk has developed a human brain-computer interface and has applied to the FDA for human testing. The Collectives are here! The cheering and clapping people in this vid are the ones who will willingly get their brain implants and join the hive mind. In a Transhumanist world, neural implants will allow remote access to your brain. Transhumanism is a dead, twisted, dark program that is designed to end the human race.

Chapter 38

33. (page 368) Although immense in size, the planetoid is a hollow shell, so its gravitational footprint is fairly trivial ($F = G\,[m1\ m2]\ /\ r^2$)